FOREVER TO ME

ERIN BRANSCOM

Forever To Me

Bridger Falls
Book 1

Erin Branscom

Content Warning

This book includes "on-page" adult content and language
unsuitable for minors.

Chapter 1
Walker

Last Call

Heads turn the moment she strides into my bar, her fiery red hair catching the light like a flame in the dark. She confidently slides onto a barstool at a high-top table across the room, her leather jacket clinging to the curves that could stop a man in his tracks. Scuffed boots and worn jeans that hug curves just right tell the story of long days. A few cowboys take notice as they tip their hats to her and sit up straighter. Hell, I can't help but notice, too. She's beautiful.

She orders a whiskey from Cash, my bartender, and pays attention to what's happening in the bar. Her eyes study me curiously over her glass as she sips her whiskey.

One cowboy, who just might be braver or stupider than the rest, leans in a little too close to the mystery redhead for my liking and says, "What's a pretty thing like you doin' here at The Black Dog?"

"Enjoying some solitude," she says coolly, giving him a tight smile that doesn't reach her eyes. I notice she doesn't make eye contact with him and keeps her distance.

"Maybe I can buy you another drink," chimes in another cowboy, this one with a crooked smile and a mischievous glint in his eye that I don't like.

Not one bit.

Neither of these assholes know how to read a room.

I hide my smirk as she turns away and gets up, completely ignoring the cocky cowboy in favor of hitting up the jukebox where she chooses 90s country classics. A smile stretches across her face as she punches buttons for a few songs.

She has good taste.

She's hands down the most beautiful woman I've ever laid eyes on. She's mysterious and sexy as hell. Throughout the night, I wonder what brings her to my bar in the middle of nowhere, Bridger Falls, Wyoming. She's probably just passing through and doesn't know that she's captivated the whole damn bar.

A long bar wraps around the front of the room along with plenty of high-top tables for folks to gather. In the back, dart boards along the walls surround pool tables to give people a place to have a good time and unwind. The bar isn't fancy by any means, but it's clean and classy. A dive bar where you can get a hot meal and hang out with the locals. We have the rare tourists that sometimes pass through our small town, but for the most part, everybody knows everybody, and we're a close-knit bunch. Which makes me wonder why she's here and where she came from.

The bar's slammed tonight, and I shouldn't spend so much time thinking about the gorgeous woman, but I can't help it. Cash and I have been busy all night. Momma Mary, our cook, went nonstop until we finally closed the kitchen down. I'm glad I hired another barback for the weekend shift because we've been slammed. I really could use another bartender, but I haven't been able to find anyone. Either they're eighty and can't drive after dark, or they just turned eighteen and still go to Bridger Falls High School with my kid. The joys of living in a small town. Not a lot of options, and like I said, everyone knows everyone.

I can't keep my eyes from drifting over to her. She's stunning and perfect. Long, rich, dark red curls cascade around her shoulders and down her back. But what really catches me off guard is the bright red lipstick that makes her striking green eyes pop. More than once, I think she catches me looking over. Her lips turn up in a smile as she drops her gaze back to her drink, as if not to put me on the spot for staring. But then I catch her staring back at me. Her eyes lock with mine, and the bar fades into nothing. It's a game we play back and forth all night. And I like this game.

"Last call," Cash yells as he starts to close things down. People trickle out as we wrap things up and wind down. Typically, I would head back to my office and finish up the paperwork. But I feel like I need to keep an eye on things.

Okay, maybe keep an eye on *her*. Rarely does a woman catch my eye like she has. Plus, I want to make sure these cowboys still lingering around leave her alone.

A few local cowboys are left finishing a game of pool when I notice one of them says something to Red. She shakes her head and turns in her chair away from him. Her body language clearly reads she's not interested. Something she's been putting out all night. But that doesn't stop the cowboy from trying again and walking up and placing a hand on her shoulder as he leans down to whisper something to her.

I grit my teeth and grip the edge of the bar. What the actual hell?

"Actually," she says, her voice rising, "I'm with him." She turns and faces me, her eyes unmistakably on me.

The two cowboys turn and stare in my direction with confusion. Then one turns back to her and gives her a challenging look before he glances back at me smugly.

Curiosity fills me as I silently watch the exchange.

She nods at me and gives me a smile that flows throughout my entire body. I watch this unfold as I cross my arms over my chest and lean back against the bar.

"Sorry, boys," she says as she stands and walks towards me, full of confidence and purpose. Her determined eyes lock onto mine, and a hint of a pleading look turns into a flirty smirk on those gorgeous red lips. She walks around the bar's edge and stands toe to toe with me. A bold move most patrons wouldn't attempt. But something is different with her. I'm not sure what it is yet, but she's something. I'm about three inches taller than her, so she's got to be around five foot nine. She has legs that go on for days. She looks me right in the eyes and says with a voice like velvet, low and smooth, "That man over there doesn't believe I'm with you. I need him to believe it, Cowboy. So, can I please kiss you right now and pretend you're mine?"

Well, fuck me with a feather.

I glance at the two cowboys as they anxiously watch our every move. My attention shifts back to Red. She's even more beautiful close-up. And she smells good, too. Like vanilla and honey. I wonder what her hair would feel like if I were to run my fingers through it.

"Well, you said please," I murmur as I snap back to reality.

A smirk spreads across her face as she takes that as a yes and puts her arms around my neck, pulling me down and crashing her lips into mine. I instinctively wrap my arms around her waist, pulling her tighter to me, her lips exploring mine, her hands gripping my back tightly and pulling me in closer.

Somehow, time stops, and my world shifts on its axis. I can't explain it. Hell, I don't think I'll ever be able to explain the way I feel right now. Only that it somehow feels right.

She kisses me passionately, her hands exploring my back like she's hungry for more. I've never kissed a stranger before, and this is so hot.

Someone in the bar whistles, and at this point I don't care who is watching us because all I can focus on is this beautiful woman in my arms, with my lips to hers, a current of electricity passing through us like we could light up the fucking world with our own power grid.

She pulls back and leans up to whisper, "Thanks, Cowboy."

I pull her close, tucking her under my chin, and murmur, "They're still watching."

I don't have the heart to tell her that I'm not a cowboy. But at this moment, I could be whoever she wants me to be.

She sighs heavily, almost like she carries the weight of the world in her body. Instinctively, I pull her tighter and cradle her to my chest. She stays in my arms, and she relaxes despite my heart racing. Out of the corner of my eye, the denim-shirt-wearing cowboy watches our every move. He shakes his head as he glares in defeat at the other guy with him. Cash passes between them.

They fucking bet on Red.

I don't know this woman, but she wouldn't have left with either of them tonight if I had to bet.

Because she's leaving with me, I'll ensure she gets home safely and nobody bothers her. I'm not sure where this urge to protect her is coming from, but I will make sure she's safe.

Then she turns to me and shocks me when she says, "Want to get out of here, cowboy?" she asks with a tinge of vulnerability and confidence.

And just like that, my rules of never taking a woman home from my bar are out the window. I am under this beautiful woman's spell, and I would probably go anywhere with her.

Chapter 2
Violet
I'm takin' you home.

The smoking hot bartender in the black cowboy hat gazes at me, sending goosebumps straight through my entire body. He has to feel this, too. If he doesn't, then I must be crazy.

He's the kind of man who turns heads without trying. Tall and rugged, his lean, muscular build hints at years of hard work. Dark hair curls slightly at the edges beneath a well-worn black cowboy hat, the brim casting just enough shadow to make his warm hazel eyes even more striking. They hold a quiet intensity that could strip a person bare with just one look.

Dressed in faded jeans that cling just right and a black shirt that stretches across his broad shoulders, he has a raw, effortless confidence. The sleeves hug his biceps, the fabric shifting over his trim torso with each measured movement. When he tips his hat, a slow, knowing smile plays at his lips—just enough to make a woman wonder what secrets he keeps. I've never met anyone like him before.

Boots scuffed, the scent of leather and cedar lingering around him, he carries himself with the easy swagger of a man who knows exactly who he is. Dangerous in all the best ways, with a voice like smooth whiskey and a touch that could burn or soothe, depending on his mood.

I'm not much of a one-night stand kind of girl, but this feels like my one chance to live wild and on the edge for once. One kiss has never turned me on this much.

That was the hottest kiss. I can still feel the tingle of his close-cut stubble from his beard on my face, and I want to reach out and trace the small scar on his jaw with my fingertips. Kissing total strangers isn't a habit, but something about this guy is familiar, even though I don't know him and have never seen him before in my life. Somehow, he feels comfortable. Safe.

And hell yeah, I asked if he wanted to get out of here. If he booked a spaceship to the moon, I'd sign up to go with him right now.

My body still tingles where his hands held me, and my ear buzzes from when he murmured his sexy words and went along with my crazy plan to make the boys go away. Truth be told, I could've handled them. I heard their plans, and I was never interested. Another cowboy caught my eye. I'd say I won the bet.

I lean back and gaze into his eyes. My momma always told me you can trust a man who has good intentions by looking into his eyes when he speaks to you. The eyes don't lie. People can talk a good game, but the eyes are the window to the soul. And that's how you find out if they have a good one or not. And right now, I feel like this one is a good one. I'd be willing to put money on that fact if I were a betting woman. Which usually, I'm not.

And when I look into this sexy man's eyes, they're kind, warm, and reassuring. Very unlike what I'm used to from men. With only two long-term relationships under my belt, and the last one not ending so great, this is new for me.

But his eyes, and the way my body practically vibrates after he touches me, tell me that this is somehow the right course to be on. None of it makes sense, and I don't even know how I got to this moment, but here we are.

I tilt my head up and meet his gaze, a slow smile spreading across my lips. "So, what do you say, cowboy?" I ask, my voice low and hopeful.

He doesn't answer right away, glancing over at the other bartender instead. They exchange a wordless look, a silent conversation that only friends working together for years could perfect. The other bartender gives a quick nod and returns to cleaning up the bar, though his gaze flicks back in our direction, full of curiosity. I don't miss it, even as focused as I am on this man in front of me and the weight of anticipation settling between us on where we're going with this.

"Wait right here for me, darlin'," he says as his warm eyes lock onto mine before he strolls over to where I was sitting and grabs my purse off the table. He stops when one guy says something to him that I can't hear. At first, they'd been harmless, but then one kept overstepping, and then when I told him I wasn't interested, I changed it up and told him I was with the bartender. I figured it would get him off my back.

But I didn't miss how the sexy bartender kept his eye on me all night. Not in a creepy way, but more in a protective way. The kind of guy you'd feel safe around. And then the way he kissed me? Hot as hell. I've never kissed like that before. Tonight is a night of many firsts, and I'm nervous and excited. I left Nashville on a mission to find myself again. A night with a hot, sexy cowboy might just be exactly what I need. And judging by the way he looks at me, it might be exactly what he needs, too.

I've been trying to figure out how old he is. I can't tell for sure, but he seems older than me. His hazel eyes look like the color of whiskey I was drinking. And I can't take my eyes off him.

"This way," he says as he grabs my hand, breaking me out of

my trance as he guides me through the bar and out the back door. The crisp, cool spring air hits me in full force, and I shiver as I follow him to his truck.

It's exactly what I would expect from him. Big, black, with a push bar on the front. Dressed head-to-toe in black, it suits him. Everything about this man is rugged, and intense in a way that draws me in. He's got the whole dark and mysterious thing down.

I wait beside the truck, my fingers curled into my palms, trying not to look at him as he rounds the hood. The night air is thick, charged with something unspoken, something I couldn't fully describe. But I feel it—heavy in my chest, warm in my stomach.

When he reaches my side, he doesn't say anything at first, just reaches past me, his broad frame so close that I catch the faintest whiff of cedar and leather, the scent of him wrapping around me like a slow, deliberate tease.

The door opens, and finally, he glances down at me, those warm hazel eyes flickering in the dim light.

"Need a hand?" His voice is smooth and steady, with just enough rasp to make me shiver.

I could have said no. I should have. But instead, I nod, my breath catching as his hands come to my hips—big, strong hands that settle against me like they belong there.

Heat surges through me, sharp and sudden, as he lifts me effortlessly. For a moment, I lose myself in the press of his grip, the way his fingers curl just right, the warmth of his touch burning straight through my jeans.

I grab onto his forearms without thinking, feeling the strength beneath his shirt, the flex of muscle as he hoists me up into the seat. For a second, just before he lets go, his thumbs brush the bare sliver of skin between my waistband and shirt, a whisper of contact that sends a shock wave through me.

Then, just as quickly, he pulls back.

I barely have time to catch my breath before he leans in again.

The cab feels smaller, the space between us nonexistent as he reaches for the seatbelt. My pulse stutters, my eyes locking onto the way his fingers move—slow, methodical, careful. He isn't touching me, not really, but I feel him everywhere.

The belt slides across my torso, the buckle clicking into place with a sharp finality.

My breath tangles in my throat.

His face is so close now that if I shifted just a little, I'd brush against the rough stubble on his jaw. His lips part slightly, like he wants to say something but thinks better of it.

For a moment, neither of us moves. The only sound is the soft hum of the night around us, the distant chirp of crickets, the wild pounding of my heartbeat.

His gaze drops—just for a second—to my mouth.

Then he exhales, slow and measured like he's fighting something. Like he feels it, too.

"Safe now," he murmurs, his voice lower, rougher.

And then he's gone, stepping back, shutting the door with a quiet click.

I let out the breath I hadn't realized I was holding. Because if that was just him helping me into a damn truck, I'm not sure how I'll survive whatever comes next.

Without a word, he rounds the truck and climbs behind the wheel. The engine growls as he adjusts the controls, cranking up the heat. Then, as if he could read my mind, he reaches into the back seat and hands me a jacket. Black, of course, and soft as butter. I slide it on over my leather jacket that is cute but not warm. He doesn't say a word, the simple gesture carrying more weight for me than it probably should. I'm not used to having a man care about me in little ways like this and anticipate my needs. Let alone a man I just met.

"I...I don't ever do this," I stammer, nerves starting to take over as I rub my palms together and slide my arms into the jacket. It smells like him, and I hope he never wants it back because I want to keep it forever.

"Do what, Red?" he asks as his lip twitches.

And I want to kiss him again.

Red.

It's not a new nickname that I haven't heard all my life with my red hair, but somehow, him calling me Red is sexy as hell. I like the sound of it on his lips.

"I mean...do you do this...often?" I ask, not wanting to be a notch on his bedpost. "I'm not judging, just wondering," I add nervously.

"You'd be the first," he says, his eyes on me, and surprise fills me at his honestly. Suddenly, I realize he might be just as nervous as I am. His eyes say it all. I'm telling you; it's always the eyes that give away a person's emotions.

He glances back over at me. "You make a habit of picking up random men and making them your fake boyfriends?"

I snort. "I've never gone home with anyone before or had a fake boyfriend," I admit as I bite my lip nervously, a habit I know I need to stop. I'm also so nervous that I keep rambling.

"Where's home?" he asks as he stares at my lips for a beat, then his gaze meets my eyes.

"I'm staying at the Dogwood," I say, and he slowly blinks, and then looks away. I can't read his expression, but something in him has shifted. It's like he's reconsidering whether he wants to do this or not, and my heart drops with disappointment, the feeling of rejection creeping in.

"I'll take you home, Red," he says softly as he puts the truck in gear and looks behind him, the scruff of his jaw sexy and dark.

I wonder what it would feel like on my skin again. What his lips would feel like on my body. My hand goes to my lips, where I still taste him and the last of the whiskey I downed hours ago. I rarely drink, and tonight was an exception. I prefer to be sober and, in my head, writing songs whenever I can, and I don't like the way I feel when I've had too much to drink. But tonight, I felt like having fun and fun is what I had, that's for sure. It was fun while it lasted, I guess.

Chapter 3
Violet

As he drives, I watch him out of the corner of my eye, wanting to trace my fingers around his biceps and feel the muscles on his forearms gripping the steering wheel. I wonder what spending the night with this hot cowboy bartender would be like. I might not find out now after what he said.

A few minutes go by, and before I know it, he's pulling into the Dogwood. "I'm in the front in room one-fifteen," I murmur.

He swings in and parks his truck in the back, even though I just told him my room is in the front. He looks over at me. "I'll walk you to your door."

"Alright." I climb out of his truck as he takes my hand and walks me to my door. Disappointment fills me, as I guess he's not staying after all. I wonder what changed his mind.

"What changed your mind?" I ask curiously as I walk next to him.

He turns to look at me, surprised. "What makes you think I changed my mind?"

I hesitate. "It feels like you're walking me to the door to say goodbye."

"Red, a good guy walks you to your door. I didn't change my mind," he says as his warm eyes search mine. "Also, I assume nothing."

I open my mouth and close it again, not even sure what to say. He's distracting me because he smells so good as he stands close.

"Why'd you park in the back?" I ask, searching his eyes for the truth.

He chuckles softly. "Well, because Maggie is a close friend of mine, and I don't want her to give me hell about you. I want to stay with you if that's what you still want. But I don't need her in my business."

I grin, knowing damn well that sounds like my aunt Maggie, the silver-haired owner of the Dogwood who also basically runs this town. And knowing that she's a friend of his makes me feel even better about him. Maggie is a stellar judge of character.

We get to my room, and suddenly, I'm so nervous. I'm sweating. The way he's looking at me now has me clenching my thighs.

He places both hands on the door frame on each side of me and leans in. He places his mouth close to my ear. "I'm going to kiss you now." He tips his head back and searches my eyes for permission before leaning in and kissing me softly.

My fists clench his shirt, and I kiss him back with a hunger I didn't know I had. The current between us is back, pulling him into me, like somehow, we're tethered together. He smells so good. Like leather and pine, and if I could bottle him up and always keep that scent with me, I would.

I moan into his kiss, the heat of it unraveling me from the inside out. I want him, and it's all consuming. No one has ever made me feel like this, like I'm on the edge and ready to fall.

"Fuck," he groans softly into my mouth as he pulls back and gazes at me. "You feel that, right?"

"Yeah," I murmur as my arms still cling to him, desire filling me like I've never felt with anyone. We're both panting and staring into each other's eyes. They way I want this man right now is practically criminal.

"What's it gonna be, Red?" he asks as his eyes search mine as if he's peering into the window of *my* soul now. And it's the most intimate thing I've ever felt with a man. His vulnerability, asking for permission, and not just assuming and taking as another man in my life has done. And it feels good to be wanted and desired right back in return.

"One night," I murmur as I reach into my purse and fish nervously for my room key.

Damn, I love it when he calls me Red. Since it's just one night, sharing names is unnecessary. I kind of like the mystery of us. Just one night and back to our normal lives. Only nothing feels normal about this.

I finally find it, my hands shaking as his hand gently covers mine. He takes the key from me and unlocks the door with ease. He pushes it open for me, allowing me to enter first, his eyes watching my every move as if he can't take them off me. Something is happening here, and it's as strong as the current of emotions pulsing through my body.

I waste no time, tossing my purse onto the chair by the table and turning as he shuts and locks the door. His hands gently cup and then trace my chin, pulling me in. He searches my eyes for permission, and he scoops me up. His arms cup my bottom, and lays me on the bed, his eyes lighting up as he admires me.

"What do you want?" he asks, his deep voice sending a shiver down my spine and igniting a spark in me.

"You," I say breathlessly. "Very much, you."

And it's not the whiskey talking. I only had one but over a span of hours. Every part of me wants to be with this man, even for just one night. He's the only cowboy I had eyes for in that bar. Nobody could hold a candle to this man in the middle of fucking nowhere Wyoming with broad shoulders, bedroom whiskey eyes, and a possessiveness when he kisses me that I'll probably never get over after I leave.

"Strip," I command with a sly grin.

He shakes his head and chuckles. "Why am I not surprised you'd be a little devil, Red?"

I quirk a brow at him and tilt my head, waiting.

He sets his cowboy hat on the table and reaches behind his neck, pulling his shirt off in one big sexy swoop to reveal a wide, broad chest that's defined but not overly muscled. He's just normal but somehow freaking fine as hell. His whiskey-brown eyes twinkle as he looks at me and tilts his head like he's waiting.

"Oh, it's my turn?" I ask innocently as I kick off my boots. I like this give-and-take game. Tonight is going to be fun.

I slide off his jacket and my leather jacket and smile at him.

"Cheater." He chuckles and takes off his boots while his eyes stay steady on me.

I reach down and slowly unbutton and unzip my jeans and kick them off, leaving me standing before him in my sexy red lacy panties and tight green sweater.

I silently thank myself for choosing these tonight because, judging by the look on his face, they were the right choice. They're hitting him just right, and he's enjoying this.

His eyes smolder, and his grin is gone. He's looking at me in a way that I can't describe. But if I ever meet another man who doesn't look at me this way, I don't want him. This is what I want from now on. The standard has now been set.

He unbuckles his belt, sliding it off in one swift motion, and it makes a snapping sound. I smirk because it's so hot and so freaking dirty. I almost come undone at the simple movement. Taking a deep breath, I close my eyes for a second.

He watches me, amused, as he slowly unzips his jeans. I can

barely hold myself back from touching him. He lowers them, and his muscular thighs bulge under his black boxer briefs. Of course, they're black briefs, and damn if they don't look good on him.

I slowly peel off my top, revealing a matching red lace push-up bra that does wonders for my boobs that I'm also glad I chose for tonight.

"Do you always wear matching lace bras and panties?" His voice croaks, unsteady.

"I have a whole drawer full of them in every color. Want to see?" I challenge as I lift a brow at him. "Beautiful lingerie is kind of my thing, cowboy."

"Later, Red," he says as he kneels before me and looks up at me with needy eyes. "I need to taste you first."

My fingers slide into his hair, threading through the soft strands, but then he pauses. His hands roam down my body, warm and deliberate, until his fingertips brush the tattoo on my upper thigh. Slowly, he traces the ink, following the delicate petals of the flowers before his fingers skim over the words etched into my skin.

He tilts his head, his expression unreadable as he looks up at me. His thumb brushes over the lyrics, a touch so light it sends a shiver down my spine.

I glance down, my breath hitching. "Just an old song. I like music."

His gaze lingers on the words, his voice quiet, almost reverent. "Beautiful song."

"It's an old favorite," I admit, heat flooding through me.

He hasn't even really touched me yet, but God, I'm already unraveling.

I hiss in a breath as he hooks a finger quickly through my panties and pulls them down, trapping me at his mercy. His fingers moving to circle my clit.

"Yesssssssss." I roll my head back, and he puts his hands on my hips and guides me to the edge of the bed.

"Tonight, you're mine, Red."

"Alright, Cowboy, show me what you've got," I say as his mouth meets my core and I arch my back, a current surging through my body as his mouth takes over.

He takes his time with me like he's got all the time in the world, making me feel like I'm going to come apart harder than I've never come apart before. He takes me to the brink and then before I come, he slows it down and takes his time, and it feels so damn good. The only two other men who've ever gone down on me did it as a pit stop or a chore before we had the most basic, disappointing, vanilla sex that left me unsatisfied every single time. I thought that was just how it was going to be for the rest of my life. No one has ever made me feel like they want me like this and actually enjoyed my body. And so far, I'm loving being enjoyed by this cowboy. Very much.

He uses his fingers and works me as he sucks and gently uses his teeth and his breath, and finally, he makes me come so hard I see fucking stars. Fucking stars. This cowboy is going to ruin me, and I'll never be the same again. I'll compare every single man I ever meet to this man from now on and the way he makes me feel. Jesus. What the hell have I done?

He then slowly trickles his kisses across my thighs and up my abdomen, and in one swift motion, he has my bra off and flings it across the room as if it offends him. Taking his time on my nipples, he makes them pebble hard, and when he seems satisfied with that, he peppers my collarbone with soft kisses and goosebumps cover my skin.

Palming my breasts in his hands like he's won them as a prize, he hums when he sucks and flicks his tongue across my nipples, taking his time with pleasure etched on his face.

Holy shit.

He trails slow, deliberate kisses down my abdomen, his gaze locking onto mine as he murmurs, "Tonight's going to be a night you'll never forget."

A shiver runs through me, but I tease, "I guess pretending to be with me was totally worth it."

His lips curve into a wicked smirk as he hovers above my skin. "Wasn't hard to pretend," he murmurs, voice thick with heat. "But I'd rather show you how real it can feel."

He works me with his tongue, and I squeeze the sheets, clenching my body, feeling everything. The scruff of his cheeks between my thighs as he uses his fingers and tongue to take me just to the edge, and before I go over, he pulls me back again, taking his time.

"What do you want now?" he asks, his gaze locking onto mine, dark and smoldering. His hair is tousled, messy from my hands, making him look effortlessly sexy—wild and completely untamed.

"I want you inside of me," I plead, breath panting, mouth salivating, and gaze glued to the rock-hard, sizeable bulge protruding from his black boxers.

He reaches for his pants, pulling out a condom from his wallet, and rips it open. He slides his boxers down, and I watch every move he makes, entranced.

Jesus, he's so sexy.

He rolls on the condom and leans over to me, kissing me and trickling his fingers down my breasts again to tease my nipples which are now rock-hard.

He works my clit again and whispers, "You're so wet, Red. Is this for me?"

I nod, unable to speak because I'm so close. He continues, watching me, kissing my ear, my cheek, my lips, and I finally can't take it anymore.

My body clenches hard on his fingers, and I see stars.

I moan, and he fists his cock and slides gently into me, making me gasp.

He gently takes me first, working his way up to a faster pace. The way he takes his time, kissing me, touching me, exploring me, it's like I'm a treasure he just discovered. Gentle, yet powerful and giving.

"More," I plead.

He gives me what I want, taking me, moving me onto all fours, and pressing me into the pillow as he pounds me hard from behind. When I feel like I'm close again, he groans, and I come hard, just from the sound of his voice.

He moves with me, as if our bodies have now become one, and I don't want this night to end. His fingers intertwine with mine. Neither of us seem to want to stop touching each other. Each touch is electric and addicting. Because I haven't felt this in a long time. True passion, true longing for someone's touch. And tonight, he's given me it all.

He grips my hands, holding me tight while both of us come down from our high.

He lies next to me, holding me, looking into my eyes.

"Hi," I whisper, unsure what to say after that.

"Hi," he whispers back, tucking a lock of my hair behind my ear.

"How was your first one-night stand from the bar with your fake boyfriend?" he teases.

"Well, I'm not sure. We might need to do it again," I say, mimicking his playful tone.

He laughs, and I love the sound of it and the way his eyes crinkle in the corners when he smiles.

"Give me a minute, and I'll give you anything you want," he chuckles.

"And what do you want?" I ask as I push up on my elbow.

"I'm pretty happy with this." He smiles as he gets up and goes to the bathroom.

I take a deep breath and look up. He seems so beautiful, sweet, kind, and considerate. All things women want in a man. Where did he even come from?

I think about how avoiding people has been my mission lately. But being with him tonight is what I need. I needed this even just for one night.

Chapter 4
Walker

I wasn't lying when I said I've never taken a woman home from my bar. Mixing work with pleasure has never been my style. Sure, I've had a few one-night stands over the years, less than I can count on one hand—but only when I've been out of town for meetings. None of them came close to what had just happened with her.

Red isn't just a one-night stand. She's a fucking sensation. The way her body responds to mine, and her touch turns me to fire—she's indescribable. Like fireworks lighting up the sky on the Fourth of July. Like a natural high that no substance could ever match. What happened between us wasn't just fun. It was unforgettable.

She was this gorgeous siren in my bar that I couldn't take my eyes off all night. And what would the chance be that she's staying at the Dogwood of all places? The motel run by Maggie, who is like a mother to me and a grandmother to my daughter, Makayla, affectionately known as Mack. That's why I have to get the hell out of here. I can't let Maggie see my truck parked here at her motel. She'll have so many questions that I won't give her answers to. And the shit she'll give me will be annoying.

The shit she already gives me is annoying. I don't need to add this to it as well. We have a unique relationship as it is with our constant jabs and sparring. But deep down, she's family to me. She's all I've got. Maggie isn't originally from here, and has family in another state, so she kind of became a transplant like me and made her own family here locally.

I quietly slide out of bed, sliding my boxers and jeans on as quietly as possible, tucking my feet into my boots, and grabbing my shirt from the floor. I see her red lace panties and snag them, tucking them in my pocket. This was a night I'll never forget. As much as I'll think about her and this night, I have a lot on my plate right now and doubt that a woman as incredible as her will stick around in a small town in the middle of nowhere in Wyoming.

She's like a dream lying there, her red wavy hair fanned out over her pillow in the moonlight shining in from the window, her perfectly plump lips parted slightly. She sleeps so peacefully after the orgasms I gave her.

I resist kissing those lips, even though I want to taste her.

I freeze when my eyes land on a battered guitar case leaning against the corner next to a small duffel bag with clothes spilling out. The sight knocks the breath out of me.

I glance back at her, surprise flickering through me. But then it's something else—something deeper. I can't stop staring, the pull toward her undeniable, like gravity itself.

I can't help but wonder about the guitar. Does she play for fun? Does she perform? Musicians aren't exactly common in this town, and another female musician is the last thing I need in my life.

She mentioned loving music—casually, like it was nothing—when I traced the lyrics inked on her thigh.

The lyrics I wrote. A song I poured my soul into years ago,

now permanently etched on her skin. She has no idea. She can't. There's no way.

When my fingers followed those words, something in me twisted, a long-buried piece of my past clawing its way to the surface. But there's no way she knows. I've spent years making sure of that, burying that part of myself so deep it's practically a ghost.

If I could ever imagine myself having a woman to call mine, it would be someone like her. Sassy, confident, and sexy. But there was a vulnerability to her, too, that is just as alluring.

This night has been nothing short of a dream. A dream that, unfortunately, has to stay just a dream. Because someone as beautiful as Red is just passing through Bridger Falls. She doesn't strike me as the type who would ever stay far from the nearest city in rural Wyoming. Which makes me wonder why she's even here. Sadly, I'll never get to find out. I have to go. It's better this way. I try to convince myself of this, anyway.

It takes everything to pull open that door and get in my truck. The loneliness that lives in me makes me want to crawl back into that warm bed with her. And take her to breakfast in the morning. Get to know her more. Ask her why that song means so much to her that she'd mark it on her body forever. Hear her laugh as many times as I can before she leaves. Because she'll leave. Everyone leaves eventually.

I reluctantly go to my truck but look back a few times, still trying to process everything that happened tonight. I've never met anyone like her. Had a connection with anyone like this before. It feels surreal.

The streets of Bridger Falls are quiet this late at night, the kind of stillness that only happens in a town where folks turn in early, where the only things stirring after dark were the occasional ranch truck rumbling down Main Street and the soft glow of porch lights left on out of habit. It's peaceful and calming here.

As I drive, the truck's tires hum over the cracked pavement, past the familiar landmarks of home. The Bridger Falls Feed and Supply sign sways slightly in the night breeze, its weathered wood a testament to years of Wyoming wind and sun. Across the street, the Harvest & Honey diner sits dark, its navy-and-white-checkered curtains drawn for the night, but come dawn, the smell of fresh coffee and cinnamon rolls will pull customers in for their daily treats.

The town square is empty now, the string lights hanging between the buildings swaying gently, casting a soft shimmer against the storefronts—the bank, the general store, the Boots and Bangs salon—all standing in quiet patience for morning foot traffic.

The last set of streetlights faded in my rear-view mirror as I cross the town's edge, the landscape opening into rolling pastures and thick clusters of pine. Out here, there are no sidewalks, no streetlights, just dark, open land stretching for miles beneath a sky full of stars.

My turnoff comes twenty minutes later, a narrow dirt road marked by a simple wooden post with my mailbox, half-covered in creeping sage. My truck rumbles onto the gravel, the tires crunching against the earth as I start down the long driveway, lined on either side by weathered wooden fencing.

My land sprawls wide, acres of open pasture rolling out under the moonlight, framed by thick pines that offered a natural border against the world. The lake shimmers in the distance, a silver ribbon reflecting the sky, its glassy surface untouched by anything but the occasional ripple from a late-night breeze.

And then, my home comes into view.

With its rustic timber beams and high-pitched roof, the

house stands proud against the Wyoming range, its windows glowing faintly from the few lights I'd left on. The wraparound porch stretches wide with deep-seated rocking chairs arranged neatly beneath the eaves, waiting for the kind of slow mornings I rarely have time for.

Not far from the main house sits the barn, its silhouette strong and familiar, the scent of hay and leather always lingering in the air. The paddocks stretch beyond, fenced and ready, even though the horses are still settled in.

And nestled just across the lake, sits the cabin. Smaller, cozier, with a stone chimney and a wide rustic front porch that overlooks the water. A place meant for quiet, solitude, and creation.

The truck rolls to a stop, the engine settling into silence. I sit there for a moment, looking at the home I've built, the space that should feel like peace.

Instead, all I can think about is the woman I left in town.

With a slow exhale, I climb out, the crisp night air filling my lungs as I head toward the house.

I unlock the back door, passing through the house, aglow with a few lamps.

I look at my watch. Four in the morning. Too wound up to sleep, I grab a few waters from the fridge and make my way down to the dock where my boat is tied up.

My cabin across the lake in the back of my house is my solace, one that has been just mine for well over the past decade. And this is the place I come to take out all my loneliness, pouring them into writing songs, and making masterpieces for other people to sing. Because that's what keeps me going. Keeps me sane. Gives me something for me.

Making music is mine and mine alone. I don't even share it with my fifteen-year-old daughter, although music is very much a part of our life in other ways. She's active in her high school band and she can play several instruments. We own so much vinyl, we could open up our own vinyl shop. Music is a passion that can never take center stage in my life ever again. That entire stage is reserved for Mack now, and it always will be. I've made a good living writing songs and selling them privately, but running the bar and being a good dad is all I want people to see when they look at me now.

When Maggie suggested ten years ago that I buy the run-down local bar in town, I balked at first. I didn't know anything about running a bar. I'm a former country musician. I retired here to Bridger Falls with more money than I knew what to do with. Now I write songs under a different name and live a quiet solitary life.

But becoming a single dad in an instant and realizing you have a whole human that depends on you for everything in life will quickly snap you back to reality. Mack didn't deserve everything that happened to her. But I've made damn sure that she's had everything she's ever needed and given her the best possible life that I could. She will always be my top priority.

I keep writing to try to feel something. And up until tonight, writing songs was the only space that gave me that.

Until Red.

I settle in my chair, kick back, and pick up my guitar, playing a melody that chased me all evening. I write a few lyrics down on the pad of paper I keep in my pocket every day. I open it and begin to sing and tweak the lyrics as I strum my guitar.

After two hours I have a song. It's not perfect, but it's a song that I'll keep working on and sharpen it until it's ready to send over to my manager. I'll sell it and then I'll write another one. Just like I do with every song. Rinse and repeat. Then I'll hear it all over the place. And I won't tell anyone that I wrote it. I thought I had everything I needed in my life. A great kid that I love, a business that I enjoy, and I get to write songs. But lately I've been feeling like things are different.

But something tells me this song is different. This song just might be for me. I might tuck this one away. I haven't wanted to do that before tonight. I think about the guitar in Red's room with the battered case. A guitar that looked well-loved and used. Not a brand new one that someone's looking to learn to play. I imagine Red and her smooth velvet voice singing a song and playing guitar, and my chest fills with warmth. I imagine myself singing this very song with Red and performing it beside her. Her plump red lips singing along as she strums her guitar.

Then I shake off the thoughts as quickly as they come. I used to share my music with someone and that nearly ruined me. It can never happen. That didn't end the way I thought it would, and opening myself back to music opens up a can of worms I can't afford to open. A risk I'm not willing to take.

Music will always be private to me. It has to be.

I make my way back to the house and head to the barn.

It's early and the animals need to be taken care of before I try to get some sleep. Although, I'm not sure I can even sleep after last night. My mind is still vibrating with energy after being with her.

I run my hands over my horses and remind them that our favorite girl will be home in a few days. I make sure they have their feed, hay and water. I'm pretty much their back up human. They love Mack so much, and I know they tolerate me taking care of them, but they miss her.

I look over at the house as I make my way back inside. When I first built this home, I dreamed of having a family here. A big house full of people, laughter, and fun. But that hasn't been the way life has worked out. So far, it's just me, Mack, and Maggie. And of course, our growing farm that Mack keeps convincing me to add animals to. And we have a good life. I'm grateful for everything that I have in my life.

Until last night, I kept my life guarded. Didn't take chances. It helps that Bridger Falls is small and there's not a huge dating pool. I also can't imagine what Mack would say if I dated. Sometimes I think she's lonely as well and deserves more people in her life, but other times I'm not sure. Maybe we're fine just the way that we are.

We're lucky to have so many good friends here in town. I can call anyone and lend a helping hand when it's needed. This town has helped me heal in ways it'll never know. It's been our refuge, and our safe place.

It's safer to keep it that way.

Chapter 5
Violet
I remember every little thing.

I sit up quickly, grasping the sheet to my naked chest as my heart pounds. Did I dream everything that happened last night? My hand slides across the empty space beside me, the cool sheets confirming what I already fear. Maybe that was all just one hell of a dream.

I groan and collapse back onto the bed, burying my face in the pillow next to me. That's when it hits me — the familiar scent of leather and pine, rugged and intoxicating. His scent still wraps me in a memory I'm not ready to let go of.

I bite my lip and smile, murmuring, "Definitely wasn't a dream."

Disappointment fills me that he left before I could even learn his name. Maybe he's a Luke. Or maybe a Ryan. Nah, he doesn't look like either of those. I consider asking Aunt Maggie later. But I don't want to give away that I was with him; he didn't want her knowing, and I won't give up our secret. And we both agreed that it would only be one night.

And it was freaking amazing. Glorious.

My first one-night stand was a night I'll never forget for the rest of my life. My mind roams back to the possessiveness of his hands, his lips all over me, and my hand instinctively goes to my neck where the scruff of his dark, neatly trimmed beard still leaves me tingling, remembering where his mouth was on my neck.

I remember the way his eyes met mine, and I almost felt sadness or loneliness a few times like there's a deepness there I wanted to explore. The way our bodies seemed to fit together, our chemistry was off the charts. I've never met anyone like him before and I don't even know his name. A cowboy bartender who works at The Black Dog in Bridger Falls, Wyoming. I hadn't planned on going out last night. But I'm glad that I did. I realize I left my car there and I'm going to have to ask Maggie for a ride to go get it.

Nice, Violet. You don't even know his name.

I get up and reluctantly take a shower, my body still feeling him from last night. I wonder what time he left. I really wish he'd stayed. Then I think about how he parked in the back even though he knew my room was in the front. My stomach drops with dread, my eyes squeezing shut in horror as I bury my face in my hands.

What if he's married? Oh my god.

I don't think he's married. He didn't strike me as the type to do something like that. There was a quiet honesty about him, something solid that made me believe he's a good man. I didn't see a ring, and his truck was spotless, no evidence of a family. I didn't think to ask, but now I wish I had, just to be sure. I'm not that kind of woman. I don't cheat, and I can't stand cheaters. After what my ex puts me through, the thought makes my stomach turn.

Shaking off the feeling of uneasiness, I finish getting ready and head to the motel office. The moment I step through the Dogwood's small front room, Maggie looks up, her expression softening with relief.

"You're here," she says, her voice warm and comforting.

I've been here just a few days now, and Maggie and I have settled into an easy rhythm together. She's my favorite aunt, my mom's older sister. And after everything I went through the past year, coming here to lick my wounds and figure out my next move with Maggie just made sense. It's been far too long since I've been back here.

"I got worried when I didn't see your car," she says as she pours me a cup of coffee from the coffee pot. She's got faded denim wranglers on, a bright pink shirt, and a denim vest with pink and blue flowers embroidered on it. Her feet wear hot pink cowboy boots. Maggie's pushing seventy and is eclectic and unique, and I just adore her. Staying here with her is healing me in ways I couldn't begin to describe.

"I left it at the bar last night," I admit sheepishly. "Can you give me a ride later to pick it up?"

She chuckles and raises a brow. "Do I want to know?"

"Probably not." I shake my head and grin. "Let's just say that the whiskey at the Black Dog was good."

And a lot of other things were very good. Like the hot cowboy bartender who cannot be named. But of course, I keep that to myself with a smile.

"Glad to see that you're getting out and doing young people stuff," she smirks as she stacks a few papers on her desk.

"Yeah, well I like hanging out with you, too," I say. "You can come with me next time to the Black Dog."

"I'd be down for supper some night," she shrugs.

Maggie and I have always been close, but one thing about her is that she isn't a gossip. She loves the people of this town and pours into them, but she's not offering up information on people that isn't relevant, and I respect her for that. In fact, that's one of the reasons why I trust her and chose to stay here for a while. Maggie is a good person deep down to her core and always has been. That's why she's my favorite aunt.

"You up for helping me with some rooms today?" she asks over her mug as she interrupts my thoughts. She looks tired again today. But then again, before I got here, she'd been running this place on her own and cleaning all the rooms by herself. And for a motel in the small town of Bridger Falls, she stays surprisingly busy. I have no idea how she was doing everything on her own.

"Of course," I say with a nod. "I'm ready. What's the plan?"

"Lots of checkouts. It's a busy day," she says as she lays out the set of master keys and a note of the rooms and special instructions next to their numbers.

When I left Nashville, I knew staying with Maggie would be the best option for me. I needed a break from my life. I love my parents, but I needed to go where I could figure things out without my parents trying to do it for me. I needed my Maggie.

Where's the best place to do that? In Bridger Falls, according to Maggie Pines, the proud owner of the Dogwood. I wouldn't necessarily say I'm hiding out, but I don't want to go home. I don't have a home to go back to anymore. Maggie seemed to find that amusing and murmured something about someone else she knew. Whatever that means. I have a feeling that the people of Bridger Falls look out for each other, and that's something I need in my life right now. I haven't had anyone in my corner for a while. And I'll admit that it feels good to have a soft place to land around someone I can trust. Maggie doesn't pry and hasn't asked me what happened back in Nashville, and I'm grateful for that. I just need time to figure everything out.

After I had been here a few days, Maggie made me a deal. If I help her out at the motel, I can stay here as long as I need to and have a job, as long as I give her plenty of notice before taking off again. I think she loves having someone here with her. The feeling is mutual.

I took her deal. And I am thankful for her every day.

We've had our routine for the past few days. I clean all her rooms for her, and then we play canasta or gin rummy until bedtime on the back porch of the Dogwood. I do all the heavy lifting for her. And we have lots of laughs, and she's full of hilarious stories that never get old. She and my mother are alike, and I think it's comforting to be near her.

I'm not sure whose soul is getting rehabbed more here, hers or mine. And despite being seventy years old, she's a freaking hoot. She comes and goes, sometimes asking me to sit at the desk and keep an eye on things. She does a lot for people around town and calls upon them when she needs something done as well. She's like the grandmother to all. She knows everything and everyone.

She's normally clad in mostly denim, and a different bright color accentuates her accessories and clothing daily with her matching cowboy boots that she must have in every color. Her hair is white and styled in a neat bob that hangs just above her shoulders. She's got class, style, and sass. I wouldn't mind being just like Aunt Maggie when I grow up.

I may be thirty next week, but I'm still figuring out my life. I guess I'm a late bloomer. I've spent the past decade playing music, making music, and that's been my life along with a few bartender jobs to get by when I wasn't making enough with music.

Her phone rings, and she answers it, smiling when she sees the caller, "Hello, sugar," she says with her thick country accent. She's probably talking to one of the many friends she has here in Bridger Falls.

She puts a hand to her hip and laughs. "Oh, you will do so good. I'm so proud of you, sweetie."

She carries on her conversation for a few minutes while I stock the cleaning cart with everything I'll need for the day.

"Alright now, sugar. Text me when you get done. Bye now."

I stock the linen cart and push it all to the back door, ready to get going for the day. If I'm being honest, it's not my favorite job I've ever had, but it's been good for my soul in ways I can't explain. I clean, I think about my life, I work songs out in my head, I get tired, and I sleep solid as a rock at night. Something I wasn't doing back in Nashville. Before I left, I was never able to sleep. Wyoming has somehow fixed that. I sleep like a baby here. Maybe it's all the fresh country air.

Cleaning has given me time to think about what I want now and what I don't want. So far, I know what I don't want. I haven't gotten to what I want yet. And that's why I'm staying in Bridger Falls until I figure it out. But what I do know is that I will never let another man lie to me or make me feel less than I am ever again. I know who I am. And last night was proof of that. I didn't go out looking for fun, but I found it all the same. My whiskey-eyed cowboy didn't make false promises of forever but gave me mind-blowing orgasms. That's all I needed.

"Sugar, how do you feel about dogs?" Maggie asks as she joins me in the back.

"I love dogs," I smile. "Why?"

"Well, good. Me personally, I don't trust anyone who says they don't like dogs. Like something's wrong with 'em or something. Dogs are good for the soul."

"Okay?" I shrug, confused at where she's going with this conversation. But that's just Maggie. She'll have random conversations that sometimes I never end up figuring out, and our time together is never boring, that's for sure. And I agree with her. I love dogs. You know why? I've never met a narcissist dog. They're just good. People on the other hand, are not always so good.

"Well, it's a good thing you like 'em because I need you to watch one for a day or so. I've been looking after one, and I need you to help me take over."

"Okay," I agree. Bet. I'll take a dog to snuggle any day. And let's just be honest. If Maggie asks me to do something, I'm doing it. I'd do anything for her. And if it involves animals, it's an automatic yes.

"Good, good. I'll bring her by later," she says as she picks up her purse and slings it over her shoulder. Pink leather that matches her boots with cowboy leather fringe. Of course, she has a matching bag. I'd expect nothing less from Maggie.

"Can't wait," I say as I watch her.

"Now I need to run a few errands. You got the rooms; I'll check in later, and we'll do lunch." She waves as she heads out.

"Alright," I call as I take off to clean as quickly as I can. I've got a song brewing in my head that I want to write down. I work out the melody while I clean. I've been struggling to write for the past week. My heart hasn't been in the place. I was in fight-or-flight mode back in Nashville. And it was more fight until I finally left and decided I was done being a puppet and being manipulated and taken advantage of by my mentor and friend.

* * *

A few hours later, I'm done for the day. I've showered and I'm sitting in the chair in my room, scripting out lyrics that are pouring out of me. Maybe my sexy bartender really was my lucky charm because right now I can't stop writing, and the creative streak is flowing.

A knock jolts me back to reality, and I look out the window to see Maggie juggling a wiggling black fur ball trying to kiss her face.

No freaking way.

I snatch open the door and squeal as I take the dog from her, who turns and proceeds to profusely lick my face. "Who is this cutie?"

"Pickles," she says and rolls her eyes. "And before you say anything, I didn't name her that ridiculous name."

"Aww," I laugh. "She's so sweet."

"She's a puppy and gets into everything, so good luck," she adds as she comes in and sets down a small bag of groceries. Maggie shows her love by bringing you food and taking care of you. And Maggie wants to be loved in return with acts of service. That is probably why we go together like peas and carrots. I like to be fed, and she likes me to help her with the motel. It's a win-win if you ask me.

"I just love her," I coo, scratching her ears.

Maggie glances over at my notebook and guitar propped against the table. "Oh good, you're getting some writing done."

"Yeah, a song came to me that I'm trying to work out," I admit as I kiss the dog's head and stroke her super soft jet-black puppy fur.

"Whose dog is this?" I ask.

She waves her hand. "A friend. I'm just lookin' after her for a few days. Or you are now, I guess." She cocks her brow.

"I could never turn down puppy snuggles," I say as I hug her to me as her mouth stretches in a big yawn and her puppy breath has me chuckling and kissing her head again.

"Good. Now let's go have some lunch. You can put her in the kennel in the front office while we're gone and Gene catches up the laundry. He's watching the front desk for me."

"I still don't have my car," I suddenly realize and look at Maggie. "Can you take me to pick it up after we eat?"

"Your car's out in front of the office, and here's your key." She reaches into her pocket, tossing it to me.

"But how did it get here?" I ask nervously, not wanting to

admit to her that I slept with the bartender last night. He made it clear he didn't want her to know. While I don't like keeping things from her, this secret feels like it's a good one to keep.

She shrugs. "Cash dropped it off and left the keys. Said you'd left it there last night."

Cash.

He must have dropped it off for me. It doesn't surprise me. He was a perfect gentleman after all. Up until he left without saying goodbye. I guess he didn't want me to come back to the bar to get it and make things awkward. That's that, I guess. No fling with the mystery man. After all, we did agree on one night.

***

Maggie and I head over to the Harvest & Honey deli. We walk in, and I notice everyone waves and smiles at Maggie. The townsfolk smile politely at me and nod as I slide into the well-worn booth. Maggie chats it up with a few people and doesn't bother to look at the blue and white checkered menu I study intently to avoid the curious stares.

The deli is tucked into the heart of Bridger Falls, a cozy little spot with a dark blue awning and a hand-painted wooden sign that reads Harvest & Honey in faded gold lettering. The scent of fresh-baked bread and smoked meats wraps around us the moment we step inside, the warmth of the space a stark contrast to the cool mountain air outside.

The walls are painted a deep sage green, full of rustic wooden shelves lined with jars of homemade jam and honey and locally cured meats. Framed black-and-white photos of Bridger Falls' earliest days hang between vintage tin signs advertising old soda brands and farm-fresh eggs. The hardwood floors are worn but well-kept, adding to the deli's lived-in charm.

A row of square wooden tables, each topped with checkered cloths in warm shades of navy and cream, fill the main seating area. Mason jars hold fresh wildflowers at the center of each table, and small, mismatched chairs add to the quaint, homey feel. The counter, a long stretch of dark oak, showcases an array of deli meats, cheeses, and house-made pickles under a spotless glass case. Behind it, a chalkboard menu lists the day's specials in loopy handwriting, complete with little doodles of sandwiches and steaming soup bowls.

Soft country music plays from an old radio behind the counter, the hum of a familiar tune blending with the quiet chatter of the few late-afternoon customers. Overhead, Edison bulbs hang from thick ropes, casting a warm glow over the space and making it feel like the kind of place where people linger long after their meal is done, just talking and sipping sweet tea.

I can already tell that it's not just a deli. It's a gathering place, an important piece of Bridger Falls' heartbeat, where stories are swapped over pastrami on rye and old friends catch up over steaming mugs of locally roasted coffee.

And in that moment, in the warm glow of Harvest & Honey, I can't help but feel a bit at home.

Maggie doesn't cook, and before I got here, she told me she went out to eat practically daily or went over to other people's houses to eat. I've been cooking every night for us, and it's been so much fun. She has a cozy little kitchen in the back of the Dogwood and a surprisingly stocked pantry for someone who doesn't eat at home. She splits her time between the Dogwood and friends' houses. I can't wait to make more of my favorite meals for her.

I decide on the grilled chicken BLT and a bowl of roasted tomato soup. As I wait for Maggie, the unofficial town mayor, to make her rounds saying hello and greeting everyone, I gaze over the glass deli case that holds various baked goods that are mouthwatering and delicious looking.

I decide that I'm going to get a piece of chocolate cake, too.

"Alright, sugar, what are you gettin'?" she asks as she slides into the booth across from me as our server arrives at our table.

I give her my order, and she nods. "Good choices. Make that two of everything," she tells the server.

"Tell me about your song. What's your inspiration for this new creative flow?" She grins mischievously like she's fishing for some information.

I play it off and shrug, "I went to the Black Dog last night and listened to some music and drank some whiskey. It was a good night."

"Hmm," she says as she watches me, missing nothing.

"Hmmm, what?" I laugh.

"Maybe it's time you meet a few more of the young locals and make some friends since you'll be staying awhile."

"You don't like my company?" I tease. "Who will play cards with you if I'm off gallivanting? And who says I'm staying awhile?"

"Oh, sugar, I love your company," she says as the server slides our food in front of us. We thank our server and dig in, eating in silence for a few moments, and Maggie says to me, "I'm glad you're here, Violet. You can stay as long as you want."

"Thanks, Maggie. I'm glad I'm here too. Thanks for letting me stay," I say as I take a small spoonful of the hot soup. Bridger Falls is growing on me. I visited as a kid but haven't been back for a long time. Usually, Maggie came to visit us.

"You're helping me more," she says with a smile. "I'm getting the better end of this deal."

"So, what do you know about the bartender at the Black Dog?" I ask casually.

"What do you want to know?" she asks, but something in her tone is guarded.

"Is he married?" I ask.

"Yes," she says, sounding surprised that I'm asking. "Cash is married and has a baby on the way."

A baby on the way.

My breath catches as I try to hide my horrified gaze, the sound of my soup sliding from my spoon with a plop.

I'm horrified as that news settles in, but I try my best to hide it. "Good to know." I jut my chin up and say, "Let's play cards."

My stomach drops like it's bottoming out. My chest grows tight, my breath stutters, and my stomach turns with nausea. I feel awful and disgusted with myself, but mostly furious at him for hiding that he has a baby and is married.

She doesn't say anything further and pulls out a deck from her purse. We play a few hands until we head back to the Dogwood.

Fucking men.

And this is why I'm in Bridger Falls in the first place. To get away from people who take advantage of and shit on others. I hope I never see that cowboy ever again. Actually, I hope I do. I'm going to give him a piece of my mind. I'm no longer tolerating anyone treating me less than I deserve. And I didn't deserve that. Neither did his poor wife.

Chapter 6
Walker
Lies Lies Lies

I'm supposed to be focused on inventory. The bar isn't open yet, which makes it the perfect time to catch up on paperwork, crank up my play list, and get things done. But instead of counting bottles of tequila, I recount the memory of her fire-red hair against the pillow, the way she laughed, and the way her lips felt on mine. When I close my eyes, I can still taste her.

I bury myself in work, or at least I've tried to. I'm desperate to keep my mind off her. It doesn't work, not even close.

Red lingers in my mind like a song, and I can't stop hearing it play over and over in my heart.

And then she pulls up in my parking lot.

My pen falls to the counter with a soft clatter.

She doesn't see me since the bar windows are tinted. But I watch her and suddenly feel nervous and excited.

"What is she doing here?" I mutter even though there is no one to hear.

My heart races. I should go back to my paperwork and pretend I don't care. It was one night. I shouldn't care this much. But her showing up here messes with my already tangled thoughts.

She looks different in the daytime. When the door shuts to the bar, sunlight pouring in around her, it almost looks like her hair is ablaze. Even her silhouette hints at the dips and curves of her body. Dips and curves I know intimately. I stand here like some lovesick idiot, watching as she makes her way toward the bar.

She's here. And I'm about to find out why.

She looks over at me through the hazy bar that is still dark because we're not open yet.

"Hi," she calls flatly. But her tone has changed. It's not playful like it was, it's serious.

"Hi," I clip a little too gruffly, nervous at her change in demeanor as I run my hand over my beard.

I hope she's not mad Cash dropped her car off on his way to the bank. I just wanted to make sure that she had it and wasn't stranded.

She stops in front of me. Then I realize she looks pissed. Really pissed.

"You, okay?" I ask hesitantly.

"No. I'm not," she hisses.

"Okay," I reply, running through reasons in my mind why she could be so mad. The only thing I can come up with is leaving without saying goodbye. Her eyes continue to flare with anger, and she looks like she wants to murder me.

"Did you forget to tell me that you're married and have a freaking baby before I had the best night of my life? What do I look like to you? Some girl you can take home from the bar and cheat on your wife with? I don't sleep with married men. I didn't think to ask if you were married before you fucked me, but apparently, I should have," she seethes.

What the hell? I look around like I'm being punked right

now. I'm waiting for Cash to come out and tell me this is a joke that these two concocted somehow.

She glares even harder at me, which I didn't think could be possible because she's pissed right now.

"Are you being serious right now?" I cross my arms and lean back against the bar.

"Dead serious. You can't just use people. You can't just screw everyone over," she says as her nostrils flare. She points a finger at me and yells, "You are *not* a good guy."

Okay, I would laugh at this misunderstanding, but she looks like she might cry. And I can't take the disappointing look she's giving me right now.

I tilt my head and say, "You came here to tell me that I'm not a good guy?"

"Yes. You suck. I thought you were good. Somehow, I felt something between us. I thought you were different. You just proved to me that you're just like the rest."

I know in my heart this isn't true, but that part hits me in the gut. What has happened to her? Who the hell is the "rest of them" and what the hell did they do to her? I want to hunt them all down one by one for putting this hurt in her.

"Who told you I was married?" I ask, calmly waiting for her answer.

"Maggie Pines," she scoffs, her eyes narrowing, hands on her hips. Hips that I remember gripping last night, and I have to shake off the memory and focus on whatever this is right now.

Running out of patience, I counter dryly, "Well, I *know* that's a lie."

Her eyes widen, and she utters fiercely, "Are you calling Maggie a liar? I'll call her up right now."

I carefully watch her and decide to call her bluff. "Do it."

"Okay," she retorts with a huff and then reaches into her purse for her phone. She scrambles to find it.

"Allow me," I grumble.

I pull my phone out, pull up Maggie's contact and call her. I put it on speaker and set it on the bar between us and wait as it rings. Her eyes stay on me, still glaring.

"Hello, Walker," Maggie says in a teasing tone. "To what do I owe this displeasure?"

"Not now, Maggie. Did you tell Red that I'm married?" I cut to the chase. We can resume our usual jabs later.

She's quiet for a moment. Too long of a moment. Shit. What the hell has she done? I maintain my poker face for Red even though I still have no idea what's happening.

"I'm assuming you're talking about my niece, Violet. And yes, I told her that the bartender at the Black Dog was married and has a baby on the way," she finally says, a hint of amusement in her voice.

And there it is. And wait, what? This is her niece? I keep my poker face in place and focus on Red. She's still really angry.

That's all I needed to know to clear up this misunderstanding.

"Nursing home, Maggie," I quip.

She chuckles, "How was I to know?"

"I'll talk to you later." I hang up the phone and slide it back in my pocket.

I know Maggie and I will have a lot to talk about later. Namely how she forgot to tell me that her niece Violet was in town. Red coming here and accusing me of being married has just now outed me and Red to Maggie. Wonderful. So much for keeping my business private in a small town. Pointless.

Her eyes are on me, and they're still angry, and she's not backing down. And it's sexy as hell.

"Do you know my name?" I ask her, now suddenly wondering who the hell she is. Maggie has a big family all over the country and several nieces. But I can't recall all their names.

I'm questioning why none of this adds up. I bet I have more questions than she has right now. But we'll get to those.

"The adulterer?" she snaps.

I growl with frustration, "Red, I own this bar. I'm *not* the bartender. Cash is my bartender. The guy who was working last night?" I look at her and wait for it to click. Relief fills me that this is not what she thought it was.

Her eyes close, and she looks down in mortification and murmurs, "Shit. I'm so sorry." Her cheeks blush a furious shade of pink to rival her bright red hair, a look of pure contrition on her face.

"I hope that clears up some things for you. Anything else you need to know, Red?" I lean back and wait, amused by this whole conversation now that I know it's bullshit.

"Nope, I'm going to crawl into a hole and die now," she admits with an embarrassed laugh.

Out of the corner of my eye, I see movement in the front seat of her car and glance back at her. "Now it's my turn. I have a few questions for you."

She looks at me apologetically. "Sure," she admits with defeat.

And fuck me if her face isn't cute as hell right now, all pink and flustered with embarrassment. There's no way this woman is a crazed fan or here for trouble. She's too hell-bent on not being a home wrecker, which I appreciate. Cash is a stand-up guy and would never do that, anyway. And I sure as hell would never be that guy, either.

"Why do you have my dog?" I nod to where my dog's head hangs out the window that's half rolled down, watching the door, probably wondering why she didn't get to come in, too.

Her mouth drops in surprise. "Pickles is yours?"

I cross my arms, waiting for an explanation. She looks even more beautiful when she's mad. I'm not even sure how that's even possible, but she's even sexier than she was last night.

"Maggie asked me to watch her," she stammers, looking confused.

I'll bet she did. She's supposed to be watching Pickles while Mack is out of town so she isn't at the house alone.

"She's supposed to watch her when I'm working. As a bar *owner*," I add with a smirk. "Not a bartender."

"Stop," she groans. "I'm so embarrassed. And technically, you were pouring drinks last night, were you not?"

I laugh and admit, "I was."

Relief fills me that she doesn't seem to recognize me. And I know Maggie would never tell her anything personal about me. She's the one person in this world that I know one hundred percent for sure that I can count on. I don't have many people like that, but I have no doubts about Maggie. That's why I knew we could call her earlier when I called Red's bluff.

"I'll go get her for you," she mumbles and heads to her car. My dog wiggles her whole body when she sees Red coming towards her. I sigh. I have the same reaction too, Pickles.

She returns a few minutes later with Pickles trotting to me, her tail feverishly wagging as her whole body wiggles when she sees me.

I bend down and pick her up, holding her to my chest.

"Can I ask you a question?" she asks hesitantly.

"Red, I think we're past formalities. Just ask," I say dryly.

"Why do you call this the Black Dog? Is it a song reference?" she wonders aloud as she glances around as if looking for clues.

I snort. "My bar has been here for over ten years now." I nod to my dog. "Hence the black dog. Before her it was Gus. My *other* black dog."

"Alright." Her mouth quirks. "Why the name Pickles?"

I want to tell her my daughter named her and that I get every pop culture reference she's throwing my way, but I'm still on the fence with her. I don't tell anyone about my personal life and not about my daughter. Something about Red feels different but still not going there. I can't. There are too many things I can't risk.

Instead, I shrug. "Just a name."

She stares at me for a beat. "Alright, Cowboy. Sorry I kidnapped your puppy, and I'm sorry I accused you of being an adulterer." She turns and leaves, and her eyes stop at the corkboard in the entryway of the bar, she looks at the bartender help wanted sign and back at me. She frowns, looks down, and heads out.

This is a plot twist I didn't see coming.

* * *

"I see you met, my niece," Maggie remarks wryly as she walks in my front door the next day, carrying grocery bags she sets on the counter. Maggie drops off groceries from time to time, and I cook for her as often as she lets me. When Mack is home, she loves cooking with me, too. One good thing about living in the middle of nowhere is that we cook most of our own meals. So, we've learned to make all our favorites. Maggie usually spends a lot of her time here, and now that she's had her niece visiting, I can see why she's not been around as much. But to be fair, we've both been busy. Me with the bar, Mack's school stuff, and her with her niece and the Dogwood.

"I did," I counter dryly as I unload the bags and set the items on the counter. "Care to explain?"

She laughs her deep throaty laugh. "She asked about the hot bartender at the Black Dog. I don't consider you the bartender, and I don't refer to you as hot, so I assumed she meant Cash.

And then Cash returned her car to the motel and dropped off the keys."

Shit, I hadn't thought about that. Although I secretly wanted her to see her again, and even though she gave me hell, I enjoyed seeing her when she confronted me. Somehow, she's even more beautiful when she's mad.

"I'll be sure to let Cash know that you think of him as hot," I tease.

"You got a thing for her?" Maggie returns with a smirk, ignoring my jab.

"I don't have a thing for anyone," I scoff as I fold and lay the empty bags flat on the counter.

She studies me for a moment. "That's too bad. Violet's a good girl, and she'll be sticking around."

Violet. The name suits her. But she's still going to be Red to me. And the things we did...I loved every minute that I spent with her.

But then I think about what Maggie said about her sticking around. Interesting. Also, a complication that I don't need right now. Or maybe I do. Maybe someone like Red is what I've been missing in my life if I were to let myself have that.

I shrug, pretending not to care. "I'm glad you'll have her around to help you."

"She's been helping me at the Dogwood and could use some friends. I was happy to hear she finally had a fun night out. She had a rough time before she came here."

Still not trusting Maggie's intentions. She's been known to be a matchmaker. And her last attempts were terrible. She is never allowed to try to fix me up ever again. And not with her niece. And I'm also curious about what happened before she came here. I wonder what her story is.

"Good, it's about time you found some help. You're too old

to be doing everything yourself down there," I say, and she glares at me at the old comment.

"I'm not doing everything myself. I have *Red* now to help me," she teases, using the nickname I gave her niece.

"That nickname suits her," she adds with a grin.

"So, you'll take her help but not help from Mack and me?" I tease.

"Speaking of Mack, did you talk to her today?" she asks as she changes the subject. She opens a package of cookies and takes one out to eat. She watches me, sliding them over as I take one, too.

"She's doing good. She mentioned she called you. She was a little sad you won't make it to her competition, but I'll take plenty of pictures and videos for you," I say, taking a bite of the cookie.

Her competition is almost five hours away, and that's far for Maggie to be gone. I have Cash to help out, but she doesn't have help like I do. Mack and I are her backup when she needs it. Which she usually won't take us up on which makes me curious why she let her niece come help her.

We eat silently for a while, and she finally says, "You know it's okay to be happy, Walker?"

I close my eyes and think about that for a fleeting moment, then reassure her dryly, "I am happy, Maggie."

"Sure," she says as she chews and watches me, obviously unconvinced. "The two of you might have more in common than you realize."

"What all did you tell her?" I turn to her as I snag another cookie.

"Nothing other than you were married and had a kid, apparently." She chuckles then grows more serious. "You know I don't talk about you to anyone. No one does."

I nod, grateful. "I know. Thanks, Maggs."

"I'm headed back to town. Just wanted to drop off some groceries so you don't starve without your child around to remind you to eat," she counters.

"I eat," I grumble as I follow her to the door, Pickles trailing behind us, wagging her tail. "And thanks for everything. And pawning Pickles off on Red. I saw what you did there."

She grins at me, knowing I caught her red-handed.

"Whatever you say. Love you, honey," she says as she lays a hand on my cheek then turns to leave.

"Love you," I wave and close the door.

I can't help but wonder what she means when she says that Red and I have more in common than I think. Maybe because of the guitar. Or the fact that she showed up just like Mack and I did all those years ago.

Mack and I moved to Bridger Falls when she was a newborn to start a new life here, where nobody knew us. We stayed at the Dogwood for the first three months until I found a place for us. Maggie and I became close; she's like the mother I've never had. She helped me through a rough time of transition in my life.

I wouldn't be where I am now without Maggie and her encouragement and support. I'm glad Red has that if she needs it.

But then I can't help but wonder what's she really doing here?

I shouldn't wonder, but I do.

Chapter 7
Violet

O kay, so I'll just stay at the Dogwood and never leave now that I've embarrassed myself with the hot bar *owner*. I really stuck my foot in my mouth. No wonder he ran out on me without saying goodbye. I'd run from me, too.

Maggie strolls into the office and sets her purse down. "I see you've officially met the owner of the Black Dog," she smirks as she watches me squirm.

"Yeah, no thanks to you for telling me he was married," I groan.

"A misunderstanding, but I'm glad you two worked that out." She grins mischievously.

I say nothing but focus intently on the computer in front of me.

"Maybe you can work it out and be friends," she replies cheekily as she watches me carefully.

"I can never set foot in that bar again," I mumble.

"Oh, whatever. This is just a little bump in the road for ya. Now, sugar, we're going to the salon today." She slaps her thighs with both hands enthusiastically. "Hair and nails."

"The salon?" I repeat, blinking in surprise. My gaze drops to my bare nails, and I wrack my brain, trying to recall the last time I did anything with my hair. It's been so long; the memory escapes me entirely. A trip to the salon? Yeah, I could use that.

I can't remember the last time someone wanted to spend time with me this way. Treating me, taking care of me. I feel like I'm wanted here and cared for. My teeth dig into my bottom lip as my nose stings, holding back a flood of emotions.

It's not so much as going to the salon, it's that Maggie wants me to go along with her after spending time together eating lunch. I'm loving this time with her. It makes me realize how much I have missed her.

"I have my standing appointment at Boots and Bangs on my lunch break, and you're coming with me. Time to meet some new young people, especially now you're apparently self-banned from the Black Dog," she says with a chuckle.

"Let me get my purse." I shake my head and grin.

* * *

The moment I step into Boots and Bangs Salon, I'm hit with a wave of heat and the scents of hairspray, perm solution, and something vaguely floral. The air buzzes with the sound of whirring hairdryers, the rhythmic snip of scissors, and the easy chatter of women who have known each other for years.

The walls are covered in vintage-inspired wallpaper—soft pink with delicate white roses curling along golden vines, giving the space a mix of small-town charm and old-school glamour. Gold-framed mirrors line the length of the main styling stations, each one reflecting a different slice of the salon's lively chaos. Beneath them, white marble counter tops are scattered with curling irons, bottles of product, and an endless supply of combs.

To my left, a row of manicure stations is already occupied. Women of all ages sit with their hands stretched out over small, cushioned pads while technicians paint on soft pastels and deep, moody reds. The sharp, unmistakable scent of nail polish and acetone fill the air, mixing with the warm vanilla aroma of whatever candle flickers on the reception desk. This place is busy and humming with noise and laughter.

Near the back, three elderly women sat under the old-school heated domes, their gray and silver curls tightly wound around plastic rollers, gossiping like it's their full-time job. One of them, probably in her eighties, peeks out from under her dome and gives me a friendly smile.

A neon pink sign in loopy cursive above the cash register reads Big Hair, Don't Care and glows faintly beneath the soft track lighting. The floor has black-and-white checkered tile, scuffed in a way that tells stories of years of boots clicking across it, of kids sitting on their mama's laps for their first haircut, and of generations of women coming here to feel beautiful.

The hum of a country song drifts through the overhead speakers, something slow and sweet, the kind of music that makes a woman want to sway in her seat. And beneath it all, laughter bubbles up from different corners of the shop—one of the stylists helping a client, another telling a wild story about her cousin's wedding disaster.

It clearly isn't just a salon. Boots And Bangs is where the women of Bridger Falls come to catch up, swap stories, and leave feeling a little lighter and bolder. And in this moment, in the warm glow of Boots and Bangs, I can't help but feel a little bit at home.

Maggie is welcomed into the salon as if she's Bridger Falls royalty with hugs and smiles just like she was at the Harvest & Honey. I stand in the doorway, taking everything in. She's truly loved and revered in this town. I wonder what it would be like to live in a town where you know everyone, where you're welcomed and people are friendly.

Maggie turns to find me holding back and motions for me to join her. "Now have y'all met my niece, Violet? She's new in town, and we're having ourselves a girls' day."

"Hi, I'm Livy and that's Emma. Good to have you in here, Violet," a pretty young woman says as she works on a woman laid back in her chair whose hair drapes over a sink getting shampooed. She looks over at Emma. "I call dibs on that gorgeous red hair."

The woman getting her hair done opens her eyes and smiles. "Hi, I'm Teresa. Nice to meet you. You'll probably meet my daughter, Cami, and my son, Ollie."

"Nice to meet you," I say as Emma motions for me to sit in a chair.

I hang up my purse and denim jacket on a hook by the mirror and slide into the chair. This is like an old-fashioned beauty shop. Like the Dogwood, this place is frozen in time and kept old, but homey. Vintage is the word that comes to mind. Think Dolly Parton from Steel Magnolias. I watch in awe as they chat about local gossip and events.

Emma runs her fingers through my hair and murmurs, "Beautiful. Do you color it?"

I shake my head. "No, it's all mine." My red hair is from my dad's side of the family.

Her eyes widen, and she smiles. "People pay good money for this color, and the good Lord just gave it to you?" she drawls.

"Suppose so." I smile. I didn't always love my hair. As a kid, I was ruthlessly teased. But recently, I've been learning to love everything about myself. I'm trying to turn a new leaf.

"What do you want to do today, beautiful? A fresh cut and style?" Livvy asks as she runs her fingers through my hair.

I blow out a puff of air. I'm not even sure. It's crazy to think that even a decision on my own hair can paralyze me. But I don't know what I want anymore.

Emma watches my face in the mirror as I'm having this internal battle and asks, "Do you trust me?"

I bite my lip and chuckle. "Sure, it's just hair. Go for it."

She smiles and says excitedly, "This will be so much fun. I'm going to clean it up and add in some fun layers."

I suck in air nervously through my teeth. I hope I don't regret this. She guides me to the sink and sets me up and proceeds to give me the best shampoo experience of a lifetime. Her scalp massage battles anything I've ever had at any salon I've ever been to. I'm so glad Maggie brought me with her.

"So, Violet, what brought you to Bridger Falls?" She shields my eyes as she rinses out the shampoo. The warm water feels amazing, and my shoulders relax.

"I came to visit Maggie and fell in love. Decided to stay awhile," I admit.

"Who'd you fall in love with?" She chuckles as she applies a deep conditioner and massages my scalp.

"Bridger Falls," I admit.

"She might be working on falling in love with someone," Maggie counters with a smirk.

"Nope, taking a break on love for a while. I play the guitar and write songs about love, though," I quip, trying to change the subject.

"She's also a great singer," Maggie adds proudly.

"How long have you been playing guitar?" Emma asks.

"Since I was eight. My parents got me a guitar for Christmas, and I've been playing songs and singing on any stage that would have me ever since."

"So, what...ten years?" she teases.

"Twenty-two," I answer with a chuckle. "I'm thirty."

"Well, you look so young. I'd kill for this beautiful clear skin and gorgeous hair."

"Thanks," I say as I look around at these women all lifting each other up. A breath of fresh air in this salon.

Maggie says gleefully, "I still can't believe you're thirty. You'll always be my young niece, Violet."

"What're you saying? I'm old?" I tease.

"I'm turning seventy-one this year, so I think I've got you beat on old," she chuckles.

The door swings open, and a young woman strides in, balancing two trays brimming with coffee cups. Her long black hair cascades over her shoulders and down her back. "What'd I miss?" she calls out, her voice bright and teasing, as she shuts the door with her foot, the bell jingling on it.

Emma takes a tray from her and says, "That's Cami."

"You're a lifesaver. I needed this," Emma say, hugging her.

"I brought a bunch, so everyone enjoy," Cami says as she sets the other tray on a coffee table and shrugs off her jacket.

"This is Violet. She's Maggie's niece and staying down at the Dogwood. She learned to play guitar at eight, and Maggie is finally getting the help she needs at the Dogwood, thanks to her niece," Emma says as she grabs the blow dryer.

"Hi, Violet! Have a coffee," she says to me, then turns to Maggie. "You heard from Mack? Is she doing okay?"

"She'll be back in a few days," Maggie answers. "She's got a lot going on right now with her school activities."

I'm trying to follow along with all the stories, and I try to put their names and faces to them. But they're all fascinating, and I've never been around such cool people. They're going to make it hard for me to leave here someday.

Listening to them talk with Maggie shows me how big of a part she plays in holding this town together. She's like the glue.

She shows up for them all in so many ways. Even me. She took me in when I had nowhere to go.

They chat as my hair gets blown out and styled and it already feels so much better after she gives me a small trim.

"Cami, how are things with you at Steamy Sips?" Maggie asks then turns to me and says, "Cami owns a mobile coffee shop, hence all the delicious coffee."

I reach for one of the coffees and take a sip, and it's very good. It has a hint of cinnamon and is rich but not bitter. Damn, the girl knows her coffee. "Thanks, Cami."

She smiles at me and says, "Business is great, can't complain. I'm thinking about opening up a brick-and-mortar store, too. I'll keep the trailer for events, but it would be nice to have a coffee shop for people to hang out."

"I don't know how you could add that to your plate and everything else you have going on, too," Teresa presses.

Cami and Teresa share a look, and she says, "I have a business to run, Mom. A business we need to help pay for the ranch. You can ask Ollie to help more if you feel I'm not doing enough."

Teresa glares at Cami, and the two exchange a heated look.

"Ollie already works as a firefighter, and he does help," her mom argues.

"I have a job too, Mom," Cami glares back at her mother.

"I just don't think you should add more," she says, her voice full of disapproval.

Maggie wasn't joking when she said that you can learn a lot about the town by hanging out at Boots and Bangs.

Cami gives Livvy a pleading look as if willing her to offer a distraction.

"I heard Jack Jessop is back in town and working out at the Jessop ranch," Livvy says quickly looking around to see if anyone is going to pick up what she puts down.

It works like a charm when all heads swivel to look at her. Cami looks like she could murder Livvy for dropping that information.

"I'm sorry," Livvy mouths to her.

"What'd you just say?" Teresa's head swivels around, her voice full of anger.

"Yep, he's running his family's ranch now," Livvy remarks as she picks up her scissors, then pauses when she realizes this might not have been the best diversion and she might be sticking her foot in her mouth even further.

Teresa scoffs. "Well, that explains your early morning rides."

"Mom!" Cami huffs. "I love my early morning rides. Those are for me. And they have nothing to do with Jack Jessop. He's the devil."

"Early morning rides?" Maggie grins and leans in for this piping hot tea.

Fascinated by all of this, my head turns to each person during these conversations, and I look at Maggie who is getting her hair dried and grinning like the Cheshire cat. Maggie might not participate in spreading gossip around town, but it seems she has no qualms over listening to it all.

"You want your nails done?" Livvy asks a beautiful blond woman.

Poppy laughs, holding her hands, "It's pointless to do my nails. They're mechanic hands. Always getting dirty and beat up."

Emma says, "Self-care is never useless. You have hard-working hands. They need to be extra pampered."

"Maybe Ollie will like them," Cami teases.

Poppy gives her a look and quirks a brow, "Want to discuss your morning rides?"

"Nope," Cami says, shaking her head and looking straight ahead.

"That's what I thought," Poppy smirks.

Teresa seems to have moved on to another conversation with someone else, letting whatever she has with Cami go for now. I think I'll get my hair and nails done more often. I like this place.

After my hair is freshly blown out in big curls and my nails are done, I feel like a million bucks. This is the most fun I've had in a long time.

"What are you wearing tonight for girls' night?" Cami asks.

"Wear something sexy," Emma adds.

"You're coming, right?" Poppy adds.

"I didn't know there was a girl's night," I add, not wanting to intrude on their plans.

"A bunch of us are meeting at the Black Dog for drinks and dinner," Poppy says. "You have to come."

I close my eyes and resist groaning when she mentions it will be at the Black Dog.

Maggie looks over and says, "You're going. Don't even think about trying to get out of it."

I'm thrilled to be included with them and hopefully make some cool new friends. No one tells you how hard it is to make friends when you're older. It's a tough world out there, y'all. I can't wait to get to know them more.

Of course, wanting to see him again is a bonus, and if I were in a group of people, maybe it wouldn't be as embarrassing. Maybe he won't even notice me. I love going out and having fun. And getting dressed up is even better. Plus, I have great hair now and an excuse to go out.

I think about what I have in my bag I can wear, and then I smile. "I know just what I'll wear."

And it will be for Walker. As an apology of course.

Chapter 8
Violet

I take my time putting on my makeup and fluffing my hair, which fills me with a new confidence I haven't had for a while. In fact, I can't remember when I last felt good like this without looking over my shoulder at someone telling me I need to look and dress a certain way and knocking me down repeatedly.

A knock at my door has me quickly finishing up my bright red lipstick and dropping it in my purse as I stroll over to open it.

Cami grins at me, her hair pulled up in a high sleek ponytail. "Well, look at you, hot stuff."

She must be the most naturally beautiful woman with her dark almond eyes and high cheekbones. Her makeup is beautifully applied, but she probably doesn't even need it. She's gorgeous.

"You look pretty great yourself." Cami has on tight jeans and a black halter top that shows off her ample cleavage, and her expertly done smoky eye and cat eye liner I'd kill for the precision to do perfectly. Everything about Cami screams strong black cat energy, and I really like her.

"Thanks, and you'll have to play some songs for us." She points to the guitar case in the corner. "We could use some live music down at the Black Dog. It gets boring in there with that old jukebox Walker refuses to update. Do you play professionally or just for fun?" she asks as she sits in one of the chairs and crosses her long legs.

"Umm, for fun, I guess." I shrug. That part of my life isn't there anymore, and I don't feel like explaining it to anyone. It's humiliating, and I'm just not going there. Ever. Music will just be for me now until I figure out what to do with my life.

Luckily, she chats with me all the way to the Black Dog about music that we both like.

We walk in and head to the back where the ladies have already begun to gather around a big table.

"Hey, everyone." I smile and slide up next to Poppy on a stool.

"Hey, glad you could make it!" Poppy says.

"Thanks, me too," I say as Cash brings over a tray of lemon drops and slides them onto the table.

"For the ladies," he says as he smiles at Maggie who gives him a thumbs up.

We all toast to girls' night and take our shots. I decline because I'm not a big lemon drop fan, more of an every now and then whiskey girl, but it feels good to be a part of girls' night with all of them. Maggie was right. I needed to get out and meet some new people.

I glance over at the bar a few times to try to see if he's here, and he's not. Maggie notices and leans over and says, "He's probably in the back."

I look at her and say innocently as I sip my water. "Who?"

She smirks at me. "You know who."

"Anyone seen Walker?" Cami asks from across the table as she glances around.

"Who?" I ask again, as I sip my drink and look around at the table, hoping I'm playing it cool. But who am I kidding, I'm not even close to being cool when it comes to him.

"Walker?" Cami says. "Have you met him? Mack's dad."

Maggie tilts her head and gives Cami a look, and Cami closes her mouth as if she suddenly remembers something and says, "Never mind."

So, he's a dad. Holy shit. To a kid who Maggie talked about being in high school. He said he wasn't married, but he didn't mention having a kid. Interesting. I look at Maggie, and she stares straight ahead as if she doesn't want to make eye contact with me. She and Walker must be very close friends if she's keeping him private like this. Even with me.

Cami turns as the door opens, and her eyes narrow when she sees a man walk in. "You've got to be kidding me," she seethes.

Two younger guys come in, and one of them comes up and puts his arm around Cami and gives her a hug. "Hey, sis."

That one must be Ollie.

Ollie looks like the kind of man who belongs on the cover of a firefighter charity calendar. He has the effortless rugged look of a man who spends his days hauling heavy hoses, scaling ladders, and running straight into danger without hesitation. His dark hair, thick and just a little unruly, looks like it's been messed up with his fingers. The ends curl slightly at his neck, giving him an almost boyish charm. He seems like a big flirt.

So far, the men of Bridger Falls are in a spectacular league of their own. But there's only one I still have my eye on.

"Hi, Ollie," she grumps. "Why'd you have to bring *him* here?"

"Don't be rude, is that any way to treat your neighbor?" Ollie scoffs as he takes a sip of Poppy's soda. Poppy makes room on her seat, and he leans in, sitting with her.

"He's not my neighbor, he's Satan reincarnated," she says with disdain as she looks at the man standing next to her brother grinning. He must be the one they were talking about who came back to run his family's ranch.

"Cami, you are looking beautiful as ever," Jack, the man she apparently despises, says as he smiles at Cami, goading her.

Cami glares back at him, taking a sip of her cocktail, "Die, Jessop."

I snort at their banter.

"Where's your boyfriend tonight, Cami?" Jack asks as he gives her a sarcastic smile.

"In my trunk. Want to join him?" she clips.

Jack snorts and shakes his head laughing. "Jesus, Cami."

Jack and Ollie pull up chairs and join us even though Cami shoots daggers at him across the table.

Music plays on the jukebox, and drinks are being poured, and I'm having a great time with all of them. I'm glad I came out for girls' night which seems to have turned into a fun night for a lot of the locals.

Poppy and I play a game of darts, which I'm terrible at. She kicks my butt twice and then plays with Ollie while I make my way back to the table.

The conversation turns to astrology, and Maggie reads everyone their horoscope for the evening from her phone, and we laugh about the results when they line up just right for each of us.

"What's your sign?" I ask Cami.

"A warning sign," Jack says as he leans forward and boops her nose with his finger.

"Fuck off," Cami glares at him but he only grins even bigger in return.

I laugh at Cami and Jack's antics before the energy changes around me, and I look over to see him.

Walker.

I'm not in a hurry to move. Not when I have the perfect opportunity to just look and see him in action.

Walker stands with the kind of presence that commands attention without asking for it—broad and steady, with an effortless confidence that comes from knowing exactly who he is. There's no pretense about him, no polished edges, just him—all raw masculinity wrapped up in faded denim and quiet intensity.

The same way he was in bed with me, and I clench my thighs at the memories.

His black t-shirt stretches across his shoulders, the cotton clinging to a chest that is every bit as solid as it looks. The sleeves hug his biceps just right, the definition in his arms impossible to ignore as he lifts a hand to adjust the black cowboy hat perched low on his head. A worn leather belt, the silver buckle dulled with age, anchors his well-worn jeans, the fabric faded in all the right places.

And Lord, those jeans. They fit him like sin, sitting low on his hips.

My gaze trails back up, drinking in the rough stubble along his jaw—just enough to make him look rugged, like he didn't bother to shave this morning. Like he woke up and ran a hand through that dark, slightly tousled hair, shoved on a hat, and walked out the door without giving a damn that he looks that good.

My stomach does an unsteady little flip, heat curling in my chest before sliding lower.

Because good is an understatement.

His warm hazel eyes, rich and deep, shift toward me, the kind that carry stories and secrets, and my breath catches, just for a second. I remember the way those same eyes darkened when he knelt in front of me, his hands gripping my thighs, his breath warm against my skin.

My cheeks flush at the memory.

And maybe it's the way he's here now, or maybe it's just the sheer force of him, standing there looking at me.

He says something to Cash, and they share a laugh. He helps a few customers at the bar and looks up as he's making drinks. I give him a smirk. He shows no response and continues to make drinks and engage with people at the bar. I just want him to look at me. And he's not. And I don't know why that matters to me, but it does.

Alright, Cowboy.

I saunter over and smile hesitantly at him as I approach. He doesn't smile back but his head tilts slightly. "What can I get you, Red?"

"I'm sorry," I admit, sheepishly. "Can we start over?"

"Nope," he says as he pours another beer and slides it down to Cash who watches us curiously as he mixes up a cocktail.

"Why not?" I slide onto the stool and lean forward on my elbows.

His eyes gaze at my exposed cleavage underneath my black sleeveless shirt and back to my eyes and he looks away, "We can't go backwards. Only forward."

"But wouldn't that be what starting over is? Like a clean slate moving forward?"

He watches me for a few beats and says, "That would be like pretending nothing happened. Is that what you want, Red?"

"Yes," I say. Then I think about what he just said. Shit. No. I don't ever want to forget about that night. I'll never be able to forget about that night.

And from Walker's wrinkled brow, I'm not sure he can either.

And based on his reaction to my answer, I don't think that was the right thing to say.

Back to square one.

Chapter 9
Walker

Red's in my bar again, and I can barely think straight as the night goes on. Every so often, I hear her laugh, and I can't focus on whatever I'm doing at that moment. As much as it fucking irritated me when she said she wanted to forget everything that happened, I can't help but replay the night we had together. Her mouth on mine, my cock buried deep inside her. Fuck, I had the time of my life with Red. It felt like more than just a night to me. But I guess it didn't to her if she's willing to forget it and move on like it never happened.

She's something else. She's changed the entire energy in my bar. Everyone seems to love her, and she fits right in here, despite me wanting to keep my distance.

Red doesn't seem to be the woman who sticks around a place like Bridger Falls. No one sticks around here, mostly they pass through. And that's exactly why I picked this place fifteen years ago. I wanted to start over in a place where it was quiet, and I could live a quiet life with my kid.

However, there's nothing quiet about Red. She's a pure fireball bottled up, and she's incredible.

Cash comes back up to the bar with a tray full of empty glasses.

"Are you cool with them setting up karaoke, Boss?" he asks, and I freeze as I bend down to put glasses in the dish bin.

"What?" I straighten.

"Karaoke," he points across the bar to Poppy, Cami, and Red with a box and speaker. "They're all excited, boss."

Oh, hell no.

"We don't do live music in the bar, Cash. You know that." I groan, but I feel like a jackass as the words come out of my mouth.

"Until now. They're passing the boot around for Wilder Ranch. It was Jack's idea, but he wants to keep it on the down low. Ollie and Cami's ranch is struggling, and they need some funds. So, all tips from tonight and the live music goes to helping the ranch," he says as he looks at me like I'm a total asshole if I say no.

I exhale, and he knows he's got me. I'd do anything to help them. Cami and Ollie have been good friends with everyone in this town. Cami's a little nuts, but she's a good person. Loyal and fierce like a momma bear. Cami used to babysit Mack when she was younger. They're all good people. Except for Teresa's ex-husband. But that's another story. I look over to see Cami and Jack sparring again at pool. If she found out Jack was passing the boot around, she'd probably kill him. Mental note to keep my eyes on them tonight. I don't need any trouble there.

Red and Cami get set up with the karaoke machine and stools in the middle of the bar under the light. She begins to sing, and people smile and listen intently. She looks nervous, but she sings beautifully, and Cami...well, Cami does not. But they look like they're having fun. Eventually, Cami gives up, and Red sings. And she quiets the entire bar with her velvety rich voice. The crowd calls out songs they want her to sing, and soon it just becomes Red singing and entertaining the bar. She seems to become more confident the more she sings.

"Alright, anyone have any songs they want to hear?" she looks over at me and smiles.

I don't smile back. In fact, I'm going back to my office to catch up on paperwork as soon as Cash has things under control up here at the bar. But my feet aren't working right now. I'm frozen in this spot.

I want to go back to my office. Hell, I'd even go catch up on the dishes right now, but I still can't move.

She's gifted, I'll give her that. She hits every note like they were made for her. I wonder how good she is with that guitar I saw in the motel room.

The crowd adores her, and people dance, and the energy is great. It's a great night, and Red made it even better.

I take out the trash, desperate to get out of here, and catch my breath in the cold, crisp air. Tonight, in the bar, every ounce of my patience has been tested. And I'm not passing any of these tests. Not even close.

The door swings open, and Maggie strolls out, looking relieved when she sees me. She pulls out a cigarette and lights it, then shakes her head. "She doesn't know who you are, honey."

"I wish you'd quit that," I say as I look away. I also hate she reads me so well.

My body is riddled with tension; she rubs my shoulder. "She doesn't know. But I told you that you both had more in common than you might realize."

I blow out a puff of air and nod. Only Maggie knows about my past. I think. I've suspected some figured it out, but no one has directly asked, and Maggie keeps a lid on this town and keeps us protected from outsiders.

"What's she even doing here in Bridger Falls?" I ask.

Maggie looks at me and looks over at the front of the bar,

where a few patrons are leaving for the night. "She went through some things back in Nashville. She's trying to start over. I don't really know what happened. She doesn't want to talk about it."

That makes my blood boil because I know what it feels like to have things go down in Nashville. And I wonder what happened. Part of me wants to find out because I know how the music industry can chew people up and spit them out. But I also know that I can't take that on. I can't help her and risk exposing who I am. And while I know Maggie didn't invite her here on purpose, I'm in a vulnerable spot here if Red were to figure out who I am. Everything would be a mess.

The night passes by in a blur. Red leaves with Maggie, and I hide in my office like a coward and wait until she leaves to head out. I can't take looking at her and thinking about those songs.

I drive home, and my thoughts are everywhere. Everything was neat and safe, and nobody bothered me here in Bridger Falls. Then I feel like Red arrived, and everything is fucking with me. And I don't know how to deal with this.

I'm off for a few days. Relieved to get out of here, I realize I need the break. I need to get her out of my mind.

* * *

After a few days out of town, I get in late after a long day of Mack's band competition in Cody. They ended up taking third place, and it was a good, proud dad moment. It was a long drive back, but I needed to get home. I have a huge list of things I need to get done in the morning with the animals and the bar.

I received a text from Maggie that she has the house and animals taken care of for me, and I'm surprised when I don't see her old truck out front. Thinking she probably parked in the garage, I grab my bag and head inside. The guest room door is shut, and Pickles isn't in her kennel, so I assume Maggie has her for the night in the guest room that she uses when she stays here.

I take a shower and wash off the long day, falling into bed, not even having more than a few thoughts before drifting off to sleep.

* * *

I wake up to the sun peeking in through the blinds and blink a few times when I hear faint music from somewhere in the house. Weird. Mack's not due back until later tonight. She's riding back with her friends on the bus.

Thinking maybe I left the TV on or something, I get up, slide on some joggers and a T-shirt, and run my fingers through my hair. I pause when I realize it's guitar music and not the TV. Who is playing the guitar in my house? I head down the hall and stop when I smell coffee and look over to see the coffee pot nearly full.

Maggie doesn't drink coffee, and I'm confused about why she'd make it. She drinks Red Bull like its water. And too much of it, if you ask me. I pour myself a cup and almost spill it when I finally realize who is playing music on my porch.

Red.

She's in my house. She made coffee, and she's playing guitar on my front porch.

No fucking way.

What in the actual fuck? Dread fills me when I think about a stranger in my house, knowing where I live and possibly telling the world. But I know Maggie would never do me dirty. Maggie is the only person I trust on the planet with my family. But I might actually send her to a nursing home someday for this.

I lean against the door frame, watching Red through the glass. She's on the porch swinging with a blanket over her legs crossed, cradling a guitar like it's a baby. Her fire engine red hair is piled on top of her head in what Mack calls a messy bun, tendrils framing the sides of her face as it shines bright in the sunlight that engulfs her. A steaming mug of coffee is perched on the railing next to her. She looks right at home.

She's stunning, and my breath hitches just watching her on my porch, looking like she belongs.

She softly strums a song and sings it quietly, like she's trying to get the notes right. She's good, but she's missing one chord, and I resist the urge to show her. It feels so strange to have someone in my life who plays music. And it's weirder that she's playing my music. A song that I wrote. In my house. I feel like I'm in the twilight zone.

I'm lost in thought, watching her hands strum the guitar with precision and grace, and I listen intently to her until her hands stop, and I realize that she's gazing over at me.

"Hey, Cowboy. Want to join me?" she asks with a grin and moves over in the swing to make room.

I shove off the door frame and slide next to her. "What are you doing here?" I ask as I sip my coffee and stare at her because I can't seem to look away.

Her knee brushes against my thigh. And she turns to me in surprise, her face closer than I realize. So close I can see the length of her lashes and how long they are. I can see how the freckles line the bridge of her nose. She looks adorably fresh faced for it being so early in the morning. Violet is like sunshine.

She looks at me watching her and says, "Maggie didn't tell you I was staying here to watch your house and animals? She told me that you asked for my help."

Pickles pops her head up from under the blanket next to Red and looks at me sleepily, wagging her tail.

Traitor dog.

I can't be mad at Maggie. She's meddling again, but I know she means well. I reach over and stroke Pickles' soft head, and she settles back between Red and me, resting her chin on my leg. I'm suddenly nervous around Red, so I am thankful for the dog distraction.

"Sure, I just forgot," I muse as I look out over the yard and notice that the flowers Maggie and Mack planted in the pots have bloomed.

I knew she was up to something. She was vague about staying at the house and watching the dog. She just said she'd take care of it. And take care of it, she did.

Her eyes widen, and she pauses. "So, you just woke up to some weirdo playing their guitar on your porch? Oh my gosh, I am so sorry. I didn't know you were here."

I snort and laugh. "You sound good. And thank you for taking care of my dog."

I want to be perturbed. I want to be mad. But I'm happy to see her.

"Of course, I'm happy to help. I'll get going now that you're back," she says as she stands.

I put my hand on her arm, and she freezes at the current between us when we touch. "Please stay, Red."

"I saw you have a little girl," she says softly and nods toward the living room where I have a lot of photos of Mack, most when she was younger.

"Well, she's not so little anymore. And if you call her little, you two might have problems." I chuckle as I adjust in the swing and sip my coffee.

"How old is she?"

"She's fifteen. She's away at a band competition," I say softly as I watch her. "She'll be back later tonight."

"I bet she's a great kid," she says with a smile and plays another chord.

Surprisingly, it felt good to share that with her about Mack.

She resumes playing her guitar and struggles with a chord.

I reach out and reposition her fingers, and her eyes follow my hands as I move her fingers on the guitar strings. She gazes up at me, and our eyes collide as we stare at each other for a beat too long, neither of us saying anything. My calloused fingers on her warm fingers. It's an intimate gesture, but I can't help myself.

I lean back, and say, "Now try that."

She looks over at me, surprised, and grins widely as she plays and hits the note. "Thanks, Cowboy. I didn't know you knew how to play the guitar."

I shrug. "I know a few songs."

If only she knew.

After watching her play together, I clear my throat and ask hesitantly, "Why do you call me Cowboy? I told you I'm not a cowboy."

"We didn't exactly introduce ourselves," she says sheepishly. "And you look like a cowboy in your hat. It's sexy."

Damn, she's so beautiful. And she thinks I'm sexy. Hmmm.

"Just Walker," I grunt. "What's yours?"

"Violet Wilson, but I like it when you call me Red," she admits with a grin.

I nod and glance around. "Now you've seen where I live. Not married, not an adulterer," I muse. "Just a bar owner, living a normal life."

She grimaces. "I still feel bad about that. I liked you, and I thought we'd had a special night. Then, when I thought you were married, I felt awful," she says resolutely.

"Liked? You don't like me anymore, Red?" I ask and wait for her response, trying not to hold my breath.

She ignores the question but grins. "You are so far from normal, Walker. What's with this house? Your house is so big it should have its own zip code," she muses as she looks around in awe.

I stare at her. "We did have a special night, Red. But there are so many reasons why we shouldn't go there again."

She cocks a brow and teases, "Like what? And also, can we not just be friends? We have Maggie in common. I'm sure she'd appreciate it if we were friends."

Shit, I just challenged her. The few interactions that I've had with Red, I've learned that she doesn't back down from a challenge. In fact, it seems to fuel her. And she's not wrong. Maggie is a huge part of my life, which means she is now, too.

"For starters, I'm a lot older than you," I insist from behind the rim of my coffee cup.

"How old are you?" she questions.

"Thirty-eight."

"Well, I'm thirty, so you're not that much older, and we're both in our thirties. Next," she commands.

"I have to put my kid first," I warn.

"I like kids and want a house full of 'em someday. And take that look of horror off your face, cowboy. You're not in the running for the job. I'm talking about way in my future. Once I find a decent man and get my life together. Other people's kids don't bother me, either. Next."

Jesus. She's not letting me off the hook. What does she mean I'm not in the running? And a decent man? What's wrong with me?

I scowl at her, finding I don't quite like this imagined future of hers.

I blow out a breath. "I need my privacy, Red. You can't tell anyone about my house, my kid, my life, none of it. It's off limits."

She watches me and then says quietly, "No one knows I'm here in Bridger Falls. I know something about wanting your life to be private, cowboy."

I stare at her and sigh. "And again, I'm not a cowboy. Not everyone in Wyoming is a cowboy."

"Fine." She rolls her eyes playfully.

This woman might be the death of me. She's funny as hell and surprises me. Very few people surprise me. Then again, I never let anyone in, so there's that.

"I'm going to take a shower and go back to the Dogwood. Thanks for letting me hang out in your zip code. I promise to never tell anyone about it." She stands and carries her guitar back into the house. Her flannel pajama pants and t-shirt cling to all her curves, and I curse myself silently for messing this up again.

I run my fingers through my dog's soft fur. I want her—God, I want her—but I'm not the guy who takes risks anymore. Risks terrify me, plain and simple. I have too much at stake to lose, more than I could ever make her understand.

Chapter 10
Violet

"How was everything out at Walker's?" Maggie asks as she stocks the linen cart.

I stare at her dryly. "He didn't know I was there, Maggie. You set me up."

But I can't be mad at her. She's had a lot on her plate with the Dogwood, helping Walker, and I know she needed my help. It's a lot easier to send me out there than it is for her to stay out there. And I didn't mind it at all.

First, Walker lives in paradise. His home is the most beautiful home I've ever seen. It's not at all what I was expecting. His words about privacy echo in my mind, and I'll never talk about his home with anyone.

She shrugs. "I thought you'd like the animals. You always loved animals."

"I still love animals. And I love his. His horses are beautiful. And the barn cats were pretty cute, too," I admit.

"See? It all worked out," she says as she nods at the linen cart.

"How many rooms do we have today?" I ask as I glance at

my watch, planning out how long I have to get the rooms done before check ins.

"Just three, it's a slow day," she says.

"Not bad," I say as I pull the cart behind me. I can do them quickly.

My phone buzzes and it's my mom. I put it on speaker and answer, "Hi, Mom."

"Hey, honey. How are things in Nashville? You get your album done?"

I suck in air through my teeth, "Well, Mom. Things changed. I'm actually in Bridger Falls."

She's quiet for a moment and then says, surprised, "At Maggie's?"

"Yeah," I say, matter of fact, like it's no big deal, hoping she'll just leave it and not ask too much.

It's not that I want to keep things from her. I don't. I just don't want to disappoint her. She and my dad have been my biggest fans and supporters. And I don't want to let anyone down by leaving Nashville and walking away from my dreams. They've always rooted so hard for me. Music has always been a big deal in my family.

"What happened? Are you okay?" she asks softly, worry in her voice.

My mind wanders as I start work on the first room, and I think about the songs I'm working on and if it's even worth it to try to start over again. I had an entire album written and was so excited. Then everything was taken from me. The album was stolen and recorded by another artist, and my label dropped me. And I'm embarrassed. I went from an up-and-coming musician to hiding out in Bridger Falls, working at a motel.

Damn. Life can change in an instant. That's for sure.

Instead of explaining everything, I don't. I simply say, "I just needed a break, Mom. Hanging out here with Maggie for a while. She needed some help, so it all worked out."

"I'm glad you're visiting with her. How is she? I need to call her."

"It's been good. Really good, actually. Been working on new songs, enjoying the town," I tell her, and that part is at least true.

"It's such a neat town. Hey, your dad is calling me. I'm going to call you back tomorrow. Keep me updated on how you're doing," she says as she disconnects.

I'm relieved that I didn't have to explain too much right now. I'm just not ready to get into it all yet.

My parents have a dairy farm in Indiana, and they're both very busy, so it didn't surprise me that she had to go so suddenly.

After I finish the final room, I return the cleaning and linen carts and restock them, switching over the laundry. The amount of laundry we do here is insane. I always try to stay on top of it for Maggie. I love helping her out.

I take a peek in the kitchen and see what she has that I can make for dinner and grab a few ingredients out of her pantry. Maggie's out, and the office is quiet. She really needs help around here. A lot of things are broken and need to be updated and fixed.

I watch from the front window of the lobby of the motel as Walker's truck pulls in and parks. He gets out and strolls up to the front door of the office, and he fixes some crumbling bricks out front before he comes in, holding the door gently behind him. He walks towards the desk and looks surprised when he sees it's me instead of Maggie.

"Red," he says with a smile.

"Walker." I smile back and nervously tuck a lock of hair behind my ear. My stomach flips when he steps in closer. My chest feels warm, and I realize I'm happy to see him. He's got such a pull on me.

"Just came over to help Maggie unclog one of her sinks," he says as he sets down a battered tool bag.

Hot.

Instead of focusing on how hot he looks with his tool bag, I reach over and grab the keys to 102 and hand them to him. "Here you go. She didn't mention you were coming, but I'm sure she'll be happy to know you're here fixing it."

He snorts. "She's at bingo. I passed her flying down the road on my way here. It's her week to call the numbers. No way she's missing that."

He looks around. "Something smells good. Are you cooking?"

I nod. "I am. I have a cowboy casserole in the oven."

He looks surprised. "I don't think Maggie ever cooks in that kitchen."

"She doesn't. But I made plenty if you'd like to eat with me. Should be ready by the time you finish that drain, plumber boy," I add with a grin, as I tilt my head.

He snorts at the plumber boy comment and turns to head out as he calls, "I might just take you up on that, Red."

I hope he does.

He's gone for a half an hour, and I take out the casserole and take down two plates just as the front door opens. He comes in and heads to the bathroom to wash his hands. He's at ease here as if he's been in here countless times before, like he's comfortable in Maggie's space. I'm glad that Maggie has him to help her out around here.

I plate up the food and set it on the small table in the kitchen that Maggie mostly uses to play cards. He walks in and stands still in the middle of the room until I motion for him to sit and hand him a napkin and fork.

"Thanks, I forgot to eat lunch, and it hit me suddenly; I'm starving," he says as he slides in and grins at me.

The fork in my hand feels heavier than it should. I take a bite, chewing slowly, my eyes flicking up to him across the table. Walker. Sitting here. Eating the food I cooked. I don't know why it feels like a *thing*. But it does.

It's just dinner. Just food. Just two people sitting at a table. Except... it isn't.

Because the air is different. Thicker. The kind that settles in your chest and makes you hyperaware of every movement, every glance, every brush of a hand too close to the other.

I keep my head down and focus on my plate, but it doesn't stop the heat curling low in my stomach. It doesn't stop my mind from drifting into dangerous territory—wondering what this looks like from the outside.

Because *this*—this quiet, this shared meal, this small act of *care*—feels like something more than it should. It feels *domestic*.

I *definitely* can't let myself imagine what it would be like if this were something *real*. But my traitorous brain? It's already running ahead of me. Already painting the picture. Already whispering in my ear—*what if?*

What if this was a regular thing? What if I got used to this? To him sitting here, stealing bites off my plate like he has a right to them. To the sound of his deep, easy laughter rolling through my kitchen.

What if I got used to *him?*

I swallow hard. Take a sip of water. Try to push down the sudden knot in my chest.

Because none of this is real.

It's just a meal. Just a quiet night. Just an *illusion* of something that was never meant to be mine. He's a friend. And Maggie's friend. I can't let anything get in the way of that.

But when I glance up again—when I catch him watching

me with that unreadable look in his eyes, like maybe he's feeling *it* too—

I know, deep down, I'm already in trouble.

I clear my throat and smile. "Not a problem. I love to cook and rarely have people to cook for," I tell him as I sit across from him, trying to play it cool.

But I'm not cool. Not even close to cool. I'm nervous as hell.

"I have a question," I ask as he takes a bite, and his eyes widen in surprise.

He taps his fork on his plate. "This is *really* good."

"Thank you," I say as I clear my throat.

"What's your question?" he asks as he looks over at me, his eyes warm and sweet.

Damn, why does he have to be so sweet? When he looks at me like that, I forget everything that I'm doing and thinking.

"I was wondering if you ever found a bartender. I saw you were looking for one," I ask.

He clears his throat and says, "I haven't."

"Oh," I say quickly, taking a bite and looking away.

"Why? Interested in bartending?" he asks as he studies my face.

"I am. I wanted to find a part-time job," I admit. "But I'll find something."

He nods, and we eat quietly. He looks at peace and says, "Red, that was the best meal I've had in a long time. Thank you."

"My pleasure. Thanks for fixing the drain. I'll take care of these," I say as I take our plates and rinse them.

"Let me help," he says as he reaches for the plates, and our fingers brush, sending a zing through my body. His touch is familiar, reminding me of our night together.

"It's okay, I've got it," I tell him as I finish putting the food away and take the dishes from him to dry.

"I insist. I always try to help Maggie, too," he says as his eyes meet mine.

"I'm glad she has you," I tell him as I hand him the dish towel.

"I'm pretty sure I'm luckier to have her. I'll keep an eye out for anyone hiring around here," he says as he searches my eyes.

"Please do," I tell him as I tuck a piece of my hair behind my ear. "I'd appreciate it."

He glances over at my guitar and the notebook with a pen tucked into it on top of the desk. An expression crosses his face, and he looks irritated for a moment, then says, "I gotta run. Thanks for dinner."

"Have a good night," I say as he heads out the door and doesn't look back.

I watch him walk to his truck and wonder what that was about. Busying myself with a few guests needing things, I tidy up the office for the night.

Walker's a man of mystery, that's for sure.

I quickly get my work done for the evening and help a few customers, but I can't help but feel like I'm floating on a cloud after spending time with him. It was a great evening.

The front door to the motel opens, and Cami and Poppy come in, their happy energies a welcome distraction. Cami smiles big and holds up a paper bag. "I brought treats."

"Hi, ladies," I smile.

"We just wanted to see how you're doing and if you're settling in, okay," Poppy says as she sits on one of the couches in the lobby.

"And I brought some lemon blueberry scones," Cami says as she sets down a bag and peels off her jacket.

"Did you guys eat? I have leftover cowboy casserole if you want some?" I offer as I nod to the kitchen.

"Oh, I bet Maggie loves having you here," Cami says as she stands to head to the small kitchen.

"Maggie does love having her here," I hear Maggie tease as she comes through the back door and hangs up her coat.

"How was bingo?" I ask as I take a scone out of the bag.

Cami, clearly comfortable with Maggie's kitchen, returns with a plate of reheated food. "This is so good. Did you have any?" she asks Maggie.

"No, I'll be making a plate. That smells really good," she says as she heads to the kitchen.

"Weird to have home-cooked food from your house, Maggie," Poppy teases.

"Hey, I'll have you know I'm excellent with a microwave," she calls as she brings her plate to the desk across from where we're sitting.

She glances at her watch. "Walker is supposed to come fix a clogged sink."

"He already came," I tell her.

All of their heads swivel at the same time to look at me. Poppy looks like she wants to say something, and Cami has a wicked grin on her face.

"Oh?" Maggie says curiously.

"He fixed the sink and had some dinner, too." Then after I say it, I realize I just added fuel to the fire.

The three of them stare at me and then exchange smirks.

"So, you had a little dinner date?" Cami asks.

"No, I just had dinner ready when he arrived, so he had some, not a big deal." I shrug.

"Oh, no," Poppy says.

"Right?" Cami adds.

"Denial," they all say at once.

"The chemistry between them is insane. You guys see it too, right?" Poppy adds.

They have a mini conversation about me as if I'm not here, and I don't know whether to laugh or tell them to shut it. But I smile because I know they mean well.

"Just friends," I protest, as I cross my legs and tap my foot.

"Yeah. Sure," Cami says as she watches me and takes a bite. "Damn, girl. You can cook,"

"I love cooking," I admit.

"Are you good at baking?" she asks.

"I'm decent," I admit.

"Well, if you ever want to help me with baking for my coffee trailer, I'd love it," she says.

"Say when."

"When. Come out tomorrow afternoon. That work?" she asks.

"I'll have to check with my boss. But usually I'm free in the afternoons," I tease.

"She's free," Maggie says with a laugh, shaking her head.

I usually get all the rooms done by then, so it shouldn't be a problem.

We all sit together and then play a few hands of cards, and I look around and take in the fun conversation and delicious pastries and think this is how friendship should be. And I'm thankful to be here in Bridger Falls, making friends with people like Cami and Poppy. I love getting invited to girls' night and getting asked to help bake. I smile at Maggie, and she's too busy laughing and laying down a card. She looks really happy, too.

Bridger Falls is starting to feel like a real home, something I was missing.

* * *

I plug in the navigation to make the drive out to Cami's ranch, which is thirty minutes outside of town in the opposite direction of Walker's. There are so many ranches around here, and they're breathtaking with the tall, looming mountains in the distance.

It's beautiful out here, and it would be a dream to call a place like Bridger Falls home. Sometimes, I think about leaving music altogether and starting over somewhere. I love songwriting, but I'm coming to terms that my career is done. And part of me feels angry and defeated about that, and then another part of me feels sad. Rejected. Like I want to make an epic comeback and show the people who took everything from me that I'm not done. Far from done. Sometimes I think about what that kind of comeback would feel like.

But we'll see. I don't know what is going to happen with my music career, but I'm happy right now in Bridger Falls. It is strangely comforting to be here in a place where people don't know the music side of me, and I don't have to talk about what happened. I'm dreading having to answer my mom's questions when we eventually talk again. But that's tomorrow's problem. Today, I get to bake and hang out with Cami.

I pull into Wilder Ranch, my tires kicking up a soft cloud of dust as I slow to a stop beside Cami's red truck.

The place is breathtaking.

The long gravel driveway winds through endless rolling pastures, stretching wide under the open Wyoming sky. Golden fields sway in the late afternoon breeze, dotted with sturdy wooden fences and grazing horses. A few cows linger lazily near the fence line, their tails flicking at flies, while further back, a small herd of goats playfully headbutt each other near a weathered old tree.

The main barn stands proud, red paint slightly faded but still charming against the backdrop of the mountains. A few smaller outbuildings sit nearby—a shed, a workshop, a little chicken coop with a white picket fence that looks like something out of a storybook.

It smells exactly like a ranch should—earthy, sun-warmed hay, rich leather, and the faintest hint of horses and fresh-cut grass.

I step out of my car, stretching my legs, taking it all in.

Before I can shut the door, Cami strides out of the barn, sliding off a pair of work gloves and shoving them into her back pocket.

She's wearing ripped jeans, boots, and a faded T-shirt that probably started black but is now more dirt than fabric. Strands of hair have escaped her messy ponytail, sticking to her forehead. She looks like she's been working since sunrise—but somehow, she still has that effortless 'badass cowgirl' aura.

"Hey, Violet," she calls, wiping her hands on her jeans. "How are you?"

I step forward, glancing around again at the picturesque ranch, the golden afternoon light spilling across the fields, the mountains standing like silent guardians in the distance.

"Great," I say, meaning it. "Thanks for having me out here. It's beautiful."

Cami grins, propping a hand on her hip, her face softening just a little.

"Yeah," she says, glancing out over the land. "It really is."

And in that moment, I can tell—this place isn't just a ranch to her. It's her whole world.

"Thanks," she says as she walks with me towards the house. "I'm glad you're here. I have a few dozen special orders that I need to make, and it would have been a very long night without your help. So, thanks for coming."

"I love baking. Happy to help," I say as she holds the door.

The farmhouse is older but looks beautiful and maintained. We step inside and walk through a doorway to the kitchen, which is big and looks like it's been updated. The island has a stainless-steel cooking space, and it's set up more like a professional kitchen.

"Wow, this is amazing," I tell her as I take in the tall cooling rack on wheels and huge double oven.

"Thanks, I do all my baking here for Steamy Sips, my coffee trailer," she says as she washes her hands in the sink to the side of the kitchen.

I follow her and do the same. After I dry my hands, she hands me an apron with a cup of coffee on it, and I slip it over my head, tying it around my waist.

"Do your mom and brother live here, too?" I ask as I look at the recipe sheet she hands me.

"No, my mom moved to town a few months ago, and Ollie is living above Poppy's dad's shop in town."

"So, it's just you out here?" I ask as I start grabbing ingredients from the shelf.

"I have my dog, her name is Love. She's a blue heeler," she says as she nods to the back porch where a dog sleeps in the sun. She gets up and stretches and trots toward me when she sees me.

"Oh," I say as I look at her and realize how much she looks like my dog. Well, my dog I don't have anymore.

"What?" she asks, searching my face.

"I had a blue heeler, too. Mine was named Rip Heeler," I tell her.

She chuckles, "That's cute. I loved *Yellowstone*."

"Me, too," I admit, as I measure out the dry ingredients.

A hollow ache settles deep in my chest, one I've tried to ignore for weeks. I swallow hard, blinking at the ceiling, willing away the sting of tears in my eyes.

I miss him. He wasn't just a dog, he was my best friend. And now I'm trying to pretend it doesn't hurt as much as it does.

Rip should be with me. And I hate that he isn't. I don't even know if he's okay.

"What happened to him?" she asks, looking up.

I open my mouth to form the words and honestly don't know where to begin. I exhale a deep breath. "My ex still has him. He wouldn't let me have him. But he was my heart dog. You know? That once-in-a-lifetime dog that you bond with. He was my best friend."

She asks me, "Why didn't he let you take him?"

I shake my head. "He was being spiteful. If I'd taken him, he'd have ruined me even more than he did."

"Where's he at now? Just so you know, I'm not above dog napping." She shakes her head, looking mad. "And ruin you? What did he do?"

"He's back in Nashville. My ex has the apartment we shared and, to be honest, he never even liked Rip. He knows he belonged with me," I say. "I'd steal him back in a heartbeat if I could."

"Wait, what happened? Why did he ruin you?" she asks again as she mixes up her ingredients, pausing to heat up the ovens.

I want to tell her. I want to open up to someone and have a friend. But the last time I did that, it blew up in my face. I don't know what to say, so I just settle on partial truth. "He cheated on me and messed up my career. I had to take off and get out of Nashville. I don't really like talking about it."

She nods. "That's fair. But if you want to talk about it, Violet, I'm here. Poppy, too."

I bite my lip and smile. "Thanks."

We work in silence for a while, the music playing softly on the radio, both of us singing along to it and mixing up scone ingredients, and by the time we slide our first batch in the oven, I feel better.

"Okay, you might just be a better baker than me," she laughs. "Where did you learn all this?"

"I grew up on a farm. My mom makes nearly everything from scratch, and I grew up helping out in the kitchen," I tell her as I get the next pan ready to switch out.

"I'm impressed. You have so much talent. You can sing, bake, and cook. Is there anything you can't do?" she asks, shaking her head in amazement.

I laugh. "I'm sure I can think of a lot of things."

We take a break, and she pours us big glasses of sweet tea, and we have scones. After all, we have to test the products.

"So good," she says as she bites into mine.

"Yours are great too," I smile.

"Are you sure you don't want to be a baker? I think you might have found your calling," she says.

I already found my passion. I just lost it all. Maybe I can be a baker if I can't get my crap together with music again.

Chapter 11
Walker

The wind rushes past Ollie and me as we cruise down the highway on our motorcycles, the hum of the engines filling the late afternoon air. We went on a relaxing ride—just two guys clearing our heads before a long night at The Black Dog for me and a shift at the Bridger Falls fire station for Ollie.

My phone buzzes in my pocket. Thinking it could be Mack, and I'd better take it, I signal to Ollie that I'm pulling over. I slowly pull off and pull out my phone and read the screen. "Hold up, Cami's calling."

"Cami?" he asks in surprise. "Why is my sister calling you?"

"I don't know." I sigh, already knowing this probably means trouble. Cami doesn't call unless she needs something. I answer on speaker. "Hey, Cam, what's up?"

Cami's voice was sharp, impatient. "Have you seen my brother? He's not answering his phone?"

Ollie pulls his phone out of his pocket and looks at it, cursing.

"Is that him? Are you together?" she asks.

"We're out on our bikes. What's wrong?" I ask.

"Violet broke down on the old county road just outside of town. Think one of you can go get her?"

Now I know Cami could go get her, but this is her way of meddling just like Maggie does, trying to get me to go get Violet. And I don't even mind. I want to be the one to go get her.

My grip tightens on my handlebars. I know I have no claim over Red—hell, we shared one night, and that was it. But the thought of Ollie riding up on his bike, Red climbing onto the back, and wrapping her arms around him? Not happening.

"No way," I bark before Ollie could even answer. "I got it."

Ollie shoots me a confused look. "You sure? I don't mind—"

I twist the throttle. "I said I got it."

Ollie huffs out a laugh, shaking his head. "Alright, man. Have fun with that."

"I got her, Cami," I clip and disconnect.

Not sticking around for any more commentary, I gun it down the highway, heading straight for Violet. I can't stand the thought of her being alone out there. We don't have much crime around these parts, but I don't want to take any chances.

Violet stands beside her beat-up car, arms crossed, scowling at the engine as if it personally offended her. Her bright red hair is pulled into a messy bun, stray strands blowing in the wind, and the sun sets behind her, casting a golden glow on her hair.

When she hears the rumble of my bike approaching, she looks up, startled. Her expression softens, then shifts to something unreadable.

"You're not Ollie," she says as I cut the engine.

"Good observation," I smirk, swinging a leg over my bike and sauntering toward her. "Cami called Ollie, but I figured I'd save him the trouble. We were on a ride together."

Red narrows her eyes. "I don't want to be a bother."

I shrug nonchalantly, even as my pulse feels like it kicks up a notch. "You got a problem with me helping?"

She studies me for a beat, then shakes her head. "No. Just surprised, that's all."

I ignore the way her voice stirs something deep in my chest. I head over to her engine and look at it. I lift a few things and turn to her. "My guess is this won't be an easy fix. Poppy will have to come get it."

She sighs and nods. "That's what I was afraid of."

I gesture toward my bike. "Come on. I'll take you back."

Red hesitates, glancing at the motorcycle, then back at me. "I, uh... haven't been on one of these before."

I raise a brow. "What, never?"

She huffs. "Not since I was a kid, and that was one of those little dirt bikes."

I hold back a grin. "Well, Red, you're due for a ride."

I grab the spare helmet and jacket from the saddlebag and hand it to her. She hesitantly slides them on. I'm glad I have extra for her just in case to keep her safe. Climbing onto the bike and steadying it, I look over my shoulder at her. "You gonna stand there all night, or you getting on?"

She rolls her eyes but moves closer, hesitating only a second before swinging a leg over and settling behind me.

"Hold on," I tell her.

She places her hands lightly on my sides, which isn't enough.

I exhale sharply. Fuck. This was a bad idea.

I grab her wrists and pull her arms around my waist, pressing her flush against my back.

"You're gonna wanna hold on tighter than that, Red," I murmur.

She sucks in a breath, but she doesn't argue. Instead, she tightens her grip, molding herself against me.

I twist the throttle as the bike roars to life, and we shoot forward, tearing down the open road.

The wind cuts against my skin, warm and sharp as we ride into the late afternoon light. The sun hangs low over the Wyoming plains, spilling gold over rolling hills, long stretches of highway, and distant, towering peaks. It's the kind of ride I've ridden through a hundred times before, but today—today, I see it differently. Today, I see it through Violet's eyes.

She's behind me, arms wrapped around my waist, hesitant at first, but now she's holding on tight. Her body molds to my back, the warmth of her seeping through my shirt, her cheek pressed to my shoulder when we lean into the turns. I can feel her breath's quick, uneven rhythm as she adjusts to the speed, the sensation of flying with nothing but the road beneath us and the sky stretching wide overhead.

She's never been on a bike before. Said so with a nervous laugh when I handed her the extra helmet, biting her lip like she wasn't sure she trusted me with her life. But she climbed on anyway, and now here we are—taking the long way back to town, because I can't bring myself to rush this.

Not with her.

The golden light stretches out in every direction, casting long shadows over the open land. Wildflowers blur in streaks of orange and yellow along the roadside, and a herd of horses grazes in the distance, tails flicking, their coats catching fire in the sunlight. I wonder if Violet notices them and if she's watching this land, drinking it in like I did the first time I ever took a ride like this.

She shifts slightly behind me, and I swear I feel her sigh. Like she's giving in, letting go.

I slow the bike, coasting easy, giving her time to take it all in. The engine rumbles beneath us, steady and low, and when I glance down, I catch her fingers curled tighter against my stomach.

"Not so bad, huh?" I call through the speakers in the helmet.

She hesitates, then says. "It's...beautiful."

I grin because that's exactly what I wanted her to see. Not just the land, but the freedom of it. The way it feels to be out here, nothing but sky and open road, nothing tying you down. It's like letting go of anything bothering me and giving it to the wind. My rides are the best way to clear my head.

I take a turn, slow and smooth, and her arms tighten around me again. I could get used to this—her holding on like she belongs here, like she trusts me to keep her safe.

Hell, I'd spend a lifetime proving that she could.

The sun sinks lower, turning the horizon into molten gold, and for the first time in a long time, I don't feel the need to rush. I don't feel the pressure of where we're going or what comes next.

All I feel is her.

And for now, that's enough. That's all I'll allow myself to feel.

I pull up in front of the Dogwood. I kill the engine, but Red doesn't move.

"That was..." she trails off, breathless.

I glance back over my shoulder. "Not so bad?"

She clears her throat. "I was gonna say kinda exhilarating."

I chuckle. "Told you."

Just then, the door swings open, and Maggie stands there, grinning as if she'd just witnessed the juiciest small-town gossip in real-time.

"Well, well, well," she drawls. "Didn't take you for the knight-in-shining-leather type, Walker."

"I'll finish up your move-in paperwork for the nursing home," I tell her.

Maggie rolls her eyes as Red hurries to climb off the bike, removing the helmet and fixing her hair like she hadn't just been wrapped around me for the past half hour. I took the long way so she could see more of Bridger Falls. Really, I just liked having her on my bike. It'll be worth the shit that Ollie's going to give me later for this.

"Bad news bears, Walker. Cash called out. His wife is in labor," Maggie says, her voice light but knowing. "Wherever would you find a last-minute bartender who has experience?"

I swing my leg over the bike and lean against it. "Why? You interested?" I know damn well the angle she's playing at, but I'm going to give her hell.

Maggie smirks and nods toward Red. "Not me. Violet."

My gaze flickers to Red.

She crosses her arms. "I do need a job, especially now that I have extra car repairs."

My lips twitched. "You sure that's a good idea? Working with me?"

Red meets my gaze, challenge dancing in her eyes. "I thought we were gonna be friends, Walker?"

I exhale slowly. Damn this woman.

Something about how she said friends made my gut clench, making me want to prove they were anything but.

"Okay," I say finally. "Be at The Black Dog at seven."

Maggie beams as Red smirks. "Guess I'll see you later, boss. Thanks for the ride."

She turns and heads toward her room, and I run a hand through my hair.

Yeah. This is a terrible fucking idea.

** * **

The bar is alive with music, laughter, and the smell of food in the air. The dim lighting gives the place a warm glow, the jukebox humming an old country tune while pool balls clack in the corner. It's busier than usual for a Friday night, and the bar, locals, and tourists blend together over drinks and the promise of a good time.

I stand behind the bar, watching Red effortlessly pour drinks and handle the growing crowd. She's a firecracker, all sharp edges, and quick wit, and it turns out she's been bartending just as long as I have.

After watching her tonight, I know she can hold her own with rowdy customers and handle herself just fine. No doubt.

But tonight, trouble walked through the doors looking for her.

Two out-of-towners, rough around the edges, have been running their mouths, pushing limits, testing boundaries. I've been watching them from the start, but I also discovered that Red doesn't enjoy being babysat. Nobody would.

Right now, she was proving exactly why she didn't need it.

"Come on, sweetheart," one man, a burly guy with greasy hair and a beer belly, slurred, leaning over the bar towards her. "Ain't no harm in a little smile. Bet you'd look real nice if you loosened up for me."

Red doesn't miss a beat, setting down a fresh whiskey glass with a hard clink. "Back the hell off."

The second man, a wiry guy with mean eyes, chuckles as he nudges his buddy. "Feisty one, huh? I like a woman with a little bite."

My body goes rigid, and I straighten from where I'm wiping down the bar. I can tell Red can handle herself, but the way these guys leer at her has my fists twitching.

Red, however, doesn't even blink.

She leans forward, planting both hands on the bar, her voice dropping to something low and sharp as a knife's edge.

"Listen, boys. If you want another drink, I'll pour it. If you want to keep running your mouths, I'll shut them for you. Your choice."

The first man sneers, glancing at his buddy. "Oh yeah? And what're you gonna do, sweetheart?"

Red smiles. The slow, dangerous smile that makes me even pause.

Oh shit. I really don't want to go to jail tonight for beating these fuckers' asses.

"I'm gonna throw your sorry asses out myself," she says easily.

The first man scoffs. "Like hell, you are—"

He doesn't even get the rest of the sentence out before Red grabs his half-full beer bottle and slams it against the bar, shattering the glass right next to his hand.

The entire bar goes silent.

Red doesn't even flinch as shards of glass skitter across the counter.

"You were saying?" she asks, arching a brow.

The second guy shoots out of his seat, his chair scraping against the floor. "You crazy bi—"

Red is faster.

Before he can move, she reaches over the bar, grabs him by the collar, and yanks him forward, planting his face flat against the sticky wooden surface.

The bar erupts into cheers and laughter, regulars banging on their tables, hooting as Red keeps the guy pinned with one hand.

"You done?" she asks him, voice dead calm.

He mutters something unintelligible.

"I'll take that as a yes."

She lets go and steps back, dusting off her hands like she's just taken out the trash.

"Now, unless you want to get familiar with the floor, I suggest you and your friend get out."

The burly guy scrambles off his stool, grabbing his buddy,

and both men stumble toward the door with their tails between their legs.

The second they're out, the bar erupts in cheers.

Sitting at the corner booth with Poppy, Cami let out a whistle. "Goddamn, Red, I think I just fell in love a little."

Poppy raised her beer. "To Red, badass bartender of the century. Walker, I hope you took notes."

Oh, I took notes. I was ready to step in at any moment, but she never needed it. She had it under control just fine.

Red shakes her head, smirking as she reaches under the bar for a broom. "Dumbasses never learn."

I lean against the back counter, watching her with an amused expression. "Remind me never to piss you off."

She grins, winking at me. "Trust me, Walker, you couldn't handle it."

And just like that, the bar returns to normal—like nothing had happened.

After the dust settles and the rowdy cheers die down, the bar returns to its usual rhythm—glasses clinking, low murmurs of conversation, the occasional bursts of laughter.

I pour drinks as Red casually sweeps up the broken glass like she didn't just handle two drunk idiots without breaking a sweat.

I'm not surprised—I figured she was tough. But tonight? Tonight, I saw something different.

Maybe it was how she'd kept her cool, never flinching, never once looking to me for backup. Maybe it was the way she had the entire damn bar eating out of her palm without even trying.

Or maybe—maybe it was that she reminded me of myself.

She never backed down. She never asked for help. And she sure as hell didn't let anyone tell her what to do.

Just like me.

I exhale, running a hand down my jaw.

I'd always thought I was the only one around here who built walls high enough to keep people out. Turns out, Red has her own fortress.

And now, I watch her crack a joke with one of the regulars, leaning on the broom like she didn't just throw two men out on their asses. I wonder what kind of story she isn't telling.

Because I know one thing is for damn sure—women build walls like that for a reason.

Something built that fire inside her. Something taught her how to fight.

And suddenly, I'm curious as hell to know what it was.

Chapter 12
Violet

Fresh coffee and cinnamon lingers in the air, a mixture of cozy small-town and early morning comfort. As I approach Steamy Sips, the small coffee trailer by the town square, I tuck my hands into my hoodie sleeves. I've craved her coffee every morning since Aunt Maggie doesn't bother with coffee. I'm not sure how she's doing life, if you ask me. Coffee is a necessity. It's kind of like having air to breathe. I need coffee to function properly.

Cami moves inside the trailer like a woman on a mission, flipping lids onto cups and chatting with a few regulars at the window. The trailer is adorable—a stainless airstream with Steamy Sips hand-painted to look like steam curling from the "S" in Sips, and flower boxes overflowing with tiny white daisies beneath the order window. It feels like a place that has a heart-beat all its own.

"Morning, Violet," Cami greets me as I step up, and she teases me. "Rough night at the bar brawlin'?"

"Very funny," I groan, rubbing the sleep from my eyes.

"You're all everyone is talking about this morning," she says with a smirk and a knowing smile.

"Not that big of a deal," I sigh. "That's a typical night at a Nashville bar."

Before I can order what I want, boots scuffing against gravel catch my attention.

A deep, familiar voice that's low and warm says, "You making her one of those caramel things? Put hers on my tab."

I turn, and Walker and Jack stand together, holding fresh cups of coffee. No man should look that good without even trying.

The way his dark hair always looks just a little too tousled, like he ran his fingers through it one too many times. The way the sun catches his whiskey-colored eyes, turning them into something rich and deep, something that makes my stomach feel a little unsteady if I look too long.

And don't even get me started on the beard. Neatly trimmed, just enough scruff to make my fingers twitch with the ridiculous, dangerous urge to remind myself what it feels like.

He's wearing that soft, worn-in flannel, the one that stretches over broad shoulders and sleeves rolled up just enough to show strong forearms. It's nothing fancy—just him. Simple. Effortless. But damn if it doesn't work.

It shouldn't matter. He's my *friend*. He made that clear that was all he wanted from me. And I'll give him that. Besides, I shouldn't get mixed up with my boss.

But damn, Walker looks so good. Too good. Like he owns the damn morning. Not fair. I'm pretty sure he stayed longer at the bar than I did. Morning came fast today, and I'm still not fully awake.

"Morning," I murmur to both of them. "Thanks, Walker. You don't have to do that."

"Morning," Jack nods.

"Didn't peg you for a caramel guy." I arch a brow at Walker.

His lips curve slightly. "I'm not. Black." He lifts the cup slightly as if to prove he's too rugged for sugar and cream.

"Black is the only fuel I need," he says to Cami. "I had to fuel up after taking Mack to school. Parenting a teenager isn't for the weak."

Cami snorts from behind the counter. "You're just mad Mack called you old this morning."

Walker shoots her a flat look. "She said I have 'dad energy.' That sounds worse than being called old."

I laugh, watching Walker's eyes soften when he talks about his daughter. Definitely a green flag.

It makes me so curious to meet Mack. I wonder if she has the same whiskey eyes as him? Or if she's funny and playful like him?

I watch Walker and Cami banter effortlessly, and the tension he usually carries eases with each teasing remark. There's something about how his shoulders loosen, the quiet pull of a smile at the corner of his mouth—it makes me realize just how rare it is to see him this unguarded. He carries the weight of so much, always steady, always in control. But right now? Right now, he's just a man, laughing with a friend. And I love watching him like this.

"Black for me, too," Jack adds, joining the conversation with a smirk, as is his way around Cami. Those two always seem to give each other hell every chance they get.

Cami snorts. "Yeah, well, maybe if you had a little sweetness in your life, you'd be more pleasant to be around, Jessop."

Jack gives her a flat look. "You saying I'm unpleasant?"

She hands me my hot caramel latte with a smirk. "I'm saying you're the human equivalent of black coffee. Strong. Bitter. A little too much for most people."

I can't stop laughing, and to my delight, Walker fights a smile, shaking his head as he takes a slow sip of his coffee.

This latte is heaven. There's sorcery in these things. I swear it.

Warm, velvety, and just the right amount of sweet—the caramel melts into the rich espresso, smooth and golden, coating my tongue with buttery warmth. The first hit is bold, the coffee strong and a little bitter, but then the caramel kicks in, swirling with the creamy milk, softening every sharp edge until all that's left is comfort.

"You're lucky you make damn good coffee, Cami," Jack mutters before turning to us. "I gotta run. Later."

"Bye, Jack. Good to see you," I call as he waves and heads toward his truck.

"You heading anywhere?" Walkers asks me.

I hesitate. "Nowhere important."

"You need a refill?" Cami nods at Walker.

He shakes his head. "Nah, I'm good. Just keeping Red company."

"Oh, *Red*," Cami smirks, wiping her hands on a rag. "Don't let me stop you two from flirting awkwardly in public."

Walker exhales through his nose. "We are not—"

"See you later, Cami," I cut in, grabbing Walker's sleeve before he can argue and make things even more weird between us.

And just like that, I find myself falling in step beside him, coffee in hand, wandering the streets of Bridger Falls.

Bridger Falls is waking up for the day. Storefronts glow with warm yellow lights, shopkeepers flip signs from CLOSED to OPEN, and a few locals sweep the sidewalks in front of their businesses and wave as we pass, giving us curious looks.

Walker and I walk side by side, unhurried, like we've done this a hundred times before. And that's how it seems to be with Walker. He's a mystery but feels familiar at the same time.

We pass the old pharmacy, its awning faded but still

standing strong, flapping in the breeze. Handwritten notes advertising "homemade salves" and "two-for-one root beer floats" fill the display window.

"You ever had one of those floats?" Walker asks, pointing his cup towards the window.

I shook my head as I sip my coffee. "Nope." It tastes like something safe, something familiar, like crisp autumn mornings and cozy blankets, like the kind of softness I don't always let myself have.

Like something I could get used to.

He stops, eyeing me like I've just confessed to something criminal.

"You mean to tell me you've never had a Bridger Falls root beer float?"

I'd never believe it could taste better than this coffee.

I smirk. "What, is that a deal-breaker for you? On being my friend," I add in quickly.

"Almost," he mutters, his eyes crinkling at the sides when he smiles. "Lucky for you, I'm big on second chances."

Green flag.

I sip my coffee to hide my grin as we continue walking.

Okay, yeah. Maybe this could work. I can be friends with Walker.

We pass the fire station next, where a few firefighters sit outside, drinking coffee. Ollie spots us immediately and waves.

"Well, well, well," Ollie called out, grinning. "First she's on the back of your bike, and now you're having morning coffee strolls, Walker? When's the wedding?"

Walker doesn't slow down. "Go play with your hose, Ollie."

Ollie laughs, shooting me a wink, and I laugh so hard.

"Don't let him pretend to be all gruff and rough," he calls to me. "Walker's secretly the town's biggest teddy bear."

Walker flips him off without looking back.

I chuckle, glancing up at him. "Teddy bear, huh?"

Walker sigh. "You and Ollie *would* get along too well."

Green flag.

We stop in front of Murphy's Auto Shop, where the scent of motor oil and gasoline mix in the air.

Poppy is under the hood of a truck, grease smeared across her cheek, and her dad stands beside her, giving her instructions.

"She's going to take over this place one day," Walker says. "Her dad won't admit it, but he's proud as hell of her. She's an even better mechanic than he is. And he's the best in a two-hundred-mile radius."

Poppy catches us looking and flashes me a knowing grin. "Morning, lovebirds!"

Walker mutters something under his breath.

I smirk and nudge him. "You make a lot of enemies in this town?"

Walker exhales. "I make a lot of nosy-ass friends in this town."

Green flag.

We eventually reach the small town square, where wooden benches sit beneath tall, sprawling oaks.

Walker sits first, stretching his long legs out. I sat beside him, close enough to feel his warmth but not close enough to make it weird.

The faded plaque on the bench catches my attention.

In loving memory of Grace Murphy. May your kindness live on in all who sit here.

"Who is Grace Murphy?" I ask, curiously.

"Grace was Poppy's mother," Walker says as he looks over at the plaque.

"Poppy's mom?" I remark, sadly, tracing the letters.

Walker nods. "She was a great lady."

The silence stretches between us, comfortable and easy. The wind picks up slightly, rustling the leaves overhead.

After a moment, I sigh, turning my coffee in my hands. "I, uh... just wanted to say sorry about last night."

Walker turns to me, brow furrowed. "For what?"

I let out a dry laugh. "You know, making a mess of your bar. Nearly starting a fight."

Walker's expression doesn't change. "You stood up for yourself."

I blink "Yeah, but—"

"I'm raising my daughter not to take shit from anyone either," he says. "So, if you think I'm gonna lecture you for standing your ground, you don't know me very well."

I stare at him, something in my chest tightening. He's right. I don't know him very well. But with everything that I'm learning, I want to know him better.

It not just the words—it's the way he says them. Like it wasn't even a question. Like he respects me for it.

A slow, unfamiliar realization settled in my bones.

Green flag.

And oh my god, there are so many.

I haven't seen this color before. Not once. My ex had so many red flags it felt like the carnival was in town. But, green? Nope.

I let myself look at him then, and before I could stop myself, I smile. "You're a good man, Walker."

He exhales, shaking his head, but I see the corner of his mouth twitch like he's fighting a grin.

"Don't go spreading that around," he mutters. "I got a reputation to keep."

I laugh, sipping my coffee as the small town of Bridger Falls moves around us like it has all the time in the world.

"Thanks for your help at the bar last night," he says, his voice low, almost gruff.

I tilt my head. "You still need me?"

A beat passes. He exhales, like he's been holding something back, then nods.

"Yeah," he says. "If you have the time. Cash needs to be with his family."

I smile, a warm feeling settling in my chest. "I have the time."

I should not be feeling like this.

Not over a motorcycle ride. Not over Walker.

And yet, here I am, clutching the warm coffee he bought me like it's some lifeline, walking beside him down the quiet streets of Bridger Falls, and trying—really trying—not to let my brain go places it shouldn't.

Like how solid he felt under my hands. How the warmth of his body bled through his shirt, steady and strong as I held on to him. How the wind tangled through my hair, the world flying by, and somehow, all I could focus on was him—how safe I felt. How much I wanted to press closer.

It was just a ride. Just a favor after my car broke down.

But now, with the town settling into a quiet hum around us, I can't shake the way my pulse still stirs when he glances over at me.

This is dangerous.

Walker is—Walker is my friend. My favorite person to banter with at the bar, the one who lets me handle things and never says a word. The guy who calls me Red with a slow, teasing grin.

He's steady. Dependable. Good.

And that ride...

That ride made me forget all the reasons we're just friends.

But it doesn't help when Walker's arm brushes mine, his

scent—a mix of leather, soap, and something undeniably him—lingering in the cool air.

"You're quiet," he says, his voice low, easy. Like he already knows I'm in my head.

I force a smirk, bumping my elbow against his. "Shocking, isn't it?"

He chuckles, and I swear it does something to my chest. Makes it tighten. Makes it ache in a way I don't want to examine too closely.

I liked that ride too much. I liked the feel of him too much.

And I can't afford to.

I take another sip of coffee, fixing my gaze on the sidewalk ahead. Just friends. That's all we are.

Even if, right now, walking next to him with the pinks and purples streaking across the sky and my heart tripping over itself like a fool...

It sure as hell doesn't feel that way.

For a second, we stand there, the space between us charged with something unspoken. Then Walker clears his throat. "We'd better get going. Maggie'll have my ass if I keep you here any longer."

"Later, Walker," I call as I head inside the Dogwood while he waits on the sidewalk like a gentleman. I'm pretending to play it cool with Walker. But what I feel is far from cool.

* * *

The smell of orange furniture polish drifts through The Dogwood as I finish wiping down the check-in counter. The afternoon light filters through the windows, casting golden streaks across the worn wooden floors.

Maggie bustles into the room, a woman on a mission,

stuffing a few things into a tote bag before shrugging on her jacket.

"Where's the fire?" I ask, sipping my coffee.

Maggie huffs. "No fire. Just heading over to pick up Mack."

I grin, because the way Maggie spoils Walker's daughter is adorable. It's the way she's always been with me. "What are you bringing her this time?"

"Just a few cookies," she says far too innocently, sliding the tote over her shoulder.

I lean against the counter, smirking. "Maggie, we both know there are at least three different snacks in there, probably a book, and knowing you, something ridiculously hilarious."

Maggie lifts her chin, unapologetic. "That girl is growing up too fast. Someone has to dote on her properly."

I shake my head, amused. "You know, Walker might fight you for the title of 'Most Overprotective.'"

I still haven't met this kid, but she seems great. I'll admit, I'm curious about her.

Maggie snorts. "Please. That man is wrapped around Mack's little finger. He pretends he's all tough, but one pout from that girl, and suddenly, he's building her bookshelves at midnight and making pancakes in the shape of horses."

I nearly choke on my coffee. "You're kidding."

"Not even a little," Maggie says, grinning as she adjusts her hair in the mirror. "I caught him doing it once. Looked embarrassed as sin, too."

I laugh, picturing a big, brooding Walker standing at the stove, flipping horse-shaped pancakes for his daughter.

Maggie gives me one of those knowing looks, the ones that see straight through you. "He's a good man, you know."

I glance down at my coffee, my heart doing that stupid fluttering thing it's been doing more often lately. "Seems like it."

She pats my arm. "Mack's a good kid too. Can't wait for you to meet her."

Warmth spreads through me at that. I say nothing, but Maggie's eyes twinkle like she knows.

She pauses at the door, one hand on the knob. "You're thinking about staying here, aren't you?"

I look around The Dogwood, the place that somehow feels more like home than anywhere else has in years.

I think about Walker. About this town that has somehow wrapped itself around my heart without me even noticing. I have nothing to go back to in Nashville and no desire to return.

I smile. "Yeah, Maggs. I think I could stay for a while."

She beams, then winks. "Well, good."

And just like that, she's out the door, off to spoil Mack with cookies and Walker with unsolicited life advice.

I shake my head, laughing to myself.

I stand by the window of The Dogwood, my hands wrapped around a warm mug of coffee.

Bridger Falls doesn't rush.

There's no honking traffic, no neon signs flashing, no relentless push to be somewhere, do something, prove something. This town moves at its own pace—steady, like a song played just right.

And somehow, it's exactly what I didn't know I needed.

I take a slow sip of my coffee and think about how easy it's been to breathe here. How the weight I'd carried for so long has felt a little lighter.

My notebook is open on the check-in counter, pages filled with half-written songs and messy lyrics, words coming to me faster than they have in years.

I thought I'd lost this part of myself—the girl who used to scribble lyrics on napkins and hum melodies under her breath just because they made her feel something.

But here? Here, the songs are coming back to me.

Maybe it's how the town breathes creativity—in the way Cami perfects her lattes like an artist, the way Poppy gets lost in her work under the hood of a car, the way Maggie just pours love into everyone. It's like a place that heals souls.

Maybe it's Walker, his quiet intensity, the way he walks into a room, making everything feel a little steadier and more real.

Or maybe it's all of it—the slow, steady rhythm of life here, the way it's wrapping around me, making me feel safe, making me feel like maybe, just maybe, I belong.

I smile to myself, fingers tapping lightly against the ceramic mug, a melody already forming in my mind.

I think I could stay here forever.

Chapter 13
Walker

The thing about small-town life is that it moves slowly. It's steady and predictable. And it's just the way I like it.

Bridger Falls doesn't change much. It hasn't in the fifteen years I've lived here. The people have stayed the same, and the town square still smells like fresh bread from Harvest & Honey deli every morning. The Black Dog, my bar and sanctuary, still have the same energy it always has. The safe and solid life that I've built for us.

And as far as I'm concerned, that's how it should be.

I pour myself a cup of coffee and lean against the bar, watching the early afternoon sun slant through the rustic windows. It's quiet now, the lull between the lunch rush and the regulars rolling in for their evening drinks and to catch up on the town gossip.

Quiet is good. Quiet is safe.

But ever since Violet Wilson walked into this town, I haven't felt calm.

And that's a problem.

I had one rule when I moved here: no more living in the public eye. No more risks. No more trusting people who could tear my life apart. And especially not my daughter's life.

And for the most part, I've kept that promise.

I still write songs, sure. Can't seem to shake that part of myself, even after all these years. I keep the small cabin out back, tucked behind the lake on my property, where I can write and record in secret. No one in Bridger Falls knows what I do out there. Not even Maggie, and she knows damn near everything. Keeping that from her hasn't been easy, either. She's nosy as hell.

I sell my songs under a pseudonym. Let the world think they come from some anonymous songwriter who wants no part of the spotlight. Because that part is true, I don't. I don't live that life anymore, and I never will.

The industry chewed me up once, and I won't give it another chance to do it again.

This town is my world now. My daughter is my entire world.

I let nothing in that could destroy the peace I've built. I don't let anyone in, period.

At least, I didn't until her.

Maggie has a soft spot for lost souls, and Violet coming here means she had something to run from.

I know all about running.

I didn't expect Violet to pull the rug out from under me and ruin the carefully built world I've built in the best way possible.

When I saw her for the first time at The Black Dog, standing in the middle of my bar like she belonged there, I knew she was different. Special. And I couldn't understand it then, but I definitely see it now.

That night, with her dark red wavy hair falling in wild

waves down her back, eyes too damn knowing, lips curled in amusement as she could already see straight through me, she looked like she knew exactly what kind of man I was and wasn't scared of anything.

And that? That's dangerous.

Because I don't let people in. I don't get involved. Even when they're running from things that make me want to protect them. Because I can't take those risks anymore.

But then she smiled at me, and I felt a crack in the armor I thought was impenetrable.

I've never met anyone like her.

The problem with Violet is that she doesn't act like an outsider.

She walks around Bridger Falls like she's been here forever. She fits in so well. It's hard not to like her. She makes it damn easy.

She's already got Cami and Poppy wrapped around her finger and already has half the town gossiping about her in that good-natured, small-town way. They all like her, too.

She's helping Maggie at the motel, taking care of things like she's been doing it her whole life.

And I don't like it.

I don't like how she can just waltz in here and kick down the walls I've spent fifteen years building up.

I don't like the way I catch myself watching her.

And I sure as hell don't like how she looks at me like she's figuring me out.

Because I don't want her figuring me out. I don't want anyone to figure me out.

I'm not a puzzle. I'm a locked door.

And locked doors don't open.

I've wanted to avoid her, but I can't. Whenever she's

around, it's a yes to anything she needs, and it's like I can't even stop myself.

It doesn't help that she's been working at my bar in the evenings, stepping in when Maggie volunteered her help with Cash out for a while.

She fits behind the bar too well, sliding drinks across the counter, laughing at things the regulars say, and tapping her fingers against the old wood like there's a melody running through her veins she can't turn off.

I tell myself it doesn't bother me.

I tell myself she's just passing through—that one day, she'll pack her bags and leave, and things will return to the way they were.

But every time I see her, that idea feels like a lie.

And that's the real problem, isn't it?

I don't want her to leave.

It's late when I finally finish closing up the bar, with only the hum of the neon sign and the faint sound of crickets filling the late-night air.

Violet is still here, drying glasses behind the bar.

I should tell her to lock up and go. Should keep my distance. But I know I won't. I'll make sure she gets a ride home and is safe behind her door.

Instead, I linger, watching how she moves naturally in my space.

She looks up, catching my gaze, and something flickers in her eyes—something warm, something knowing.

"You gonna keep staring, or you wanna help me with these glasses?" she teases.

I smirk, shaking my head as I grab a towel. "Didn't realize I was staring."

She chuckles, handing me a glass. "Oh, you were. It's alright, though. I know I'm fascinating."

I roll my eyes. But damn if she isn't right.

She leans against the counter, watching me dry the glass with a lazy kind of amusement.

"What made you come to Bridger Falls?" she asks suddenly. "You've been here what—fifteen years? What made you pick Bridger Falls of all places?"

I glance at her, startled by her question. I should have expected it. I'm surprised that she hasn't asked sooner. "Needed a fresh start. Seemed as good a place as any."

Her lips curve. "That's vague."

I smirk. "You ask every man you meet for his life story?"

"Only the ones who are hiding something."

Damn. She's good.

I let out a slow breath, weighing my options. She's already got one hell of an instinct for bullshit, and if I dodge too hard, she'll just keep coming. I need to give her something.

Something true.

Something that won't lead her straight to the past I left behind.

I keep my voice even. "Had a baby to raise. Wanted somewhere quiet. Somewhere safe."

That part? That part is real.

Violet doesn't say anything right away. She just studies me, like she's trying to decide whether or not to believe me.

And for a second—just a second—I wonder if she can see right through me.

But then, she just smirks, drumming her fingers against the table.

She studies me for a beat like she's picking apart the layers I don't want her to see.

"Guess I can understand that," she says finally. "There's something about this place. Feels... safe."

Safe.

I swallow, looking away.

She has no idea how hard I've worked to make it that way.

By the time we finish cleaning up, it's past midnight, and the air outside is cool and still.

She stretches, letting out a little satisfied sigh, and I have to force my eyes away.

"Thanks for letting me help," she says. "You need me tomorrow?"

I know what I should say.

I should tell her no.

I should tell her I don't need her.

But the words don't come.

"Yeah," I say instead, my voice quieter than I mean it to be.

She smiles, slow and soft like she knows exactly what just happened.

And just like that, I realize I'm in trouble.

Because I don't let people in.

But Violet Wilson is already halfway through the door, and I feel like I couldn't stop her even if I tried.

We lock up and head out to my truck as I dump the trash in the dumpster.

The night air is crisp, carrying the distant scent of pine and the lingering hum of the town settling in for the night. The streets are quiet, and it's my favorite time of night.

Except now, I'm standing next to Violet, watching her pull on a hoodie over her tank top, her hair a little messy from a long night, and I can't ignore the familiarity of it.

She looks just like she did that first night.

The night I told myself was just a one-time thing. And that one time that I can't get out of my head. No matter how much of a perfect gentleman I try to be.

I clear my throat. "You ready?"

She looks at me, then at my truck parked outside The Black

Dog. "Are you asking me nicely, or are you gonna tell me you're taking me home whether or not I like it?"

I smirk. "That depends. Are you planning on arguing?"

She grins. "Always."

I roll my eyes and gesture toward the truck. "Come on, Red. Before you start walking and I feel obligated to follow you like some damn lost puppy to make sure you get home safe."

She laughs, hopping up into the passenger seat like she's done it a hundred times before. And that's the problem, isn't it? It feels easy. Feels familiar. Feels like I haven't worked hard to pretend I don't remember exactly how she felt in my arms that night.

I slide into the driver's seat and start the engine, the rumble breaking the silence between us.

But not for long.

Because, of course, Violet's the first to break it.

"You know," she muses, resting her elbow against the window, "this is oddly familiar."

I glance at her in surprise, pretending not to know what she means. "What is?"

She turns her head, giving me a look that says I know damn well what you're doing.

I shake my head, shocked that her words precisely mirror what I was thinking, as I laugh softly to myself. Because of course, we even think alike.

"This," she says, motioning between us. "Late night. You driving me home? Me, pretending I'm not thinking about—"

She stops herself, eyes flicking toward me, watching for my reaction.

I grip the steering wheel tighter. "Not thinking about what?"

Her grin is all mischief and amusement. "Nothing. Forget I said anything."

I sigh, shaking my head. "Red—"

"Relax," she teases. "I just meant it's funny, that's all. You, driving me home, me pretending I don't notice how your truck smells like cedar and bad decisions."

I snort. "Bad decisions?"

She tilts her head, eyes sparkling. "You telling me the last time we were in this truck together wasn't a bad decision?"

I don't answer right away.

Because part of me knows damn well it wasn't a bad decision.

It was a mistake to let her get close. But that night? That night wasn't a bad decision.

She lets out a dramatic sigh. "It's fine, Walker. I get it. It was just a one-time thing. No big deal."

I glance at her. "You're really enjoying this, aren't you?"

She grins. "Oh, yeah."

We pull up to The Dogwood. The light is on, casting a warm glow over the front of her door.

She unbuckles but doesn't move to get out right away. Instead, she turns toward me, her expression softer now, less teasing.

"Thanks for the ride," she says, voice quieter.

"Anytime," I murmur, surprised to find that I actually mean it.

She hesitates for a second, then smiles—not her usual playful smirk, but something smaller, something real.

"Thanks for being my friend, Walker."

And that? That hits.

Friend.

The word sticks in my chest like a splinter I didn't see coming. Friend zoned for real.

Because I know she means it. And maybe I should be relieved, or maybe I should be grateful that she's willing to see me as anything other than the guy who pushed her away.

But instead, it feels like a punch to the gut.

Because if she's calling me a friend, then it means I'm doing exactly what I set out to do. Keeping my distance. Keeping it casual. Keeping my walls up.

And yet, why does it feel like I'm losing something?

She gives me one last look before stepping out, pulling her hoodie tighter around her as she heads up the steps.

I watch her go, my grip tightening around the steering wheel, the word still ringing in my ears.

Friend.

I should be okay with that.

I should.

So why the hell am I not?

* * *

I should've known better than to step foot in The Dogwood Inn without my guard up. Maggie gives me hell on a good day. But today I feel like she's got an even bigger plan to drive me crazy.

Maggie has that look. The one that means she's about to meddle in my love life like it's her God-given duty.

I've barely walked through the front door when she pops up behind the counter, eyes twinkling like she's about to ruin my day in the most affectionate way possible.

"Well, if it isn't Walker, the man who's been circling my niece like a lovesick hound dog," she says, crossing her arms.

I sigh. Loudly. "Hello to you too, Maggie."

She grinned. "Saw you two having a lovely stroll through town the other day."

Shit. Can no one leave me alone in this town?

I force a casual shrug. "We were just having coffee."

Maggie narrows her eyes. "Uh-huh. And you just so happened to be glued to Violet's side the whole time?"

"Glued?" I scoff. "That's dramatic, even for you."

She waves me off. "Please. You were looking at her like she hung the damn moon. And the way you puffed up when Ollie teased you? Whew. I could feel the testosterone all the way over here at the Dogwood."

I scrub a hand down my face. "You're seeing things and need to get your vision checked before you move into the nursing home. Also, what, do you have a gossip phone tree going? How do you even know all of that?"

Maggie lets out a sharp bark of laughter. "Honey, I've been watching stubborn men deny their feelings since before you were born. You're not slick."

I lean against the counter. "You got a point, or are you just here to make my life harder?"

"Oh, I always have a point." She smirks. "And my point is—when are you gonna quit dancing around that girl and do something about it?"

I open my mouth. Close it. Because the truth? The truth is, I want to. I want Violet. But she is...Violet. Stubborn, smart-mouthed, and too good for me. She deserves better than what I can give her.

Maggie watches me like a hawk. "That's what I thought."

I exhale sharply. "It's not that easy."

"Oh, honey." She pats my hand like I'm the biggest idiot she's ever met. "Love is never easy. But you? You're making it much harder than it needs to be."

I drag a hand through my hair. "Maggie—"

She cuts me off with a knowing smile. "You can fight it all you want, sugar, but that girl is yours. Everyone sees it. The only one still pretending otherwise is you."

I let my head drop back, staring at the ceiling. God help me.

Maggie's voice goes all sing-songy. "You know I'm right."

I mutter a curse. "You always think you're right."

"Because I usually am." She pats my arm before walking off, humming to herself. "I'll see you later."

And I, fully exasperated and maybe a little rattled, did the only thing I could—got the hell out before she could meddle even more.

Chapter 14
Violet

"I swear to God, Violet, if you've been driving this thing with the check engine light on for months, I'm gonna revoke your car privileges personally."

Poppy's voice is muffled from under the hood, but I can still hear the judgment dripping from it.

I lean against the wall of the garage, arms crossed. "I wasn't ignoring it. I was—" I pause, searching for a reasonable excuse.

She peeks her head out. A single brow arched as she waits for my lame excuse. "Yeah?"

I sigh, holding up my hands in surrender. "Okay, I was procrastinating."

Poppy laughs, wiping her hands on an old rag. "At least you admit it." She leans against the workbench, shaking her head. "Girl, I don't know how this thing didn't leave you stranded on the highway."

I wince. It did. And it has before. This time I was just lucky that Walker came to my rescue.

I had a taste of Bridger Falls hospitality when my car died. Cami called Walker, and somehow, instead of my car being rescued, I ended up wrapped around Walker's back, riding through town on the back of his damn motorcycle.

I try not to think about that. Friends don't think about their friends like that.

"Well," I say, kicking at the floor, "at least I made it here in one piece."

Poppy snorts. "Yeah, yeah. Let me work my magic and see if I can keep you from breaking down again."

She turns back to the engine, completely in her element, and I find myself watching her.

I like Poppy.

Poppy Murphy has the kind of beauty that doesn't need effort. She's all natural, all effortless, all completely unfair.

Her blond hair, thick and wild, is pulled into a messy bun on top of her head, but loose strands have broken free, framing her bright blue eyes—the kind of blue that made you think of summers spent under an open sky. Even with a smudge of grease on her cheek, she still looks like she belongs on the cover of some western romance novel, the kind where the heroine tames the rugged cowboy with nothing but a smile.

Dressed in her grease-stained mechanic's coveralls, sleeves rolled up to reveal toned arms and smudged hands, she looks like she's just rebuilt an engine with nothing but determination and a wrench. And yet, somehow, she still manages to shine bright and bring the sunshine wherever she goes.

She's unapologetically herself, all confidence and moving around the shop with effortless ease. She doesn't hesitate, doesn't doubt herself. It's refreshing to be around someone who... knows who they are.

I used to know who I was, and I used to have that kind of confidence.

But somewhere along the way, I lost it.

Or maybe—maybe it was stolen.

Actually, there's no maybe. It was. And that's why I'm determined to get it back.

"So," Poppy says, her voice casual as she tightens something under the hood, "are you thinking about sticking around here?"

I blink. "What?"

She doesn't look up. "In Bridger Falls. You gave passing-through vibes when you first got here, but now..." She glances at me, smirking. "You got a job, you're helping Maggie, you're—what's the word—assimilating?"

I scoff. "Assimilating?"

"Yup." She tosses a wrench onto the workbench. "Next thing you know, you'll be baking pies and talking about how the 'city just doesn't have the same charm' like the rest of us townies. Also, Maggie mentioned it."

I snort, laugh, and roll my eyes, but the teasing lands deep in my chest.

Because she's right.

I was passing through. At least, that's what I told myself. But somewhere between helping Maggie at The Dogwood, working at The Black Dog, and getting roped into small-town daily life, I started... staying.

And it doesn't feel like a mistake.

I sip the coffee I picked up from Steamy Sips earlier, the caramel warmth grounding me. "I don't know what I'm doing," I admit.

Poppy raises a brow. "No one does."

"Seriously, though. I never meant to stay here. But I like it." I hesitate, then add, "This place is good for the soul."

Her expression softens. She leans back against the workbench, arms crossed, considering me for a moment. "Yeah," she says finally. "I get that."

Something about the way she says it makes me think she really does.

I've had friends before.

At least, I thought I did.

The kind of friendship where everything is easy and fun—until it's not. Until one day, you need them, and instead of showing up, they disappear.

I haven't talked about it. Not to Maggie or even to think about it myself if I can help it.

But standing here in Murphy's Auto Shop, watching Poppy casually fix something I should have taken care of months ago, I realize something.

She's not being nice to get something in return. Sure, I'm paying her to fix my car, but outside of that? She's been a friend.

She's been a friend because she wants to be my friend.

And I appreciate that.

I exhale, pressing my palms against my thighs. "Okay, not to be dramatic, but you fixing my car might actually make me emotional."

Poppy laughs. "If you cry, I'm kicking you out."

I grin. "Fair enough."

She snorts, going back to work, and for a second, I let myself just be here.

It's been a long time since I've had this—the kind of easy banter that isn't hiding anything sharp underneath. No competition. No pretending. No waiting for the other person to stab me in the back.

Just laughter. Just understanding.

And I like it.

After another fifteen minutes, Poppy steps back, wiping her hands on her coveralls.

"Alright," she says, "your car probably won't explode. But I have to order a few parts."

I give her a look. "*Probably* won't explode?"

She grins. "Look, I'm a genius, but even geniuses have their limits. You gotta start scheduling regular maintenance."

I shake my head, laughing. "Alright, I will."

I glance around the shop at the old photos on the walls, some of them of Poppy's mom, Grace, who she mentioned passed away ten years ago.

There's history here. Genuine history.

Bridger Falls isn't just a town. It's layers of stories, stitched together over time, carried by people who still give a damn.

And somehow, I've found myself inside one of their stories.

I exhale, stretching my arms over my head. "You know, this place is a pretty great place to call home."

Poppy smirks. "Careful, Violet. If you start calling it home, you'll never leave."

The word home makes something catch in my throat.

I don't know what to say.

But maybe, for the first time in a long time, I don't need to.

"Alright, get out of my shop," Poppy says, smacking a grease-stained rag in my direction. "Before I find something else wrong with your car and make you stay even longer."

I laugh, heading toward the sidewalk. "Noted. Thanks, Poppy. Seriously."

She shrugs, but I see the warmth in her expression. "Anytime."

I slide into Maggie's truck, turn the key, and the engine hums to life.

For the first time in a long time, so does something in me.

I don't know what it is yet.

But as I drive away, windows down, air crisp against my skin, I think—

Maybe this is what it feels like to start over.

Maybe this is what it feels like to finally belong.

* * *

It's past nine, and The Black Dog is in full swing.

The neon sign out front hums against the glass, the jukebox in the corner plays a mix of old country, and the scent of whiskey, beer, and fried food fills the air.

I'm finally getting the hang of this place with the rhythm of pouring drinks, remembering the regulars' orders, dodging Jack and Ollie's relentless flirting from the other side of the bar. I know they're doing it on purpose to get under Walker's skin. And by the looks of it, it's working.

Walker left to run an errand, but when he's here, I can feel him watching me sometimes.

Like he's still trying to figure me out, like a puzzle he can't find all the pieces for.

Like he doesn't quite know what to do with me yet.

Join the club, Walker.

"Hey, Violet," Momma Mary, the cook calls from the kitchen. "Can you grab another bottle of whiskey from Walker's office?"

We've been slow and have been restocking the bar and kitchen area before our dinner rush.

I nod, wiping my hands on a rag. "On it."

I head toward the back hallway, past the emergency exit sign that flickers like it's one day away from giving up and finally reach Walker's office. He has a whole little space separate from the bar back here with a living area, a place for his dog, and a desk. He also has a row of storage shelves in the back where he keeps extra inventory.

I push the door open—and stop dead in my tracks.

There's a girl sitting in his chair, boots kicked up on the desk like she owns the place, petting Pickles who is curled up in her lap. The dog wags her tail when she sees me.

She's scrolling through her phone, popping a piece of candy in her mouth, and barely spares me a glance.

She's dark-haired and carries the same brooding energy as her father.

And I know immediately—this is Mack.

Walker's kid.

The one Maggie dotes on, the daughter that Walker would burn the entire world down for.

And she's sizing me up.

Oh, this is going to be fun.

"You lost?" she asks, arching a perfectly unimpressed brow.

I cross my arms. "Nope. Just came to grab a bottle of whiskey."

She smirks. "Figures. You look like you drink a lot."

I snort. "You look like you get away with too much."

She grins. "I do."

There's a beat of silence, then—we both laugh.

Okay. I like her already.

I lean against the door frame, watching her lazily toss her phone onto the desk. "So, let me guess—you come back here to hide from your dad, steal candy from his drawer, and pretend you don't like being at the bar."

She blinks, then points at me. "That was freakishly accurate."

I flash a grin. "It's a gift."

She studies me for a second, then tilts her head. "You're Maggie's Violet."

I raise a brow. "Maggie's Violet?"

She shrugs. "She's been talking about you non-stop. 'Oh, Violet is staying with me at the Dogwood. Violet is working with your dad at The Black Dog. Violet has great hair and would be a fantastic girlfriend if only stubborn Walker would wake up and see it.'"

I choke on air.

She grins, clearly pleased with herself.

"Wow," I say, pressing a hand to my chest. "That was disturbingly accurate. You sure you don't have a gift as well?"

"More like talent for mimicking small-town meddling."

I grin, definitely liking her even more.

And something about Mack feels... easy. Natural. Like bantering with her is the most effortless thing in the world.

The door creaks open behind me, and I don't need to turn around to know who it is.

Walker clears his throat, and Mack and I both turn toward him like we got caught red-handed.

His arms are crossed with his usual grumpy expression in place, but I don't miss the flicker of surprise in his eyes as he watches us.

"Everything okay in here?" he asks, voice low, unreadable.

Mack smirks, absolutely eating this up. "Oh yeah, Dad. We were just bonding. I was getting to know my new mommy."

Walker narrows his eyes at her as if he's giving her a warning, then flicks his gaze curiously to me as if he's gauging my response at her teasing.

I laugh at her comment and fight back a grin. "She insulted me within the first thirty seconds of meeting me, so... yeah. I'd say we're off to a great start."

Mack shrugs, popping another piece of candy in her mouth. "She can take it, Dad. I respect that."

Walker exhales, rubbing the back of his neck like he doesn't quite know what to do with this.

"Alright, kid," Walker finally says, shaking his head at Mack. "You done interrogating our friend, Violet?"

Our *friend*. And the way he obnoxiously emphasized the word friend. There he goes with the friend shit again.

Mack shrugs, looking too pleased with herself. "For now."

Walker mutters something under his breath before turning to me. "Whiskey's on the bottom shelf."

I salute him. "Sir, yes, sir."

Mack cackles. "I like her, Dad."

Walker mutters another curse before heading out.

I turn back to Mack, and we stare at each other for a moment—two smartasses in a standoff. Then we both crack up at the same time.

And just like that, I know.

I like this kid.

A lot.

* * *

Walker's bar is quiet for once. Most of the customers here are the regulars, and the jukebox hums something old and slow in the background. I'm just about to steal the last fry from Mack's plate when the front door flies open with the force of a full-blown tornado.

And that tornado has a name.

Aunt Maggie.

"MAKAYLA LEIGH!"

Mack's fork froze halfway to her mouth. "Shit."

Walker, not even fazed, leaned against the counter, amused as hell. "And here I was, thinking this night was about to get boring."

Maggie stomped inside, hands on her hips, eyes blazing. I was pretty sure if Mack had been a less stubborn human, she would have bolted out the back door.

But Mack?

Mack just chews her bite real slow, swallows, and grins. "Hey, Maggs. Want some fries?"

Maggie looks like she's contemplating homicide. "I went out

to the house, and you weren't there. You didn't tell me you were at the bar."

I take a very long sip of my drink and wait for the fireworks.

"It is a school night, Mack." Maggie's voice is all sharp edges and exasperation. "Do you know what responsible people do on school nights?"

Mack nodded seriously. "Stay up late and eat bar food?"

Maggie eyes her. "They sleep. And do homework."

"Well, I'll get to the sleep eventually. And I already did my homework."

Maggie inhales very slowly, probably to pray for patience or suppress the urge to shake Mack by the shoulders.

Walker chuckles under his breath, sliding a fresh plate of mozzarella sticks onto the table like he's setting out snacks for a live show. "Mack, why didn't you tell Maggie you were staying in town?"

Mack mumbles, "Sorry, Maggie. I forgot."

Maggie gives him a look as he drops off the mozzarella sticks. "You're an enabler."

Walker smirks. "I prefer 'gracious host.'"

Maggie sighs dramatically, pulls out a chair, and sits down next to Mack. "Well, if I'm going to scold you, I might as well eat while I do it."

Mack pumps a fist. "Yes! Corrupting Maggie, one mozzarella stick at a time!"

I grin, watching them dig in. And against my better judgment, I join them since we're slow.

Walker arches a brow. "You too?"

I shrug. "What? This is the best entertainment I've had all week."

Maggie shakes her head as I grab a mozzarella stick. "I don't know why I even try. You're all bad influences."

Mack snorts. "Oh please, you love me the most."

We just eat, order fries, joke around, and throw a few fries at Pickles, who's curled up under the table, snoring like an old lady.

Maggie even steals the last mozzarella stick from Mack's plate, which makes Mack gasp like she's been personally betrayed.

"Maggie, that was mine!"

Maggie bites into it, totally unrepentant. "Possession is nine-tenths of the law, sugar."

Mack turns to me for backup. "You saw that! She's turning against me."

I nod solemnly. "This is how it starts. First, she steals your food. Next thing you know, she's taking over your entire life."

Maggie rolls her eyes but tries to hide a smile behind her drink.

"She already does that," Mack grins.

Walker lets out a low chuckle from behind the bar, his gaze drifting between the three of us. He hasn't said much all evening, just watched.

Like he likes seeing us all together.

And I love this. Growing up with Maggie for an aunt was super special. Seeing her with Mack and knowing that Mack has that too is a good feeling. The warm and fuzzy kind.

I meet his eyes for half a second, my stomach doing something weird and warm. But then Mack tosses a fry at me, and the moment is gone.

By the time Maggie finally drags Mack home, stuffed with food and still whining about bedtime, Pickles is up and ready to play, and Walker still watches me like he hasn't quite figured me out yet.

And honestly?

I'm not sure I want him to.

I don't even know what I'm doing.

Chapter 15
Walker

The drive to The Dogwood is quiet tonight.

Violet sits in my truck, legs tucked up, fingers playing with the hem of her sweater. I can tell she wants to say something, but she doesn't. And I don't push.

I pull up to The Dogwood, the porch light casting a soft glow over the old wooden steps to her door.

She shifts, undoing her seatbelt. "Thanks for the ride, Walker."

I nod, watching as she grips the doorhandle, hesitating for half a second before turning back to me.

"I like your kid. And I had fun tonight."

I glance at her, a flicker of warmth settling in my chest. "Yeah," I murmur. "She's something."

She smiles, soft and real, then steps out into the night.

I wait until she reaches the door until I see her disappear inside.

Then, and only then, do I drive away.

I drive slowly, the engine's hum steady beneath my hands, but my mind's not on the road. It's still back there.

Still back on the porch, watching Violet disappear inside her room, still hearing the way she'd said it.

"I like your kid. And I had fun tonight."

Simple words. Casual, even. But somehow, they settle deep, lodging themselves right in my chest.

I grip the wheel a little tighter, exhaling through my nose. I shouldn't like this. Shouldn't like the way she looked sitting across from Mack and Maggie tonight, laughing over fries, tossing fries at Pickles like she belonged there.

But I do like this.

God help me, I really do.

I saw it happen tonight. The way Mack, my impossible, sharp-tongued, full-of-hellfire kid, started gravitating toward her, the same way she does with Maggie. How Violet met her head-on, matching her wit for wit, teasing but never condescending, treating her like a person instead of just a kid.

Mack doesn't let many people in. Neither do I.

But I could tell that she likes Violet.

And Maggie? Hell, Maggie's been waiting for this moment like she's been secretly planning this all along.

She watched the two of them at that table tonight—Violet and Mack, feeding Pickles, stealing food off each other's plates, bickering over music—and she looked at me with that knowing glint in her eye.

Like she knew exactly what was happening.

Like she knew that no matter how many walls I put up, they were already crumbling.

And she's right.

Because when Violet sat there laughing with my family like she'd been a part of it all along—

I knew.

I'm in trouble. Real trouble.

Because this is what I've always wanted. I didn't think that I could have it.

Until now. Now, I'm rethinking everything.

* * *

The ringing wakes me out of a dead sleep. I've only been asleep for a few hours because after I dropped Violet off, I worked on a few songs at the cabin.

I pick up my phone, hit the button and put it to my ear, blinking at the ceiling, my body on high alert before my mind can catch up. Calls in the middle of the night usually aren't the friendly checking-in kind.

Then I hear the urgency in Poppy's voice. "Walker—The Dogwood's on fire."

I'm already moving before she finishes the last word, my heart pounding against my ribs.

"Is everyone out?" I demand, shoving my boots on and grabbing my keys as I brace myself for the answer.

"Everyone got out safely. But it's bad."

"I'm on my way," I clip, disconnecting the call.

I'm already up the stairs and running down the hall, pushing open Mack's door. She blinks awake and sits up, confused. "Dad?"

I don't waste time. "Come on. We gotta go, honey. The Dogwood's on fire."

She's on her feet in seconds, throwing on a hoodie. Panic in her voice, she asks, "Maggie and Violet?"

"Everyone got out," I say, more to myself than her.

I don't exhale until we're in the truck, tires spitting gravel as we speed toward town. Mack is strangely silent. I can feel the worry from the passenger seat.

"Hey, it's gonna be okay," I reassure her, reaching over and patting her arm.

"What's going to happen to Maggie? She loves The Dogwood. That place is her whole life," she says with turmoil on her face.

"I don't know, but she's safe. And she can stay with us until she figures it out," I promise her.

By the time we get to town, the air is thick with smoke, the sky glowing in the distance like the sun decided to set in the wrong direction. A sharp, acrid smell hits me first: burning wood and earth and a pungent chemical odor. It's the kind of smell that clings to you, seeps into your skin, and settles deep in your lungs.

I pull up, my truck's tires crunching over the pavement. The flashing red and white lights from the firetrucks cast eerie shadows against the charred structure, flickering across the gathered crowd of townsfolk—because in a place like Bridger Falls, a fire isn't just a call for emergency services.

It's a call for the whole damn town.

I spot Jack first. He's standing near the truck, sweat and soot smeared across his face, talking fast with the firefighter crew. Our fire department's small—mostly volunteers, mostly men and women who've got regular jobs during the day but show up when the sirens wail, no questions asked.

And tonight, they're all here. Because when one of us goes down, we all show up.

I see Poppy standing near the fire truck, her blond hair pulled back tight, streaks of black on her arms where she must've wiped sweat and ash away. She's talking with another firefighter, her expression tight, eyes scanning the crowd.

And then there's Ollie, all business, all firefighter mode, directing the last of the containment. His crew moves fast, securing the area, knocking down lingering flames while steam rises up in thick, angry clouds where water meets fire.

I step out of my truck, my boots hitting the ground hard, my chest tight with something I don't have a name for yet.

Because standing here, watching my town—the people I know—band together in the face of disaster and destruction...

It does something to me.

Because this is Bridger Falls.

This is home.

And no matter how much I tell myself I don't get attached or try to keep my distance, it pulls me in.

I take a step forward, scanning the scene, my heart hammering as I spot one person in particular in the crowd.

Violet.

And when I see her—standing near Maggie, her arms crossed, eyes locked on the blaze with something unreadable written all over her face—

Everything else falls away. Something tightens in my chest.

Mack rushes to Maggie first, wrapping her arms around her.

Maggie looks up, and when she sees me, her shoulders sag just a little with relief.

Forgetting my boundaries, I can't help it when I step up to Violet and pull her into my chest, my arms wrapping around her protectively, utterly relieved that both of them are okay and safe. Violet leans into me, pulling me close, needing the hug.

"Hey," I murmur. "You both alright?"

Maggie nods, but her voice is hoarse. "Everything's gone."

"I'm so sorry, Aunt Maggie," Violet whispers as she reaches for her hand.

Maggie squeezes her hand. "They're just things, sugar. I'm so glad everyone is safe."

I watch Violet swallow hard, her throat working like she's trying to keep something down. But I know better.

This isn't just stuff to either of them. It's not just things lost in the fire.

I see it—the grief, the fear, the weight of it all—sitting heavy in their eyes. The kind of weight that doesn't just come from watching a place burn—it comes from knowing what could've happened. From what almost did. And I can't let my brain go there. I can't.

I exhale sharply, rubbing the back of my neck. I can't stand it.

"Come on," I say, my voice firm, leaving no room for argument. "You're coming with us."

She blinks. "What?"

I gesture toward Maggie and Mack. "You're both staying with us. End of discussion."

Violet hesitates, chewing her lip, her gaze flicking to Maggie, then back to me. She's torn.

"I can go stay with my parents in Indiana," she says, but there's a quiet edge to it. A reluctance. "But... I don't want to leave you."

And maybe it's the smoke in the air, maybe it's the way the firelight still flickers in her eyes, but the truth hits me like a hammer to the chest.

I don't want her to go anywhere else. Sure as hell not Indiana.

I find Ollie and clap him on the back, relieved he's okay, too. This was a nasty fire. "What the hell happened?"

He shrugs, wiping sweat from his brow. "Not sure. We'll know more tomorrow. Just glad we got everyone out safe."

Maggie and Violet finish getting checked out by the paramedic, finally clear to go. I see them scan the crowd for me.

"Thanks, man. I'm going to get Maggie and Violet home."

He nods and returns to cleaning up his equipment.

The truck is quiet on the way home.

Maggie and Mack talk softly in the back seat, but Violet stares out the window, her fingers curled around the blanket still draped over her shoulders.

I don't say anything.

Not until we pull into my driveway, the house looming against the backdrop of trees and night.

I cut the engine. "We're home," I murmur.

Violet lets out a soft, shaky breath.

Then, finally, she nods. As if she's trying to convince herself of something.

Inside, Maggie and Mack head upstairs to settle in. Mack brings down clean pajamas for Violet and hands them to her, looking sad for her.

But Violet lingers in the living room, arms wrapped around herself like she's trying to hold something together.

My room and bathroom are on the main floor of the house, a guest room with a bathroom on the other side of the house. Upstairs is Mack's room and three other bedrooms, one that Maggie uses when she stays. Maggie has a lot of her things up there already, thankfully, and has extra clothes here.

Violet has nothing now. All her things were in that motel. And I know it's not just things. She had that guitar, her notebook I've seen her writing songs in. Everything she has is gone.

"Hey, come on," I murmur as I lead her to the guest room. I check for bathroom towels and ensure she has everything she might need.

She still looks a little shell-shocked, so I hug her. "It's okay."

She leans into me, holding me. "That place was Maggie's home and her livelihood. She lived there for over thirty years," she whispers.

I know she lost a lot, too. But her concern for Maggie is selfless, and I can tell she cares as much as I do. I hate seeing the loss Maggie is facing.

"I know. I'm just relieved that you're all safe." I rub her back.

She steps back and nods. "Yeah, you're right."

"Get some sleep, Red. It's gonna be okay."

I linger in the doorway after she disappears into the guest room, my fingers curling around the frame, my pulse still too damn uneven.

That hug—Jesus.

I can still feel the way she leaned into me, her body pressed against mine, her fingers gripping the back of my shirt like she needed something to hold on to. Like she needed me to hold on to.

And I didn't hesitate. Not for a second.

When Maggie needs me, I show up. Her niece is like family, too. I try to tell myself this, anyway.

She wasn't just some woman standing in the smoke, watching her things burn—she was wrecked. And seeing her like that, hearing the ache in her voice when she whispered about Maggie's home—

It undid something in me.

I close my eyes, pressing my knuckles against the doorframe.

I'm falling.

Hard. Fast. Without a goddamn safety net.

And I'm starting to think—maybe I don't want a safety net.

* * *

The next morning when I wake up, Maggie and Mack are in the kitchen making coffee and talking about getting pet ducks. But they're both in good spirits, and that makes me happy. All things considering, I hope the duck idea passes because we don't need ducks right now. Or ever.

I glance around for Violet, and Maggie points, "Front porch."

I glance out and see her in the same position I saw her in a few weeks ago. Only no guitar and notebook. Then it hits me. That's what she was missing last night. Her guitar is gone. And the songs that were in that notebook she carried around.

I watch her for a second before heading into my office. When I return, I'm carrying a guitar I keep in my office.

The screen door creaks as I step out and hold the guitar out to her.

She looks up, brows knitting together. "What's that?"

"For you. You can keep it."

She blinks, eyes flickering between me and the guitar. "Walker, I—"

"Just take it."

Her hands are hesitant at first, but when she finally curls her fingers around the wood, I see how her grip tightens, like it's something solid she wasn't ready for.

I figured she'd like it, but I didn't expect her to look at it like it might break her. She stares at it in her hands, her fingers ghosting over the worn wood, tracing the edges like she's afraid of it. Her breath hitches when she blinks at me, her eyes glassy.

Shit.

I feel something tighten in my chest, something that pulls so hard it almost hurts.

She runs her fingers over the strings, testing them lightly, and the softest note hums through the air.

Then she looks up at me, her voice quiet, and I can tell she's trying to make light of it so she won't cry. "You just... have this amazing guitar lying around?"

I exhale, shifting my weight. "Just...it's not a big deal."

I'm not doing this again with her. Not talking about my music with anyone.

She doesn't know that this guitar, the one I've kept locked away for years—is one of the last pieces of the life I left behind. She doesn't know that, before this town, before The Black Dog, before Mack, this was all I had too.

She doesn't know how much it guts me to see that same lost look in her eyes.

Because I know exactly what it feels like to lose everything.

I know what it means to start over with nothing but a few broken dreams and whatever strength you can scrape together.

And right now, in this moment, this guitar and whatever's left of the songs in her head? That's all she has left in the world.

So, I shake my head, pushing away the weight of my past.

"Just... play," I murmur. "You'll feel better."

She studies me for a long second—like she sees something in me I don't want her to.

But then she nods and strums another note, and just like that, I know she's already finding her way back. And damn it, so am I.

* * *

I finish the barn chores, and when I step back into the kitchen, chaos is already in full swing.

Maggie whips batter in a mixing bowl like she's on a mission. Mack sits on the counter, barefoot and smug, flipping through her phone. Violet, still in her borrowed sweatpants and hoodie from last night, leans against the fridge, grinning at both. Pickles runs back and forth, excited that so many people are here.

"What is happening?" I ask, crossing my arms.

Maggie gestures at the mess of flour and butter across the counter. "Making breakfast, obviously."

I arch a brow. "Yeah, but why are *you* cooking?"

"Oh, don't be dramatic," she scolds, swatting me with a dish towel. "We're celebrating."

Mack looks up. "Celebrating what?"

"Being alive," Maggie says.

The words land heavier than they should.

For a second, we all get quiet.

Because last night could've gone a lot differently.

Violet's gaze flickers to me, and I see the weight of it in her eyes too.

Maggie claps her hands together, breaking the moment. "Anyway! Waffles fix everything."

Mack rolls her eyes. "That is a lie, but I'll allow it."

Violet chuckles, looking over at me. "You gonna let her burn those waffles, Walker?"

I exhale, shaking my head. "I will if I want to live, apparently."

Maggie smirks. "Smart man."

We eat at the big farmhouse table, plates piled with waffles and syrup.

It's loud—Mack and Violet throwing sarcastic comments back and forth, Maggie fussing over how much syrup everyone uses. The truth is, we kind of need the syrup to cover up the taste of the waffles. Maggie is a terrible cook, but we say nothing and dig in.

And somehow, it feels normal.

Like this isn't temporary.

Like they've always been here.

Mack teases Violet relentlessly about something—probably how she nearly fell on her face earlier when she tripped over my dog in the hallway.

"That was a velociraptor attack," Violet says, pointing her fork at Mack.

Mack smirks. "She was literally asleep."

"I think she moved last second," Violet accuses.

"Riiiiiiight," Mack counters.

"Walker, tell your daughter that your puppy is an energetic velociraptor," Violet pleads.

I sip my coffee, pretending I don't hear her.

She groans. "You're both terrible. It's like you have a mini version of you, Walker."

Maggie pats her hand. "Welcome to the chaos, sweetheart."

Violet stills for half a second. Then she smiles, soft and real.

I swallow, but I'm not sure why that feels as good as it does. I like having her here in my chaos.

Chapter 16
Violet

Even though the fire is gone and the embers have cooled, I still feel the heat on my skin, the panic sitting heavy in my chest. Even though it's over, I'm still shaking off the feeling of the smoke. That was the scariest night I've ever lived through.

One second, I was sleeping peacefully in my bed at the motel, curled under my blankets, dreaming peacefully about songs. The next thing I knew, I was choking on smoke. Maggie was shaking me awake, her voice urgent but calm, telling me we needed to get out.

The flames weren't at my door yet, but the air was already thick, making it hard to breathe and hard to think.

I barely remember grabbing my shoes or how Maggie's hand felt tight around mine as she led me outside, past the smell of burning wood and lost memories.

But I remember the fear. The way we went up and down and banged on everyone's doors until Maggie was certain we got everyone out, even the elderly gentleman and his dog.

All I can think about is how I probably would have died in

my sleep because I wouldn't have woken up if Maggie hadn't come to get me. And I think about what would have happened if I had lost Maggie. Maggie means everything to me. Other than my parents and sister, she's the closest family member that I have. I can't think about what would have happened if I had lost her.

Everything I had to my name was inside that motel.

My guitar.

My notebook that was full of the songs I had written. The only pieces of myself I still carried.

Gone.

When I first came to Bridger Falls, I really thought I had nothing other than Maggie coming here. And now that is ironically true. Now I really truly have nothing. And I'd give everything up again just to make sure everyone was safe.

Then Walker hands me a guitar the next morning like it's nothing.

Like it's just some extra thing he had lying around.

But I knew that wasn't true the second I ran my fingers over the wood.

This is a real instrument. A piece of history. The kind of guitar people pass down, the kind musicians spend their whole lives looking for.

I strummed it once, and the sound was smooth as butter, rich as whiskey, deep and true.

I stared at him, stunned. "Walker, I—"

He had looked away and shook his head like he didn't want me to ask questions. I'll never forget the look on his face, because I still have a million questions.

Random people don't just own vintage guitars like that.

Random people don't just hand them over like they don't mean anything.

But Walker?

He just stood there, arms crossed, waiting for me to accept it. If I had turned it down, he looked like he would have been so offended.

Now it's the next morning, and I'm dying to ask him again, and he still doesn't want to talk about it.

I tighten my grip on the neck, searching his face. "Where did you get this?"

His jaw twitches. "Doesn't matter."

"It kinda does."

"Red." His voice is a warning.

I hesitate, but I know a locked door when I see one. And I'm also not going to make him feel like I'm ungrateful or interrogating him. He didn't think twice about letting me stay here with Maggie. Sure, she's like family to him. But me? I'm not his family, and he still took me in, without a thought. And he's been so kind to Maggie. I'm glad she has Walker and Mack.

So, I don't push.

Instead, I run my fingers over the strings again, letting the sweet, golden sound settle into my bones.

I lost everything in that fire.

But now—he's given me this.

And I don't really know what to do with that.

But somehow, that guitar feels like hope. Like a blanket of reassurance that everything is going to be okay. Maggie's safe, and that's all that really mattered to me. I can rewrite the songs. They're in my head, anyway. I can buy another guitar and give this one back to Walker. But I can't replace Maggie.

* * *

Maggie decides we need to go into town.

"Supplies," she says, listing things off on a piece of notebook paper. "Clothes. Shoes. Shampoo. Probably some snacks, because I'm not living in a house full of hungry people without emergency cookies."

She refuses to dwell on the fire, refuses to let us sit around and feel sorry about it. At first, I wondered if she was handling everything okay. But this is just her way. She pushes through it and makes it fun.

I love that about her.

So, off we go.

Walker stays back, saying he has things to do. But I think he saw the writing on the wall and didn't want to be dragged to a million stores to shop with us. Instead, he hands Maggie his credit card and heads out to the barn.

Maggie grins and holds it up. "Who wants to go on a shopping spree?"

I shake my head, laughing, glad my phone still holds a way to pay for my things.

Maggie doesn't take us to some big-box department store to replace what we lost.

She takes us to the Bridger Falls Thrift Shop.

Before we can even enter the store, about a dozen people stop us and tell Maggie and me how sorry they were about the fire and that they were all safe and to offer help if we needed anything.

God, I love this town and these people. They rally around Maggie and give her the love that she deserves.

The thrift store is amazing. It's chaotic and wonderful, packed with old books, weird lamps, and clothes that should have remained in past decades.

Mack groans as we step inside. "If you try to make me wear someone else's old moldy jeans, I swear—"

Maggie pats her cheek. "Hush, child. You're gonna love this."

Mack just sighs, already resigned to whatever is about to happen.

But me?

I love places like this. I love thrift stores. I love finding treasures.

Because sometimes, the best things in life aren't new. Sometimes, the best things are the ones that have been loved before.

Twenty minutes later, we are deep in the trenches. And I mean deep. It's chaotic, hilarious, and the most fun I've ever had. I've never laughed so hard at all the ensembles we're putting together.

Mack and I are trying on the most ridiculous outfits we can find, and Maggie is cry-laughing when Mack steps out in a floral blazer straight out of the '80s with puffed sleeves.

I spin in a hideous sequined prom dress, arms wide. "Maggie, be honest. Could you see me wearing this?"

Mack shakes her head. "If I ever see you in that in public, I'm pretending I don't know you."

Maggie wipes away tears of laughter. "Oh, honey, you look like a Vegas lounge singer on her last night before retirement."

Mack collapses against the dressing room door, howling.

Well, I'm glad I can provide the entertainment. And it feels so good to see them smile, despite how shitty the past twenty-four hours have been.

By the time we leave the thrift store, our arms are full of clothes, accessories, and a few things Maggie insisted we needed, like a hideous owl-shaped cookie jar. Where she plans to put that, I don't know.

Mack groans as we load up the truck. "I cannot believe we spent over two hours in there. I'm so hungry. We need food."

Maggie beams. "And we had so much fun."

I settle into the passenger seat, exhaling slowly.

This morning, I woke up feeling uncertain about everything.

But right now, I feel full.

And not just because of the ridiculous amount of stuff Maggie made us buy.

Maggie loves Mack and Walker fiercely, I can see it in every tiny action—the way she fusses over Mack's hair, the way she playfully slaps Walker's arm when he gets too broody, the way she looks at them like they're the best thing she ever helped build.

And somehow, she's dragged me into this circle, too.

Like she's decided I belong.

I don't know what to do with that.

I don't know if I should trust it.

But as Maggie drives us to more errands, the sun dipping low over the town that has somehow wrapped itself around my heart, I think...

Maybe I want to.

Maybe I'm ready to.

For the first time in a long time.

If Maggie can let them in, maybe I can stop being a big baby and let them in, too. But the problem isn't with me. Walker doesn't seem to want to let me in. Although, he is letting me stay at his home. That's something.

By the time we pull into the Bridger Falls General store, my stomach is growling, and Mack is already plotting a snack heist like we're about to go on a twelve-hour road trip instead of buying comfort food snacks and planning an epic sleepover.

"We need all the essentials," Mack declares as we step inside. The automatic doors barely have time to shut before she beelines for the chip aisle.

I glance at Maggie. She gives Mack a look like they have

an inside joke between the two of them. "I swear, if this turns into another 'let's see who can eat the most sour gummies without puking' contest again, I'm leaving you both at the store."

Mack waves her off, already shoving a family-sized bag of Hot Cheetos into our basket. "Maggie, please. This is a sophisticated operation. I'm grown up now. I don't barf when I eat junk like I did when I was nine."

Maggie snorts. "You say that like you won't be double-fisting those hot Cheetos and soda in an hour."

Mack pauses. "Fair." Then she grabs two more bags for good measure.

I grab a cart and start piling in every piece of candy I can get my hands on. Reese's, M&M's, Skittles—if it has sugar in it, it's going in the cart. I'm going to make a candy salad. It's going to be epic.

Maggie eyes my growing stash. "Are you planning on running a black-market candy shop out of Walker's guest room?"

I shrug, tossing in another bag of gummy worms. "No. But if I was, you'd be my first customer."

Maggie laughs, but I don't miss the way she sneaks a pack of Oreos into the cart.

Mack pops up behind me, clutching a can of whipped cream like it's a treasure map. "This is a necessity."

I blink. "For what?" I mean, I'm not disagreeing. Whipped cream is always a necessity in my book.

"Midnight whipped cream shots."

"Put it in the cart," I motion. "Absolutely."

"It's like there are two of you now. Two peas in a pod." Maggie looks like she's reconsidering all her life choices. "Why did I bring you both here?"

Mack grins. "Because you love us."

Maggie mutters something about regrets but doesn't take the whipped cream out of the cart.

After the sugar apocalypse has been secured, we move on to drinks.

"I'm thinking Dr Pepper and maybe some energy drinks," I say, scanning the shelves.

Maggie immediately vetoes. "No energy drinks. The last time Mack had one, she tried to bribe the mailman to let her drive the mail truck."

Mack sighs. "That guy had no sense of fun."

I hold back a laugh and grab two bottles of soda instead. Mack swaps one out for a neon blue sports drink that looks vaguely radioactive.

Maggie side-eyes it. "That looks like something that would fuel a spaceship, not a human body. Walker's going to kill me, isn't he?"

"Probably." Mack grins.

By the time we make it to the register, our cart looks like it belongs to a group of unsupervised teenagers at a gas station.

The cashier is a high school kid who looks both impressed and mildly concerned as he slowly scans each item.

"Big night?" he asks.

Mack nods seriously. "Sleepover."

Maggie sighs. "More like a scheduled descent into madness."

He looks over at Maggie and says, "Sorry to hear about the fire, Maggie."

She smiles at him. "Thanks, honey."

I go to swipe my card from my phone and pause while Mack grabs a pack of gum at the last second, and we haul our loot out to the truck, barely fitting all the bags in.

As I shut the door and slide into the passenger seat, I glance at Maggie, who's staring at the massive pile of junk food like it personally offended her morals.

"Not one vegetable," she murmurs, shaking her head.

Mack rips open a bag of Hot Cheetos and pops one in her mouth. "There's corn in these."

Maggie laughs and starts the truck.

This is going to be a fun and hilarious night.

We grab some pizzas from the local pizza shop, because why not? What's a few more junk food items. Walker's going to think we're all a bunch of raccoons when he sees all the food we bought at random.

The second we hit the road, Mack is already rummaging through my play lists, mumbling about how I have "the most tragic excuse for a playlist" and how it's her duty to fix it.

Maggie sighs dramatically. "God help us on what she's going to choose."

Mack pushes a button on the audio, and suddenly, the familiar bassline rumble fills the truck—Fleetwood Mac.

"Oh, hell yes," I say as *The Chain* kicks in, that slow, haunting guitar creeping through the speakers.

Maggie throws her arms up like we've just hit the chorus at a sold-out concert. "NOW we're talking!"

She cranks the volume, and just like that, we're flying down the road, the windows down, the crisp night air whipping through the cab, singing like we're on a damn world tour.

Maggie is the first to start drumming on the dashboard.

Mack leans forward from the backseat, pointing at her. "You're into it."

Maggie scoffs, still tapping her fingers to the beat. "I will neither confirm nor deny."

Then the chorus hits, and suddenly, we're all shouting at the top of our lungs—

"YOU WILL NEVER BREAK THE CHAIN!"

I laugh and sing as the cool Wyoming air rushes in, carrying our voices out into the night.

When *Go Your Own Way* starts, Maggie is all into it, throwing her head back and singing without hesitation.

And for the first time all day—after the fire, the stress, the uncertainty—we're just here. In this truck, on this road, together.

And I think we're all okay. Or we're going to be.

Chapter 17
Walker

Maggie, Mack, and Violet headed into town to pick up clothes and essentials.

I didn't go.

Mostly because I don't need to witness that chaos firsthand.

I get work done around the property while they're gone, trying not to think about the fact that this morning was the first time my house has felt like more than just a house. It felt like a home. Full of laughter, noise, and people. I liked it.

The sound of the truck pulling in catches my attention, but it's not the engine that makes me look up.

It's the laughter that pours out of the windows.

Hers.

Soft, rich, and completely unguarded. A sound that wraps around me like a warm breeze, catching me mid-step as I wipe my hands on a rag.

And then she steps out.

Violet.

Her vibrant red hair's down tonight, loose and wild, streaked with golden strands in the sunlight. It falls over her shoulders in soft waves, some of it sticking to the side of her neck from what I can only assume was a day of chaos with Mack and Maggie.

But it's not the hair that gets me.

It's the dress.

A sundress. Light green. Thin straps that leave her shoulders bare, the hem swishing around her legs as she steps out of the truck.

I swallow my throat feeling tight. I've always thought she was beautiful. But this? This feels different.

The dress hugs her curves in a way I'm pretty sure she's completely unaware of. The fabric is doing a hell of a job wrecking my focus. And when she shifts the paper bags in her arms, the neckline dips slightly, revealing the slightest hint of golden skin that makes my pulse stutter.

I blink and drag my eyes to her face, only to find her laughing at something Mack just said, her eyes crinkling at the corners, her cheeks flushed from the wind. Her smile is wide and real—completely unguarded in a way I don't see often.

And that's when it hits me.

She doesn't just look beautiful.

She looks happy.

And God help me if that doesn't knock the breath out of me harder than the dress does.

The night air feels warmer suddenly. My heart picks up, and that slow, familiar ache—the one I've been pretending not to notice for months—settles in my chest.

I'm falling.

And it's not just about the way she looks tonight. It's how she lights up when she's with Mack, doesn't hesitate to throw herself into Maggie's chaos, and is here, standing in my driveway, laughing like she belongs.

Because she does.

Mack slams her door and bolts toward me, waving a bag of

Hot Cheetos. "Dad! We bought half the store! And Maggie almost got kicked out for arguing about coupons, again!"

Maggie groans as she climbs out of the passenger seat. "That cashier was a child with a calculator, not a professional."

Believably, she'll argue to give them crap. It's the Maggie way. Then, next week, she'll drop off a treat for the cashier, and they'll be besties again.

Violet laughs, and my eyes snap back to her.

She's looking at me.

And when our gazes lock, everything inside me stills.

Her smile softens, her lips parting slightly, and for a second, it's like the noise around us fades into the background.

"Hey," she says, shifting the bags in her arms as I reach for them.

I clear my throat, desperately trying to look unaffected. "Hey. New dress?"

She glances down, brushing at the hem self-consciously and proclaims proudly. "Yeah. Epic thrift store find. New with tags."

"It..." I hesitate, searching for words that won't give me away. "Looks good."

Her cheeks turn the prettiest shade of pink, and she gives a small smile. "Thanks."

Mack picks that moment to practically tackle her, sending one of the bags tilting sideways. A bag of Sour Patch Kids hits the pavement and bursts open, candy spilling everywhere.

Violet laughs and bends down to pick it up, hair falling forward over her face.

And I can't help it.

I stand there, watching her in the soft glow of the porchlight, my chest tight with something I don't want to name.

Because if this keeps up—if she keeps looking like that, laughing like that, fitting so damn easily into my world—

I'm done for.

Maggie unloads the rest of the bags onto the kitchen table. It's mostly junk food which makes me laugh. They seemed to have had a fun time.

Mack flops onto the couch, dramatic as hell. "We survived."

Violet drops into the chair next to her. "Barely."

I cross my arms, smirking. "Didn't kill each other?"

Maggie snorts. "Came close."

Violet sighs. "We disagreed on important things."

Mack nods solemnly. "Like whether denim skirts are a crime against humanity."

I blink. "I feel like this is not my conversation."

"It's not," Maggie confirms.

I raise my hands in surrender and head toward the door.

Violet perks up. "Where are you going?"

I hesitate. "Checking on the horses."

Her eyes light up. "Can I come?"

I try not to read into the way that makes something stir in my chest.

Instead, I nod. "Yeah. Come on."

I hear Maggie and Mack whispering, and when I turn around, they give me fake smiles. "Have fun," Maggie calls with a wave.

I roll my eyes and pull the door closed behind me.

The pasture stretches wide, the afternoon sun hanging low. The barn doors are already open, a soft breeze filtering through the stalls.

Violet walks ahead of me, turning in slow circles like she's trying to take it all in.

"You have no idea how much I love horses," she says, her voice almost awed.

I watch as she approaches Maximus, my black quarter horse, who immediately nuzzles against her palm.

She laughs softly, running a hand over his muzzle.

"You ride?" I ask.

"I used to," she says, and something shifts in her expression. "Haven't in a long time, though."

I don't ask why.

Instead, I nod toward the gate. "We can go for a ride sometime."

She glances at me, brows raised.

I can't help but think back to the night we shared. Hell, I think about that night more than I probably should. I wonder if she's taking an entirely different meaning from my words about going for a ride. I decide to play it off innocently.

I shrug. "If you want." I'm trying to play it cool, but I'd love to go for a ride with her.

She smiles. "Yeah. I'd like that."

And damn it, I would too.

Violet starts talking to Winnie and murmuring to her as she pets her and turns to look at me. She stands close to Maximus' stall who apparently is jealous that he's not getting the attention.

Sure enough, Maximus gives her a solid nudge right between the shoulder blades.

Violet lets out a startled yelp, and stumbles right into me.

I react fast, my hands wrapping around her upper arms just as she crashes into my chest. The impact knocks the wind out of me, but I barely register it because she's flush against me. Her chest is against mine, my hands still holding her steady.

Her breath hitches, a sharp sound in the quiet barn, and she turns her head slightly. I catch the surprise in her eyes.

Every muscle in my body is tight. I know I should let her go. She's my *friend*.

But I don't. Not yet. I like how we're close.

My jaw tenses, and my throat bobs with a hard swallow.

She doesn't move either. I can feel her hesitating, like she's caught between laughing this off or doing something reckless. Like she knows that if either of us goes the reckless route, things are going to change for us.

Then, Pickles bounds up to us, tail wagging.

Violet turns and breaks free, pointing a sharp finger at Maximus. "You did that on purpose."

Maximus snorts at her and blinks as if he's completely innocent. Liar.

Violet laughs as she kneels down for the dog like she's her new favorite person.

"Oh, I forgive you for earlier," she coos, squatting down to scratch behind her ears.

I playfully roll my eyes. "I thought she was a velociraptor?"

She grins up at me. "She's just a wild baby."

I shake my head, watching as she fits too easily into my world.

I knew letting her in was a bad idea.

But I don't think I can stop it now.

That evening, after dinner, we sit together, watching the sky fade into the familiar deep oranges and purples.

Mack and Violet are still bickering about whether Ty or the new guy is better on the show they're watching, Heartland.

Maggie listening, but she watches me.

I ignore her.

Mostly. Because I know she's trying to tell me something. Something along the lines of like, look at what's happening here. Isn't her niece great? Yeah, she is. But I'm not telling her that.

Eventually, Mack yawns. "I'm gonna go to bed."

She stands, stretching. Then, without thinking, she leans down and hugs Violet.

Violet freezes for half a second, then melts into it.

And I don't know who that moment is bigger for.

Maggie smiles knowingly.

I clear my throat. "I'm gonna lock up."

Maggie follows Mack upstairs, leaving just me and Violet on the couch.

She exhales, looking out at the night sky through the floor-to-ceiling windows. "Your home is beautiful, Walker."

I glance at her, the glow from the candle on the coffee table casting soft shadows over her face.

It's not just the house that's beautiful. She's stunning.

I walk beside her towards her room, keeping my hands stuffed in my pockets so I don't do something stupid. Like reach for her.

Because damn it, I want to.

She's close to me, too close. Barefoot, her hair up in a messy bun, her t-shirt slipping off one shoulder like it's begging to be touched. She looks soft and sleepy.

I glance at her and say, "At least when I walk you to your room, you don't live that far."

She huffs out a soft laugh. "Yeah, well, I usually live farther than down the hall from you."

We reach her door, but I don't stop, and I step in a little closer, watching the way her breath hitches and her fingers twitch at her sides.

"Guess I don't have to worry about you being safe," I murmur.

She rolls her eyes but her lips curve, "I think I've always been safe here in Bridger Falls."

She doesn't move and neither do I.

Something stretches between us, thick and heavy.

I glance down and find her staring at me, her lips parted slightly. My gaze drops to her mouth before I can stop it, before I can remind myself that we're supposed to be just friends. I can't go there. I'm not supposed to go there.

She sucks in a breath, and I watch her throat bob as she swallows.

Hell.

I've said goodnight and dropped her off a bunch of times. Watched her step inside, made sure she was safe.

But this time feels different.

We both jolt when a door creaks open somewhere in the house, snapping apart like we've been caught.

She exhales, then clears her throat. "Night, Walker."

I take a step back. "Night."

I head down the hall and realize I'm not sleeping tonight. I can't sleep after that.

* * *

Mack barely waits for the truck to come to a full stop before she hops out, slinging her backpack over one shoulder.

"Be good," I call after her.

She throws a smirk over her shoulder. "No promises. Bye."

I shake my head as she disappears into the school, already chatting with a group of her friends. Fifteen going on twenty-five.

Pulling away, I tell myself I'm heading back to The Black Dog to handle some invoices. But somehow, I end up parked outside Steamy Sips instead. I need a coffee, and I like to support Cami and check in.

The second I approach the coffee trailer, Cami's face lights up like she's been waiting for me all morning.

"Well, if it isn't just the man I wanted to see," she says, handing off a latte to another customer before turning her full attention to me.

I narrow my eyes. "Why do I feel like this is going to be bad?"

Cami glances around like she's about to commit a federal offense, then leans over the counter.

"I need a favor," she says, voice low.

I sigh. "Cami—"

She waves me off, eyes darting left and right before locking back onto mine.

"Look, I know you have contacts back in Nashville."

I school my expression into neutral territory. My face betrays nothing—not my past, not my history, and definitely not the truth behind what she just said.

Even though some people around here know who I used to be, we kind of have an unspoken thing that we don't talk about it. And it's been great. Until now.

Cami waits, watching me closely. I don't confirm or deny it. I just cross my arms.

"What do you want?" I grunt, defeatedly.

She leans in closer, practically whispering. "Do you think you could get someone to steal Violet's dog back from her shit-head ex? He's in Nashville."

I blink. "What?"

Cami nods seriously, glancing over her shoulder like we're plotting a heist. "I think it would cheer her up to have Rip Heeler back."

I process that sentence slowly.

Her dog is named Rip Heeler?

I exhale, dragging a hand through my hair. "What happened to her dog?"

Cami straightens, her expression darkening. "That jackass ex of hers stole him. When she left, he said she didn't deserve to keep Rip, even though she's the one who raised him. And now she's here, trying to move on, but she's heartbroken over that dog. I saw the way she got so sad when she saw my blue heeler and she really misses her dog. And you know Violet—"

I do.

I know how her face softens when she talks about animals. I know how her fingers linger on Pickles' fur every time she comes trotting up to Violet like she's her favorite person.

I know how she loves horses and how her smile looks different around them, like something inside her untangles.

I didn't know about her dog.

And now I do. And now I can't just let this happen. I would want my dog if someone took her. I love my dogs. I even named my bar after my dog.

Damn it.

Cami sighs. "I just... I think it would mean everything to her."

I lean against the counter, arms crossed. "Cami, we can't just go around stealing dogs."

She gives me a flat look. "You say that like we're talking about swiping a stranger's dog from their front yard. This is her dog, Walker. He's the thief. We're just... correcting an injustice."

I shake my head. "I don't know."

But the thought sticks.

Follows me all the way back to my truck.

By the time I pull into The Black Dog, I'm still thinking about it.

I don't call my manager, Will, very often. And I definitely don't ask him for favors.

Haven't had a reason to. We're a well-oiled machine. I write songs, he sells the songs and gets me paid. It's a perfect arrangement, even though I bet he'd love for me to do more.

But as I sit in my office, staring at my phone, I realize I'm about to make an exception.

I pull up Will Maren's number and hit call.

He answers on the second ring. "Well, well, well," he

drawls. "If it isn't Walker, calling me out of the blue. Thought maybe you'd finally decided to come back to civilization."

I grunt. "Not likely."

Will chuckles like he expected that. "What can I do for you, buddy?"

I hesitate for half a second.

Then I say it.

"I need someone to get a dog out of a bad situation. With no one knowing," I add.

There's a beat of silence.

Then, surprisingly, Will just hums. "A dog?" he repeats. "You want me to steal a dog?"

"Yeah. One that belongs to someone here in Bridger Falls. Her ex in Nashville has him, and I want to get him back for her."

Will chuckles again, but there's something sharp in it this time. "Damn, Walker. Didn't take you for a dog thief."

I roll my eyes. "Are you gonna help or not?"

Will exhales. "What's the ex's name?"

I hesitate. "I don't know yet."

"Then find out. And send me whatever you can on the guy —where he lives, if he's got security, that kind of thing. If you have a picture of the dog, even better."

I pause. "You don't think we'll get caught, do you?"

Will laughs. "Relax, Walker. I know a guy who knows a guy. If this dog really belongs to your girl—"

"She's not my girl. But yes, he does."

"—Then I'll see what I can do."

I rub my jaw. "Appreciate it."

A beat of silence.

Then, Will says something that makes me stiffen. "If I do this, will you do a favor for me?"

I narrow my eyes. "Depends."

A smirk edges into his voice. "Must be an important girl if you're willing to break a few laws for her."

I grunt. "What do you want?"

"I don't know yet."

I exhale, already regretting this. "Maybe."

Will hums, pleased. "Good enough."

There's a rustling on the other end of the line. Then, "What's the girl's name?"

I hesitate for half a second too long.

Then I say it.

"Violet Wilson."

Silence.

Then—interest.

"Well, well," Will murmurs. "Now that is interesting."

My grip tightens on the phone. "Why?"

"Let me do some digging first," he says smoothly. "I'll be in touch."

The line goes dead.

I sit there for a long moment, staring at my phone, that uneasy feeling creeping in.

Will knows something I don't. I could hear it in his smug voice. Will is a good guy to his core. When I left Nashville years ago, I made it a point never to work with anyone who was dirty or bad. I wanted a clean break. When I started over here, I wanted to ensure that I was good with who I worked closely with and only with people I could trust. I know that I can trust Will. But I don't know what he's going to want.

Will is very connected in Nashville. He has no problems selling all the songs I write for him. He can get the job done quickly and privately. And that has kept an abundance of income coming in for me. When I left the industry, I had enough to set us up for life if we lived modestly. But I still have dreams. I wanted to build a home and a life here that Mack deserved. I wanted her to have everything. Without the glitz and glamor of stardom, because that isn't really what people think it is. Paparazzi and reporters can be vicious and vile and can ruin you if they want. The industry is corrupt and not a world I want my daughter to be a part of. I've kept her out of it on purpose.

And I have a feeling I won't like what Will wants in return. But deep down, I know I can trust him, so there's that.

I lean back in my chair, staring at the ceiling.

I should leave it alone.

I should have told Cami that it's too much trouble—that I don't get involved in other people's business. Because I typically don't.

But then I think about Violet's face when she talks to my dog. And I remember how close Mack and I were to Gus and now Pickles. If my ex had kept my dog, I would have been so wrecked. I love my dogs. Mack, Maggie, and I were so sad when Gus passed. Sure, he was old, but he was our family. He grew up with Mack. They were the best of friends. I knew I had to get another dog when he passed. Mack was thrilled when we found Pickles at a local shelter.

I think about how Red tilted her head when she ran her fingers over that guitar last night like she didn't understand why I'd given it to her.

I think about how she looked at The Dogwood Motel's remains, holding herself together even though she was clearly breaking inside.

And suddenly, I know.

We gotta get that damn dog back.

Even if it means making deals with the world that I swore I'd left behind.

Violet Wilson, you have no idea what you've started. I never thought I'd be the guy who would burn the whole world down for a woman, but I'm getting there. And shit it scares me.

Chapter 18
Violet

I take a deep breath before pulling up my mom's contact. I know this isn't going to be a fun conversation to have. No mother wants to get this call. Maggie asked me to call her and tell her what happened. Maggie's handling everything so well, but talking about it seems to make her upset so I offered to do it. Currently her default is pretending that nothing happened and going shopping for new things. I'm not judging her; it's been awful, and I'll do anything she needs to make it easier.

The phone rings three times before my mom picks up.

"Violet?" Worry fills her voice, and I brace myself as she asks. "Is everything okay?"

I exhale slowly, trying to keep my voice steady. "Yeah, Mom. I'm okay. Maggie's okay, too."

A pause. "Did something happen?"

Damn. Her mother's intuition is strong today.

I close my eyes and press my fingers to my temple. "The Dogwood burned down."

Silence.

Then—a sharp inhale.

"Oh, honey," she murmurs, her voice softer now. "Are you both safe? Where are you? Why didn't she call me?"

I shift on the bed, curling my legs beneath me. "We're staying with... a friend of Maggie's. We're both okay. Maggie's just been busy."

Technically, it's not a lie.

Mom exhales, relieved but still rattled. "Thank God. I was already worried about you being out there, and now I'm even more worried. And I feel terrible for Maggie."

"Really, we're fine, Mom," I tell her. "I'm still with Maggie."

I don't mention Walker.

I don't mention his big house on the edge of town, or his quiet protectiveness. The way he gave me that guitar like it meant nothing, even though I know it means everything. I'm still trying to figure that one out.

She doesn't need to know any of that.

"Well, as long as you're okay." She hesitates, then lowers her voice. "You're planning on staying, aren't you?"

I look around the bedroom where I've slept since the fire— the soft, lived-in feel of the place, the way Maggie already put fresh towels in the bathroom like she knew I'd need them. I think about the groceries I picked up earlier, already planning to make meals for everyone this week. Walker's kitchen is a dream kitchen to cook in, and I can't wait to try it out.

I think about Mack and how she hugged me before bed last night. I needed that hug. God, I really like that kid.

I think about Walker and how he hasn't once made me feel like I don't belong here.

I don't answer right away.

But I don't deny it either.

"Yeah, Mom," I say softly. "I think I am. I really like it here."

"What happened back in Nashville to make you want to leave? Did you break up with Brice?" she asks.

"Yes, we're done," I say softly. Something in my tone must make her stop pushing because she doesn't ask details. But my mom has always known when to back off, and I love that about her. She's nosy, but she doesn't push. She knows I usually tell her when I'm ready.

We talk for a while and catch up, and after I hang up, I sit cross-legged on the bed, my new notebook in my lap.

I lost the songs I was working on in that fire.

Thankfully they're still in my head. These songs aren't gone like the ones stolen from me before.

I need to get them down before they disappear and or get buried beneath the weight of everything else that has been on my mind.

The pencil moves without hesitation, words flowing, melodies humming under my breath.

I don't even realize I'm singing out loud until I hear a quiet shift near the door.

I freeze and look up.

And there he is.

Walker leans against the doorframe, arms crossed, watching me with an unreadable expression on his face.

"You were listening?" I ask, voice hoarse.

He doesn't look guilty in the slightest. He doesn't even pretend he wasn't.

"Yeah," he says, his voice low, honest. "You're really good."

My throat goes dry. My palms feel sweaty. I'm so nervous.

I never meant for anyone to hear them. Not yet. Not like this.

"Thanks," I murmur, looking down, pretending to fiddle with my pencil even though my hands are suddenly too unsteady to hold it properly.

He doesn't leave, and he doesn't say anything else.

I glance up, meeting his gaze. "Ready to talk about that guitar yet?"

And I see it.

The warning in his eyes. The walls slamming back up.

He doesn't want to talk about it.

His jaw tightens, just slightly.

Then—a shift. A change of subject.

"Come on," he says, voice gruff. "Let's go for a ride."

I tilt my head at his invitation and think, *you know what, why not?* I set the notebook and guitar aside and stand.

"What kind of ride?" I ask Walker with a smirk.

He grins at me. "A horseback ride."

Excitement fills me when I think about riding again. It's been such a long time. I'm giddy thinking about the stirrups under my feet, the weight of the reins in my hand, and the wind in my hair as I ride. I am here for this.

I follow Walker out to the barn, Pickles chasing after us, clumsily tripping over her own feet. She's still in that awkward puppy stage.

I know he's busy and probably has a million other things to take care of, but he's making time for this. And for that, I love it. I'll treasure this.

The barn is warm and familiar, the scent of hay and leather grounding me as I step inside.

Walker moves easily through the space, hands brushing over bridles and saddles, boots scuffing against the old wooden floor.

"How long has it been since you've ridden?" he asks, grabbing a saddle.

I smile. "I grew up on a farm. It's been a long time since I left home, though. I was a city girl for pretty much the past decade."

His lips twitch, but he doesn't give me the satisfaction of an actual smile.

Instead, he nods toward a deep chestnut mare in the nearest stall.

"This is Winnie," he says. "She's Mack's horse, and she's gentle. Unlike Maximus who can be a brat sometimes."

He runs his hand over her and pats her side.

I step closer, running a hand down her sleek chestnut colored neck, the warmth of her velvet fur on my fingertips.

She exhales, soft and steady, and something in me untangles.

Walker watches me carefully.

"You're good with them," he murmurs.

I glance at him, raising a brow. "Surprised?"

He shrugs, tightening a strap on his saddle. "A little."

I smirk, but I don't push.

"I didn't know you grew up on a farm," he says softly.

"A dairy farm," I admit. "But we had horses, too. We actually had all kinds of animals. My dad could never say no. Kind of like someone else I know."

The rhythm of the horse beneath my fingers matches my breathing, steady and even.

"What was it like?" he asks.

"Hard work, but fun. My sister and I had chores, and we learned a lot about hard work. We lived about an hour from the nearest town, so we found ways to entertain ourselves. For me it was music. For my sister, it was writing. She's a romance author now," I add with a smile.

Walker focuses on his task, but the way he looks over and his eyes meet mine show me that he's listening. That's one of the things that I love about him. He is a good listener.

After the horses are ready, we swing up into the saddles, and already I feel at home. There's something about riding horses that is so relaxing. Takes me back to the farm. Where life was simple. Maybe that's why I love Bridger Falls so much. It reminds me of home.

Walker rides beside me. His posture is relaxed, but his watchful gaze never strays far.

I don't know if he's looking at me or looking out for me.

Maybe both.

The land stretches out, vast, endless golden fields rolling toward the tree line. It's beautiful.

I exhale, tilting my face toward the sky, feeling the sun on my face.

"You don't talk about it," Walker says suddenly.

I glance at him. "Talk about what?"

He doesn't look at me. "What you're running from."

My stomach tightens and I focus on the horizon, the weight of the reins in my hands.

"There's nothing to talk about."

He exhales through his nose. "Bullshit."

I huff out a short, humorless laugh. "Oh, so you can shut down every time I ask about that guitar, but I have to spill my guts?"

His jaw flexes, and I know I hit a nerve. But I don't regret it.

His secrets are just as heavy as mine. Maybe heavier.

We ride in silence for a while and we don't say anything else. But something settles between us.

Something I don't know how to name. Like an understanding that we both will have to open up at some point if we're going to keep going with whatever we're calling this.

The sun is lower when we return, stretching long shadows over the barn.

Walker slides off his horse, stretching his legs, and steps beside me, holding his hand out to help me down as he watches me carefully.

His hands reach out and guide me down, landing on my

hips and guiding me off of the horse, my legs shaky since I haven't ridden in a while.

His hands feel so good on me, I lose my train of thought, completely lost at his touch and how much I love it.

"I meant what I said," he murmurs.

I blink up at him. "About what?"

"Your music," he says. "It's good."

I don't know what to do with that and the way his voice sounds when he says it. Like it's the truest thing he's ever told me.

Something burns in my chest. Something I'm not ready to face.

So, instead, I give him a small, tired smile. "Thanks, Walker. That means a lot."

And for now, that's enough. I guess we both have our secrets.

* * *

The bar hums with the kind of quiet that only happens after last call. We flip chairs upside down on tables while the scent of spilled beer and fried food lingers in the air and the hum of the old fridge in the back provides a steady, familiar soundtrack.

I sit at the bar, sipping water, my feet aching from a busy shift. My hair's a mess, my makeup is smudged, and I'm pretty sure there's ketchup on my shirt. But it's one of those nights where your heart is full and you're the good kind of tired. I had a good time tonight. I love chatting up all the locals and getting to know everyone.

Walker's behind the bar, wiping down the counters with that effortless, end-of-night focus. His sleeves are rolled up, forearms flexing with each swipe of the towel. He looks like the kind of guy who belongs in some black-and-white whiskey ad. His dark hair tousled, a neatly trimmed beard shadowing his jaw, and those damn whiskey-colored eyes that miss nothing.

He catches me staring and one eyebrow quirks. "What?"

I shrug, trying to play it cool. "Nothing. Just wondering if you've got any moves besides being a bar owner."

He snorts. "Moves?"

"Yeah. Like..." I glance toward the old jukebox in the corner. "Dancing."

He laughs softly, shaking his head. "Red, if you're looking for entertainment, I can turn on the jukebox. You can dance your little heart out."

I roll my eyes and hop off the stool, wincing when my feet protest. But I make it to the jukebox, scroll through the selections, and hit the button for *Forever and Ever, Amen*. The machine crackles to life, skipping a beat before Randy Travis's smooth voice spills into the empty bar.

I turn to face Walker, heart thudding a little harder than it should. "Dance with me."

His towel freezes mid-wipe. He blinks like he didn't hear me right. "You want to dance with me?"

"Yeah." I cross my arms, suddenly nervous. "Unless you're afraid my moves will show you up."

His mouth twitches into that crooked half-smile. "Oh, Red. You're in way over your head."

Just what I thought. He won't turn down a challenge.

He tosses the towel on the bar and steps around it. My stomach flips as he moves toward me with an easy, confident stride. He stops just close enough that I catch the faint scent of soap and leather and the lingering smoky warmth of the grill.

His hand extends, palms up. "Let's see what you've got."

I slide my hand into his, and before I can say a word, he tugs me into his arms. His other hand settles on my waist, firm and sure, while mine lands against the solid wall of his chest. I feel the warmth of him through the soft cotton of his shirt, the steady beat of his heart under my palm.

The music flows around us, lazy and familiar. And then, without warning, he moves.

He steps back, leading me effortlessly into the rhythm. One step, then another, his body guiding mine with practiced ease. He spins me once, pulls me back, and sways us into a smooth turn.

"Wait—" I stumble. "You actually know how to dance?"

His laugh rumbles low in his chest. "What happened to all that talk of showing me up? Let's see what you've got, Red."

I cling tighter as he dips me, his hand strong against my back. My heart leaps into my throat, my pulse racing. He pulls me upright again, his smile cocky and devastating.

"No one said anything about you being a ballroom cowboy," I mutter, breathless. Damn, he's good. I was just fibbing. I actually don't know how to dance, but damn, he does.

"Didn't think I had to." He spins me again, the kind of spin that makes my hair fly.

"Well, good job. You're full of surprises, Walker."

He grins, slowing the pace until we're swaying again, the energy softening into something that makes my chest ache. His thumb brushes against my waist, and my breath catches.

I should step back. Crack a joke. Do something to break the tension.

Instead, I tilt my head up, and our eyes meet.

The jukebox hums the last line of the chorus, and the air grows thick, crackling with something unspoken. His gaze drops to my mouth, just for a second, before he looks away, exhaling hard.

"This is dangerous," I whisper.

His lips quirk. "I know."

His grip tightens just a little like he doesn't want to let go.

I don't either.

Walker's hand rests low on my back, warm and steady, his thumb drawing circles through the thin cotton of my shirt. His broad chest, strong arms, and the scent of leather and soap that always makes me want to breathe him in when I'm near him.

I should've never asked him to dance. I'm playing with fire now, and I know it. The problem is that I can't stop. I don't want to stop. Now it's like a game of emotional chicken, and I'm about two seconds away from swerving off the road entirely.

Because this isn't how friends dance. This is how people who are falling in love dance, and we both damn well know it.

The song ends, and the noise in the bar fades into a low hum. I can feel the weight of his gaze without even looking.

I finally lift my eyes to his.

His jaw is tight, his whiskey-colored eyes sharp and unreadable. But underneath that? There's heat. Slow, simmering, and far more dangerous than I'm ready to deal with.

My heart kicks hard against my ribs. "What are we doing here, Walker?"

His head tilts, and the corner of his mouth curves, but it's not his usual cocky grin. It's softer. Deeper. "What do you want to do here, Red?"

His voice is low and rough, with a tone that should come with a warning label. And the way he says *Red*? Like it's a challenge. A dare.

I swallow hard. "I...I don't know."

He steps closer. My toes bump against his boots. His thumb strokes along my side, slow and deliberate. "Yeah, you do."

I open my mouth to argue, but he dips his head just a little, his lips a breath from mine. I can see the faint scar by his eyebrow, the gold flecks in his eyes.

I should step back. Make a joke. Laugh it off. That's what we do.

Instead, I stay exactly where I am, heart racing, pulse thrumming like a live wire.

He doesn't kiss me.

But God, he makes me want him to.

Walker sighs, his forehead resting against mine for half a second before he steps back.

"It's getting late," he says, his voice tight. "We should get home."

I nod, even though I'm not sure I can remember how to walk right now. "Yeah."

He hesitates for a second like he wants to say something else. Then he turns and walks away, his shoulders tense under that damn worn flannel.

I stand in the middle of the floor. What do I want to do here?

God help me. I know exactly what I want.

I just have no idea what the hell I'm supposed to do about it. I don't know if he wants the same thing.

Chapter 19
Walker

My phone rings before the sun's even up. I groan and reach for it. I'm a night owl, and this is too early for this shit.

I stare at the screen, already knowing who it is before seeing the name.

Will Maren. My manager. And the guy knows I work nights and sleep in the mornings. If he's calling me this early, he must have a reason.

I exhale sharply, dragging a hand over my face before answering.

"This better be good, Maren." I groan. I think I've only been in bed for a few hours at this point.

Will's voice is too damn smug for this early in the morning. "Oh, it's good, alright."

I rub my temple, already regretting this. "Tell me you have the dog."

"The dog's coming through Wyoming on a tour bus this week. I don't have an exact day or time."

I sit up straighter. "What? What tour bus?"

"Kelsie Turner's bringing him. She's another one of my artists."

I blink, trying to catch up. "Kelsie Turner? *The* Kelsie Turner?"

She's a huge country music star. Sold out stadiums huge.

Will snorts. "Relax, Walker. She's doing a couple of shows out west and offered to take a minor detour to bring your delivery."

I groan. "She can't come here."

Will is silent for a beat. "Do you want the dog or not?"

I grit my teeth. He knows damn well I do. I asked for this. And I appreciate him doing it.

"We got him," Will says, like this was a casual favor, not a logistical nightmare, which it probably was. "You're welcome by the way. I don't think that guy was very nice to him, so it's probably a good call that we got him out of there. He was a mean little shit at first, but now he's growing on everyone. Kelsie even brought him on stage on her show last night. That dog likes music, apparently. He'll fit right in out there with you."

I run a hand down my face. "Where's the drop-off?"

"She'll be passing through Bridger Falls in a couple of days. You can figure out a way to be discreet."

I scoff. "There's nothing discreet about Kelsie Turner in a town this small, and you know it."

Will chuckles. "That's your problem, Walker. Not mine."

I exhale, rubbing the tension out of my neck. "You are a pain in my ass."

"And yet, you called me for this favor that you're now complaining about," he reminds me. "Which brings me to my next point."

I frown. "What now?"

There's a pause. Then, in a tone too damn careful, he says—

"Do you even know who Violet Wilson is?"

Something in my stomach goes cold. Because, honestly, I don't.

I sit up and ask, "Why?"

Will sighs. "She was with Royce Records. And she's a talented musician. How did you find her, anyway?"

The words hit like a punch.

My grip tightens around my phone. "What did you just say?"

"She was signed to Royce."

I curse under my breath, pressing my fingers against my temple.

Royce Records.

My ex-wife's label and my old label. The same label that damn near ruined me. The same label I swore I'd never be within a hundred miles of again.

"She was dropped," Will continues. "Don't know all the details yet, but it wasn't pretty. Word on the street is that she left town, and no one knows where she is... well, except you, apparently."

I stand, pacing the length of my office, my pulse thudding. "I don't like this, Will. Fuckin' Royce Records?"

"Yeah, well," he says, tone dry. "You're the one who hooked up with her."

I grit my teeth. "That's not what's happening here."

Will laughs like I'm full of shit. "Keep telling yourself that. You had me commit a crime for her. Which you still owe me for, by the way."

I don't respond. Because I don't know what the hell I'm supposed to say. I'm still shocked. I had no idea.

My past and whatever she is to me now have collided in a way I never saw coming.

And the worst part?

I have no idea what to do about it. But I'm in deep now.

*** * ***

By the time I get moving for the day, I'm still a mess.

Royce Records.

Violet Wilson was signed to Royce.

It's not saying much. Royce Records signs so many artists. They're running a scam. They're known for treating their artists like garbage. Like they're a dime a dozen. False promises and using their artists. I've seen them do so many dirty things, it's not even funny.

The name makes my blood run hot, a thousand old wounds threatening to open.

I should've seen it. Should've known the moment I first heard her sing and play the guitar.

But I didn't.

And now, I don't know what the hell to do with it.

I rub a hand down my face as I step inside—

And freeze.

Because the house doesn't feel empty.

There's music playing, the warm scent of something cooking curling through the air, and laughter—Mack's laughter—coming from the kitchen.

My chest goes tight at the warmth pulsing through me. My house feels like a home.

I round the corner and find Mack sitting at the kitchen counter, her schoolwork spread across the surface.

Maggie's in the nook by the window, sorting through a stack of paperwork.

And Violet's at the stove, barefoot, singing softly as she stirs a pot.

Violet Wilson, a musician, one good enough to be signed to a label, casually cooking dinner for my family in my kitchen.

I lean against the doorway, taking in the scene.

The warm glow of the overhead lights.

The sound of Mack scribbling notes and chewing on her pen like she always does.

The easy, unhurried rhythm of it all.

I don't say anything at first.

Just watch. And damn if this doesn't make me happy to come home to.

Mack looks up first, smirking when she sees me. "Hi, Dad. Did you know Violet can sing?"

She says it like it's some earth-shattering revelation.

Like it's a fact that should change the world.

If only she knew.

I shift my gaze to Violet, who pauses for half a second before recovering, shooting Mack a playful glare.

"Mack," she warns, stirring the pot. "I told you it's no big deal."

Mack grins. "Yeah, it totally is."

I cross my arms, watching her closely. "How's your home-work coming along?"

Violet doesn't look at me and continues to focus on what-ever she's cooking like it's the most fascinating thing in the room.

I spent the entire drive home thinking about her.

Thinking about what it means that she was with Royce Records.

Thinking about who hurt her and made her feel like she had to come here and hide her music. And then I thought about how I could find them and make them pay for hurting her.

Because I have no doubt that she was hurt.

You don't get dropped by a record label like that without scars. And especially that record label. Something happened. And now I want to know. But if I try to find out, it opens me up to having to answer questions for her.

Maggie clears her throat, breaking the moment and waves a handful of papers in the air. "Alright, I have news."

Mack perks up. "Good news?"

Maggie's eyes sparkle. "I'm going to rebuild The Dogwood even better than it was before."

Violet pauses, turning to face her fully. "You are?"

Maggie nods, spreading the papers across the table. She gestures for me to come closer, and I do, glancing at the blueprints, the notes, the sketches.

And damn if it isn't impressive.

She's not just rebuilding it—she's making it a hell of a lot better. The Dogwood needed an upgrade, that's for sure. As old as it was, I'm not surprised it burned down. Everything was falling apart in that place. So much needed to be updated and brought up to code. It was a disaster waiting to happen.

"I thought about just retiring," she admits, tucking her hair behind her ear. "Thought about taking this as a sign to slow down."

She looks up, eyes warm and determined. "But this place is my home," she says. "And I'm not done yet."

I scan the plans, the layout, and the small, thoughtful details Maggie always includes in everything she does.

A wraparound porch by the office. A bigger kitchen. Twenty additional rooms. A small swimming pool.

A guest house on the property—one that wasn't there before.

I raise an eyebrow. "You're adding a guest house?"

Maggie shrugs, but I see the way she looks at Violet.

"I enjoy having company."

Violet's eyes go soft.

Mack nudges me. "You're not gonna cry, are you, Dad?"

I shoot her a dirty look. "No."

But I don't say anything else. Because the truth is—this moment does something to me.

Seeing Mack happy.

Seeing Maggie excited about something again.

Seeing Violet here, in my house, looking like she belongs. When I see her with Maggie and Mack, I know she didn't deserve whatever happened to her before she came here.

* * *

I'm not jealous.

I'm not.

But this friendship between us? It's bullshit. I thought I could do it. I thought it would be fine until I saw her with *him*.

I'm just...*observing*. Yeah. Observing the situation across the bar where one of our regulars, Mason Carter laughs way too hard at something Violet said.

And she's laughing too. *Way* too much. Like, what the hell is so funny? That guy is definitely not funny. He's not even remotely funny.

Mason leans closer, his stupid white smile flashing in the low bar lights. His hand lands on her arm, and Violet doesn't pull away. No. She *smiles*. Then they laugh again. And I'm trying not to come unglued.

My grip tightens on the glass I'm holding. I should probably stop before I smash it into oblivion, but I can't.

"She looks like she's having a good time," Maggie says from across the bar. Her voice is casual, but I know better. Maggie loves stirring up trouble more than a raccoon loves a trash can.

I ignore her. I'm not taking the bait.

Next to her, Cami smirks into her wine glass. "She sure does," she says. "Violet's practically glowing."

I clench my jaw. *Glowing?* What does that even mean? She

doesn't glow. She—okay, maybe she's glowing a little. Her cheeks are flushed, her eyes are sparkling, and—dammit—she's flipping her hair.

This motherfucker needs to go.

"She does look happy, doesn't she, Cami?" Maggie drawls, eyes dancing with amusement.

"Ecstatic," Cami agrees, nodding sagely. "Maybe Mason's her type."

I snort. "Yeah, right."

Maggie perks up. "Oh? And why's that?"

I shift, wiping the same damn spot on the bar for the fiftieth time. "He's...too polished."

"Polished?" Cami chuckles. "Like he showers regularly? Dresses nice? Real deal-breakers there, bud."

"He looks like he moisturizes." I throw the rag down and grab a glass to polish instead.

Maggie's eyebrows shoot up. "Moisturizes? Since when is that a crime?"

"Does Red go for guys like that?" I gesture toward Mason, who's currently showing Violet something on his phone. She leans closer, and I swear my blood pressure spikes. "He probably irons his jeans."

Cami chokes on her drink. Maggie bursts into laughter.

"Oh my God." Maggie wipes her eyes. "Walker, you are *so* jealous."

"I'm *not* jealous," I clip.

"Jealous as a rooster locked outside the henhouse," Cami adds, grinning. Then she makes a rooster noise that makes me glare at her even more.

"I'm *concerned*. She doesn't know Mason like I do."

"Right," Maggie says, smirking. "Because you're obviously just worried about her safety."

"Exactly!" I point at her with the glass. "That guy's too

smooth."

Maggie arches an eyebrow. "You sure you're not worried he's got a little *too* much charm?"

"Nope," I lie.

"Oh, sugar." Maggie pats my hand. "Bless your heart."

Cami's laugh turns into a snort. "You've been scowling for the last twenty minutes like Mason just stole your girl. Face it, man—you're jealous. And the entire bar knows it."

I glance around. Sure enough, half the regulars are sneaking looks my way and whispering. A couple of guys from the pool table actually give me an encouraging thumbs-up.

Fantastic.

I grit my teeth and turn back toward the bar. "It's not jealousy. I'm just protective."

Maggie hums into her wine glass. "Sure. Protectively jealous."

My glare does nothing to dim her amusement.

Across the room, Mason says something else that makes Violet laugh. Then she rests her hand on his arm.

That's it. I'm done.

I slam the glass down and march around the bar. Maggie cackles behind me, calling out in encouragement, "Go get your girl, Walker!"

I don't stop. I'm too busy stomping across the floor toward Red, who's now twirling a lock of hair around her finger while Mason leans even closer.

I come up behind her and rest my hand on her back. She startles and looks up at me, wide-eyed.

"Hey, Red," I say, my voice low. "Can I steal you for a sec?"

Mason opens his mouth to protest, but I don't give him the chance. I slide my hand into Red's and tug her toward the back hall.

She stumbles after me. "Walker, what the hell—"

We reach the hallway near the storage room, and I stop, turning to face her.

She's breathless, eyes flashing. "Why did you just drag me away from Mason?"

My voice comes out rough. "I needed to talk to you."

"Why?"

I rub the back of my neck, searching for words that won't make me sound like a possessive idiot.

"You looked like you were having fun," I say eventually. "With him."

She blinks, confused. "I was. Until you turned into Captain Caveman."

I blow out a breath. "Yeah, well...I didn't like it."

Her jaw drops. "You didn't like it? *What* didn't you like? Me laughing? Talking to someone who doesn't shut me out on the important details of their life?"

"I didn't like seeing you with him." The truth slips out before I can stop it. "And you're one to talk. You keep things from me, too."

The hallway goes dead silent. Red's mouth opens, but no sound comes out. She's got me. I just admitted to keeping things from her and here we are. A fork in the road.

Finally, she asks, "Are you...jealous?"

I lean a hand against the wall beside her head. "What if I am?"

Her breath catches. Her eyes drop to my mouth, then snap back up. "Then maybe...you should do something about it."

Heat licks through me. My pulse pounds in my ears.

I don't give myself time to overthink it. I close the gap and kiss her. Not like last time. This time I take my time. I savor her.

She lets out a soft moan, but she doesn't hold back, either. Her hands fist in my shirt, and she grips me like she's afraid I'll pull away and she needs me right now.

And I need her.

I take her deeper, tilting my head, pressing in, tasting her. She's sweet like honey and vanilla, warm, and when she sighs a contented sigh against my mouth, I groan, dragging my hands up her body, framing her face like she's my prize I've just won.

She meets me right there in the moment, pressing up onto her toes, her lips parting even more for me as I take my time exploring, my tongue sweeping slowly against hers, teasing her, and tasting her.

Her body melts into mine, and hell if that doesn't make me grip her even tighter, my chest burning with a need I can't even begin to describe.

I stroke my thumb along her cheek and feel the way her body trembles beneath mine.

She's breathing hard, lips swollen, and when she pulls back, and looks at me with those green eyes, I nearly come undone.

Because this wasn't just a kiss. It was *the* kiss.

Somewhere in the distance, I hear Maggie yell from across the bar, "Called it!"

Red rests her forehead against mine.

"Your fan club's proud of you," she whispers.

I grin and kiss her again. "Yeah. But that was great. Even if we did have an audience."

Chapter 20
Violet

I can still feel his kiss lingering on my lips from last night.

Even now, long after, my lips still tingle from the feel of his mouth on mine. Soft and demanding. Rough and tender.

God help me, I'm trying to be his friend. But friends don't kiss each other like that. Friends don't have the kind of chemistry we have. Even I can't deny it. It's the strongest attraction I've ever had to a man. I can't explain it. I've never felt this way before with anyone.

I press my fingers to my lips, like I can somehow press the memory deeper into my skin.

I should've known and should've seen it coming. The way he watches me when he thinks I don't notice. The way he shows up without asking, always there, always steady. The way my chest tightens every time he says my name.

And then that kiss.

His hand, warm and sure, sliding to the back of my neck like it belonged there. The scrape of his thumb along my jaw, gentle but possessive. The way he tilted his head just before his lips met mine, like he was giving me one last second to stop him.

I didn't.

I couldn't.

Because the second his mouth touched mine, I forgot how to breathe.

There was just him. His taste—whiskey and something darker. His scent—leather, smoke, and Walker. His body, strong and solid against mine, like gravity finally figured out where I belonged.

And when he deepened the kiss—when his hand tightened in my hair and his breath hitched in that low, desperate way—

I melted.

God, I'm in trouble.

Because I wasn't supposed to feel this. Not like this. Not with him.

But here I am, my body still craving his like a compass desperate to find north.

I close my eyes, and there he is again.

Walker.

With his easy smile, his ridiculous banter, and the kindest damn heart I've ever known.

I tried so hard not to fall for him. I tried to just be friends like he wanted.

And then he kissed me. And I forgot about being friends with him.

The bar is packed tonight with regulars and a few out-of-towners who heard about The Black Dog from God knows where. The jukebox hums with old country, the kind of music that makes you want to sip whiskey and make bad decisions. I support both things as long as it doesn't result in a bar fight or a mess.

I've been here long enough to fall into the rhythm of it all, and it's been so much fun. Even pouring drinks, wiping down the bar, and chatting with the regulars. I've loved getting to know everyone in town better. Walker thinks I'm doing him a favor by helping him out. He's doing me the real favor. I'm saving up to pay for my car repairs, which aren't going to be cheap. Poppy had to order an expensive part that she's waiting on.

I look up when a large bus pulls up in front of the bar. The type of bus that I've seen plenty of back in Nashville but is uncommon here in Bridger Falls. Like a tour bus. And at Walker's bar. Concern fills me, and I crane my neck to look harder, curious to who it might be.

Then it gets crazier because, holy crap, Kelsie Turner just walked into The Black Dog. She stops and looks around, smiling and nodding to a few people.

The Kelsie Turner.

I freeze, bottle in midair in my hand, my brain short-circuiting. Did my two worlds collide? I've seen plenty of famous musicians while working on music row back in Nashville. Both singing and bartending. I'm so used to it, that I'm not much on fan girling. And in Nashville, musicians are just normal. But this is not what I expected to see tonight here in this small town in the middle of nowhere. Especially, not her.

Kelsie freaking Turner. And she's even more stunning in person. Sure, I follow her on social media. But I don't know her. And she sure as hell wouldn't know me. This is completely wild.

She's country music royalty. The woman whose songs have been played in every bar, truck, and heartbroken girl's bedroom for over the last five years. She's won awards and has sold-out shows. She's nothing short of incredible.

And she's standing right here, right now, in Walker's bar in the middle of nowhere. I glance around, looking for the joke. Surely, this is a prank.

I blink to make sure I'm not hallucinating.

Nope. She's still there.

She leans against the bar, her long dark hair cascading over a dark leather jacket that probably costs more than my car.

She leans over and asks, "Walker here?"

How does she know Walker? And why is she here, in his bar, asking for him? I'm so confused.

I scan the bar, expecting someone else to react, but no one does. I don't think they realize what's happening. Just me.

I swallow hard, my mind spinning with so many questions. These questions might not even be my business, and I have no business wondering.

Then, I clear my throat and smile. "I'll go get him."

My feet somehow make their way down the back hall, thankfully remembering how to walk because my brain isn't working right now. I push open the office door without knocking.

Walker is behind his desk, focused on paperwork because, of course, he is.

He looks up, surprised to see me, as if he was lost in his work. "What do you need, Red?"

I open my mouth, but I have no idea how to say this. So, I blurt it out. "Kelsie Turner is in your bar. Like, IN YOUR BAR."

The air goes thick. His entire body goes still. There's an expression on his face, but I don't understand it. Is it surprise? Is it shock? I can't tell.

For the first time since I met him, I see Walker, unshakable, steady Walker actually shaken.

Our eyes lock.

And in that moment, I realize something I should've realized before now.

There is an entire world of things I don't know about this

man. Way too many dots aren't connected. And right now, they're starting to connect.

I follow him back to the bar, my heart beating too fast.

Kelsie's still leaning against the counter, looking completely at ease. Her eyes light up when she sees him. "Walker," she says, like she knows him.

And then—they hug. And she whispers something into his ear. He casually pats her on the back.

It's quick, nothing dramatic, but my stomach still twists. I don't like this.

I don't know why.

Why is she touching him?

They continue to murmur something to each other, voices too low for me to hear, and then she tilts her head toward the door.

Walker nods. And follows her.

Out of the bar.

Onto her damn tour bus.

I stare after them, heart in my throat.

Walker.

The man who doesn't talk about his life and is insanely private. The man who acts like his magic guitar knowledge doesn't exist.

Just got on a tour bus with Kelsie Turner.

I turn back to the bar. I shouldn't be jealous. I have no business being jealous.

But what the hell is going on?

It feels like hours, but it really was just a few agonizing minutes later as Walker steps off the bus.

And he's not alone.

He's holding a leash.

And at the end of that leash is a familiar dog with pointed black ears and warm brown eyes.

A dog I thought I'd never see again.

My best friend in the whole world.

Rip Heeler.

My throat closes. My chest tightens. Tears spring to my eyes.

No freaking way.

I must be dreaming right now. This can't possibly be happening.

I stumble forward, barely registering my movement.

But I don't care.

Because Rip is here.

Rip Heeler crashes into me like a storm.

His tail wags so hard his entire body moves with it, his paws pressing into my thighs as I sink to the ground, grabbing fistfuls of his fur, burying my face against his neck as he covers me with kisses and whines.

"Rip," I whisper, wrapping my arms around him and pressing my face into his fur as he cries, having the same visceral reaction as me.

He smells and feels exactly the same. Like grass, sunshine, and all the good and familiar parts I thought I'd lost forever. My boy.

His ears twitch at my voice, and he lets out a long and soft, familiar whine, the same one he always did when he wanted to be held closer.

Like he missed me, too.

Tears slip down my cheeks as he licks my face, and I laugh through the sob, overwhelmed, unable to believe this is real.

I pull back just enough to look up at Walker, my voice shaky.

"Walker," I breathe, still kneeling on the ground, my hands tangled in Rip's fur. "How did you know to get my dog?"

He's standing there, completely still, like he's afraid to move, afraid to break whatever's happening. His usual gruff, unreadable mask is gone. He looks like he's watching something he didn't know he needed to see.

Like this moment, the way I'm clutching Rip, the way I'm crying and laughing all at once is hitting him somewhere deep. Like maybe he didn't expect this to matter so much. But it does.

His mouth parts slightly, like he wants to say something but doesn't know what. His jaw clenches, his throat bobs with a hard swallow, his fingers flex where they hang at his sides.

And his eyes—God, his eyes.

There's something soft in them. Something careful. Something I don't think he means for me to see. Then he says softly, "Cami told me. He belongs with you. I reached out to a few friends to make it happen."

My body reacts before my brain does, and before I can register what I'm doing, I wrap my arms around him in a hug, pulling him in, and burying my face in his neck. "Thank you, Walker."

He hugs me back and pats my back, rubbing circles with his hand.

Suddenly, I realize that the bar is silent around us. Or maybe it just feels that way because my heart pounds in my ears, my breath uneven as I sink back to my knees, clutching Rip like he's my lifeline.

Rip wiggles and whines, pressing his whole body into me like he can't quite believe I'm real.

I know the feeling. I bury my face in his fur, letting the relief crash over me one more time. And when I finally look up, I realize I'm not the only one watching. People have stopped mid-drink, mid-conversation, their eyes locked on me and Rip and... Walker.

The whole damn bar sits watching this unfold because small towns don't miss a thing.

They see how my shoulders shake and my hands grip Rip's fur as if I'll never let go.

They see Walker standing there, looking at me like he didn't expect this to hit him the way it did.

And they see what I see—that Walker did this. He made this happen.

That somehow, some way, he brought my dog to me.

Cami is the first to speak. I didn't even see her come in, so that tells you how wrapped up in the moment I am. She steps forward, crossing her arms, her lips twitching in a mix of amusement and something softer. "You really made this happen, Walker."

Walker hears it but doesn't say anything. His jaw tightens, his fingers flex at his sides, but he doesn't deny it.

Doesn't brush it off.

I look over at Cami and mouth the words, "Thank you." I stand and pull her into a hug. "This means everything," I tell her.

"It was a group effort." Her voice is gentle, but there's a knowing edge to it. Of course she was in on this. Cami is a fierce and loyal friend who would do anything for the people she loves.

And Walker? He just exhales sharply and looks away, like the weight of what he's done is suddenly too much. Like maybe he didn't expect it to feel this big.

But Cami? She just watches him, her smirk fading into something almost... proud. She doesn't say anything else. She doesn't have to. Because everyone in this bar already knows.

Knows that Walker isn't the kind of man who does things halfway.

Knows that if he did this—if he went out of his way to bring Rip home—then maybe, just maybe, it means something.

Maybe, just maybe... *I* mean something.

And that? That thought is almost as terrifying as losing Rip in the first place.

I stand slowly, my knees shaky, Rip's leash still in my grip. I look at Walker, and he looks right back. The air between us crackles, charged with something unspoken. Something too big for words, too real for either of us to admit.

His throat works like he wants to say something. But then— he doesn't.

Instead, he just nods once, tight and controlled, then turns back toward the bar like it's just another night.

Like he didn't just change everything.

But I know better. Everyone here knows better. Because whatever this is? Whatever just happened? I'll never forget it.

This means the world to me.

* * *

The bar buzzes with energy, a crackling mix of music, laughter, and the kind of night that feels bigger than itself. But no matter how loud it gets, my mind keeps drifting to the back.

I steal moments between pouring drinks, slipping away whenever I can to check on Rip where he lounges on the dog bed in Walker's office next to Pickles, the two of them quickly bonding now hanging out together.

Maggie brought Mack to the bar, and when I peeked into the office, I found her curled up on the couch with my dog.

She's put on the show Bluey, grinning as she nudges Rip with her foot. "Come on, boy. You gotta watch your show."

She is loving this. And I can't say I blame her because Rip is the shit. I love that dog so much. He's that once in a lifetime heart dog. The dog that stays with you in your heart forever. And he's mine again.

Rip, ever the loyal companion, rests his head on his paws,

eyes half-lidded, content as can be. His tail flicks at the sound of my voice, and the second he sees me, it thumps harder, his whole body wiggling despite his lazy sprawl.

I lean against the doorframe, my heart tight in my chest. I still can't believe he's here. That Walker made this happen. That after everything, I finally got my best friend back.

His eyes drift closed, completely content like he's always belonged right here.

Something in my chest goes tight. I cup his face, whispering, "You were always mine." His tail thumps in agreement as I make my way back to the front to work my shift.

Kelsie Turner and her band stick around. She's down to earth and so cool. So far, I'm too nervous to talk with her other than bring her beers and food.

They drink, play a few songs, and the whole town loses its mind. People are recording them, and I notice Walker disappeared to his office.

I watch from behind the bar, pouring drinks and dodging questions, still trying to wrap my head around what the hell just happened.

Because Walker isn't just some grumpy small-town bar owner. I have no idea who Walker is. He knows Kelsie Turner. He somehow got my dog back.

And I have no idea what to do with any of this.

At some point, Kelsie catches me staring while they're on break from playing. Her band is hanging out, playing darts and pool now.

And then Kelsie Turner slides onto a barstool across from me. She props her elbows on the table, watching me with a lazy kind of amusement. "So," she says, taking a sip of her drink. "Hell of a dog you got there."

I look up, full of gratitude for this woman. "Thank you so much for bringing him here."

Kelsie smirks and chuckles. "It really was my pleasure. He's a great dog."

I smile at her and nod, still nervous and unsure what to say.

"He is a good boy," she says, glancing back at me. "Worth the trouble."

I sit up straighter. "Trouble?"

She grins. A slow, knowing grin. She leans forward, lowering her voice. "Do you really want to know how we got him?"

My pulse picks up. "Yes."

Kelsie chuckles, shaking her head. "Alright, then. Here's how it went down."

I lean in closer.

"You ever met Will's kid?" she asks.

I shake my head. "I don't know who Will is."

Kelsie grins. "Will Maren, my manager. Anyway, Will has a daughter, Harper, in college, in Nashville."

Will Maren? Holy shit. I know who Will Maren is. One of the best managers in the industry. I'm not at all surprised that he manages Kelsie.

I blink. "What happened?"

Kelsie takes another sip of her drink, her eyes sparkling. "Well," she says, "Harper and her boyfriend Collin decided to run a little dog-walking side hustle through one of those apps. And guess who signed up for their services?"

It hits me instantly. I gasp in surprise. "No way."

Kelsie nods, smirking. "Yes. Your ex. He hired them to walk Rip. Never suspected a damn thing."

I press a hand to my chest, trying to process this. "You're telling me Will Maren's kid stole my dog through a dog-walking app?"

Kelsie shrugs, unapologetic. "Let's call it reunification."

I stare at her. "How?"

She grins. "They picked up Rip for a 'walk' and never brought him back."

My jaw drops.

"Oh my God," I breathe. "That's insane."

Kelsie laughs, tossing her brown hair over her shoulder. "Nah. That's called doing the right thing. I heard your ex is a piece of work."

I glance back up at Kelsie, my brain still struggling to put all the pieces together.

"So let me get this straight," I say, shifting in my seat. "Will's kid stole my dog, and you brought him to Wyoming on your tour bus?"

Kelsie grins, tipping her drink toward me in a mock toast. "That about sums it up."

I shake my head, in awe of the sheer absurdity of it. And I love it. Serves Brice right. He knew Rip was mine. Then another thought hits me like a train.

Walker made this happen.

He set this in motion.

I glance over toward the back, where Walker leans against the wall, arms crossed and watching the bar with his usual broody intensity.

Kelsie follows my gaze. Her smirk softens just a little. "Hell of a man, that one," she murmurs.

I tear my eyes away. "Who the hell is he?"

Kelsie tilts her head, considering me. Then, with a knowing smile, she says, "Oh, sweetheart. That's the question, isn't it?"

Chapter 21
Walker

Red and I clean up the bar in record time, moving together like a well-oiled machine. We work in sync without even thinking about it—passing each other bottles, wiping down the counters, stacking chairs. It's easy. Natural. Like we've been doing this forever.

Bringing her in to cover for Cash? One of my better decisions.

Even if it's costing me.

Because working this close to her, spending hours in her orbit, watching the way she moves, the way she laughs, the way she fits into this place like she's always belonged—

It's getting harder to ignore what's happening between us. What's been happening from the second she walked into my life, no matter how I try to fight it.

And then, I do things I have no business doing. Like getting involved in something I should've stayed the hell out of. But when I saw the look on her face when she dropped to her knees and clutched that damn dog like he was the last piece of home she'd ever had...

It was worth it.

On the way home, the road stretches dark and quiet ahead of us, the only sound the soft hum of the truck's tires against the pavement. The stars are bright over Bridger Falls, but I focus on the yellow lines flashing beneath my headlights.

Violet is next to me, silent for once, her fingers tangled in Rip's fur as he stretches across the seat between us, his tail giving the occasional lazy thump when she pets him. He seems like a good dog. Mack and Maggie liked him. And I didn't miss the looks Violet kept trying to give me. She's been sneaking glances at me since we pulled away from the bar. I can feel it.

And I know what's coming.

"How did you do this?" she asks, her voice soft but insistent. "Just please tell me, Walker. How do you know Will Maren?"

I tighten my grip on the steering wheel, my jaw already clenching. I knew this conversation was coming, but that doesn't mean I want to have it.

"Just leave it, Violet."

She huffs out a breath, not letting it go. "No," she presses, shifting to face me fully. "You—" she pauses, shaking her head like she doesn't even know where to start. "You play guitar like a damn pro. You know famous people in Nashville. You own a guitar that most musicians would kill for, and you just—" she gestures toward me, frustration laced in her voice, "—*gave* it to me. Who the hell are you, Walker?"

I exhale sharply, shaking my head. "Just stop. Please."

She stares at me. But I don't say anything else. Because there's nothing to say. And so much to say. So much that I won't say. Opening up to her is something I can't undo if it doesn't go well. I'm nervous as hell to tell her the truth.

She sighs, leaning back against the seat, her fingers absent-mindedly scratching behind Rip's ears.

"I used to think," she murmurs, staring out the window,

"that when I made it, when I got a record deal, everything would fall into place."

I glance over at her. Something about her tone pulls me in.

"I had this dream, you know?" she continues, her voice distant. "Of writing music, that meant something. Of playing on stage and feeling free."

Her laugh is bitter.

"And then I signed with a record label that made my life hell. It was called Royce Records."

My stomach drops. Just hearing this from her lips sets me on edge. My hands grip the wheel so hard my knuckles go white.

I say nothing. Mostly, because I can't say anything. I'm frozen by her words.

She swallows hard, still not looking at me. "Anyway, I had a best friend back in Nashville who is also in the music industry," she says, voice tight. "We did everything together. Wrote together, played together. I trusted her with everything. She was like a mentor to me. I actually thought she was helping me. It turns out that she was just getting me to write a bunch of songs that she could steal from me."

My heart clenches at the pain and betrayal in her voice.

"She was toxic," Violet says flatly, like she's learned to make peace with the words, but I know better. "Took my songs, except I wrote them. Every damn lyric. Every chord. She just put her name on them, recorded them, made them into an album."

My chest burns, rage curling in my gut.

Violet's voice is quieter now. Rough around the edges.

"And when I called her on it when I told her she knew damn well those songs weren't hers?" A humorless laugh slips from her lips. "She told me if I said a word, she'd make sure I never worked in the industry ever again."

I swear, my pulse actually stops.

She keeps going.

"But those were mine, and I worked hard on those songs. They were my stories," she says pointing at her chest as she looks at me.

"Then she got me dropped from my label," she says, still petting Rip like she needs something to ground her. "Then to top it off, I walked in on her in my bed with my boyfriend."

The air in the truck goes heavy.

Violet turns toward me again, and when I glance at her, I wish I hadn't. "I guess my songs weren't enough to steal. She took my boyfriend, too. Whatever she wanted, I guess."

Because her eyes are full of hurt.

Not in the way that says she's still broken. In the way that says she's had to rebuild herself from nothing.

And I know exactly how that feels.

"Red," I start, my voice lower than I meant for it to be.

She shakes her head, forcing a small, too-casual smile. "It's fine," she says. "I mean, it sucked. It broke me for a while. But I got out, and I got away."

She swallows hard. "And now I'm here. And I'm not telling you all of this for you to tell me anything. But I just want you to know why I am the way that I am."

I don't say anything for a long moment. Because I'm glad she's here. But I hate that she's here for those reasons.

Because what the hell am I supposed to say?

I know what it's like to watch someone steal from you, to watch someone you trusted turn into a monster.

I know what it's like to walk away from everything you thought you wanted, because staying would have destroyed you.

I glance at her again, and the weight in my chest feels unbearable.

"This is why you don't talk about your past," I say quietly.

She nods. "Yeah."

I grip the wheel tighter. "Your ex—" I grit my teeth, exhaling through my nose. "He took Rip to hurt you, didn't he?"

She hesitates, then nods again.

Something inside me snaps. Because I hate that I know this game.

I hate that I know exactly what kind of person would take a dog to make someone suffer.

I hate she had to learn it the hard way too.

I hate that this world and this industry spits people out and doesn't care. It shouldn't be that way.

And I hate that I still care.

Even after all these years, music still has its hooks in me, tangled somewhere deep in my chest where I can't reach. I think it always will.

No matter how much I tried—still try—to escape, it will always be a part of me.

I slow the truck as we near the house, pulling into the long gravel driveway, headlights sweeping over the front porch.

For a second, neither of us moves.

Violet finally exhales, her voice quiet. "And now you know."

Yeah.

Now I know.

And I wish like hell I didn't. Not personally, and not from her story.

I stare out the windshield, my thoughts spiraling into places I don't want to go. I look at her then, really look at her, and something cracks inside me.

"Now tell me what happened to you," she whispers softly.

She watches me, quiet.

"I lost everything," I tell her, my voice lower. "And I rebuilt all of this," I exhale, shaking my head.

Violet's expression softens.

I glance around at the house, the land stretching behind it, the stillness of it all.

"But I want this quiet life more than I want what I lost."

She doesn't say anything right away.

Then I say softly, carefully, "I think I want this too."

And for the first time in years, I don't feel like I'm the only one running from the past.

Maybe, just maybe, I don't have to run anymore. Maybe I could let her in.

*** * ***

The sky is painted in soft hues of gold and lavender, the Wyoming sun starting its slow descent behind the mountains. There's a stillness out here that I've never found anywhere else. A quiet that settles in my chest, grounding me.

And tonight, it feels different.

Not just peaceful.

Full.

The barn doors are wide open, a gentle breeze carrying the scent of fresh hay and warm earth. The horses shift in their stalls, ears twitching as Mack skips past, Rip Heeler and Pickles darting happily at her heels.

I lean against the fence, arms crossed, just watching. This is the kind of life I built for her. A place she could have her animals and be happy. Live a life that I dreamed of having for her.

Maggie smiles at me from her favorite spot on the porch, sipping her iced tea like she's watching a Hallmark movie play out in real-time.

"Never thought I'd see the day Walker would have a full house," she muses, eyes twinkling.

I shoot her a less than amused look. "Nursing home."

She hums in amusement, completely ignoring me. "I think Rip sure likes it here. Care to explain that?"

"Nope," I smirk.

I glance back at Pickles and Rip, now rolling in the grass, completely at ease.

Yeah. He does like it here.

And so does his owner. Red's taken over my kitchen, making the most amazing dinners. I won't ever tell Momma Mary at the bar, but she cooks even better than her, and Momma Mary has been cooking for over thirty years. Call it whatever it is; I love it. Tonight, she's making some sort of pasta I can smell all the way out here. My mouth is already watering.

Violet calls out the back door, "Dinner's almost ready!"

Mack groans from where she's petting the dogs. "Five more minutes?"

"One," I tell her.

Mack brushes her hands off on her jeans, giving Rip one last scratch behind the ears before heading toward the house. Rip and Pickles trail behind her.

I linger behind, taking it all in.

The barn. The land. My daughter laughing. My dog's happy. Violet's dog here. Everyone is happy.

Life doesn't get much better than this.

And for the first time in a long time, I don't want it to change.

When I enter the kitchen, it smells damn near illegal.

Garlic, butter, basil—a mix of everything good and holy in this world.

I step inside, and Violet is at the stove, stirring a pot of what I can only assume is the best-smelling pasta I've ever encountered in my life.

She's barefoot, her hair piled up in some messy twist that's barely holding together, a smear of flour dusting her cheek. And she looks... happy.

Maggie is perched at the kitchen table, wine in hand, watching Red like she's witnessing a miracle.

"Did you know my niece can cook?" Maggie asks, eyes wide, like Violet just pulled off an exorcism. "I mean, really cook?"

Violet snorts, shaking her head. "I literally just threw together some ingredients."

Maggie waves her off. "I thought when you said you were cooking that you meant, like, 'making boxed mac and cheese without burning the house down' kind of cooking."

Violet rolls her eyes, but she's smiling. "Nope, that's you Aunt Maggie."

Mack, hovering way too close to the garlic bread, sniffs the air dramatically.

"This is next-level, Dad," she declares, nudging me. "You better prepare yourself. Our standards are about to go way up."

I cross my arms, smirking. "Oh yeah?"

Mack nods seriously. "Yup. Your cooking? Not gonna cut it anymore. You and Maggie are fired."

Maggie gasps, clutching her chest. "Excuse me?"

Mack grins. "You literally tried to microwave eggs once, Maggie."

Maggie narrows her eyes. "I was experimenting."

Violet laughs, pulling the bread from the oven, and the smell alone has me questioning everything I thought I knew about life.

"Alright," she says, setting the food on the table. "Eat before Mack stages a mutiny."

Mack grabs a slice of bread before the plate even fully touches the table.

"Oh my God," she groans, eyes rolling back dramatically. "Violet, this is insane."

Red smirks. "Good insane?"

Mack gestures wildly at the bread. "I never knew garlic bread could taste like this."

Maggie takes a bite and actually moans.

"Don't expect this kind of food in your nursing home," I tease.

Maggie waves me off. "Shut up and eat, Walker."

I grab a plate, piling on more pasta than I probably need, and take my first bite.

And holy hell. Yeah, I needed all of this. Probably seconds.

I freeze mid-chew.

Violet watches me with a knowing glint in her eyes. "Well?"

I swallow, then clear my throat. "This is..." I shake my head, pointing at my plate. "You made this from scratch?"

She shrugs like it's nothing. "Yeah."

Mack leans forward, grinning. "So, Dad?"

I raise a brow. "What?"

Mack gestures between Violet and the food. "Can we keep her?"

Red chokes on her wine.

Maggie laughs so hard she nearly tips over her glass.

I glare at my daughter. "She's not a stray, Mack."

Mack shrugs. "She comes with a dog. Rip is basically part of the family now. And I like her food."

Red sets down her fork, wiping her mouth, her eyes full of mischief. "Wait, wait," she says, feigning offense. "You like my dog first? And then me?"

Mack nods, completely serious. "I mean, the food is really good, but Rip is, like, next level."

Violet pretends to glare and murmurs. "Unbelievable."

Maggie, grinning over her wine glass, winks at Violet. "Don't take it personally, hon. Walker was just telling me how much he likes having you around."

I choke on my drink.

Red raises a brow. "Oh, really?"

I shoot Maggie a warning look, but she's got that damn twinkle in her eye.

Mack gasps dramatically. "Dad, do you have a crush on Violet?"

I groan. "I'm gonna eat my food in the barn now."

Violet laughs, shaking her head, and something in my chest unwinds. God, I love her laugh.

I don't know what the hell is happening.

But I know one thing—

I don't want this to end.

Chapter 22
Violet

The porch is quiet, the late-night air cool with the scent of pine and earth. We just had a relaxing thunderstorm, and I can still smell the dampness in the air. It's the perfect sleeping weather. But I have a song I need to get down on paper before it leaves me.

The sky is a perfect shade of deep indigo. Stars scatter across it like someone spilled a jar of glitter all over. It reminds me of Walker. He's a mystery just like the night sky, but beautiful, dark, and comforting at the same time.

And here I am on the porch, with my notebook, his guitar, and a heart that finally feels like it has something to say again.

I strum a chord, then another, letting the notes hum into the night.

It feels good. Better than good.

For the first time in a long time, music doesn't feel like pressure. It doesn't feel like an expectation. It feels like mine.

My pencil scratches across the paper, the lyrics pouring out faster than I can keep up.

I hum a melody, tweaking it as I go, my foot tapping lightly against the wooden boards of the porch beneath me. The swing creaks as I lean over to my notebook.

And just as I hum the chorus, something shifts in the air.

I feel it before I see it. A presence. I glance up and there he is. Walker leans in the doorway, arms crossed, listening.

Rip's tail thumps on the floor of the porch, and he tilts his head up when he sees Walker.

He doesn't move and doesn't say anything.

I freeze mid-lyric, the last note hanging in the air like an unfinished confession. He just stands there, leaning in the doorway with his broad shoulders, shadowed jaw, and those eyes. The ones that always seem to see through me no matter how hard I try to keep things light.

He watches me with those beautiful, sharp, and unreadable eyes like he's trying to figure something out.

I playfully narrow my eyes at him. "How long have you been standing there?"

His lips twitch like he's amused. "Long enough."

I groan dramatically, tossing my pencil down. "Walker. Creeping is not polite."

He smirks, stepping onto the porch. "Neither is stopping in the middle of a good song."

He moves across the wooden boards with that easy, unhurried confidence of his—like the night bends around him instead of the other way around.

And suddenly, the night feels smaller. More intimate.

I strum another soft chord, letting the moment settle.

Then his voice speaks, low and even. "So, what do you plan to do now?"

I glance at him. "With what?"

"With music," he says, tilting his head toward my notebook. "Now that you don't have a label taking advantage of you."

I run my fingers over the strings, letting the question sit in my chest. I know the answer. I've known it for a long time.

"I don't know," I admit, shrugging slightly. "I just know I was put on this earth to write songs. And music will always be a part of my life, even if it's just mine."

His expression doesn't change, but something flickers in his eyes. Something quiet and knowing. He understands. Somehow, I know he does.

I tap my fingers against my guitar, tilting my head at him. "What about you?"

He frowns slightly. "What about me?"

I arch a brow. "What do you do out at that cabin of yours?"

His shoulders stiffen, just barely. "What do you mean?"

I smirk. "I see you, you know. When we get home from the bar late at night. You head out there sometimes. And sometimes I hear music across the lake."

He exhales through his nose, shaking his head. "You really don't let things go, do you?"

"Not when they're interesting."

He gives me a long look, like he's debating whether or not to tell me.

Then, finally—

"I write," he mutters, rubbing the back of his neck.

I blink. "Like... stories?"

"No." He exhales, looking away. "Songs."

The words echo like a sudden clap of thunder. Walker writes songs. My mind scrambles to catch up, memories flashing like snapshots—the way his fingers always drum the bar when a good song plays. The way he hums under his breath when he thinks no one's listening. All this time, he's been holding on to music just like me. And I never knew.

Silence.

Then—pure, unfiltered shock bursts out of me that I can't

hold back any longer. He's given me a piece of him right now, but I'm also completely shocked that I didn't figure it out until now.

"Walker. No way."

He groans, pinching the bridge of his nose. I can tell this is a weird conversation for him to have and he says with a groan, "Red."

"You write songs?" I stare at him, my mouth hanging open. "And you didn't think to mention this earlier? Like, I don't know, maybe when I was sitting here writing songs?"

He grumbles something under his breath that I don't catch. His jaw ticks. Just once. But I see the way his shield going up, the careful distance settling back into place. He's sitting beside me, but I can feel him pulling away like he's bracing for me to push too hard, too fast. Like the music is something fragile he's terrified to share.

But I see the way his jaw tightens, the way he shifts slightly like this is a conversation he'd rather avoid.

And that's when I realize—he's serious about keeping this private.

It's not just something he does. It's something he protects. I press my lips together, softening. "You don't play them?" I ask, quieter this time.

He shakes his head.

I let that sink in. And even though a million questions burn in my throat, I don't push. Because I know what it feels like to lose music for a while. To love something and still walk away from it.

I know that instinct—the need to protect the pieces of yourself that matter most. So I don't press. I don't ask for lyrics or melodies or explanations. Instead, I strum another chord, soft and familiar, inviting him to stay without saying a word.

The night settles around us, the sound of crickets filling the silence.

Rip stretches out at our feet, snoring lightly.

Walker leans back on the swing, his arms resting along the top, his fingers almost brushing my shoulder.

I strum another soft chord, picking up the melody from before.

His head tilts slightly, listening.

And when I start to hum again, picking up where I left off—

He stays.

Listens.

Doesn't run.

And for now, that's enough. Walker has his secrets. But tonight, he let me in. Just a little bit. I'm not going to push.

Walker writes songs.

I stare at him, the words circling in my head, refusing to settle.

Walker. Writing. Music.

It doesn't compute.

Not because I don't believe he's capable of it. I do.

Hell, I knew there was something about him. The way he listens to music. The way his fingers twitch on the bar counter whenever a song plays in the background like he's unconsciously counting beats, feeling rhythms.

But he never would tell me. He wouldn't let me in. Until now.

And that?

It feels huge. Even if it's just a little movement.

I glance down at my guitar, running my fingers over the strings, trying to process.

Music is... everything to me. It's woven into my DNA, the only constant I've ever had. And for a long time, I thought losing my place in the industry meant losing music altogether. I thought I was alone in that feeling.

But Walker? Walker gets it. He knows what it's like to hold on to music like a lifeline. And yet, he's been keeping it to himself. That's what hits me the hardest. This isn't some hobby for him. This is something he protects. Something he keeps locked up, far away from the world.

Away from me.

And now I'm sitting here, wondering why. I look at him; really look at him. He's got that closed-off expression again, the one I recognize now. The one that says he's waiting for me to push too hard. For me to ask questions he doesn't want to answer. And maybe a few weeks ago, I would have.

But not tonight.

Tonight, I let the knowledge settle inside me, warming me from the inside out. Because I get it now. Walker isn't just a small-town bar owner. He's a songwriter. A real one. A damn good one, I bet.

And suddenly, it's not just my music that feels exciting again.

The night folds around us, the music filling the silence between breaths. His arm rests along the back of the swing, his warmth just close enough to make me aware of every nerve under my skin. And as I hum the chorus again, I feel it—the unspoken truth between us.

This music isn't just mine anymore.

It's ours.

* * *

I should have known better than to go along with Mack, Cami, and Poppy's plan. The truth is, I've been so happy to have friends and do fun things with them that I think I left my judgement behind somewhere.

"What the hell is this?" I screech, holding out my arm.

It's not bronze. It's not golden. It's... Cheeto orange.

Poppy stifles a laugh from her spot on the ground where she's sprawled out like a starfish, arms and legs airplane-wide, because Cami swore we had to "air-dry for optimal results."

"You look like a traffic cone," Poppy says, gasping for air.

I glare at her. "Don't laugh, Oompa Loompa. You're literally the color of a carrot."

She sits up and looks down at herself, then shrieks. Her legs are streaked like a damn tiger. Dark orange lines running down her calves like someone finger-painted them.

Cami, standing in front of the mirror, groans. "I said light, even layers!"

"I *did* even layers!" Mack protests. "Y'all look ridiculous. I'm glad I didn't do it."

I throw my arms up. "We *did* light, even layers! The bottle said 'tropical bronze'! Look at us! We're like the cast of Willy Wonka."

Poppy collapses into giggles, clutching her stomach. "I can't —" she wheezes. "I literally can't breathe. Violet, your knees... your knees are glowing."

I look down. My knees are neon orange. Like Halloween pumpkin bright.

"Dear God," I whisper. "This is how it ends. As an internet meme."

We gather in front of the mirror, horrified but fascinated. I can't stop looking at all of us; we look so ridiculous.

Cami's arms look like a human Rorschach test—uneven patches everywhere.

Poppy's legs are striped like a tiger, and Mack somehow missed her left foot entirely.

My knees and elbows are so neon they might glow in the dark.

"Okay," Mack says, wiping sweat off her forehead, leaving a tan stripe. "We can fix this."

Poppy sits on the floor, still laughing. "Fix it? What are you gonna do? Power-wash us?"

Mack brightens. "Actually... yeah."

Five minutes later, we're in Walker's backyard, standing in nothing but old shorts and tank tops, while Cami uncoils the garden hose.

"This is a terrible idea," I say, arms crossed.

Poppy's already giggling again. "What if someone sees us?"

I gesture toward Mack, who's aiming the hose like she's about to blast us off the planet. "We look like escaped circus performers. We're practically a tourist attraction."

"Even the horses look concerned," Poppy laughs as she points to them watching us, their tails swaying, curiously.

Mack twists the nozzle. "Hold still."

The first blast of water hits me square in the face, and I sputter. "Mack!"

"Oops!" she says, not looking remotely sorry.

The next blast hits Poppy, who lets out a high-pitched squeal and drops into a defensive crouch. "It's like being attacked by a fire hose!"

"Stop squirming!" Cami yells. "We have to get the streaks off!"

"I swear to God, if I die via hose attack—"

Suddenly the water pressure surges. The nozzle flies from Mack's hands like a missile, spinning wildly, and blasts Poppy right in the chest.

She goes down like a sack of potatoes.

I'm screaming. Cami's screaming. Poppy's lying on the

ground, soaked, orange streaks running down her legs like she lost a fight with a paintball gun.

And then we hear it.

A low, rumbling laugh.

We whip around and see Walker, Ollie, and Jack standing on the other side of the fence, beer bottles in hand, grinning like idiots. Jack covers his mouth with his hand sheepishly as Walker glares at him for laughing.

Then, Walker's eyes lock with mine. He takes one look at my neon-orange knees and wheezing laughter spills out of him.

Ollie bends over, hands on his knees. "Oh... my God. What... did you *do*?"

Cami groans and slaps her forehead. "We tried spray tans. Mack assured us it would be fine."

"That's what you get for listening to a teenager," Ollie smirks.

Mack picks up the hose and aims it at Ollie, "Say that again, Ollie."

Jack chokes on his beer. "Y'all know no one here tans. We just burn and go back to flannel."

Walker, still laughing, tips his chin at me. "Nice knees, Red."

I point at him. "Laugh it up, Walker. One day, you're gonna need my help, and when you do, I'm bringing this moment up."

He grins even wider. "Oh, I hope you do."

Cami lunges for the hose nozzle in Mack's hands. "I will spray you all!" she practically bellows.

Walker backs away, hands up in surrender. Ollie and Jack bolt. Poppy's still on the ground, gasping through laughter. And me?

I'm standing in a puddle of muddy self-tanner, my pride long gone, my abs sore from laughing, wondering how the hell this is my life.

Maggie texts me later, saying, "Saw the video of y'all. Why didn't y'all invite me to the spray tan party?"

Chapter 23
Walker

I know Mack and Maggie are up to something before I even step foot in the damn kitchen.

Their whispers travel down the hall, their voices full of poorly disguised mischief.

I pause in the doorway, crossing my arms. "Alright," I say, narrowing my eyes. "What the hell are you two scheming now?"

Mack and Maggie both freeze, eyes wide like I just caught them burying a body. Then, simultaneously, they scramble to look innocent—Mack shoving something behind her back, Maggie suddenly very focused on stirring her coffee.

I glance between them, already losing patience.

Maggie clears her throat as she glances at the barn. "We were just discussing..." She hesitates. "Hay."

I blink. "Hay."

Mack nods vigorously. Way too vigorously. "Yeah. A big hay conspiracy is happening. We'd better stock up for the horses, Dad."

I stare at them. "You two are ridiculous."

Maggie nods, completely straight-faced. "Oh, we know."

I run a hand down my face. "Do I even want to know?"

"Nope," Mack says quickly.

"Definitely not," Maggie agrees, sipping her coffee like she's innocent.

They're up to something. And I don't like it. I move toward the coffee pot, fully aware that they're still watching me. They're not even being subtle about it.

Mack leans in, whispering something to Maggie, and Maggie smirks. That damn smirk. The same one she always had when she used to try and set me up with every single person she came across in town.

It finally clicks.

I turn around, arms crossed. "This about Violet?"

Maggie and Mack both feign innocence at the same time.

"Who?" Mack asks, blinking way too much.

Maggie shrugs. "Doesn't ring a bell."

I scowl. "You two are the worst liars I've ever met."

Maggie grins, completely unbothered. "Walker, sweetheart, you should know by now—we don't lie." She lifts her coffee cup, raising a brow. "We strategically rewrite reality."

I groan. "Oh, I know."

Mack snickers.

I grab my coffee and head toward the table, but the second I sit down, Mack perks up. "So, Dad..." she starts, way too casually.

I immediately regret being in this kitchen.

She props her chin on her hand, looking entirely too smug. "Violet sure is happy here, huh?"

I take a slow sip of coffee, pretending I don't hear her as I fix my plate of food.

Maggie grins. "Oh yes, she fits in so well. The way she's helping at the bar, making home-cooked meals..." She sighs dramatically. "It's like she was meant to be here."

I set my coffee down. "I strongly dislike both of you at this moment."

Mack beams. "No, you don't."

I scowl at them. "I don't know what kind of scheme you two are running, but whatever it is, stop."

Maggie tilts her head. "But sweetheart, if you don't like her, why are you getting all grumpy?"

"I'm always grumpy."

Mack snorts. "Yeah, but this is different. You're extra grumpy."

I groan, pinching the bridge of my nose. "You're insufferable."

Maggie pats my hand like I'm a poor, lost soul. "We just want what's best for you, honey."

"And for Violet," my daughter adds.

"And Rip," Maggie tacks on.

Mack nods seriously. "Rip loves it here. And for the goats."

"We don't have any goats." I give her a look.

Maggie clicks her tongue. "So much undeniable evidence in favor of this arrangement."

I glare. "This isn't a damn trial."

Mack leans forward, smirking. "Okay, fine, but if this was a trial, the jury would already be so on our side."

Before I can argue, the screen door creaks open, and the woman in question walks inside, humming to herself, her Velcro dog, Rip, trotting behind her as he usually does.

She's wearing my damn hoodie, her hair messy from sleep, and looking so comfortable in my house that my brain short-circuits.

Pickles, who had been dozing by the door, immediately jumps up and trots to her and Rip, tail wagging like she hung the damn moon.

Maggie and Mack both exchange looks. And I want to throw myself out the nearest window.

Violet pauses, raising a brow at the three of us. "Okay," she says slowly. "What's going on?"

I open my mouth—

And Mack ruins everything.

"Dad was just saying how much he likes having you around."

I choke on my coffee.

Violet's eyes widen slightly, a smirk creeping onto her lips.

"Oh really?" she asks, way too amused.

I shoot Mack a glare that could set fire to a forest.

Mack grins, completely unrepentant. "Yup. Big softie, this one."

I swear to God, I'm going to send this child to a nursing home with Maggie. Maybe they have a two for one deal.

Violet grins, shaking her head. She walks past me, giving Pickles a scratch behind the ears before stealing a piece of toast from my plate like it's the most normal thing in the world.

And the worst part?

I don't stop her. I simply watch as she heads back out to the porch, Pickles and Rip trotting behind her.

Maggie leans back in her chair, looking smug as hell.

"Well, well," she hums, sipping her coffee. "Would you look at that?"

I narrow my eyes. "Don't say it."

She grins. "Looks like we're keeping her after all."

Mack cheers.

And me? I sit there, watching her, watching this, and I know—

I'm so screwed.

* * *

The bar is halfway through the afternoon rush, and Violet and I are behind the counter, moving like we've been doing this together forever.

She's pouring drinks, throwing in that easy charm that makes her a new favorite among the customers, while I handle inventory and keep an eye on everything.

I barely notice the door swing open until a familiar voice cuts through the noise.

"Well, damn. You replace me already, boss?"

I turn, and there he is—Cash, grinning like he never left.

"You look too well rested for someone who has a newborn at home," I say, crossing to give him a hug and clapping him on the back. "How're Codi and the baby?"

Cash laughs, clapping me on the back as he settles onto a barstool. "Yeah, yeah. I needed a break, but I'm ready to come back if you'll have me. Everyone is good."

Violet walks over, setting a beer in front of a customer next to him. "Hi, Cash," she muses.

Cash smirks. "Hey, Violet, how's my job?"

She grins. "Good, you ready to have it back?"

Cash laughs. "I will admit that I missed this place." Then, he lowers his voice. "Also, I heard this wild rumor that Kelsie Turner was here?"

I pause.

Cash leans in. "Walker. Tell me it's not true. I missed that?"

I sigh, rubbing a hand down my face. "It's true."

His jaw drops. "What the hell?"

Violet laughs, crossing her arms. "Oh, you should've seen it. Full-on country music royalty, waltzing into The Black Dog like it was nothing."

Cash shakes his head, staring at me. "You really gonna act like this isn't the craziest thing that's happened since this place opened?"

I shrug, grabbing a rag and wiping the counter. "It was just business."

She snorts. "Yeah. Just business."

Cash narrows his eyes at me. "You're hiding something, but I'll get it out of you eventually."

I change the subject. "You looking for more hours?"

Cash nods. "Yeah. I need the work."

I glance around the bar, at the growing crowd, the endless responsibilities, the way I barely have time to do anything but keep this place running.

Then, an idea hits me. A crazy one.

One that might actually make my life easier.

I lean on the counter, leveling Cash with a look. "How would you feel about being the bar manager?"

Cash blinks. "Come again?"

I cross my arms. "I'm looking to hand off more responsibility. You've been here long enough. You know the place inside and out. Thought you might want a promotion."

Cash stares at me and grins. "You're serious?"

"Dead serious."

He lets out a low whistle. "Damn. Didn't think I'd walk in here today and get a promotion."

Violet leans on the counter beside me, grinning. "You should take it. He needs someone to keep him from growling at customers all the time."

I shoot her a look. "I do not—"

"You do," Cash and Violet say at the same time.

I roll my eyes.

Cash leans back, running a hand through his hair. "You know what? Yeah. I'll do it."

I nod. "Good."

Violet grins at him. "Welcome to management, boss."

Cash chuckles, raising his beer. "Guess I better start acting important, huh?"

I smirk and playfully toss him a rag. "Yeah. Start by cleaning tables."

He groans and laughs. "Already regretting this."

The rush picks up again, but something inside me feels lighter. For the first time in a long time, I feel like I can breathe. With Cash stepping up, I don't have to do this by myself anymore.

And maybe, just maybe—I don't want to.

I glance at Violet, who's already tossing a rag at Cash and laughing when he dodges it. She fits here. Too damn well. And with the weight of the bar shifting off my shoulders, I finally have the time to focus on what matters. My daughter. My music.

And the woman who's making it harder and harder to imagine life without her.

* * *

I find her behind the bar, wiping down the counter, lost in whatever song she hums under her breath. She hasn't noticed me yet. For a second, I just watch her. It's ridiculous how easily she fits here, how natural it feels having her behind my bar, moving like she's been here for years instead of weeks.

And that's exactly the problem.

Because the longer she stays, the harder it's getting to picture this place and my life without her in it. I clear my throat, and she finally looks up, a slow smile pulling at her lips.

"Well, if it isn't Walker, looking like he needs me for something," she teases, leaning against the counter.

I roll my shoulders back, ignoring how my cock twitches when she looks at me like that.

"I don't like to ask for favors," I mutter.

Her grin widens. "Yet here you are."

I exhale sharply, dragging a hand over the back of my neck.

Maggie's busy. The Dogwood rebuild takes up a lot of her time, and I don't like Mack being alone at night. Cash is taking over more of a manager role, but I still need help at home.

I could ask anyone. Could find someone else to help. But I don't want someone else.

I want her.

"I need someone to stay at the house with Mack when I'm working," I say finally. "Make sure she gets to school. Pick her up."

Her eyes widen slightly, like she wasn't expecting that. Hell, I wasn't expecting it either.

She blinks up at me, like she's waiting for the punchline. "You want me to help?"

I meet her gaze. "Yeah."

I expect her to hesitate. To say she's too busy, that it's too much. But instead, she smiles. Soft and real, like the idea of helping means something to her. "Of course, Walker. I'd love to."

Something shifts in my chest. Like I was bracing for something that never came. Like maybe, I was waiting for her to give me a reason not to do this.

She doesn't. Instead, she just says yes.

She doesn't know what that means to let someone into my life like this. And for the first time, I think—maybe I'm okay with it.

"Hey, Walker?" she asks with a hint of teasing in her tone. "Yeah?"

"Can we write together in your secret cabin?"

I stare at the ceiling, "Don't push it, Red."

But I'd love to write music with her. I'm dying to write

music with her. But she's already slipping into all the other corners of my life. Music is my only safe space now. The door I swore I'd never to open to anyone.

If I let her in, she'll see it all. She'll see how much I still love it. How much I still need it, even after all these years of pretending I don't. She'll see the parts of me I don't let anyone else see. And worse?

She'll make me want it again.

And if I let myself want it, if I step back into that world, even for her—

I don't know if I'll survive it a second time.

* * *

I've been doing my best to avoid Red and her questions about songwriting. I don't regret telling her, but now I'm just not sure where to go from here. For over fifteen years, this has been a part of me that I kept private. I don't know how to share that with anyone, let alone Violet.

I should've known something was up when Jack and Ollie cornered me at the bar.

Jack sits on the barstool he always claims as his with his legs stretched out, arms crossed, and that shit-eating grin already in place. Ollie leans against the counter, his firefighter uniform still dusty from a call earlier, and a look that says, "I'm here to cause problems on purpose."

I grab a rag and wipe down the bar, ignoring whatever ambush they're brewing. "You two need something? Or just here to loiter like the freeloaders you are?"

Ollie smirks. "I'd take a burger and fries. I'm starving."

Jack straightens, pushing his hat back on his head. "We need to talk about Violet."

I freeze for half a second, then continue wiping down the bar like I didn't hear him. "No, we don't."

"Yeah," Ollie says, voice smug as hell. "We do."

I exhale through my nose and brace myself. "I don't know what you're talking about," I say, tossing the rag aside and heading toward the cooler.

"Bullshit." Ollie grabs a soda from the cooler. "You're into her. We've all seen it."

Jack nods, his grin widening. "Maggie said you practically stare at her like she's a stack of pancakes every time she walks into the room."

I groan. "Jesus, why is Maggie involved in this conversation?"

"Because she's Maggie," Jack says, shrugging. "And she loves meddling in all our lives."

Ollie sips his soda. "So, what's your plan here, Walker? Keep standing around all broody while Violet thinks you don't care?"

"I don't stand around broody."

They both laugh.

"Dude." Ollie points at me. "You have literally been brooding about her since she got here."

Jack holds up a hand. "Wait—do you remember the first night she bartended with you? The man looked like he was ready to propose."

Ollie slaps the bar. "Yes! And when she laughed at the Oompa Loompa fiasco last week? Walker made this weird face —like he got hit in the gut. He's a goner."

I scowl. "I did not make a weird face."

Jack tilts his head. "It was weird."

"Super weird," Ollie confirms.

I grit my teeth. "You two are idiots."

"Maybe," Jack says. "But we're right and you like her."

I rub a hand over my jaw. I could lie. Tell them they're off base. But I can't.

Because they're right.

I like her. More than like her. And now that she knows about the songwriting, how I've been holed up in that cabin, pouring my soul into notebooks for years, the line I've tried to keep between us doesn't exist anymore.

I let her in.

Jack's voice breaks through my thoughts. "Walker, you've always been a damn hermit since we've known you. And we get it. We do. But Violet's different. We like her for you."

Ollie nods. "She gets it, man. She's one of us."

I swallow. Yeah. That's the terrifying part. Because I can see her here as one of us. But what if she ends up leaving?

"I don't know if I can let her in," I mutter. "Not all the way."

Jack sighs. "You mean you don't know if you can let yourself be happy."

I shoot him a glare.

He grins. "You're not denying it."

The silence stretches across the bar. I stare at the worn wooden surface, trying to find some excuse, some reason to keep everything locked down. But the truth is there, staring me in the face.

Violet isn't like anyone else.

She fits here. With me. With Mack. With this entire town. And damn if I expected this. Or was even looking for it. I wasn't waiting around for someone to walk into my life and make me feel like this. But she did.

She makes me laugh. More than I've laughed in a long time.

I like her so damn much.

She makes the world feel brighter. Like there's color where there was darkness before. And she's so beautiful. And I've been standing on the edge, pretending I don't want more. Pretending that night with her didn't undo me. Pretending that being near her doesn't make me ache with something I haven't let myself feel in years.

I want her. And I want her to know the parts of me no one else does. That scares the hell out of me.

Ollie slaps the bar suddenly, making me jump. "Enough with the broody act, Walker. She likes you. You like her. Stop being a wussy and go get your girl."

I barked out a laugh. "A wussy?"

"Yeah." He grins. "A big ol' wussy."

Jack chuckles. "I mean... he's not wrong."

I shake my head, biting back a smile. "You two are relentless."

"Because we're right." Ollie points his soda at me. "And because she's worth it."

The words hit harder than I expected. Because yeah, she is.

And suddenly, I'm not so sure I want to spend the rest of my life not letting her in. Maybe it feels scary because it's right.

I want more.

And maybe... maybe it is time to stop being a damn wussy and go after it.

Chapter 24
Violet

I should've known something was up when Maggie knocked on my door early this morning, wearing sneakers and smiling like a woman on a mission.

Maggie doesn't wear sneakers. She wears cowboy boots and judgment. So, when she hands me a clipboard and says, "We signed you up!" with that mischievous glint in her eye, I absolutely know that my day is about to go straight to hell.

"Signed me up for what?" I ask, gripping the clipboard like it might contain answers and save me from whatever mission she's signed me up for.

Maggie's smile widens. "The best event of the year in Bridger Falls."

I turn to Mack, who stands behind her with an expression that practically screams mischief as well.

"Oh, yeah," Mack says, eyes dancing with glee. "You're gonna love it."

And that's how I end up standing in the middle of Bridger Falls' annual "Ranchers vs. Townies" contest, glaring at Maggie, Mack, and half the town.

I've had so much delicious food from all of the food trucks. Who knew that this was such a popular event in Bridger Falls?

Apparently, Bridger Falls does this once a year in the summer to bring the town together. The town people and the ranch owners all get together, eat good food, play games, and it's all in good fun.

It has been a full day of events. And it has been so much fun. Until now. Because apparently, Walker is now my partner.

In a three-legged race in front of everyone.

And the way the crowd watches our every move? I'm convinced this was less about town spirit and more about a collective matchmaking scheme from everyone.

Walker stands beside me, scowling down at the thick rope binding our legs together.

His jaw is tight. His hands rest on his hips. His t-shirt stretches over his broad shoulders, and the way his biceps look should be illegal.

I try not to look. And fail.

"Tell me again how this happened," he mutters.

I cross my arms. "Your daughter and Maggie are agents of chaos, that's how."

Mack waves from the sidelines, beaming like she's never been prouder. "Don't mess this up, Dad!"

Walker sighs, rubbing his jaw. "I should've seen this coming."

I smile. "You're slipping."

His eyes flick to mine warm, sharp, and full of challenge. "You sure you can handle this, Red?"

The air thickens. Just slightly. His voice is low and rough around the edges, like a sandpaper tease against my skin.

"You sure you can keep up, old man?" I shoot back, trying to ignore the warmth creeping up my neck.

He huffs out a breath, muttering something under his breath about how he can "definitely keep up."

I grin. "What was that?"

His lips curl at the corner. "Nothing."

Liar.

The announcer steps up to the mic, adjusting his cowboy hat. "Alright, folks! Time for our favorite event: the three-legged race!"

The crowd cheers like maniacs. The Betty Lou Bandits from the quilting club wave a banner that says: "TEAM WALKER & VIOLET: WILL THEY KISS OR CRASH?"

I groan.

Walker sees it and curses. "This town's insane."

"Yeah." I swallow hard. But I can't help but secretly love it.

His eyes linger on mine for a beat too long. Something shifts in my chest.

Maggie shouts from the sidelines: "Go get 'em, sugar!"

Walker groans. "Maggie, your paperwork's officially getting sent in for the nursing home."

Maggie just winks. "Hurry up! We want to see if Cami and Jack kill each other. They're up next."

The announcer lifts his hand. "Ranchers vs. Townies—GO!"

We take off, our legs tangled and steps uneven, already doomed. Walker wraps an arm around me to keep our balance, but it distracts me and makes me lean into him and glance at him, making me almost trip. Then it doesn't help that I can feel his body heat where we're connected.

Walker tries to match my stride, but his ridiculously long legs have me practically hopping to keep up. His fingertips hold me steady, but we're already a mess of limbs.

"Damn it, Violet—move your leg!"

"You move your leg, Walker!"

Geez, who knew Walker was so competitive?

We lurch forward, limbs flailing, like a drunken octopus trying to run a marathon. We both laugh but stumble and almost fall.

Behind us, Cami and Poppy wipe out spectacularly, landing in the dirt in a tangled heap.

I cackle—but that laugh costs me when I lose focus. Walker yanks me forward, his hand gripping my waist, and my heart skips a beat.

"Eyes on the finish line," he growls. The sound of his voice sends a traitorous shiver down my spine.

"What finish line?" I gasp. "All I see is my impending death."

Walker laughs, and damn it, that deep, rich sound does something wild and dangerous to my pulse.

"Just keep moving, Red," he huffs.

Somehow, miraculously, we find a rhythm. His thigh brushes mine with every step. Heat rolls off him, amplifying the leather, soap, and sweat smells and mixing with the dust in the air.

I glance at him. Grinning. Breathless. "We might actually win this thing."

And that's when we step in a pothole.

We go down. Hard.

The ground rushes up to meet me, and I land with a bone-jarring thud. Walker's half on top of me, his arm braced by my head, his body heavy, warm, and solid as hell.

The crowd erupts in laughter.

Mack is howling. "You were so close!"

I groan. "So very close."

Walker lifts his head. He's propped on his elbows above me, his face inches from mine. I go completely still. His weight presses against me in all the wrong—or maybe right—places. His breath fans against my cheek.

God help me, this man smells like a sin I want to commit twice. His eyes drop just for a second to my mouth, and everything fades. The crowd. The dust. The entire town shouting in the background... they all disappear until it's just us.

The heat between us is impossible to ignore. My skin tingles and my heart races. I feel his breath and his muscles tense. His thumb brushes against my hip. I lick my lips. His eyes track the movement. His jaw tightens. His fingers flex. His gaze turns molten.

God. We're one wrong move from a full-on public indecency charge.

And then—

Maggie's voice cuts through the haze. "KISS HER, YOU IDIOT!"

Walker groans, his forehead dropping to my shoulder. "I hate this town."

I laugh, breathless and wrecked, but damn if I don't feel the exact same way. He rolls off me, muttering under his breath as he starts untying the rope around our legs. I sit up, brushing dirt from my jeans. My pulse still races.

Maggie hollers: "YOU COULD'VE KISSED HER!"

Walker's head snaps up. "Maggie, for the love of—"

Mack walks over, hands on her hips. "So... does this mean you lost?"

Walker sighs. "Yeah. We lost."

I nudge him with my shoulder, still giddy from whatever the hell that moment was. "But we had fun."

His eyes flick to mine. He smiles, just a little, and his gaze drops again to my mouth. His voice is quiet. Rough. Just for me. "Yeah. We did."

We walk back to the truck, our shoulders brushing every

few steps. The sun dips lower in the sky. The crowd cheers for the next round. Maggie's still yelling something about romantic tension.

Walker's hand brushes against mine. I feel it like I would an electric shock. "Told you I could keep up," he murmurs, voice low and wicked.

I force out a laugh. "Was that before or after we face-planted?"

He stops. Turns to me. His eyes are pure trouble, his mouth quirking up on one side. "Maybe next time... we try something with less rope."

The air thickens again.

My mouth goes dry, and I can't breathe. Because "next time" sounds a whole lot like a promise.

And God help me—I want it.

* * *

I know something's wrong the moment I push open the garage door. Normally, there'd be music blasting from the old radio or the sound of Poppy swearing at an engine. But today?

Silence.

Poppy stands next to my car, leaning against the hood with an expression that screams guilt.

"Poppy..." I narrow my eyes.

She smiles—too wide, too innocent. "Hey, stranger! Here for your car?"

I glance past her to my dusty Subaru that hasn't seen daylight in weeks. I run my hand along the roof like I'm greeting a long-lost pet. "Yeah, you know... since it's been in car jail for half a century."

Poppy chuckles and pushes off the hood. "Funny thing about that..."

I cross my arms. "Funny how?"

She rubs the back of her neck, her eyes darting everywhere except at me. "So... it's been fixed."

My mouth drops open. "What?"

She winces. "For... a while."

I blink. "How long is a while?"

She cringes. "I'm sorry that I'm not sorry."

"Poppy!" I try to be mad, but I can't hide my grin.

"Wait!" she says, holding up both hands. "Before you get mad, let me explain!"

I narrow my eyes to hide my amusement. "This better be good."

She flashes a grin. "Okay, so... watching you and Walker do the whole 'grumpy cowboy drives the stubborn redhead around town' thing? It was like the cutest damn reality show I've ever seen. We all agreed it was best for... you know... morale."

"Morale?" I sputter. "You kept my car hostage for entertainment purposes?"

"Don't act like you didn't love it."

I open my mouth to argue, but before I can, the side door swings open. Cami walks in, carrying a tray of iced coffees, her eyes immediately lighting up. "Ooooh! What's this? Trouble in paradise?"

Poppy cackles. "Oh, yeah. Violet just found out about the Walker chauffeur conspiracy."

"Ahh." Cami sets the tray of coffees down, picks one up, and sips it. "Yeah, that was a good run."

I groan. "Wait—you knew, too?"

Cami shrugs. "Of course. The whole town knows."

I sit heavily on the nearest rolling stool. "Wait. Are you telling me the entire town has been... watching us?"

"Watching is a creepy word," Poppy says, already smirking. "We've been... encouraging."

Cami nods. "And placing bets."

I blink. "Bets?"

"Yeah." Cami sips her drink, totally casual. "We have a pool going."

"A pool."

"Mhm. On when you two will finally get together."

I groan and drag my hands down my face. "Oh my God. You people need hobbies."

"This *is* our hobby," Poppy says with a grin.

Before I can respond, the side door swings open again. Mack walks in, eating a popsicle like she owns the place. She stops, surveys the room, and grins. "Ah. The Walker and Violet bet."

I point at her, not able to hide the grin this time. "No. Just— no. Go... do algebra or something."

Mack shrugs. "I don't need algebra when I can read body language." She leans against the workbench, crossing her arms. "And yours screams 'in denial'."

Poppy howls. Cami almost spits out her coffee.

"How," I demand, "did I become the main character of this small-town gossip?"

Poppy wipes her eyes. "Babe, that happened the second you showed up and started making googly eyes at Walker."

I groan. "I do not make googly eyes."

"You absolutely do," Cami says, voice muffled as she opens a bag of Skittles she apparently brought for this event. "That thing you do when he walks into the room? It's like watching a deer spot a predator and freeze. Only you look way thirstier."

"Thirstier?" I choke.

"Bone dry, sweetheart."

Mack hops onto the workbench, swinging her legs. "It's true. I've seen it. It's gross."

"This is your dad. We shouldn't be talking about this," I groan.

Mack shrugs. "I got a text from Poppy. She said, 'Come witness the moment Violet finds out she's in love with your dad.' So... here I am."

I whip toward Poppy. "You summoned witnesses?"

She doesn't even pretend to look ashamed. "Obviously. This is historic."

I stand up too fast, knocking the stool over behind me. It hits the oil drain pan, which tips, and luckily, Poppy uprights before it can spill.

Mack whistles. "Well. That's symbolic."

Poppy's trying to wipe away tears from laughing. Cami's texting—probably live-updating the town gossip page. Mack, of course, looks delighted. "You okay?" she asks sweetly.

I glare. "No. I'm being emotionally waterboarded by my friends."

"That's fair," she agrees, licking her popsicle.

Poppy snorts. "Come on, Red. Just admit it—you've got it bad."

I groan. "You're all insane."

"And yet," Cami says, "you love us."

"Against my will." I look down at my shoes, my heart pounding harder than it should. Because they're wrong. And they're also right. And I hate that I don't know what to do about it.

Luckily, I don't have to think about it too much longer because Cami gets a text and frowns as she reads it. She looks up and says, "Who wants to do a little breaking and entering tonight? My pie is in a contest to win in the local category, and word on the street is Maggie cheated and had someone make one that rivals mine. And we'll see about that. I need that prize money, you guys."

We all stare at her in shock and silence.

"It's for a good cause?" she raises her eyebrows. "And we can eat the pie that we steal..."

We all raise our hands and giggle.

* * *

At 10 p.m. sharp, the four of us stand across the street from the community center, wearing all black like we're auditioning for a low-budget spy movie. Walker is at the bar, hopefully unaware that I'm helping corrupt his daughter.

Cami adjusts her mask. "I can't believe we're actually doing this. This is so exciting!"

Poppy wiggles her fingers like is warming up for something. "We've got one shot, ladies. One pie. Let's make it count."

Mack salutes. "I'm ready."

I rub my temples. "We're going to end up on the Bridger Falls police blotter."

"Worst-case scenario, we bribe Sheriff Matthews with a slice," Poppy says with a shrug.

Fair point. He probably will want a piece if this pie is as delicious as they say. Just sayin'.

We sprint across the street, ducking behind bushes despite the town being dead quiet all while Cami hums the *Mission: Impossible* theme song.

"Why are we whispering?" I hiss as we crouch by the side door.

"Stealth," Mack whispers back. "We're pie ninjas."

Poppy jiggles the door handle. Locked. "Plan B," she says, pulling a tiny kit from her pocket.

"You can pick locks?" I whisper in awe.

She winks. "High school wasn't all algebra, babe."

Thirty seconds later, the door clicks open.

"Holy crap," Cami mutters. "She's good."

"You're going to have to teach me that," Mack says in awe.

"Don't encourage her," I say, stepping inside.

We creep down the hallway to the kitchen. The overhead lights hum faintly, the air thick with the smell of cinnamon, butter, and stealth.

Mack freezes beside me. "Do you smell that?"

"Peach pie," I whisper.

"Victory," she corrects.

We find the pie on a stainless-steel prep table, golden and perfect, covered with foil, and labeled, "MAGGIE'S. TOUCH AND DIE."

Cami reads the note. "She's bluffing."

Poppy raises a brow. "Maggie never bluffs about baked goods."

"I can't believe she's trying to win the prize over me," Cami huffs.

"We've come this far." Mack's voice is steely with determination. "We take the risk."

"This child is terrifying," Cami whispers. "She's going places. Maybe not Harvard. But places."

"Prison if we get caught! Hurry!" I say as we giggle collectively. We carefully lift the foil and inhale pure dessert heaven.

"Okay," I say, pulling out the plastic forks Poppy brought. "One piece each. We take it so we leave no evidence."

Poppy holds up her phone. "Wait, selfie first."

So, there we are: four idiots, crammed together in the dim kitchen, taking a triumphant selfie over a stolen pie in our black stealth ninja clothing. We each take a bite and another selfie.

It's pure magic. Buttery crust. Sweet peaches. A hint of cinnamon.

"Whoever made this is a genius," Cami moans, eyes closed. "My pie didn't stand a chance."

"Not true, your baked goods are so good," Poppy says.

"If she finds out we did this, we're dead," I say, licking peach filling off my thumb.

Mack takes a second bite. "Worth it."

We're halfway to the door when it happens. The motion-sensor alarm we somehow missed when we came in the other door goes off. The alarm shrieks like a banshee. Lights flash. The oven timer starts beeping for no reason.

"Run!" Poppy yells.

Mack grabs the pie.

"Leave the pie!" I shout.

"Never!" she yells, sprinting for the exit.

We bolt through the kitchen, slipping on the tile like cartoon characters. Poppy knocks over a stack of mixing bowls. Cami crashes into a mop bucket. We burst through the side door just as Sheriff Matthews's patrol truck rounds the corner. His head-lights catch us mid-sprint.

Poppy throws herself into a bush. Cami dives behind a trash can. Mack still holds the pie, frozen in place like a criminal caught mid-heist. Naturally, I trip over my feet and face-plant in the grass.

The truck door opens. Sheriff Matthews gets out, arms crossed. "Let me guess," he sighs, looking directly at me. "Pie-related shenanigans?"

I groan into the grass. "Yes."

Mack holds up the pie triumphantly. "But we got it!"

Fifteen minutes later, we sit on the curb, still wearing ski masks covered in grass stains. Sheriff Matthews sits on his tail-gate, eating a slice of Maggie's pie right from the pie plate.

"You gonna arrest us?" I ask.

"Nah," he says, taking another bite. "Maggie said to call her if you tried anything. I'm just supposed to take a picture for the town Facebook page."

Poppy groans. "I knew it."

"Say cheese!" he says as he holds up his phone and snaps a picture.

Cami snorts. "Bridger Falls: Land of No Secrets."

Mack licks pie filling off her finger and shrugs. "Worth it." And damn it, she's right.

But we also just had the best damn night of our lives.

Chapter 25
Walker

The bar is quiet now. It's our last night working together since Cash is back tomorrow, and Red will shift her focus to helping me out more at the house. And damn if I don't love having her at my house. My home has always been meant to be full of people. And I'll admit that I'm really going to miss working with her. She makes the bar come alive when she's here. The whole energy in the place changes when she's around. She's one of the hardest workers I've ever met, and our customers love having her here.

The last of the customers are gone for the night, the lights are dimmed, and the only sounds left are the hum of the jukebox on low and the quiet clinking of glasses as Violet puts them away.

We've fallen into this simple rhythm, her working beside me, moving through my world like she was always meant to be here.

It's dangerous.

Because every night she closes the place down with me, it gets harder to picture this bar without her.

Harder to picture my life without her.

I glance up, watching Violet lean against the counter, humming to herself as she wipes down the bar. Rip is sprawled out on the floor, completely dead to the world, his tail flicking lazily whenever Violet shifts. He stays back in the office all night, but comes out here to watch her while we close up. He's never far from her.

She fits here. And her dog. Seeing her happy with her dog has been worth it.

I should say something. Tell her goodnight, tell her... something that isn't the truth that claws at the back of my throat.

But instead, I just watch her. And, of course, she notices.

"What?" she asks, smirking as she tosses the rag over her shoulder.

I shake my head, grabbing my keys. "Nothing."

She follows me toward the door, her presence at my side too familiar now. Too right. And then, right as I flip the sign to Closed, she says it. "You ever get tired of me hanging around?"

She says it lightly, like it's a joke, but there's something else in her voice. Something uncertain.

Like she's testing me.

Like she's still not sure if she belongs here.

Like she still thinks she might leave.

And before I can think about it, before I can talk myself out of it—the words just come out. "You're stuck with us, Red."

She goes still. Her eyes widen just a little, searching my face like she's not sure she heard me right. "Yeah?" she murmurs.

I swallow, my grip tightening around my keys. "Yeah."

She doesn't say anything right away. She just looks at me, and for the first time, I think she finally sees what I've been too damn stubborn to say out loud.

That she's not just passing through. That I don't want her to.

She tucks a loose strand of hair behind her ear, something

soft and unreadable in her expression. Then, smirking just enough to break the tension, she bumps her shoulder into mine. "Well, lucky you," she teases. "I'm pretty good company."

I chuckle, shaking my head as I push open the door. "Yeah. You are."

And for the first time in a long time, I know I mean every damn word, but I can't let the moment get too serious. I nudge her shoulder. "So... how'd you enjoy your life of crime?"

Her steps falter. "What?" She asks it all innocently, pretending not to understand. But I know what they did. And I have to give her crap about it. I've been waiting for the perfect moment to tease her about this. "The pie heist." I grin, shoving my hands in my pockets. "You, Mack, Cami, Poppy. Disguises. Busted by Sheriff Matthews. Ring any bells?"

Her mouth drops open. "How do you know about that?"

"Sheriff Matthews showed me the footage." I chuckle. "You should really work on your getaway skills."

She groans, tipping her head back. "There's footage?!"

"Oh yeah." I lean against the doorframe, enjoying this way too much. "My favorite part? You, tripping over a bush while Mack screams, 'Save the pie!' like you're both in an action movie."

She slaps a hand over her face. "Dear God. I'm never showing my face in town again."

"Too late." I grin. "A private viewing is scheduled for the next town meeting."

Her eyes snap to mine. "You're lying."

"Nope." I pull out my phone and pretend to scroll. "Maggie's bringing popcorn."

She groans again. "I can't believe it."

"Believe it. Funny you all thought you could get away with it. You should have known Maggie would get the last laugh."

Her mouth opens to argue, but she stops. Because she knows I'm right.

The tension shifts again from playful to something heavier. Thicker. We stand in the doorway. Inches apart. The air between us crackles like a live wire.

Her eyes lift to mine. My gaze drops to her mouth.

I know better.

But she's looking at me like she's just as wrecked by this as I am. And that's when I know I'm done for. I lean closer. My hand drifts toward her waist.

She sways toward me, just slightly.

God. I want to kiss her. So damn bad.

"Walker," she breathes.

I swallow hard. "Yeah?"

Her lips twitch, mischief sparking in her eyes. "Next time we rob a pie, you're driving. Because clearly, I can't be trusted on foot."

I bark out a laugh, the tension shattering like a dropped dessert. "Deal."

She grins. "And we're bringing disguises that don't make us look like raccoons committing tax fraud."

I shake my head, still chuckling. "Noted. I'll handle the getaway car. You handle not face-planting."

She groans. "One bush! I tripped over one bush!"

"It looked like an aggressive bush," I deadpan. "Jumped out of nowhere."

She throws her hands in the air. "Exactly!"

I smirk, arms crossed, and I chuckle as I walk her to her car. She slides into the driver's seat, Rip jumping in beside her.

My chest feels tight. My head's a mess.

She rolls down the window, and I rest my forearms against the door. "Night, Red," I murmur.

Her gaze meets mine. Soft. Searching. "Night, Walker."

She pulls away, taillights glowing red in the dark. And I stand there long after she's gone, the night air cool against my skin.

Because I just told Violet Wilson she's stuck with me.

And for the first time in years... I hope like hell she believes it and sticks around.

She heads home, and I finish things up at the bar, getting it ready for tomorrow. When I pull in a little later, I notice a light on in the barn. I catch Violet in there, talking to Maximus like he's her therapist, looking so at home in my world that it messes with my head.

So, of course, I do the dumbest thing possible. I saddle up the horses and tell her, "Come on. Let's go on a middle of the night ride."

And now? Now, she's riding next to me, hair spilling loose from whatever mess of a bun she had it in, my hoodie drowning her frame, and I have no clue how to handle any of this.

We stop at the ridge overlooking the house, the glow of the stars twinkling in the sky.

Violet exhales, taking it all in. "Wow."

I'm not looking at the view, I'm looking at her. At the way the big, beautiful moon lights up her face, the tension in her shoulders easing like this is the first time she's breathed all day. The silvery light touching her face, highlighting her soft skin, makes her look like she came straight out of a fairy tale.

She catches me staring. "What?" she asks, voice quieter than before.

I shake my head. "Nothing."

She smirks, tilting her head. "You're a terrible liar, you know."

I huff out a quiet laugh. And now, somehow, she's looking at me the way I've been trying not to look at her.

Like something is about to happen.

Like she's waiting.

Like maybe I don't have to hold back anymore.

I should move. I should say something to break this ridiculous tension. Instead, I just sit there, watching her, my eyes flickering down to her lips before I can stop myself. She shifts as she feels it, too.

"Walker..."

I lean in. Just barely. Her breath catches. And right when I think she's gonna meet me halfway, Maximus snorts loud enough to shake the damn earth.

I jerk back, cursing under my breath.

Violet lets out a laugh, pressing a hand to her chest. "Wow. Thought that was about to be a moment."

I glare at my horse, who looks far too pleased with himself. "Maximus, I swear to God—"

"Has terrible timing?" she offers, grinning.

I sigh, adjusting the reins, trying to ignore the fact that I was about two seconds away from doing something stupid. "Come on, Red," I mutter. "Let's get you home."

She doesn't argue. But as we turn the horses around, the air between us is different now.

Like she knows.

Like I know.

* * *

"Hey, Red, I have a delivery coming today at around noon. Can you be available?" I ask as she stirs a pan of eggs on the stove for breakfast burritos.

"Sure, what are you having delivered?" she looks up curiously. She has on one of my flannel shirts over some leggings. And I will never get tired of her stealing my shirts.

I lean in closer and whisper, "Baby goats. But don't tell Mack. It's a surprise."

Her eyes widen, "What? Oh my gosh, no way!"

"Way. She's been asking for them for a while now. She's probably forgotten by now. But they're coming. She'll be excited."

"Heck, I'm excited, Walker," she says excitedly. "You know you're going to have an entire zoo by the time she's done asking, right?"

I roll my eyes playfully. "Not happening. Just a few goats, Red. It's really not that big of a deal." I got them because they'll be good to clean up the weeds around the property, and plus, they did look really cute in the picture.

* * *

Later that evening, I pull into the driveway, already knowing something's wrong. For starters, the flowerpots on the porch are tipped over. The flowers that were planted in them are gone, and dirt is everywhere.

Rip Heeler and Pickles run around in wild circles, barking their heads off.

And there are goats. Everywhere. So many goats.

I grip the steering wheel and take a slow breath. What. The. Holy. Hell.

Then the screen door swings open—and a goat sprints out of my house.

Out. Of. My house.

Maggie, sitting comfortably on the porch like she's enjoying a damn TV show, sips her sweet tea and tips her glass toward the chaos.

"Welcome home, Walker. I see you got some goats."

I climb out of the truck, eyes scanning the battlefield.

Horror fills me. What the hell? One goat stands proudly on the hood of Violet's car, another perches on the porch railing, and—

Jesus Christ. Another is on the roof of the barn.

"Okay," I say slowly. "I'm afraid to ask."

"Good choice," Maggie says, taking another sip. "Just enjoy it like I've been."

Then I spot Mack and Violet, standing in the middle of the yard, looking like they're plotting something.

Mack grins, and Violet is covered in dirt, holding an open bag of potato chips like she's negotiating a hostage situation.

A goat nudges her knee, and she yelps. "No! We are not doing this again, you tiny demon!"

The baby bleats loudly, clearly disagreeing.

Mack bursts into laughter.

I rub my temples. "Someone start explaining."

Mack bites back another laugh, wiping her eyes. "Okay, first, thanks for the baby goats, Dad. I mean, you totally overdelivered on this one. They are totally adorable and so much fun. And second, Violet is amazing."

Violet glares at her. "I am not *amazing*. I am a *victim*."

Maggie cackles.

I cross my arms. "Explain."

Maggie points at Violet, grinning. "She took a goat to the knee, Walker. It was a Nancy Kerrigan figure skating move."

Mack bows to Violet. "You didn't even go down easy. You just took the hits like a champ."

Violet turns to me, wild-eyed. "Your goats are evil."

The herd makes its way back to the pen now, somehow. Probably has something to do with Rip Heeler herding them all back in.

However, one still watches from the roof.

"Why are there so many?" I ask, panicked.

"They said you ordered two dozen," Violet says as she shoos the one at her feet into the pen.

"I asked for two. Two!" I protest, rubbing the back of my neck. "Not twenty-four."

Maggie chuckles, shaking her head. "This is the funniest damn thing I've seen in years."

I glance at Violet, still clutching the chip bag like it's a lifeline.

"Dare I ask why you're bribing them with potato chips?"

Violet throws a hand in the air. "Because it works!"

Mack nods. "She's right. The goats respect snack-based negotiations."

I pinch the bridge of my nose. "What are we supposed to do with twenty-four goats?"

Mack looks at me oddly. "Is this a bad time to tell you that some of them look like they are with child?"

I stare up at the sky and curse my good deed decisions that are now coming back to bite me.

Mack throws an arm around Violet's shoulder, still grinning. "We should do this again sometime."

Violet turns to her, dead serious. "If you ever say that again, I swear on Maggie's peach pie, I will fake my own death, move to Alaska, and live among the moose."

Mack bursts out laughing.

Maggie wipes a tear from her eye, she's laughing so hard. "The best entertainment I've had in years."

I shake my head, watching them, and something tightens in my chest. Because as ridiculous as this scene is, Violet fits in here.

She's covered in dirt, arguing with my kid like they've been doing this for years. She's standing in my yard, dealing with my animals, and not running away screaming. And I don't know when it happened, but...I can't picture this place without her anymore.

Violet groans, pointing at me. "Walker, I swear, if one of these goats gets inside your house again, I'm moving out."

Mack smirks. "But you don't even officially live here."

Violet freezes.

I freeze.

Maggie grins like the devil.

"Well," she says sweetly, sipping her lemonade, "maybe it's time she does."

Mack high-fives her.

Chapter 26
Violet

Mack and I have fallen into our usual post-dinner ritual where we curl up on the couch under a pile of mismatched blankets with a bowl of popcorn balanced between us and *Heartland* on the TV.

Rip sprawls across my legs, snoring softly, occasionally kicking like he's chasing something in his dreams. Probably goats. Pickles is curled up in Mack's lap.

Mack is fully invested in our show, her eyes glued to the screen as a brooding cowboy delivers a heartfelt speech that will probably lead to some dramatic, slow-burn kiss.

"This man needs therapy, not a horse," she declares, tossing a piece of popcorn into her mouth.

I laugh, sipping my root beer float. "Accurate. But I wouldn't say no to a troubled cowboy falling in love with me." The words are barely out of my mouth when I hear it—a low voice from the other couch, quiet but unmistakable.

"You don't need a cowboy, Red."

I freeze.

Mack doesn't. She grins like she just won the lottery. "Ooooh, he heard that."

Walker sits across from us with his arms crossed like he's trying to keep it together, but the slight flush creeping up his neck gives him away.

"I wasn't listening," he mutters, but it sounds weak even to him. "She's watched this show a hundred times."

I arch a brow. "So you just happened to respond?"

His jaw tightens. "Drop it, Red."

Mack smirks, shoving another handful of popcorn into her mouth. "Face it, Dad. You're down bad."

Walker exhales sharply, like he's wondering how he ended up here with a teenage daughter who has no mercy and a woman who makes it impossible for him to keep his walls up. "I'm going to the cabin."

Mack and I exchange a look. Then, in perfect unison—"Goodnight, troubled cowboy," we say and then laugh.

Walker mutters something under his breath and disappears down the hall, but not before I catch it, the tiniest hint of a smile he didn't mean to let slip.

There's something about quiet nights here that feels like they belong in a song.

After we finish our show, we settle in outside on the porch. The sky is so dark it's almost velvet, the stars sharp and endless. The only sounds are the breeze rustling the trees, the occasional creak of the porch swing, and Rip snoring softly at my feet. If you're quiet and listen closely, you can hear the faint sound of music from across the lake, making me itch to go over there and join him. I would love to see what he's working on. I'm dying to know what's inspiring him to write his songs.

Mack and I sit side by side, swinging gently. It's a routine now—our thing. When I'm not with Maggie, I'm with Mack. And we've been having so much fun.

Mack sighs, kicking her feet lazily. "I like having you here, you know," she says, her voice soft.

I smile, turning my head toward her. "Yeah?"

She shrugs. "Yeah. You fit in here with us."

That word hits harder than it should. Fit.

I shouldn't let myself think about that. I shouldn't let myself get used to this and to her, to this house, to the way Walker seems to soften when I'm around.

"You're fun," she adds, nudging my arm. "And you keep my dad on his toes, which is chef's kiss entertainment."

I laugh softly. "Glad to be of service."

She turns serious, her eyes meeting mine. "You're not leaving, right?"

My heart stumbles.

I want to give her a simple answer. I want to say no, of course not, but I can't make promises I'm not sure I can keep. "I don't know, Mack," I say softly.

Mack frowns like that's the wrong answer.

"Well," she says firmly, "you should stay. Because we need you."

Her words settle like stones in my chest, heavy but grounding. I swallow the lump in my throat. "I think I need you too," I whisper.

A throat clears behind us. I jump, twisting around to find Maggie standing in the doorway, arms crossed, her silhouette framed by the soft glow of the porch light.

Walker pulls up down at the dock on his boat, and man he looks good. He ties up the boat and heads up the lawn, taking in all of us on the porch. Hesitating like he's trying to decide if he wants to say what's sitting on the tip of his tongue.

Mack grins like she's been caught red-handed but doesn't care. "Told you," she says, way too smug. "Violet should think about sticking around."

I shoot her a look. "Mack."

She shrugs, sips her float, and then says, "You're welcome."

Maggie's gaze lingers on her for a second, then shifts to me. "Y'all just having a girl's night without me?"

"We waited up for you," I protest. "Plus, how was bingo?"

She shrugs, "It was boring, so I left early."

Which means she wasn't winning.

Mack's gaze bounces between us, grinning like a lunatic, and she finally hops to her feet.

"Well, I'm going inside," she announces, "because this is getting awkward in the best way."

"Mack," Walker says.

She turns back and gives him a quick hug. "Have fun, you two."

"I'm heading up to bed. It's old lady time," Maggie grins.

The door clicks shut behind her, leaving just me and Walker, standing in the soft glow of the porch light. The silence is heavy now, filled with everything unsaid.

"I don't want you to go, either. If anything I think matters," he says softly.

"Never said I was going anywhere," I say softly.

His mouth turns up and he looks relieved.

"I really like your kid, Walker," I admit.

"Just my kid?" he asks. His jaw ticks. I see it—the way his fingers flex against his knee, the way his whole body goes still like he's bracing for impact.

I lick my lips, my heart pounding. "I like you too," I whisper.

His eyes darken, his entire focus narrowing in on me like he's trying to memorize every detail of this moment.

Like maybe he wasn't expecting me to admit it. Or maybe, he's just been waiting too damn long to hear it. The space between us suddenly feels too small. His hand moves, like he wants to touch me—but he hesitates. Like maybe he's still waiting for me to take it back. Like maybe he doesn't quite believe it yet.

So, I do the only thing I can think of to prove it. I reach for his hand, slowly, deliberately, letting my fingers brush against his.

His breath shudders. "You mean that?" he asks, voice barely above a whisper.

I nod. "Yeah. I do."

His fingers tighten just slightly around mine. He leans down and presses his lips to mine, softly kissing me, and it immediately takes me back to that night. Walker kissing me lights up my world like the Fourth of July.

It knocks the breath out of me when he says, "I came back to get something, and I'm going back to the cabin. Goodnight, Red."

I wish he'd take me with him. I watch him walk away after I confess that I like him and he kisses me. Which pretty much tells me he feels the same. But damn, his walls are high. So high, it's like a fortress I can't seem to scale no matter how hard I try.

It's not just that Walker is good-looking in that rugged, broody cowboy way. It's not just that he looks at me like I'm a puzzle he's still trying to figure out. It's more than that. So much more.

It's the way he takes care of people without thinking twice. The way he worries about Mack but lets her find her own way. The way he never treated me like I was temporary—even when I thought I was.

And damn it, I've fallen for him.

And his kid. Hard. Both of them have me wrapped around their hearts. I don't even know when it happened.

Maybe it was when he drove me around town like it was no big deal that my car was "mysteriously" still broken. Maybe it was when he gave me that vintage guitar like it wasn't the most priceless thing he owned. Maybe it was when he brought back Rip Heeler, just to see me smile.

Or maybe it was just every single damn day, every time he looked at me like I was something worth showing up for.

Maybe, I was always supposed to end up here.

Right beside him.

* * *

Dropping Mack off at school should be simple. But nothing in my life is simple anymore. Because the second she hops out of the truck, she rolls the window down and shouts across the parking lot. "Hey, Mr. Shores, wanna buy a goat?!"

Mr. Shores—the very startled high school teacher—pauses mid-coffee sip and blinks at her like she just asked if he'd like to participate in an illegal gambling ring.

I lay my forehead against the steering wheel. This is my life now. And I might secretly love every bit of it.

"You have to stop trying to sell people goats," I say as Mack leans into the window, grinning like a menace.

"Oh, come on," she says, propping her elbows on the door. "We have too many, and I'm just doing some light marketing."

"This is not light marketing," I deadpan. "This is borderline harassment."

She shrugs. "One man's harassment is another man's business opportunity."

From across the lot, Mr. Shores slowly backs toward the school entrance, clutching his coffee like a life preserver.

Mack waves. "Think about it, Mr. S! Eco-friendly lawnmowers!"

He practically runs inside the building.

I groan, rubbing my temples. I point a warning finger at her as she backs away toward the school doors. "Have a good day," I tell her, shaking my head.

She cackles and disappears inside as she waves to me.

I sigh, shaking my head as I pull away from the school. If I don't get coffee immediately, I will lose my mind. Steamy Sips it is. Plus, I could use some catching up with Cami.

By the time I pull up, Cami's already at the order window, grinning like she knows I just went through some fresh hell. "Rough morning?" she asks. "I heard about your goat fiasco."

I groan. "Mack has been trying to give everyone a goat this morning. It's like the Oprah episode when she gave everyone a car. This time it's a goat. You get a goat, and you get a goat!"

Cami chokes on her coffee. "Oh my God, I'd totally take a few off your hands."

"I'll send Mack your way for negotiations," I grin. "But be warned, she's ruthless. She's out here pitching livestock like it's a door-to-door subscription service."

Cami snorts. "I love that for her."

Just as I'm about to steer the conversation back to sanity, my phone buzzes. I glance down and immediately curse under my breath. It's Walker. His name shows up on the screen and Cami notices.

"Oooh," Cami teases. "Walker's calling."

I answer, bracing myself. Walker's voice comes through, low and unimpressed. "Red."

I grin. "Walker."

"Did you know my kid just emailed the entire town an ad for 'Gently Used Goats: Negotiable Pricing'?"

Poppy and Cami absolutely lose their minds laughing.

I close my eyes, and chuckle. "No, but that's hilarious."

And Mack? That kid is definitely going places.

But also? Maybe she's a little bit my hero, too.

* * *

I should've known better than to call my mother.

Not because I don't love her, I do. But because she is a menace. If she even sniffs that there's something she can meddle in, she will sniff it out like a bloodhound.

And, apparently, Maggie is the same way. Sisters who have that in common. Meddling.

The second Mom picks up, I barely get out a "Hey, Mom," before she launches in.

"Well, it's about time you called me. You know, some mothers get regular updates from their daughters, but me? Oh no, I have to get my information secondhand from my sister."

I roll my eyes, already bracing myself. "Mom—"

"Anyway, she tells me you're staying with a handsome single young man," she says with a voice full of glee.

My entire body freezes. Oh. Oh no. I inwardly groan.

"Tell me about him," she prods, her tone way too interested.

I clear my throat, playing it cool. "Not much to tell."

"Uh-huh," she hums, clearly smelling a lie.

I twist my hoodie's hem—okay, it's Walker's hoodie, so not the point right now—and force a casual tone. "He's just a guy." Silence.

Then—"Oh, sweetheart," she says not believing me.

I groan. "Mom."

"No, no. I just—" She exhales dramatically. "I didn't think I'd live to see the day my daughter downplayed a man. Usually, I hear about every tiny little detail, but now? Oh, now, he's just a guy? What makes this one so special?"

"He is just a guy," I insist, pacing the room. "Just a regular, broody, infuriating cowboy bar owner guy."

Mom gasps. "A cowboy? Violet, are you living in a romance novel?"

I nearly choke. "Absolutely not."

"Oh, honey." She sighs dreamily. "It's finally happening. Please tell me everything."

I pinch the bridge of my nose. "What is finally happening?"

"You're smitten."

I let out a hysterical laugh, probably further giving myself away. "I am not smitten."

She laughs like she doesn't believe a word I'm saying. "What's his name?"

"Walker," I grumble.

"Oh." She pauses. "That's a good name. Sounds very... masculine."

I groan louder. "Goodbye, Mother."

"Wait, wait, just one more question—"

"Nope. Hanging up now."

"Is he good with his hands? Because a cowboy bar owner sounds—"

Click.

By the time I pull up to the Dogwood, Maggie is standing outside, hands on her hips, surveying the ongoing demolition like a queen overseeing her kingdom. She has on a pink hard hat that apparently the contractor gave her.

I hop out of the truck and march right up to her. "Thanks for telling Mom about Walker."

Maggie smirks. "Oh, is he supposed to be a secret?"

"No, but—"

She crosses her arms, completely unbothered. "Then what's the problem?"

I open my mouth. Close it. Try again.

Maggie waits patiently, clearly entertained.

Finally, I huff. "She's insufferable now. So are you."

Maggie chuckles. "I'd imagine so. Your mother is a very smart woman."

I narrow my eyes. "You are not helping."

Maggie gives me a sweet, innocent smile that I don't buy for a second. "I'm just saying," she muses, "I couldn't have picked a better man for you if I tried." She lifts a brow. "Which, by the way, I didn't. You showed up here at my doorstep if you recall."

I shift my weight, suddenly very interested in the ground. "That's—"

"And I'm glad you did," she adds, her voice softer now.

I glance up at her, that warmth in her eyes knocking the breath out of me. Because I'm glad, too.

And it's not just the town. It's not just the people I've grown to love. It's him. The way he makes the world feel a little steadier. The way I don't feel like a stranger here anymore—not when he looks at me like I already belong.

I don't say it out loud. I don't even know if I *can* say it out loud. But I feel it.

Deep in my chest, my fingers curl into my sleeves, and my heart isn't racing to run anymore.

Because for the first time in forever, I don't want to.

Bridger Falls wasn't supposed to stick. I was supposed to visit, help Maggie, and move on. But this place? It crept into my heart. The friendly hellos, the ridiculous gossip, the sense that every person here has already claimed me as one of their own.

It feels like home.

Maggie squeezes my arm gently, like she knows.

Hope's a tricky thing. It sneaks in when you aren't looking. And when you notice it—warm, familiar—you wonder if you're supposed to chase it away or invite it to stay.

I've been chasing it away. But maybe... maybe this time, I won't.

"Come on, sweetheart," she says, nodding toward the Dogwood. "Come help me make something new out of this mess."

I take a breath. And then I follow her inside.

Chapter 27
Walker

She wasn't supposed to fit in here so damn well. She wasn't supposed to laugh her way into my house, my kid's life, my bar, and my heart.

But she did.

And now, she's everywhere.

She's in my kitchen, dancing in her socked feet while she makes breakfast for everyone.

She's in my truck, singing off-key just to make Mack laugh.

She's at my bar, tossing out sarcastic remarks like she was made to be here, like she belongs.

She's on my damn porch swing at night, playing my guitar like she's always had it, like it was meant for her.

She makes everything louder, funnier, more alive.

I like her.

And not in the way I used to like people. Not in the easy, surface-level way I let people in.

I like her so much it's messing with my head.

And now, here I am, standing in the doorway of my cabin, staring at my messy, scribbled lyrics on the desk, debating whether or not to let her all the way in. Whether or not to share this part of myself—the part I don't share with anyone.

I tell myself it's not a good idea. That music isn't something I share with other people anymore. That I keep it to myself for a reason.

Because I know what happens when you mix love and music.

Because I've seen what happens when you let someone too deep into this part of you.

Because the last time I let a woman into my music, I lost everything.

I tell myself all of that. And then I think about the way Violet looked at me that night on the porch, eyes shining, fingers plucking my guitar like she was born with it in her hands. The way she said music will always be a part of her life, even if it's just for her. She gets it. She lost everything, too.

And the thought of her writing alone, singing alone, keeping it locked inside just like I do—it doesn't sit right.

I don't want her to go through what I went through. It's a lonely place to be. I head back to the house in the boat and park it and sit for a while, staring out at the cabin. I don't want her to think she has to shove her music into the shadows like I have. And maybe—maybe I don't want to anymore, either.

Footsteps behind me pull me out of my thoughts. I look up, and there she is. Violet, standing on my dock, smiling like she doesn't know she's about to undo me just by standing there, looking so beautiful.

"Hey, Walker," she teases. "Hiding out again?"

I huff out a laugh, rubbing the back of my neck. "Something like that."

Her eyes flick towards me, curiosity flickering across her face. "You know, for someone who doesn't play music anymore, you sure have a lot of instruments just lying around."

I should tell her to drop it. I should say something gruff, something to make her laugh and move on. But instead, I hear myself say it—"You want to come with me sometime?"

Violet blinks. "Yeah, I'd love to," she whispers.

And I swear I see the exact moment when she realizes what I'm asking. This isn't just about going to my cabin. My writing space. This is about stepping into something bigger.

This is about trust.

And when she smiles, soft and real, my chest tightens—because I already know.

I'm letting her in. And there's no going back.

* * *

A few days later, I get home early for once. We finish cleaning up and relax in the family room after dinner. Mack has run off to work on homework, and Maggie has retired to her room with her book. Before I can chicken out, I say, "I want to show you something, Red."

"Coming," she says and winks at me.

I close my eyes. Fuck me.

She turns and grabs her guitar and follows me out the back door. I can tell she's excited to go to the cabin, and that makes me even more nervous about what I'm about to show her.

We get down to the boat, and she laughs nervously. "I've never ridden in a boat."

I hold it steady, and she gets in and looks a little uneasy. Reaching out, I hold her hand, steadying her.

Her eyes meet mine, and she says, "This isn't the part where I find out you have a creepy clown doll collection hidden at your cabin, is it?"

I give her a look and shake my head as I tuck her guitar between us. I sit on the other side and crank the engine.

She looks up at the stars and shivers, goosebumps on her arms. "It's so beautiful out here. I can see why you guys love it here so much. This place is so special."

I look around as I steer the boat. "Yeah, it's a pretty special place."

We pull up at the dock across the water, and I tie up the boat. I help her out and grab her gear. Suddenly I'm nervous, so I take a deep breath. There's no going back now.

"So, is this like your lady lair?" she waggles her eyebrows at me. "Where you take all of your ladies and write all of your love ballads?"

"Something like that," I say, and she looks at me with surprise. I roll my eyes, "I'm kidding. I've never brought anyone out here before now. Can you keep this private?"

But I know she will. Something in me tells me that I can trust her.

She opens her mouth and shuts it again. "Now you're kinda freaking me out, Walker."

I take a deep breath and unlock the door, which is kinda funny that I lock it anyway, considering we're in the middle of nowhere, but there's a lot of expensive equipment in here, and you never know.

"Mack and I used to live here before I had the house built about ten years ago," I say as the door swings open, and I turn on the light.

She moves slowly, eyes scanning the rustic space, and I imagine what she sees as she looks at everything. The couch we opened Christmas presents on. The one where I used to sleep when Mack was still getting up all throughout the night. The old wooden dining room table covered in notebooks of scribbled lyrics. The shelves full of notebooks of melodies I never intended anyone to ever see.

Then, finally, she turns to me.

Her mouth opens. Closes. Opens again.

Then—"You're Asher freaking Wyatt."

Shit. I rub the back of my neck.

"Holy shit!"

"Technically, Asher Wyatt Walker," I mutter.

She spins around a full circle, pointing at everything in rapid-fire accusation.

"The GRAMMY?! The CMA Award?! The walls of lyrics—Walker, you wrote every single hit song on the damn radio!"

I clear my throat. "Not every song."

"Oh, I'm sorry," she says, waving wildly at my entire life. "Would you like a round of applause for being slightly humble about your secret GRAMMY-winning, chart-topping legendary career?!"

I sigh. "Violet—"

She cuts me off with a sharp gasp, her hands slamming onto a pile of notebooks. "Oh my God—did you write *If the Whiskey Could Talk?!*"

I shift on my feet and look out at the lake. "Maybe."

"Maybe? MAYBE?!" Her mouth drops open in shock. Then she stomps toward the fireplace and picks up the coveted golden gramophone, holding it up like she can't believe what's in her hand. "You know, most people put something subtle on their mantle, like a nice family photo, or even a candle, or literally anything. No, not you. You have a freaking GRAMMY!"

I exhale slowly. "You done?"

She points at me with the damn thing. "Not even close, buddy."

I swallow and nod, waiting for this to fully sink in. It's been a long time since anyone has realized who I used to be and understood the gravity of it. Hell, sometimes it still feels like a fever dream to me.

"I had sex with Asher freaking Wyatt!" She covers her mouth. "Oh my God."

I roll my eyes and exhale a deep breath. She looks like she needs a paper bag to breathe into, and she's really freaking out.

She shakes her head and looks at me, "The fuck!"

"What?" I shrug, waiting for the rest of her freak out moment to unfold.

"You let me struggle to play your songs right in front of you!" She points at the notebook where she found the song I wrote and looks at me accusingly. "You freaking wrote that song!"

I swallow nervously and nod.

"And my tattoo! It's your lyrics! You said nothing!" She starts to take deep breaths and holds her chest. She covers her face and tries to walk around me to the door.

I reach out and stick my arm out to stop her, and she whirls.

"You let me embarrass myself by playing your song in your bar. You didn't say anything!"

"For the record, you sang it beautifully," I add.

She stares at me and shakes her head slightly. "People talk about you. They think you're dead. No one has seen you. You really just up and disappeared."

I snort. "I'm sure there are a few people who wish I was dead." I walk over to the old wooden cabinet, pull out a bottle of whiskey, and pour two glasses.

Violet narrows her eyes. "What's this for?"

"Every time you freak out," I say, handing her a glass, "I pour us another drink."

She squints at me. "I'm gonna be wasted by the end of this, aren't I?"

I shrug. "Probably."

She glares. Then downs the whiskey in one go.

I pour her another.

"Asher freaking Wyatt." She shakes her head and stares at me as if she's trying to determine whether I'm real or not.

"You can quit saying that anytime now." I stare at the ceiling. "I think I'd rather go with Cowboy at this point."

"Easy for you to say, you didn't just meet your idol."

I snort. "Your idol. You were Mack's age when I ended my career."

"Yeah, and my parents were so sad. So many people mourned the loss of you. You were everywhere for a while, and then you just disappeared. And apparently, you never really ended that career. Look at you still going," she says as she waves her hand at the room containing my life's work.

"I came to Bridger Falls with a baby," I tell her as I pour more into our glasses.

"What happened to her mom?" she asks.

"She and I were married, but that's a story for another time," I say as I tip my glass back and finish it.

For the next two hours, I tell her everything. Well, almost everything. It's a lot for one night. And every time I drop another piece of my past, we drink.

"I walked away from Nashville because the industry nearly ruined my life." (One drink.)

"I still write songs and sell them under a pseudonym." (Another drink.)

"Yeah, I was supposed to be the next big thing. And yeah, I didn't want any of it." (Drink, drink.)

"Maggie's known this whole time." (Violet shakes her head and drinks twice.)

Somewhere around the time we finish the bottle, she's sitting cross-legged on the floor, flipping through one of my old notebooks, giggling to herself.

And me? I'm sitting next to her, watching how her hair falls over her shoulder, how her smile keeps lingering, and how she's completely, entirely in my world now.

She looks up, her whiskey-drunk eyes soft and teasing. "You know," she murmurs, "you're not nearly as grumpy as you pretend to be."

I huff a laugh. "Only with you, Red."

She grins, tipping her head to the side. "Oh, so you're admitting I get special treatment?"

I lift a brow. "You want me to start treating you like everyone else?"

She pretends to think. "Mmm. Nope. I like this version of Walker. Asher Walker." She smirks and shakes her head in disbelief.

Her eyes flick to my mouth. And I swear the entire world tilts. Because I'm drunk. And she's drunk. And she's looking at me like she's about to do something incredibly stupid. Which is why I should stop this.

I should be a responsible adult. I should—her fingers skim my jaw.

And just like that, I'm gone.

I close the space between us, my hand tangling in her hair as I kiss her slowly, deeply, and recklessly. She melts against me, whiskey-sweet and warm, her hands sliding into my shirt like she's needed to do this for weeks. And maybe she has. Because I know I have.

I don't know how long we sit there, tangled together, her lips pressing against mine like she's learning every damn secret I haven't told her yet.

But then—a loud thump.

We pull apart, blinking. The GRAMMY has fallen off the fireplace and onto the floor.

Violet bursts out laughing. "Wow," she gasps. "Even your trophies are trying to stop you from making bad decisions."

I shake my head, groaning.

She leans in, still grinning. "You gonna regret that kiss in the morning, Walker?"

I look at her, her eyes glassy, her lips still kiss-swollen, her laugh still lingering in the air.

And the worst part? I know I won't. Not even a little. But instead of saying that, I smirk. "Guess we'll find out."

Chapter 28
Violet

Walker's not here, yet. He dropped me off and went back to pick up some snacks and drinks we forgot. And I have to say, coming back over to his cabin has been exciting. Something about this place makes me want to write all of the songs. It's magical out here.

Which means I should probably not be snooping around in his cabin like a nosy little gremlin.

But. In my defense—

1. He left me alone in here.
2. There are literal stacks of notebooks just *sitting out in the open.*
3. He is a retired country music legend, and I am a curious woman with zero impulse control.

So, really, this is his fault. At least, that's what I tell myself when I flip open the notebook on his desk. The pages are a mess of scribbles, half-written lyrics, and notes in the margins. It's chaotic, but also weirdly beautiful. Like him.

Most of the songs are unfinished. Ideas. Rough drafts. And then I see it. One title, underlined twice:

"Red."

My heart flutters. I skim the first verse. Then the second. By the time I reach the chorus, my stomach flips over itself.

Because this song—this song is about me. The lyrics are all there. A song completely scripted out. And it's beautiful.

- The way I walked into his life unexpected.
- The way he wasn't looking for something but suddenly couldn't look away.
- The way he wants me to stay.

It's all there, in his words, scripted out beautifully in his handwriting. Like he's been writing me into his life before he even knew how to admit it.

I press my hand against the desk, trying to catch my breath. And that's exactly when he walks in.

I don't hear the door open. But I feel him.

I look up, and he's standing there, framed in the doorway, his jaw tight, his eyes locked onto the notebook in my hands.

For a second, neither of us speaks.

Then—his voice comes out, rough. "Violet."

I swallow hard. "You wrote this?"

He doesn't answer. Doesn't need to. Because the guilt is written all over his face.

I take a shaky breath. "This song—" I shake my head. "You wrote this *about us*."

His fingers flex at his sides. "Red—"

"How long?" My voice is barely above a whisper. "How long have you been feeling like this?"

His jaw ticks. But he doesn't look away. Which means I get to see the exact moment he gives up trying to hide it.

Walker exhales, slow and deep. Then, finally, finally, finally —"Since the night I picked you up on my bike."

I suck in a breath.

His voice drops lower. Rougher. "Since you walked into my bar like you already belonged there."

I clutch the notebook tighter, my heart slamming against my ribs.

"Since you started taking care of Mack like she was yours."

His gaze drops to my lips.

And suddenly, I can't breathe.

"I didn't mean to write about you, Red." His voice is like gravel, low and thick and dangerous. Then he adds, "I didn't mean to want you this much, either."

We're too close now. I don't know who moved first. Maybe him. Maybe me. Maybe we've been moving toward this for weeks.

All I know is that his hands are on me now, gripping my hips, pulling me forward, closing the last bit of space between us.

All I know is that his breath is warm against my skin, and my fingers curl into his shirt, and I want him. Not just in a fleeting, reckless way. Not just because he's Asher Wyatt, a country music legend. But because he's my Walker.

The man whose heart holds mine. The man who eats dinner with us, takes care of his family, and would do anything for the people that he loves.

And I have never wanted anyone more in my entire life. Never felt this deep for anyone. When I look at him and picture my life without him, I can't bear the ache it leaves with just even the thought.

His forehead drops to mine. "Tell me you want this, Red."

I don't hesitate. "I want you."

And then he kisses me. And holy hell, it is everything. It's slow and deep and messy, his lips sliding over mine like he's been waiting to do this for too long.

Like he's been writing songs about it. Well, he kind of has.

Like he's been trying to fight it and losing every damn time. That he has done, too.

My hands tangle in his hair, pulling him closer, drinking him in. He groans against my mouth, and the sound sends heat straight through me straight to my core. Just that sound alone can simply undo me.

I feel the edge of the counter press into my back, and I don't care.

I feel his hands gripping my waist like he's afraid to let go, and I don't care.

I want him to hold me so tight and never let me go. Because this? This is exactly what I wanted. Him and me. Nothing between us. No secrets, just us.

Walker drags his mouth from mine, breathing hard. His forehead presses against mine. "I'm scared I'll mess this up. Things are good between us," he mutters.

I let out a breathless laugh. "You already wrote a song about me, Walker. You're past that point now."

He chuckles, but it's low and dark and wrecked. His hands tighten on my waist. "If I kiss you again, I'm not stopping."

I bite my lip, my pulse racing. "Then don't stop."

His fingers flex. His resolve cracks. And then?

He kisses me again. And this time, we don't stop at all.

We waste no time on a strip tease this go 'round. It's been a long time since we first had that one-night stand at The Dogwood. This is different. This feels like forever.

We both take off everything as quickly as we can, only stopping every few moments to continue to kiss and touch each other. We can't keep our hands off each other, I want him so badly. I cup his jaw, kissing him down his neck and under his ear. He groans, and I pant with desire. God, I want him.

He reaches between my legs, and his eyes meet mine, "Damn, Red. You feel so good."

"How good?" I murmur.

"So good," he whispers in my ear as his finger works my clit. He uses his fingers, working me until I feel like I'm going to explode, and he takes me all the way there. Not stopping.

"Walker..."

"Come for me, Red. Come hard for me," he pleads because I know he wants me just as bad as I want him.

I can't even see straight, and the room spins as my body tenses and fireworks shoot through me, my body so spent when it's over. "Oh my God," I murmur, panting and leaning against him.

He picks me up, and I wrap my legs around his waist as he carries me down the hall and lays me on the bed. He gazes down at me and kisses me softly, taking his time.

"I love you, Violet," he says as he gazes into my eyes with nothing but love in his eyes.

The feeling is the most beautiful thing that I'm not sure I could even begin to describe. "I love you so much, Asher," I whisper and tip my head to his lips and kiss him.

He takes his time, playing with my breasts, sucking and blowing on my nipples until I feel like I could come again.

He finally takes his cock in his hand and reaches into the drawer and pulls out a condom, rolling it on, and why does he even make that look hot, too? I don't know how, but he does.

He takes his time at first, watching me, giving me time to adjust to him because he fills me up so good.

"Walker," I cry as he gets me almost there again. "More."

He fills me harder, faster, taking me to the brink, and then before I can help it, I'm coming and he is, too. His face is beautiful as he contorts in pure ecstasy, and buries his face into my neck, a satis-fied groan filling my ears, sending little aftershocks through me.

He lays his head next to me on the pillow and looks over at me. "How did I get so lucky, Red?"

I turn and smile at him. "Lucky? Baby, look around. You worked hard for everything you have here. There's no luck in that. You're a good man, and you deserve everything that you have."

He kisses me softly. "I guess you made me work for this."

I laugh. "You made me work for it, too. But that's what makes it worth it. You were never going to be just one night. I don't know how, but I felt that from the first night. You mean so much to me, Walker."

He smiles and says, "That night when I drove away from you, I didn't want to leave. I wanted to take you to breakfast and stay with you. I wanted to know your name and everything about you, Violet Wilson."

"I felt the same way. I was so sad when I woke up that morning and you were gone. I thought you were a dream," I admit.

Later that night, we go back to Walker's home and shower. Together. And have another round of glorious sex that I can still feel when I close my eyes. When I stretch up to kiss him and head back to my room, his fingers trail down my arm and around my hand as he pulls me into his bed with him. He shuts off his lamp and pulls me in, not saying anything, just tucking me into him, and we fall asleep that way.

Then I wake up with the sun peeking through. I've always been a morning person, and it's a habit I've gotten back into again since I've been getting up with Mack every day.

I love him.

God. The words still burn through me, leaving my chest raw

and aching, but in the best possible way. Like breathing fresh air after a lifetime of holding it in.

I've spent so long running from things like this, from feelings that dig in too deep, that threaten to stay. But now? I don't want to run. Not from him.

Because Walker just told me he loves me last night.

And I told him right back. No hesitation. No fear. No second-guessing.

And now I lie here, completely wrecked in the best possible way, my pulse still racing, my body still humming, knowing—truly knowing—that this is real. That this isn't just some fleeting, temporary thing.

That he's mine.

And I'm his.

And somehow, that doesn't scare me.

I think about all the times I tried to push this feeling away. Tried to tell myself I was imagining the way he looked at me. That the heat between us was just chemistry and nothing more. That the way he touched me—like he couldn't help himself—wasn't the beginning of something unstoppable.

I was so damn wrong. Because this? This is everything.

I glance at him now, watching him in the soft glow of the morning sun, the way his chest rises and falls, steady and sure.

The same man who once kept himself locked up so tight he barely let anyone see past the surface. The same man who just let me all the way in.

And it hits me all over again, knocking the air out of my lungs.

God, I love him. This grumpy, stubborn, beautiful man who looks at me like I hung the damn stars. Like I belong here. With him. And the wildest part?

I do, I think as I drift back off to sleep.

* * *

I wake up to the smell of bacon and the sound of Maggie humming. *Humming.* Which can only mean one thing.

She knows.

I lean over and kiss Walker softly and slide out of the bed, creeping down the hall to my bedroom and throwing on a hoodie. Shuffling into the kitchen, I brace for impact.

Maggie stands at the stove, flipping bacon and looking entirely too pleased with herself. "Mornin', sugar."

I grumble in response, pouring myself coffee.

She turns off the stove, plates the bacon, and leans against the counter, smiling like a damn fox in a henhouse. "So," she says, far too casually, "How was your night?"

I freeze mid-sip. Then I slowly lower my mug. "I still can't believe you kept that from me."

Maggie just shrugs, all innocent-like. "Walker is just a guy. Country music legend. Secret hit songwriter. Owner of *several* prestigious music awards. But to me? He's my friend. My family."

I blink and grin in disbelief. "You *knew all along.*"

She pats my arm. "Oh, sweetheart. Of course, I knew."

I gape at her. "And *when* exactly were you planning to share this information?!"

Maggie sips her coffee, completely unbothered. "Wasn't my information to share."

I drag both hands down my face. "Oh my God. I did kind of make a fool of myself."

"Oh, *honey.*" Maggie laughs. "You really thought you were just living with a *regular* guy? That Walker was just some *random* bar owner? That his broody, secretive, 'I don't talk about my past' thing wasn't *a massive red flag?*"

"I—I don't know! I thought maybe he had *trauma* or something!"

She snorts. "Well, technically, he does. *Music industry trauma.* Just like you do."

I groan into my coffee. "I feel like an idiot."

Maggie grins, entirely too delighted. "Oh, sweetheart, it's *adorable.*"

She slides into a chair across from me, resting her chin on her hands. "So... what's it like living with a *former* country music star?"

I scowl. "Exactly the same as before, except now I know his guitar collection is worth more than my *soul.*"

Maggie cackles. "Oh, don't worry, dear," she says. "We all saw this coming."

I blink. "Saw *what* coming?"

"You two," she says, gesturing vaguely. "The tension. The pining. The whole 'oh no, we're just friends, but also I look at you like I want to climb you like a tree' situation."

I choke. "Maggie!"

She winks. "I'm just saying, if I was writing this as a romance novel, you two would've *already* had a dramatic rain-soaked kiss in the middle of town."

I groan, burying my face in my arms. "I *hate* that you're enjoying this so much."

Maggie just pats my head. "Oh, sweetheart. I have never enjoyed anything more."

Chapter 29
Walker

I pull my truck into my driveway and hit the brakes.

There's a goat. Tied to my damn mailbox. With a For Sale sign hanging around its neck, the letters painted in what looks like hot pink glitter glue.

The goat—big, bearded, and pissed—lowers its head and rams the post box so hard the whole thing shakes. I sigh, put my truck in park, and climb out. The goat lifts its head and gives me a death glare.

"Son of a—MACK!" I holler toward the house. "What the hell is this?"

The front door swings open, and Mack steps onto the porch like she hasn't just pulled some unhinged small-town Craigslist stunt. I'm not even sure this is legal.

"Oh, good! You're home!" she calls. "Billy's for sale." She says this like this is the most normal conversation we've ever had.

I pinch the bridge of my nose to keep from losing it. "You can't just tie a goat to the end of the road like a yard sale lamp, Makayla Leigh."

She crosses her arms. "Why not? You always say people

impulse buy crap. I thought maybe someone would see him and think, 'Damn, I need a goat today.'"

Billy lets out a deep, guttural bleat, eyes glowing like Satan himself, and lunges at me. The rope jerks him back, but not before I dodge a solid attempt by him to the shins.

"Yeah, real sellable," I grumbled, grabbing the rope.

Mack waves a hand. "That's why he's out there! That one's a billy goat, and he's mean as hell, Dad. He's gotta go."

I stare at her. "And instead of, I don't know, asking me first, you figured you'd just slap a sign on him and park him roadside like a free couch?"

Mack shrugs. "Could've worked."

I exhale hard. "We're taking him back to the barn before someone calls the sheriff."

Mack groans but follows as I lead the goat back toward the barn, muttering about the lunatic I'm raising. Billy fights me every step of the way, pulling and bucking like an overgrown toddler who doesn't want to leave Target.

As we reach the barn, Mack huffs. "Fine. I'll try something else."

I'm already skeptical as I glance at her. "Something else like what?" I'm actually afraid to hear her answer.

Mack lifts a shoulder. "I'll take him to the bar."

I stop mid-step and turn to her slowly. "The hell you will."

She grins. "C'mon, think about it. Saturday night crowd? Drunk people make terrible decisions. I could get double what he's worth."

I press my fingers to my temple. I feel a massive headache coming on. "Mack."

"Dad."

I exhale and look up at the barn ceiling, whispering a prayer for patience. I know that I did this. I encouraged her to be independent, entrepreneurial, and problem-solving. And now, I have to own it. Plus, the goats are my fuck up.

Apparently, twenty-four damn goats are my fuck up.

Billy the Demon bleats.

I sigh.

Maybe if we put a For Sale sign on Billy at the bar, that wouldn't be such a bad idea.

* * *

It's late. The house is quiet.

Maggie's asleep. Mack's asleep. Violet should be asleep.

This is why I don't think twice when I walk out to the back porch, pick up my guitar, and start playing.

It's a habit. A ritual. Something I do when the words get too heavy in my chest. It's the perfect way to wind down.

I pick at a melody, my fingers moving on instinct. Then, before I even realize it, I'm singing. And that's when I hear it.

A sharp inhale.

I look up—and there she is.

Violet. Standing in the doorway with a blanket wrapped around her and her hair falling down around her shoulders. Watching me.

We lock eyes, and I freeze mid-verse. She just stands there, staring at me like I'm her prize.

I clear my throat. "How long have you been standing there, Red?"

She swallows. "Long enough."

Shit.

She takes a slow step outside, eyes still locked on me. Then another. And another until she stands right in front of me, close enough that I can smell the vanilla and coconut in her shampoo.

I set my guitar down, suddenly feeling exposed in a way I

haven't in years, even when I showed Violet the cabin. Singing and playing for an audience is a piece of my soul I never thought I'd share with anyone ever again.

"You sound..." She shakes her head, almost disbelieving. "Holy shit, Walker."

I grunt, crossing my arms. "It's just a song."

She lets out a breathless laugh. "It's not just a song."

I narrow my eyes. "If you start fangirling, I'm out."

She grins. "Oh, I'm definitely fangirling."

The way she looks at me right now makes my heart hitch, skip a damn beat, do funny shit. I shake my head, leaning back against the couch. "Violet. What am I gonna do with that mouth?"

"Fuck it," she says, dropping onto the armrest beside me.

I love her smartass mouth. And the images that flood my brain are all I can think about. I try to push them aside, but they're there now, thanks to her. I chuckle. "I mean it."

She grins so widely it should be illegal. "You, sir, have been holding out on me. Now I want all the private performances that I can get."

She grins at me as if she's not just talking about music. Fuck. Me.

I groan and tease. "I knew this was a mistake."

She smirks. "A very sexy mistake."

I tilt my head, unamused.

She hums, mock-serious. "I feel betrayed, honestly."

I groan again.

She pokes my knee. "You sound like sin wrapped in whiskey."

I rub my face. "You are so damn dramatic."

She shrugs. "Sorry, I just—" She shakes her head, looking at me with something new in her eyes. "I can't believe I live with you, and you've been hiding this."

I exhale through my nose. "I wasn't hiding it."

She raises an eyebrow.

I sigh. "Okay, fine, I was hiding it."

Her grin gets wider. "So, you admit it?"

I narrow my eyes. "I am this close to throwing you into the lake."

She ignores me, grabbing my guitar off the couch. "Play me another one."

I blink. "Absolutely not."

"Come on, Asher." She wiggles the guitar at me. "One more song."

And fuck me, if I don't love her saying my name. No one ever calls me that. But hearing it come from her...it just does things to me.

She doesn't back down. And before I know it? I'm strumming. And she's watching me.

I'm singing for her. And this time, I don't stop. I don't know how long we sit there.

I just know something has changed. The woman I've fallen completely head over heels for holds my heart in the palm of her hands. I couldn't stop and wouldn't stop even if I could. I'd do anything for this woman.

Because when the song ends, and the last note fades between us, she's still staring.

And this time, it's not funny. It's not teasing. It's real.

Her voice drops, quiet, soft in a way I don't think I've ever heard before. "That was beautiful, Asher."

Something in my chest tightens. I swallow, fingers flexing over the guitar strings. "Thank you."

She shakes her head. "You're beautiful. Everything about you. Your heart, your soul, and your music. It's all so beautiful."

And damn it, I think she might actually see me. The real

me. The one I've been hiding. The one I've kept locked up for way too long.

I shift, exhaling hard. "Don't make it a big thing."

She smiles, but it's softer this time. "Asher," she murmurs, voice like a promise. "It already is."

She makes me play three more songs. Demands. And I do it because I'd do anything for her. And I love singing to her. There's something so beautiful and intimate about singing to someone you're in love with. I didn't realize that until now.

I grouch about it the whole time.

She ignores me.

And when I finally walk her to her room, she looks up at me, and grins.

"G'night, rockstar."

I roll my eyes. "I hate you."

She laughs. "No, you don't. You love me."

She's right. I really, really do. I tried not to, I really did. But I love her.

She turns to go, but I don't let her. I don't even think, I just wrap my hand around her wrist, tugging her back, and before she can say another smart remark, I press her against the wall, my body crowding hers, my hands braced beside her head.

Her breath hitches, her eyes go wide.

I tip my head down, my mouth so close to hers that I can feel her breath. "You love me too, huh?" I say in a rough voice, teasing her.

She licks her lips, and says, "Maybe."

I kiss her. Not softly, not careful.

Desperately. Like she's the last drink I'll ever have. The last moment that I'll ever capture. And hell, does she kiss me back. She feels so good and tastes even better.

This time, she's all mine.

* * *

I do not like being woken up at two in the damn morning. Especially not by the sound of my fifteen-year-old daughter pounding on my bedroom door like she's got a warrant to serve.

"Dad! Get up! Emergency!"

I groan, barely cracking an eye open. "Unless the house is on fire, go back to bed."

"It's worse."

I scrub a hand down my face. "If this is about a goat—"

"Oh, it's absolutely about a goat."

Five minutes later, I'm outside, shirt in my hand, boots half-laced, freezing my ass off as I trudge toward the barn, deeply regretting every decision that led me to this moment.

Violet, who should be asleep like a normal person—already stands by the barn door, wrapped up in one of those big, cozy sweaters that make her look soft and comfortable. Too comfortable, considering I'm out here suffering.

"What the hell are you doing here, Red?" I grumble, shoving on my flannel but not bothering to button it.

"Mack woke me up," Violet says, smirking. "Figured it had to be good."

"Oh, it's great," Mack announces, throwing the barn doors open. "Because, surprise! Dot had her babies."

I step inside and exhale hard, still half asleep. "Who is Dot?"

There's Dot, my supposedly-not-pregnant goat, standing over two tiny, shivering babies. Two more goats to the collection. But damn, if they're not cute.

Violet lets out a soft gasp. "Oh, they're adorable."

"They're a damn inconvenience," I mutter.

Mack grins. "You say that now but wait till you name them."

"I am not naming them."

"You totally are," she says smugly. "It's part of the process."

I groan and survey the barn. "They're freezing. We need to warm them up."

Violet is already moving, crouching beside the babies with a towel. "On it."

I reach for the smallest one at the same time as she does, and of course my hand lands directly on hers. Warm. Soft. I freeze. So does she. Neither of us pulls away. We just sit there, holding hands over a goat like absolute idiots.

Then Mack makes it worse. "Oh my God," she says, way too loudly. "Are you guys holding hands over a goat right now?"

I jerk my hand back so fast I nearly fall over. "No."

Violet smirks. "Technically, yes."

"Oh my God," Mack cackles. "That's so gross. Are you gonna, like, gaze into each other's eyes and talk about your feelings?"

I glare at her. "Mack—"

"Or maybe you should just kiss right now and get it over with."

Violet chuckles, standing up and tossing a towel at my chest. "Tempting."

I catch it, scowling. "You're not helping."

"Not trying to."

Mack grins like a damn hyena. "Oh, this is the best night of my life."

I exhale hard and start rubbing down the baby goat, ignoring the way my neck feels too damn warm. "I'm basically a goat farmer now, aren't I?"

Violet pats my shoulder. "You did this to yourself, big guy."

I groan and look up at the ceiling, praying for patience. Then I look at Mack, who smirks like she absolutely enjoys this way too much.

And they're right. I did this to myself. But I love it, and I love them. I love every adventure with them.

* * *

I slap the sign onto the bulletin board at the bar and step back to admire my work.

GOATS FOR SALE–CHEAP.

Healthy. Mostly friendly. Some have anger issues.

Buy one, get a second one free (you won't regret it, but I will).

See Walker before he loses his mind.

I rub my eyes and yawn so hard my jaw cracks. It's been three days since Dot decided to drop a surprise litter, and between dealing with newborn goats, my actual ranch work, and Mack trying to sneak one into the house because "it looked cold," I haven't slept more than a handful of hours.

Cash whistles behind me. "Heard you're a goat farmer now."

I turn to face him, squinting. "Heard you're a bar manager now."

He smirks. "Yeah, but I picked that career on purpose. Can't say the same for you from what I've heard."

I groan and drop onto the nearest barstool, yawning again. "Look, man, I just need a few suckers—uh, fine upstanding citizens—to take some of these goats off my hands before Mack gets even more attached and then they're part of the family."

Cash leans against the bar, arms crossed, grinning like an idiot. "How many we talkin'?"

"Twenty-four. Actually, twenty-six now."

His grin disappears. "Jesus, Walker. You running a damn petting zoo?"

"Not by choice," I mutter. "One minute, I had a few goats. Next thing I know, they're multiplying."

Cash chuckles and shakes his head. "You puttin' 'em on a payment plan? Or is this a take-a-goat, don't-look-back kinda deal?"

"Cash, I will straight-up put a goat in your truck right now for free."

"Tempting, but no." He holds up his hands and laughs.

I wave a tired hand at the bar regulars. "Fine. Someone here wants a goat. I know it."

I turn toward the first man I see Bobby Ray, who's halfway through his second beer. "Hey, Bobby. You ever wanted a goat?"

Bobby Ray scratches his beard. "Hmm. Do they eat weeds?"

"Absolutely," I lie. I think they do, but I'm not entirely sure. I mean, they ate all my flowers. But no way am I telling him that.

He nods, considering. "Do they eat cans?"

I blink. "What?"

"Like in cartoons. Have you ever seen that? A goat just gnawin' on a tin can?"

I sigh. "Bobby, if you take two goats, I will personally test-feed them a damn soup can and report back."

He nods slowly. "Alright. Put me down for two."

Two down. Twenty-four to go. I'm back at square one.

I turn to Jolene, who's shaking her head before I even say anything. "No," she says firmly.

"You don't even know what I was gonna ask."

She narrows her eyes. "You were gonna ask if I want a goat."

"...Okay, but what if I wasn't?"

She smirks. "Were you?"

I groan. "Just take a damn goat, Jolene."

"Pass."

"Cash will give you free beer for a week."

Cash looks up. "No, I won't."

I glare at him. "Not helping."

He grins. "Not trying to."

I move down the bar and lock eyes with Earl, an old rancher who hasn't said a word since I walked in.

"Earl," I say, using my most serious rancher voice. "You need a goat."

Earl squints at me. "The hell I do."

"Earl," I say again, slower this time. "You need a goat."

"...Do I?"

I nod.

He sighs. "Fine. One."

"Two," I correct. "It's a bogo thing."

Earl grumbles but holds up two fingers. "Fine."

Two more down. I drag a hand down my face, exhausted. "Anyone else?"

Silence.

Then, from the corner booth, a cowboy I don't even know raises a hand. "You got any of them fainting goats?"

I squint at him. "Why?"

He grins. "They're funny as hell."

I have no idea if any of my goats faint, but at this point, I'll say whatever it takes. "Sure do."

"Hot damn. I'll take three."

I slap the bar in triumph. "Hell yes, that's the spirit. Now they're bogo, so that means you get four."

Cash shakes his head. "You're a mess."

"I'm a desperate man." I yawn again, stretching. "Now, if y'all excuse me, I'm gonna head home before Mack tries to get these goats registered as emotional support animals."

Cash chuckles as I stand up. "Good luck with that, Goat King."

I glare at him. "I hate you."

He grins. "No, you don't."

I sigh. "Yeah, whatever."

Then I walk out of the bar, several goats lighter, and pray to God that by this time next week, I won't still be drowning in them.

Chapter 30
Violet

I've never seen Cami nervous. At all. She's one of the strongest and most confident women I know. Nervous? Never.

She's not even frazzled when she's running her coffee trailer in the middle of a morning rush. Not when she's elbow-deep in a fight with a local town employee about parking permits for her trailer.

She doesn't ask for help. She is quick to help everyone else and makes things happen. So, when Cami walks into Murphy's Auto, finds me leaning against Poppy's workbench, and says, "I need help," my entire world tilts.

Because her voice is quiet, and there's something raw in her eyes. And because she looks scared.

I set my coffee down slowly and move closer to her. "What's wrong?"

Cami exhales hard, crossing her arms. "You know how I *never* ask for anything?"

Poppy, sitting nearby with her feet kicked up on an over-turned bucket, snorts. "Oh, this should be good."

Cami gives her a vulnerable look. "Not now, Pops."

Poppy holds up her hands in surrender. "I'm just saying, this is a *historic moment*."

Cami doesn't take the bait. Instead, she looks at both of us, jaw tight, shoulders stiff, like she's holding herself together with sheer willpower. "I'm gonna lose my family's ranch," she says.

My stomach drops. "What?"

She swallows hard. "My mom's given up and has moved to town. Ollie's given up and apparently lives upstairs above your shop. The bank gave us an extension, but we need money. *Fast*."

"What can we do to help?" Poppy demands. "We'll do whatever it takes."

I reach out, grabbing her arm. "Cami..."

She shakes her head and stares at us with desperation and turmoil etched on her face. "I can't lose it. It's all I have left. I have to fight."

I nod, my chest tightening. "Okay. What can we do?"

She takes a slow breath. "The county fair has agreed to let me do a fundraiser concert at the fair."

"Oh!" I say, relieved. "That's great! The whole town loves stuff like that. You'll raise a ton of money."

Cami nods once. "Yeah. But... I need you to perform."

I freeze. Then blink. Then laugh. "Wait, what?"

Cami's face is stone cold, serious.

"I haven't performed in a really long time," I say, shaking my head. "Not since..." My stomach turns. "Not since Nashville."

"I know," she says. "But I really need you. Remember the part where I said I never ask for help?"

I open my mouth, then shut it. Panic climbs up my throat. She's right. She needs me. But my heart is in my throat right now. Panic fills me just thinking about what she's asking me to do.

Perform? On stage? With people watching?

I can't. I can barely perform for the horses when no one's looking.

Cami watches me, reading my hesitation. "Please. You did karaoke at the bar."

I look at Poppy, who is very much not getting involved but taking all this in. Rubbing my hands over my arms, I cradle them to me. "I'll think about it."

There's a big difference in singing with friends at the bar and doing an actual performance at the bar. I sang covers and other people's songs there. But a performance is more raw, vulnerable, and especially triggering since I left Nashville with my tail tucked between my legs about performing.

Cami nods. But I can tell—this means everything to her. I have to do it.

* * *

Later that night, I sit on the porch, watching Walker build a goat house because, apparently, that's just a normal part of our life now.

And I have to say that the whole rugged cowboy, tool-wielding thing should be illegal. Damn, he looks good. Too good. Like distractingly good.

The kind of good where you can't even begin to focus on anything else when he stands there without a shirt on, his forearms flexing as he grips the tool, sweat sliding down his chest. His Wranglers shape to him every time he bends to grab another plank of wood.

He looks up, sweat on his brow, eyebrows raised. "You gonna keep staring, or are you gonna tell me what's on your mind?"

I roll my eyes. "What makes you think something is on my mind?"

He smirks, tossing a piece of wood aside. "I can tell."

I take a deep breath. "Cami wants me to perform at a fundraiser concert to raise money for her ranch."

He pauses and watches me. "And?"

"I told her I'd think about it."

He nods and sets his hammer down, wiping his hands on his jeans. "If you don't want to do it, don't do it."

"I *do* want to help her," I say quickly. "I just... I don't know if I can."

He tilts his head and asks softly. "What are you afraid of, Red?"

I look down, fingers twisting together. "Remember when I told you that my ex-best friend tried to sabotage me? How she spread lies about me all over Nashville and got me dropped from my label? Well, now..." I exhale, shaking my head. "Now I can't even sing in public without feeling like I'm gonna choke."

"I remember," he says, looking pissed all over again on my behalf. It's the same look he had the night I told him all about it.

I swallow, the hurt still raw. "I'm finished in Nashville, Walker." I tell him, humiliation creeping in all over again and making me feel sick to my stomach.

The memories of the social media posts and how nasty people were to me, completely oblivious to the truth. To the fact that the whole story was actually the other way around.

"Whoever she is, she's a horrible person. You didn't deserve that," he says as he glares at the goat house and shakes his head.

I nod, agreeing, "She sucks."

Walker watches me for a long moment. Then, carefully, he says, "What if you did a practice concert at The Black Dog?"

I blink. "Like... what do you mean, practice?"

He tilts his head. "Just family, friends, a few regulars. Get comfortable on a stage again. Work through the nerves. You're a performer, Red. You've got this. You can do this. And whoever that woman was back in Nashville, she can't touch you here in Bridger Falls. You're one of us now."

I chew my lip. "And what if it's a disaster?"

He shrugs. "Then, at least you'll know before you step onto a county fair stage."

I stare at him, my pulse uneven. Then, I ask him softly, "Would you help me practice and get over my fears?"

His jaw ticks. His eyes darken. "You want me to help you?" His voice is low, rough.

I nod.

For a second, he doesn't say anything. Then his lips twitch. "I'll help you," he murmurs. "But only if you promise me that you won't let this horrible person ruin your career. You don't want some of the regrets that I have."

"You have regrets, Asher?" I ask softly.

He nods, "I do. I left like you did and never got to see how far I could have taken my career. Yeah, I did good here, and I have a good life. But I backed down to the bullies. What if you didn't? What if I helped you?"

"I might need a paper bag to breathe into," I admit. "This is *a lot.*"

He smirks, leaning against the railing, watching me. "You're gonna be fine, Red."

Something in his voice settles me.

Maybe I really can do this. Maybe I can face my fear. And maybe... just maybe...

Having Walker by my side makes it feel a little less terrifying.

* * *

I shouldn't be this turned on over a damn guitar lesson.

And yet, here I am.

Sitting this close to Walker in his cabin, hands grazing, bodies angled toward each other like we're about to do something much filthier than write a song. I wish we were, honestly.

He strums, slow and easy, watching me like he's daring me to break first.

I probably will. Because holy shit, this man is *hot*.

"I don't know what songs to play," I admit, shifting on the couch.

Walker lifts an eyebrow. "What do you mean?"

I exhale, frustrated. "Well, I had a brand-new album ready. So many songs. And they're *gone* now. Well, technically they're out in the world. But they aren't mine anymore. They're stolen."

His eyes darken as he hears me.

I let out a dry laugh. "I guess I could just sing covers."

Walker shakes his head. "Nah. That's not you."

I scoff and tease him. "Oh, and *you* know what's me?"

His eyes flick to mine, unreadable. "I have a few you could sing," he murmurs.

I blink. "What?"

He shrugs, setting his guitar aside. "Songs I've written. Stuff I never sold. Just sitting in my notebooks, gathering dust."

I swallow hard. "You'd let me sing one of your songs?"

Walker tilts his head. "Or we could write one together."

I stare at him, heart hammering. "You—you'd write a song with me?"

Walker smirks. "You sound surprised."

I am. Because this is his world. This is the part of himself he's kept locked away from everyone. And now he's just... offering it to me?

And I'm no dummy, I'm going to take it. I'm going to learn from the *best*. I know what he's offering me here, and it's a once in a lifetime chance to learn songwriting and performing from a legend. But doing all of this with the man I love? That feels pretty damn great, too.

Not even sure how I got this lucky. It's not that he's Asher Wyatt Walker, country superstar. It's also that he's the most incredible human being, and he's mine. Writing a song together feels more intimate than sex somehow.

I lick my lips, nodding. "Okay."

He picks his guitar back up, strumming something slow and sultry, something that curls heat low in my stomach.

I close my eyes, letting the rhythm settle. Letting the words come. And then, softly, I start to hum. Walker stills, watching me. The moment stretches, thick and charged.

Then, quietly, he starts playing along.

My breath catches. Because it fits. It's natural, easy, like we've been doing this forever.

I tilt my head, eyes locked on his hands. The way his fingers move over the strings, the easy confidence in his touch. The way he's looking at me now, like he's playing just for me.

And suddenly, writing a song doesn't feel like just writing a song.

It feels like undressing. Like laying every part of yourself bare. And Walker is letting me see him. I shift closer, our knees touching. He doesn't move away.

His voice is low, raspy. "Any lyrics come to you, yet?"

I bite my lip. "Something's coming."

He smirks. "Good."

I start singing, soft, hesitant at first.

And Walker? He watches like I'm the only thing in the world.

I feel his eyes on my mouth. The way he leans a little closer every time I hit a note just right. The way he lets his fingers brush against mine if we accidentally touch. My whole body tightens.

This is more than music now.

I strum, mimicking his rhythm, our hands moving in tandem. Walker watches, expression dark and unreadable. Then, he sings too. And holy hell. His voice knocks the air right out of my lungs.

It's rough, low and deep, a little gravelly, and stupidly, unfairly hot.

I forget my own lyrics. Forget how to function as a human being. Because Walker singing right next to me is a full-body experience. And right now?

I want him in every damn way possible. This is the hottest foreplay I've ever experienced.

We hit the last note, the sound lingering thick between us. I'm breathless. Walker hasn't moved.

We're too close now. His fingers skim my wrist. I swear, my pulse stutters and I suck in my breath. He looks at me like he's thinking about kissing me. And damn I want him to kiss me so badly. I lean in, and before I know it, I'm kissing him. And he kisses me back, and I never want to stop.

But before I can do something irresponsible, like climb him like a tree, he shifts back, exhaling hard.

I blink. Walker clears his throat. "That was good."

I nod, still dizzy. "Yeah."

Silence. Then, a smirk.

"You wanna write some more?"

I groan, dropping my head into my hands. "Walker."

He chuckles.

And me? I know I'm in way too deep. Walker is still watching me. The cabin is too quiet, the air too thick, my body too wired. We just wrote a song together—or maybe we just undressed each other with lyrics and guitars and long, lingering stares—and I do not know how to come back from that.

I need a second. Or several.

But of course, the universe has other plans.

Because just as Walker shifts, his eyes still dark, still unreadable, his phone buzzes loudly between us.

We both startle. Then we stare at it like it personally dragged us back to Earth from whatever dangerous, gravity-defying moment we were having.

Walker sighs, rubbing a hand down his face before grabbing the phone. "Yeah?"

A pause. Then—he groans. "What the heck, Mack."

He puts her on speaker, and I bite back a smile at the sound of his daughter's voice, dead serious, no-nonsense. "We have a crisis."

Walker pinches the bridge of his nose. "That so?"

"Yeah," Mack huffs. "We're out of syrup."

I snort.

Walker glares at me before turning his attention back to the phone. "That's your crisis? Syrup?"

Mack sighs, dramatic as hell. "Dad. It's waffle night."

Walker mutters something under his breath before responding, "There's some in the pantry."

"Nope. Maggie used the last of it for something *probably delicious*, and now we're all gonna starve."

I laugh, still feeling drunk on whatever just happened between Walker and me.

Walker shoots me a look. "You think this is funny?"

"Yes," I say immediately.

Mack perks up. "Is Violet there?"

Walker sighs. "Yeah."

"Put me on video!"

Walker grumbles something unintelligible, then reluctantly switches the call to FaceTime. Mack's face pops up, eyes narrowed. "You're laughing, *Red*."

"I mean," I tease, flashing her a grin, "syrup is a serious matter."

Mack nods gravely. "Thank you."

Walker just shakes his head, muttering.

"So, Dad?" Mack presses. "Are you going to the store, or am I making a public plea for assistance on Facebook? Hey, maybe I could trade some syrup for a goat or two."

Walker stares at her. "Are you bartering our goats now?"

Mack shrugs. "I mean, I could do a swapsie."

I lose it and snort laugh.

Walker sighs, defeated. "Fine. We'll go grab syrup. Ask Maggie what else she needs."

Mack grins, triumphant. "Cool. See you soon. Love you, Dad. Love you, Violet."

I freeze. Walker does too.

Mack immediately panics. "I mean, like, in a *cool* way. Not in a 'you're my new stepmom' way. Forget I said it. Never mind. Bye." And then she hangs up.

Walker stares at the phone.

I stare at Walker.

Silence. Then I burst out laughing.

"Oh my God." I gasp between laughs. "Your *kid* just dropped the 'L' word."

Walker groans. "That kid."

I lean against him, still giggling, still lightheaded from everything. "Well, come on. We have a syrup crisis to solve."

Walker shakes his head, muttering, but I catch the ghost of a smile on his lips.

And just like that, we're back to real life. But my skin still tingles where he touched me. And the way he's looking at me tells me we're not done yet. Not by a long shot.

We're just getting started, and I love it.

Chapter 31
Walker

Violet hums the melody under her breath, tapping her fingers against the body of her guitar. She's been sitting across from me on the couch in the cabin for the past hour, looking unfairly gorgeous in my old green and black flannel and a pair of leggings, her hair piled up in one of those messy buns that makes my hands itch to pull it loose.

We're supposed to be writing a song. But hell, how am I supposed to focus when she looks so beautiful in my space, wearing another one of my damn shirts?

I strum a chord, watching her. "What if we take the second verse up a notch?"

She tilts her head. "You mean make it sadder? Or sexier?"

I swallow hard. "I was thinking...both?" Big mistake. Now I can't stop thinking about her voice, low and breathy, about how damn thing she says sounds like it was made to wreck me.

Her lips curve. "Bold choice, Asher."

I love it when she says my name.

She jots something down in her notebook, biting the end of the pen. I watch her mouth, completely losing my train of thought.

She lifts an eyebrow. "You got something, or are you just staring at me?"

Busted. I clear my throat and lean forward, resting my forearms on my knees. "Maybe something about knowing you shouldn't love someone, but you do anyway. Like, 'I know this isn't supposed to happen, but I'd still burn it down for you.'"

The second I sing it, I know. It's not just a song. It's the truth. She's fire, and I'm the fool who'd burn the world down for her.

Her breath hitches. She blinks at me, something unreadable flickering in her emerald-green eyes. "That's..." She swallows, her voice softer now. "That's good."

We sit there for a second, the air thick. I don't know if it's the late hour or the low glow of the fire, but suddenly, the space between us feels way too small.

She licks her lips. "Sing it."

I grab my guitar, strum the opening chords, and let the words roll out low and rough.

"I know this isn't safe, but I'd still cross that fire for you...

One step, one touch, and I'm burned right through..."

When I look up, her expression is unreadable. But her eyes are locked on mine, deep and wanting.

Screw it.

I set the guitar aside, reach for her, and pull her into my lap. She gasps, but it's swallowed when my mouth covers hers.

The kiss is slow at first, hesitant, like maybe she's still testing the waters. But then she fists her hands in my shirt and presses closer, and every rational thought I have flies straight out the window.

I used to be worried about everything. But now I'm not. I don't care about the risks, the lines we swore we wouldn't cross. All I care about is how good she feels and how right this feels. For once, something feels right, and I love it.

Her taste is like wild honey and temptation, her breath warm as she sighs against me. I slide a hand into her hair, letting it free, running my fingers through it, tilting her head to deepen the kiss. She melts into me, soft and perfect, and I know there's no going back.

She is the kind of woman that ruins a man for anyone else. And I think I was already ruined since our first night together.

This isn't a maybe for me. This isn't a mistake.

This is everything I didn't know I needed.

* * *

Sunlight filters through the curtains, spilling golden light across the room.

Violet's still asleep, curled up against my side with one arm draped over my stomach. Her hair is a mess, her lips are a little swollen from last night, and I swear, I've never seen anything prettier.

I could wake up like this for the rest of my life. And the worst part? I don't even feel panicked by that thought. It just feels...right.

I run my fingers down her back, watching her breathe.

But all I can think is, God, I love her. I can't imagine myself not being able to love her.

I should be scared. This should freak me out. But it doesn't. Not anymore. Not even a little. And then, like it comes out of nowhere, another thought hits me.

I don't just love her. I want to build something with her. Not just a life. But something real and that matters.

Something like a record label.

I've spent years avoiding the music industry because I hated how it chewed artists up and spit them out. But maybe that's the problem. Maybe the only way to change it is to step in and build something better. Be a safe place for artists who can create in peace and not be taken advantage of.

The idea clicks into place so fast that I almost laugh. It's like it's been there all along.

I'm sick of labels like Royce Records screwing over artists. Sick of watching people like Violet get stolen from and cheated. Artists deserve to be treated fairly.

What if I built something better? Something independent, something fair?

Violet stirs, her fingers curling against my chest. She lets out a sleepy little sound and blinks up at me. "Why are you awake? Stop thinking so loud."

I grin. "I've got an idea."

She groans, burying her face against my shoulder. "No ideas this early."

"Oh, I think you'll like this one." I trail my fingers down her spine, and she shivers. "What if I started my own record label?"

She lifts her head, eyes still heavy with sleep. "Wait. What?"

"Red, I'm serious. I want to do this." I shift to face her. "I know music. I know the business. And I know I'm sick of watching talented artists get screwed over."

She blinks. "You're serious."

"Dead serious." I brush her hair back. "What do you think?"

She studies me for a long moment, then leans in and kisses me soft, slow, and deep. Pulling back, she whispers, "Okay, I take it back. I love your early morning ideas."

And just like that, I know this is a good idea. This is going to change everything.

I haven't been this keyed up in a long time. I'm so excited about all of this. My mind whirls and buzzes with energy. I don't want to sit around and wait on this. I know exactly who I can talk to more about this.

Will picks up on the second ring.

"You got five minutes, Walker," he says. "I'm about to walk into a meeting with Royce Records where I have to pretend to be nice, smile like I don't want to strangle someone, and resist the urge to flip a table."

I smirk. "I'll make it quick. I'm starting my own label."

Dead silence. Then, "I'm sorry, what?"

"You heard me. I'm done watching Royce screw people over. I want something better. Something fair."

I expect him to call me crazy. Hell, I half expect myself to call me crazy. But the second I say it out loud, it clicks. This isn't just an idea. It's a damn good one.

Will exhales. "Well, shit. I can't even make fun of you because that's a damn good idea."

"You can still make fun of me. I know you want to."

"Oh, I will. Later." He pauses. "How's Rip Heeler doing?"

I grin. "He's living the dream, chasing goats. Thanks again for that, Maren."

"Alright, so remember when I asked you for a favor for that?" he says.

"Yes," I say hesitantly.

"What if I kick this meeting, and we sign my artist to your future label? Sure would like to deal with you and not Royce ever again."

I grip the back of my neck. "That's exactly why I want to do this."

Will hums. "And this has nothing to do with the fact that you're madly in love with Violet Wilson?"

I scowl. "That's..."

He sounds amused as hell. "Because last time I checked, you were a grumpy bastard, and now you're out here playing 'Love Me Tender' on your guitar like a damn fool."

I sigh. "Are you done?"

Will laughs. "Oh, I'm not even close to being done. But just know that the next time we talk, I'm bringing popcorn to watch you trip all over yourself for this woman."

I should deny it. I should roll my eyes. But instead, I just smirk and say, "I already fell, Maren."

And I don't want to get back up. I'm a goner for Violet Wilson.

* * *

Violet paces back and forth like a caged animal, mumbling song lyrics under her breath while clutching her guitar like it might strangle her if she lets go.

We're only a week out from the county fair, and tomorrow night is her practice run at the Black Dog. But with every passing hour, her nerves grow.

I lean back against the couch, arms crossed, watching her and wondering when she'll wear herself out.

She's doing that thing again, winding herself up until she's ready to combust. And damn, if it isn't kind of adorable. She chews on her bottom lip and mutters under her breath like she's trying to bargain with the universe. I should let her burn off some of this nervous energy, but if I don't step in, she's liable to wear a hole through my damn floor.

"Red."

No response.

"Violet."

Still nothing. She's muttering to herself now, something about forgetting chords and making a fool of herself.

I sigh. "Baby."

That gets her attention. She stops mid-pace, whipping her head toward me at the new endearment. "What?"

I nod toward the chair in front of me. "Sit."

"I can't sit! I have to do something. I—"

"Sit, or I'm carrying you over here."

Her eyes narrow. "You wouldn't dare."

I arch a brow. "You wanna test me?"

She mutters something about bossy cowboys but plops down in the chair, gripping the guitar like it's a damn life raft.

I kneel in front of her, resting my forearms on her thighs. "You nervous?"

She lets out a sharp laugh. "No, I just love sweating through my shirt for fun."

"It's not a good look on you, anyway. Maybe take it off," I tease.

She groans, dropping her head back. "Walker, I'm being serious. What if I mess up? What if I completely bomb? Cami is counting on me. I am *not* ready. I just keep hearing the voices telling me I shouldn't do this anymore."

I reach out, plucking the guitar from her lap and resting it against mine. My fingers instinctively find the strings, a soft chord ringing out as I strum. It's automatic and easy like breathing.

It always comes back to this. The weight of a guitar in my hands, the feel of the strings against my fingers. No matter how much I try to bury the musician in me, it never left. And right now, I feel like that part of me is waking up again, but not for me. For her. For Red. And for future artists.

"You're not gonna bomb," I say, nodding for her to watch my hands. "You just need to trust yourself. And the music."

She huffs. "That's easy for you to say. You've done this a million times."

I shrug. "And you think I never got nervous?"

She hesitates. "Did you?"

"All the damn time." I pluck a simple melody, letting the sound settle between us. "But here's the trick. Half of performing is looking like you belong there, even when you're freaking out inside. You have to practice putting on your poker face. Sometimes every damn time."

She watches my fingers as I play, her bottom lip tucked between her teeth.

I pause and lean forward. "Look at me, baby."

She does. Her eyes are still laced with worry, but there's something else there, too.

God, those green eyes. I could drown in them if I let myself. And the worst part? I don't think I'd fight it.

"You know this song like the back of your hand," I say. "So, when you step up there, don't think about everything that could go wrong. Just feel the music. Let your body move with it, keep your breath steady, and if you get lost, just come back to the rhythm. It'll be there for you."

She swallows. "And where do I look?"

I smirk. "Depends. If you wanna make 'em swoon, pick someone in the crowd and sing like you're telling just them a secret."

Her brows lift, and she grins. "I guess I could do that."

"It works." I grin. "If you're nervous, pick a point above their heads. No one knows the difference."

She nods slowly, rolling the advice over in her mind. Then she leans forward slightly. "And what about staying in tune?"

I can't help it; I laugh. "Red, if you go off-key, just take a breath, regroup, and jump back in. No one's gonna throw tomatoes at you... probably."

She gasps. "A new worry unlocked!"

I grin. "You'll do great."

She shoves my shoulder, but she's smiling now, the tension finally breaking. I reach for her hand, sliding my fingers between hers, playing with them absently.

She watches me, eyes tracing over my face. "You miss this, don't you?"

The question catches me off guard. I pause, running my thumb over her knuckles. "I don't miss performing and being in the spotlight." I glance down at my hands and how they rest so easily on the guitar. "I think those days might be over for me."

She frowns. "But?"

I take a breath, letting the truth settle before I say it. "But I'm really excited about the label." I look back at her. "Helping artists. Giving people a chance without having to sell their souls to the industry. That feels right."

And maybe, just maybe, I'm starting to believe I can build something real. Something worth holding onto. Just like her.

Something shifts in her expression. She squeezes my hand. "You're gonna change a lot of lives, Walker."

I let out a breathless laugh. "I hope so."

Her lips part slightly, like she's not sure if she should kiss me or shove me for getting too deep. So I make the decision for her.

I set the guitar aside, reach up, and pull her down into my lap. She gasps as she lands against my chest, straddling me, her hands instinctively landing on my shoulders. I smirk up at her. "Better?"

She breathes out a laugh. "You are so—"

Whatever insult she had on her lips leaves when I thread my fingers into her hair and kiss her. Hell, I should've done this sooner. Maybe then I wouldn't have spent so long fighting this with her. Because this kiss is everything.

She melts into me immediately, hands curling into my shirt, pressing closer like she can't help herself. Her lips are warm and soft, and when she sighs against my mouth, I deepen the kiss, tilting her head to claim more of her.

Her fingers slide into my hair, tugging just enough to make my pulse slam.

I groan against her lips. "You keep doing that, and I'm not gonna be responsible for what happens next."

She grins, challenging me. "Oh? What's going to happen?"

I grip her hips and flip her onto the couch, pinning her beneath me before she can blink. She gasps, and my grin is slow and wicked.

"You were saying?"

Her breath catches. She tilts her chin up, eyes locked on mine, daring me to kiss her again.

So I do.

If I was lost before, I'm completely gone now. This is it. This is her. And no way in hell am I letting go.

Chapter 32
Violet

I am going to be sick.

Like, full-on, knees-shaking, stomach-clenching, might-pass-out-on-stage sick.

The Black Dog is packed. People crowd around tables and line up around the bar, waiting for the music to start. The warm glow of string lights casts a golden hue over everything, making the whole place feel too intimate, too real.

So much for it just being close family and friends. Word travels fast, and the whole town must be here.

I wipe my sweaty palms on my dress and grip the neck of my guitar like it's the only thing keeping me upright. Well, because it is. I'm holding onto it like it's my lifeline at this point.

I've done this before. I've performed in bars, small concerts, and venues where I didn't know a single face in the crowd. And back then? That was easier. Because those people? They were just strangers. They'd listen, maybe clap, maybe forget me the second they walked out the door. But these people?

I scan the crowd and feel my stomach tighten.

These people, I love. And what they think? It's all that matters to me now. It matters so much to me. And partly because when I left Nashville, something about performing in front of people broke inside me. My so-called friend who stole my songs ruined one of my last performances by showing up and singing my songs. And then she made damn sure I never had another performance after that. And that still haunts me. This feels like dipping my toes back into it, and it brings all those painful memories back.

This time it's different. I have so many people around me who care about me. And I'm doing this for Cami. Knowing that my singing here and at the fundraiser matters to her and helps her is what keeps me going. I know I can't live a life without music in it.

I think about all the people here tonight to cheer me on and that's what keeps me going.

Maggie. My aunt, who is like my second mom, sits up front with that knowing little smile that says she believes in me more than I believe in myself. She always has. She sits with Mack, and they're both smiling and happy.

Poppy. My newest best friend who somehow bulldozed her way into my life with oil-stained hands and her funny sharp wit. The girl who keeps the entire town laughing even when she's running on fumes. She catches my eye and gives me a huge thumbs-up, her grin wide and unapologetic. As if I haven't spent the past twenty minutes telling her I'm going to throw up. Her confidence in me is ridiculous. But it's also kind of comforting.

And then there's Cami. My other best friend. Listen, friend trauma is real, y'all. I had a best friend who encouraged me and was there for me. Until she got what she needed from me, then she destroyed me. It was so hard letting people in and trusting them again. But these two never took no for an answer in the best possible way. They showed up for me and reminded me that they were there for me when I didn't want to trust or believe it. They've healed that in me, and for that, I'm grateful.

Cami pushes through the crowd, makes a beeline for me, and grabs my hands.

"Vi." Her blue eyes are wide and glassy like she's one breath away from crying. "I can't tell you how much this means to me. You standing up there tonight? Singing your songs? Doing all of this for the ranch?"

I squeeze her hands, trying to keep my own from shaking. "Cami, you don't have to thank me. This is your family's legacy. Of course, I want to help."

She shakes her head fiercely. "No, Violet, you don't get it. Without you stepping up like this or organizing all of this, I don't know what I would've done. This fundraiser, this event, it's all I have left. You're giving me a fighting chance."

I swallow hard. Damn it. My nerves were bad before, but now there's a lump in my throat because Cami deserves this. She deserves to keep her home and her family's ranch afloat and fight for what's hers. And now? It's up to me to help make that happen.

Cami pulls me into a hug, squeezing the life out of me before whispering, "You've got this. You're gonna blow them all away."

Jack and Ollie are in the front, waiting and holding their beers, and they smile and wave when they see me. I love it so much that they're here too.

Then she's gone, slipping into the crowd, leaving me standing there, heart pounding.

And then...there he is. Walker leans against the bar, arms crossed, watching me with those deep, whiskey-colored eyes— eyes that see right through me. There's no judgment there, no pressure. Just unwavering belief.

That's the part that undoes me.

Because *he also believes in me*. More than I believe in myself at this moment.

And that makes standing up here, about to perform the song we wrote *together*, all the more terrifying.

It's one thing to sing in front of strangers, but *him?* The man who knows every note, every lyric, every place where I hesitated while writing it? That's different.

That's *intimate*. It's like sharing us with the world. We're not in the cabin, holed up writing together anymore. We're in the bar together in front of our town. It feels very official, and nerves get me with that, too.

My palms are clammy against my guitar, my pulse hammering so hard I can feel it in my throat. But when my eyes finally meet his, he does the one thing that steadies me, he smiles.

Not just any smile. A slow, warm curve of his lips, filled with nothing but pride.

Like he already knows I'm going to be incredible. Like I *can't* fail. Like I'm his favorite thing to watch.

Like he's proud of me.

And somehow, that's enough to make me take a breath, grip the guitar a little tighter, and believe, just for a moment that maybe he's right. We've got this.

God, he's calm. Always so damn steady, like nothing ever rattles him. And here I am, gripping my guitar like it might strangle me, when all I really want to do is go stand next to him, lean into him, let him tell me everything will be okay in that low, gruff voice of his.

But I can't do that.

I have to do this.

Cami steps up, taps the mic, and announces me.

"Hey, y'all. Tonight, we have something special planned for everyone. Violet is a fantastic singer and songwriter. She has a few songs she'd love to share with you tonight. This is brand-new music that no one has ever heard. Not a cover, but her very own songs that she wrote. I'm so excited! Let's give it up for our very own, Violet Wilson!"

The bar erupts in applause and whistles. My legs shake as I walk up and settle onto the stool at the mic stand. I fumble with my guitar, adjusting the strap, my fingers numb from clutching the guitar so tightly. The crowd quiets.

Too quiet.

I clear my throat, bringing the mic closer. "Uh, hey, everyone." My voice is shaky. "I, um, I wrote this song with someone special recently, and—"

There's movement in the corner of my eye. A shadow stepping onto the stage. I turn my head—and there he is.

Walker.

A guitar slung over his back, his smirk slow and easy, like he planned this.

"What are you doing?" I whisper as he slides onto the stool beside me.

He grins. "Singing with you."

Oh. *Oh.*

The crowd erupts—cheering, clapping, hooting like they just won the damn lottery.

Because Asher Wyatt—the man who swore his singing days were behind him—just stepped onto the stage, guitar in hand, in front of a crowd that only knows him as Walker.

They've never seen *this* side of him before. The legend, the raw talent, the man who once owned every stage he set foot on. But he's still in there.

And for the first time in years, they're about to witness the man he tried to leave behind.

He tunes the strings, then turns to me, his knee brushing mine, his voice whispers low. "You're not doing this alone, Red."

My breath catches. I don't know how he seems to know,

seems to always see me, really see me, even when I don't say a damn word? Walker can read me like a book.

He gives me a look, are you ready? I nod, my hands settling on the strings. And then we play. The first chords hum through the speakers, filling the room, and suddenly, everything else fades.

I don't hear the chatter at the bar. I don't see the crowd.

I see him.

His eyes flick to mine, warm and knowing, and I swear we're somewhere else—somewhere without walls, expectations, or past lives. Just us. Just this. And I get lost in the moment. So lost, like the kind of lost where when you finally come up for air, you forget where you are and what you were doing.

We sing.

Oh God. This is different. This is more than just singing. The way his voice blends with mine, the way our bodies move in perfect time, it's like we were always meant to do this together. Like we're pulling the song straight out of the air like it's been waiting for us to find it.

His voice is low and rich, wrapping around mine, guiding me, anchoring me.

I lean closer, tilting my face toward him as we sing the chorus. His eyes darken, his voice roughening just slightly, and I swear, for a moment, we forget.

Forget that there are people watching. Forget that this is supposed to be a one-time thing.

Forget that he's a bar owner now and not the country music legend he used to be.

But the way he looks at me as we hit the last note? That's not a man who's done with music. That's a man remembering who he is. The powerhouse, the artist, the musician who healed hearts and gave so much joy with his music.

The last chord fades, and the entire bar explodes into

applause. But neither of us moves. We still sit knee to knee, breathing hard, staring at each other like we just stumbled into something dangerous and completely inevitable.

His eyes drop to my lips. I don't think. I just move. I lean in, and he meets me halfway.

The second our lips touch, the crowd loses their damn minds. I hear Maggie's delighted screech, Cami shouting "FINALLY!"

A few whistles make it all the way from the back, but it all blurs because his hand slides into my hair, his fingers curling against my scalp, and his mouth, God, his mouth.

The kiss is slow. Deep. He feels so good. Like he's making sure I know exactly how much I mean to him. My heart swells so much with his touch. I never want this moment to end.

When we finally break apart, I'm breathless. His thumb brushes my cheek, his eyes flicking between mine.

And then, from the front row, Maggie lets out the sharpest whistle I've ever heard and shouts, "Well, hell! That wasn't just a performance, that was the show of the damn century! Somebody put it in the books! We just witnessed history!"

Walker groans, laughing, dropping his forehead against mine.

Cami yells, "Forget the fundraiser! Y'all could charge admission for *that*!"

I shake my head, grinning. "We are *never* gonna live this down."

Walker smirks. "No, we are not."

The world feels *different* after that performance. Like something inside me cracked open, something raw, real, and impossible to ignore.

I can still feel Walker's voice tangled with mine, the heat of his knee pressed against mine, the weight of his gaze pulling me in like gravity. How he looked at me—like I was *his*—was enough to make me believe it, even if just for a few minutes.

And then the kiss.

God, the *kiss*.

I'm still catching my breath, still floating in the electric charge of whatever we just created, when I feel it—*the shift*.

Not in me. In *him*.

Walker stiffens beside me, his body going rigid, his easy, breath-stealing smile vanishing like a candle snuffed out in the wind. His jaw locks, his shoulders tense, and something dark flickers in his whiskey-colored eyes.

I barely have time to register it before I feel it, too. The weight of a stare. The kind that burns, sharp and cutting, even across a crowded bar.

I turn my head, and there she is.

Stella.

I recognize her instantly. Because how could I not? She's the woman who has haunted my nightmares and the voice in the back of my head that tells me I don't belong in the music industry anymore. The person who stole everything from me.

She stands near the back, watching us, her arms crossed tight, her manicured nails digging into the sleeves of her coat. She's tall and blonde, every inch of her sculpted to perfection like she stepped straight out of a high-end music video and into *my* worst nightmare.

But it's her expression that hits me hardest.

She's not surprised to see *him*. She's pissed to see *me*.

Her ice-blue eyes flick between us, her gaze narrowing, her lips pressing into a thin, unforgiving line.

She saw it. *All of it.*

The song. The way Walker looked at me. The way he *touched* me. The way we kissed like the rest of the world had fallen away. Her being here ruined what should have been the best moment in my life.

And now?

She looks like she wants to rip my throat out. Like she wants to destroy something else of mine.

But why is she here?

My stomach churns as she starts moving toward us, the sharp click of her heels cutting through the noise of the bar. Everyone around us watches as this unfolds and confusion rests on everyone's faces.

This isn't just a coincidence.

She's here *for him*.

And I have a sick feeling she's about to make damn sure I know it.

"Hey, *baby*."

Baby.

The word is like a bomb dropping into the middle of the bar. The way she says it, slow, intentional, like she's *staking her claim* makes my stomach lurch.

Walker doesn't move. His jaw is tight, his fingers twitching at his sides, and I can *feel* the tension rolling off him like he knows her.

My stomach *drops*. Because I know that face. I know *that smirk*.

No. No, no, no.

She flicks her long blonde hair over her shoulder, her familiar expensive perfume reaching me before her voice does.

"Well, well." Her eyes drag over me, slow and calculated, before she lets out a little laugh. "This is *rich*."

I can't move. I can't *breathe*. Because standing in front of me, smirking like the devil herself, is *Stella*.

Stella. My former best friend.

The girl I trusted with everything—my songs, secrets, and dreams.

The same girl who *stole everything from me.*

The same girl who took the songs I wrote and put her name on them.

She called me a thief and made me lose my record deal while I had to leave town and rebuild my career and life. The woman who broke *me. No fucking way.*

The air is too thick, the voices around me suddenly too loud. I feel Walker shift beside me, his hand brushing my arm, but I can't look at him.

I can't not look at *her.* She's the epitome of evil. Someone I trusted and now could never trust again.

Her lips curve. "Oh, Violet."

She laughs again, shaking her head like this is the funniest thing in the world. "I *cannot* believe this. You and Asher?" Her eyes flash with something cold, something *vicious.* "I mean, I knew you liked my leftovers, but *damn,* girl. You really went all in this time. Congratulations on this. Really, you truly played this game hard."

My stomach twists so hard I think I might be sick. What is she talking about?

I swallow, forcing my voice to be steady. "What are you doing here, Stella?"

She tilts her head. "Oh, you know. Just passing through. Thought I'd check in on *my husband.*"

She reaches out, dragging a manicured finger down his arm, and I feel my pulse slam into overdrive. "I *missed* you, baby."

What the actual hell? This is Walker's ex-wife? Oh, hell no. How could the universe be so freaking cruel?

Walker yanks his arm back, his expression sharp, but I don't even register his reaction.

Because all I see is *red. How dare she?*

She already stole my songs. She already stole my career. And now she thinks she can waltz in here, flick her hair, flash that *look-at-me* smile, and stake a claim on *him*, too?

She smirks, like she can read my mind.

"Oh, don't look so threatened, Vi." She tuts, crossing her arms. "You *do* remember how this goes, right? I take what I want." She shrugs, her eyes gleaming. "And I always get what I want. But it's cute you thought you could win."

The room tilts. I can't move. I can't breathe. And suddenly, I don't know if I can handle what happens next.

I'm still catching my breath, still floating in the electric charge of whatever we just created, when I feel it—*the shift*.

Not in me. In *him*.

Walker stiffens beside me, his body rigid, his easy, breath-stealing smile long-vanished like a candle snuffed out in the wind. His jaw tightens, his hands flex at his sides like he's *bracing* for something.

My stomach twists.

No.

The air leaves my lungs in a single, brutal punch.

Mack. This is Mack's *mother*.

Funny in all the years I knew her, she never mentioned being someone's wife or mother. Never thought that was an important part of her.

Suddenly I can't think of anything but Mack and what she must be thinking right now. I know how badly her mother not being around has affected her, and now, for her to drop in like this and especially to be so horrible? She's got to be so upset right now. I quickly scan the crowd and see Maggie with her arm protectively around Mack as they watch all this unfold in horror.

My pulse pounds in my ears. I look at Walker, at the tension coiled so tightly in his frame, at the way his throat bobs like he's swallowing back something ugly, something *painful*. Something *familiar*.

And I know that pain. Because she did it to me, too. And now I'm fucking pissed that she was the one that did it to them. The one who *broke him*. It's *her*. Oh *God*.

I take a half-step back, my legs suddenly weak beneath me, the weight of this realization crushing the breath from my lungs. It hits me like a punch to the face.

Walker *was married* to Stella.

Stella, the woman who stole my music, my dreams, *my future*. The person who used me, took everything I ever confided in her, and ran straight for the spotlight with my songs in her damn hands.

And all this time? I had no idea. Did he know?

I whip my head toward him, my chest tight, my voice barely above a whisper. "Walker."

His jaw ticks. His fists clench. He's *shaking*. And that's my answer, isn't it?

He didn't know. Just like I didn't.

Oh, *hell*.

I can feel the weight of the bar pressing around us. People are still talking, still drinking, still *celebrating* the moment we just had. The moment that now feels like a cruel joke, like something sharp waiting to slice me open.

I stare at him, trying to find words, trying to *breathe*.

He turns to me then, finally, and the look in his eyes is like a blade to my ribs. Like he's just as wrecked as I am. Like he's wondering the same damn thing.

If *I* knew.

The realization slams into me like a freight train. Does he think I *knew*? That I knew he was Stella's ex-husband? That I *let* this happen, let him fall into something real with me while I was carrying this secret?

"No," I whisper, shaking my head, the words catching in my throat. "Walker, I didn't—I *swear* I didn't—"

"Violet." His voice is low and raw, his shoulders rigid. He exhales sharply, like he's trying to *contain* whatever he's feeling. And right now, anger radiates off of him. Like he's barely hanging on.

I don't get the chance to say anything else.

Because Walker is already on his feet, as he takes Stella by the arm and pulls her toward the door. He doesn't speak. But I know this is far from over with Stella. She doesn't leave anywhere without *wrecking everything*.

Chapter 33
Walker

I don't say a word as I grab Stella's arm and haul her toward the door.

She stumbles in her too-high heels, yanking against my grip, but I don't stop.

I *can't stop.*

The second I saw her standing there, smirking like she owned the place, like she *owned me*, the air in my lungs turned to pure fire and rage.

The *audacity.*

She doesn't get to be here. Not in *my town.* Not in *my bar.* Not near *my daughter.*

I shove the door open and drag her out into the cool Wyoming night, the door swinging shut behind us. The distant hum of music and conversation is swallowed by the silence outside, the only sound between us is the sharp click of her heels against the pavement as I *let her go.*

She smooths out her shirt, her lips curving into that same smug, *infuriating* smile that used to make me lose my mind—in every damn way.

I used to love that smile. I used to think it *meant something*. Now?

Now, it just makes my stomach churn. It's a smile I never wanted to see again.

Because that smile? That smile is nothing but destruction. A wrecking ball disguised as lies and expensive perfume. And I'll be damned if she comes back here, after all these years, to tear down what I've built. What I've worked my ass off to create. The life I made for Mack. The life I made for myself.

I inhale sharply, working to contain the rage pulsing under my skin. She doesn't get to do this. Never again. Not after what she put me through. Not after the wreckage she left behind, wreckage I barely crawled out of.

And now she's here? Acting like she has the *right* to step back into our life?

She has no right. She signed those rights away and left our baby all alone just hours old. But my anger isn't just about me. It's about *Mack*.

She's in there, in the bar, probably trying to act like she's fine, but I *know* my kid. I know when she's putting on a brave face. And even if she's indifferent now, this *will* affect her. How can it not? And I'll be damned if I let Stella hurt her, too.

I force the words through gritted teeth. "What are you doing here, Stella?"

My voice is low. Rough. Barely restrained.

She lets out a breathy, almost *laughable* little sigh, pressing a manicured hand to her chest.

"Asher—"

I shake my head. "*No.* Cut the shit. Why the hell are you here?"

Her lips press together, the mask slipping just enough for me to see something else beneath it, desperation. The need to control the situation and manipulate it to her benefit.

"I fucked up," she whispers, her voice small. "I *know* I fucked up."

I say nothing. Because *what is there to say?* She's right. She *did*. In more ways than I can count.

She swallows, eyes darting over my face like she's searching for a weak spot.

That used to work on me. She used to look at me like that, and I'd soften. I'd let her in. I'd believe whatever bullshit she fed me because I thought I could fix things, fix us. But I'm not that man anymore.

Not after what she did and not after what it cost me.

"I just...I want to make amends," she says softly. "I want to see her. I want to see *my daughter*."

The words hit me like a kick to the gut. I go *still*. My body moves before I think, stepping closer, my voice dropping to something dark, something *dangerous*.

"You don't get to call her that." My hands curl into fists at my sides. "You signed away your rights. You don't even know her *name*, Stella."

She flinches. But only for a second before she tilts her chin up, all faux confidence and arrogance wrapped in a designer coat.

"That's not fair," she breathes. "You kept her from me."

I *laugh*. A sharp, bitter sound. "That's not true at all, and you *know* it. You walked away and left her alone in the hospital. You didn't even wait for me."

She shakes her head, eyes wide, dripping with the same manipulation she's always used. "You don't know what I went through, Asher. You don't *know*."

That name. That *damn* name. I hate hearing her say my name.

My fists tighten. My jaw *locks*. I grind my teeth together.

"Don't call me that." I love it when Violet says it but when Stella says it, it sounds patronizing.

Her lips curve. "It's who you are."

I don't wait for her to say another word. I turn back toward the bar and push the door open. Inside, Maggie waits, her arms crossed, her eyes soft but knowing.

I exhale, rubbing my jaw. "Take Mack to my office. Keep her there until Stella leaves."

Maggie nods, already moving. "Come on, sweetheart," she says gently to Mack, who looks more confused than anything.

Mack frowns, looking at me. "Dad, I'm fine."

I shake my head. "Just... *go* with Maggie, okay?"

I need to know she's safe. I need to know she's *away from this*.

Mack sighs but follows Maggie. As soon as the office door clicks shut, I let out a slow breath, pressing my hands to the bar.

And then, before I can even think about what happens next, Violet is in front of me, eyes blazing.

"Did you know?" My voice is quiet, dangerous. "Did you know *before tonight* that she was my ex?"

Violet's mouth opens, then closes. "No," she breathes. "Of course not."

I want to believe her. I *should* believe her. But, like Stella says, this is really convenient. How could we both have the same enemy? And how did she even find us? Did Violet lead her right to us? How else could she know?

But after everything I've been through, after what *Stella* did, my chest tightens with something ugly.

Violet sees it. And it shatters her. Her face falls, her arms dropping to her sides. "You don't believe me."

I exhale, trying to fight the doubt, trying to *push it away*. But I don't answer fast enough. And that silence? That's what kills her.

She shakes her head, stepping back. "Wow." Her voice is thick, raw. "Guess I don't know *you* as well as I thought either."

Then she turns and walks out.

* * *

I wake up with a pounding head and the sharp sting of regret pressing heavy on my chest.

The cabin is dark, the only light coming from the early morning sun filtering through the curtains. My mouth is dry, my body heavy, the remnants of last night's whiskey still burning low in my stomach.

I don't drink like that. *Not anymore*. But last night?

Last night, I needed something to numb the ache in my chest, to drown out the feeling of her, the way she looked at me when she walked away, when I let her.

So, I came here. To my *safe place*.

I tried to work on a song, thinking maybe I could *get it out of me*, the anger, the confusion, the damn *hurt*, but nothing came. No words. No melody.

Just silence.

Except now, sitting up in bed, I realize something. It doesn't feel safe anymore. It feels *empty*. Because she's everywhere.

Her coffee mug still sits in the sink, the one she always used because she swore it made the coffee taste better. One of her hair ties is on the nightstand, forgotten, like she just stepped out for a second and might come back.

And then, I see the flannel. It's draped over the chair by the fireplace, the one she always curled up in when she stayed over. I don't even have to pick it up to know it still smells like her.

I do it anyway. The scent is *faint*, but it's *there*. Vanilla and coconut. Something that smells like *home*. I inhale sharply, clenching my jaw.

Damn her.

Damn the way she's in every corner of this place. Damn the way I can still hear her laugh, see her curled up on the couch, wearing my flannel and pretending like she wasn't stealing it.

Damn the way I pushed her away.

I step out onto the porch and lean on the railing, trying to ground myself.

I rake my hand through my hair, trying to pull myself together, when suddenly, I hear it.

Click. Click. Click.

The sound of cameras. I freeze. Then—the shouting starts. Voices just beyond the tree line.

"Asher Wyatt, over here!"

More cameras. More clicks.

I shove the flannel down, my stomach *twisting*. How the *hell* did they find me here? I go inside and close the door. Clenching my jaw, I move toward the window. Sure enough, past the porch, a group of them stands on my property, cameras raised, flashes going off even in the early morning light.

"Jesus Christ."

I grab my phone off the nightstand, dialing fast. It rings twice before a deep, steady voice answers.

"Matthews."

"Sheriff," I grit out. "I need your help. Now."

A pause. "What's going on?"

I exhale sharply. "Reporters. They're on my property. Trespassing."

His voice turns sharp. "I'll send out help."

"Thanks."

I hang up and immediately text Maggie.

Me: *There are reporters at my cabin.*

A second later, my phone buzzes.

Maggie: *They've been at your front damn door too.*

I curse under my breath. Because I know exactly how they found me. I know exactly who led them here. The one person who is hellbent on destroying me. She didn't get what she wanted last night, so now she's doing this. I know it.

Stella.

Rage coils in my chest. My fists clench, my jaw tightens, at how she's exposed me. Told the world exactly where to find me, where to find Mack.

I shove open the front door, only to see Maggie standing on the cabin's porch, her arms crossed, eyes sharp as she glares at the people with cameras standing beyond my fence.

Damn it, she must have driven back here. "Where's Mack?" I ask her, needing to know that she's safe. But the one person I can't bring myself to ask about is Violet.

"She's getting ready for school, you lunatic. Now get yourself together and come deal with all of this."

I swear and grab my stuff and follow her out, ignoring the chaos.

This was supposed to be my sanctuary. The one place I built from the ground up where no one could touch me, where no one could touch Mack. And now? Now the vultures are circling.

"How the hell did they get here so fast?" I grind out.

Maggie exhales, shaking her head. "When I got up this morning, *this* mess was already happening." She jerks her chin toward the chaos. "Your *ex-wife* wasted no time, did she?"

My teeth grind together. "She just couldn't help herself."

Maggie sighs, stepping closer. "Walker, listen to me—"

"No." My voice is sharp, cutting. "You *know* who did this, Maggie. You *know* how she operates."

Maggie studies me for a long moment, then says something that makes my stomach churn. "You know who wouldn't do this?"

My fists tighten. "Maggie," I warn.

But she doesn't back down. "She's my niece," she reminds me, voice steady. "And you know damn well she wouldn't *purposely* set you up like this. You're acting like an asshole to the wrong person, Walker."

I let out a sharp breath, scrubbing a hand over my face. "Then why else would she be here so randomly? And she was friends with Stella."

Because it doesn't make sense. None of it does. The timing, the connection, the way this whole damn thing blew up the second she walked into my life. I don't believe in coincidences. Not anymore. And if she didn't know and was truly innocent in all of this, then why does it feel like I've been set up all over again?

Maggie's eyes flash. "Because she *loves* you, you damn fool. She never came here for you. She came here to find a safe place to land. Which turned out to be you. She never meant for any of this to happen, it just did."

Maggie and I ride in her truck over to the house, leaving the boat to deal with for another time.

Before I can open the door to the house, it swings open. Mack steps outside, her arms crossed tight over her chest. She glances at the camera crew perched at the end of the driveway, then at me. "Seriously? Why would you mess things up with Violet?"

I don't have an answer for that. Because I *don't know*. Because the truth is—I know that this is all very bad. Also, I don't know how far Stella will go.

I don't know what game she's playing, or what her end goal is. But I do know one thing.

She's a viper. And I don't trust a damn thing that comes out of her mouth.

I exhale sharply, looking at Mack. "How are you doing with all of this? Do you want to talk to her?"

Mack hesitates. Just for a second. Then she says, "Part of me, yes. Because I'm *curious*." She swallows hard. "But part of me, *no*. Because she seems so... toxic."

I nod, throat tight. "When someone shows you who they are, believe it. She's shown us."

And that's what terrifies me. That Stella will find a way to sink her claws into Mack. That even after all these years, she'll find some twisted way to manipulate her, the same way she did to me. Mack says she doesn't need her, that she doesn't even want her, but she's fifteen. And I know what it's like to want answers. To wonder if the person who left ever really cared and then brutally find out that they actually didn't.

Maggie sighs, rubbing Mack's shoulder. "Sweetheart, whatever you decide, just know you don't owe her anything."

Mack nods. But then she turns on me, and her glare is almost as sharp as Maggie's. "You're being an idiot," she announces.

I blink. "Excuse me?"

She glares harder. "Why are you letting Stella *win*?"

My chest tightens. "I'm not—"

"You are," she interrupts. "You know that, right?" She throws up her hands. "Violet is our family now, Dad. And you just threw her away."

Maggie exhales. "She's got a point, Walker."

I clench my jaw. "I needed to think."

Mack scoffs. "To think? Or come up with an excuse?"

The words hit harder than I want them to. Because deep down, I know she's right. I didn't push Violet away because I needed to think. I pushed her away because I'm scared. Because it's easier to shove people out before they can leave on their own. Because what if she knew? What if she's not the person I thought she was? And worse, what if I let myself believe in something real again, only to have it ripped away?

But Mack isn't finished.

"You're mad at the wrong person, Dad." Her voice cracks. "You're mad at Stella. Not Violet."

I swallow hard, my chest twisting.

Maggie nods, arms crossed. "Walker, if you keep this up, you're going to lose Violet. She stayed at Cami's last night."

I don't answer. Because I don't know what to say. Because they're right. Because the anger is still there, boiling under my skin, but the doubt is starting to creep in, too.

And I hate it.

I exhale sharply and pull out my phone, my fingers already dialing before I can stop myself.

Maggie and Mack watch as I put the phone to my ear.

A few rings, then, "Walker?" Will Maren's voice is groggy, like I just woke him up.

"I need help," I grit out.

Will sighs. "If this is about the label, I already—"

"It's not about that." I exhale sharply. "It's about Stella."

Silence. Then, "Shit."

"Yeah."

Another beat of silence. Then Will mutters, "Tell me everything."

So, I do.

And as I talk, as I lay it all out, something shifts.

Because for the first time, I finally start to see how badly I might have just screwed up.

Chapter 34
Violet

Cami's ranch is peaceful.

Or at least, it *should* be. But I am not at peace after what has happened. I can't make sense of any of it.

Of all the bars in all the towns in all the world... how the hell did I end up falling for a man whose ex-wife is the same woman who tried to ruin me?

What kind of twisted, cosmic joke is this from the universe?

The universe had to be bored when it cooked this one up. Like it sat back with a drink, looked at me and Walker, and thought, "Let's see how much chaos they can handle before they completely break." Because this? This isn't just bad luck. This is just plain cruel.

How is it even remotely possible that the man I love—the man I trusted, the one person who made me believe in something good again, was married to her? The same woman who stole my music, my career, my future? The same woman who took everything from me and left me with nothing? And now, here she is, waltzing back into both of our lives like some twisted ghost, smiling like she hasn't already burned the world down around her.

The wind rustles through the fields, the horses graze lazily in the paddock, and there's the warm scent of hay and fresh earth in the air. It's the kind of place that should bring me peace. Should make me feel grounded. Should remind me that life goes on, even when it hurts.

Instead, I sit on the back porch, nursing a glass of wine, while Poppy stands on a rickety old chair, trying to string lights up over the beams.

"If I fall and break something," she grumbles, "you will lie to the paramedics and say it was something cooler than 'she fell hanging string lights like an idiot.'"

Cami, lounging back in her chair, boots propped up on the railing, takes a slow sip of her beer. "What about 'she fell while fighting off a mountain lion'?"

Poppy considers it. "Acceptable."

Maggie, who just walked outside with a fresh basket of biscuits Cami had in the oven, snorts. "I'll tell 'em she was *running* from a mountain lion."

Poppy glares. "Wow. Betrayal."

Mack, curled up in the chair beside me, laughs around a mouthful of mashed potatoes as she tells Poppy. "If you die, I get your antique truck, right?"

Poppy narrows her eyes. "If I die, I *haunt* you. And that truck is not antique! It's vintage."

"Fine. But it's older than dirt."

I shake my head, smiling despite the heaviness still lodged in my chest. Because they are the only thing keeping me from completely unraveling right now. I was relieved to see Mack and Maggie show up earlier to spend some time with me. Everything feels horrible right now.

Walker should be here.

But he's not.

Because he's off figuring out his crap, and I refuse to sit around waiting for him to decide whether or not I'm worth fighting for.

I check my phone. Still nothing.

Cami nudges my leg with her boot. "You still thinking about him?"

I exhale, setting my wine down. "I'm thinking about how he made me feel when he accused me of knowing who Stella was."

The weight of his words still lingers in my chest. It wasn't just that he was angry, it was that he doubted me. Where he could have trusted me, he hesitated. I've been here before. I've watched people I love walk away from me like I don't matter, watching them decide I wasn't worth believing in. And I told myself I would never let it happen again. Never let myself be put in the position of proving my worth to someone who should already know it. But here I am, doing it again. And it stings. I thought things were different with him. Maybe not.

My throat tightens, but I push forward. "I get it, okay? I do. He's been burned before, bad. And the person who did it just showed up to do it again."

Poppy groans. "Yeah, but that doesn't mean he gets to throw you under the bus just because his trust issues got set on fire."

Maggie, ever the diplomat, sighs. "Walker's a good man, honey."

I nod. "I know." And that's the hard part. It makes me feel like I'm not the good one.

"But he's also a damn idiot," she adds.

I snort, and Mack grins. "Finally, someone says it."

Cami shakes her head. "It's just dumb. All of it. Stella is evil. Walker should know you had nothing to do with this."

I swallow hard. "I told him. But he didn't believe me."

Mack says, "Anyone want more potatoes? I'm getting more." We shake our heads, and she heads inside.

And that's the part I can't let go of. The part that hurts. The part that makes me feel like it's happening all over again, watching someone I love walk away because they decided I wasn't worth it.

Cami sighs. "That woman is a plague."

Poppy leans forward. "What exactly did she do to you?"

I let out a slow breath, my chest tight. "She slept with my boyfriend. Took my album. Used me for my talent and then ruined me when she didn't need me anymore." I clench my jaw.

Cami leans forward, eyes dark. "When the devil couldn't reach you, he sent an insecure, self-victimizing 'friend' who craved male validation, had no empathy, and used manipulation to take what she wanted. Sounds like she has a pattern with this."

Poppy whistles. "Damn. Say it again, but slower."

Maggie blinks. "Cami, that was kinda poetic."

Cami shrugs. "Been holding that one in for a while."

Maggie snorts. "You're not wrong, though."

I stare down at my hands, exhaling. "She took everything from me."

Cami nudges my knee. "Not everything. You still have us."

Something sharp wedges itself in my throat.

Maggie reaches over, giving my hand a squeeze. "And I know Walker. He might be lost in his own damn head right now, but he's not going to let her take anything else from him. And that includes you."

I wish I could believe that. I wish I could hold onto that certainty, that trust. But right now, I don't know. And I don't have the energy to fight for someone who isn't willing to fight for me back.

I chew my lip, staring at the sky. "Maybe. Maybe not. But I'm not waiting around for him to figure it out."

Poppy tilts her head. "So, what now?"

I shift in my chair. "I don't know."

Cami perks up. "Yes, you do."

I give her a look. "Oh, do I?"

She grins. "You're going to perform at the county fair."

I blink. "Uh—"

Maggie slaps the table. "The show must go on, honey. Show Walker what he's missing."

Cami nods. "It's literally the best way to remind yourself who the hell you are."

I hesitate.

Mack settles back into her chair with her food and raises a brow. "What? You gonna let Stella win?"

That hits me like a slap. Because no. No, I am not. I square my shoulders. "Fine."

Poppy beams. "Hell yeah."

Cami raises her beer. "To Violet, reclaiming her damn career and not letting that viper win."

Everyone cheers, and I laugh, shaking my head.

I glance out over Cami's ranch, the pastures stretching wide, the horses grazing under the Wyoming sky, the old red barn that's stood here longer than any of us have been alive.

This place matters. It's been in her family for generations.

Now, I can see why Cami is fighting so damn hard to save it. Why we're doing this fundraiser in the first place. It's more than just land—it's history, legacy, and home. And looking at it now, I understand something I hadn't before.

This isn't just about me. It's about fighting for the things that matter. And I'll be damned if I let Stella take anything from anyone I love ever again.

Mack stretches out, then sighs dramatically. "Is this a good time to confess my sins?"

Maggie eyes her warily. "What did you do now?"

Mack winces. "So... I may have taken a video of you and Dad singing at the bar before all hell broke loose."

Maggie groans. "Makayla Leigh Walker, I am too old for this nonsense."

Mack holds up her hands. "In my defense, I was proud of you guys! It's not every day you have famous parents!"

I freeze. She's not talking about Stella. She's talking about me. And her referring to me like that melts my heart.

Poppy whistles as she scrolls through her phone. "Damn. This thing went VIRAL viral."

Cami shakes her head, grinning as she leans over and looks. "Like, actual internet-breaking viral."

Maggie fans herself. "Lord, Walker is going to lose his damn mind."

"I mean, he kind of already has, so what's one more thing, right?" Poppy asks as she scrolls through the comments. There are thousands.

Holy shit. I blink at Mack, who now holds onto the rocking chair for dear life.

"So, your dad doesn't know about this?" I ask, my voice wavering with nervousness.

Mack stares at me, completely deadpan. "No."

I tilt my head. "He will soon."

Mack swallows. "And I'm going to be grounded for life."

Cami laughs. "I give you one to two business days of freedom, tops."

Poppy nudges her. "Say your goodbyes now, Mack."

I exhale. "I should be panicking."

Cami grins. "But you're not."

I shake my head. I know I shouldn't watch it. But the second

Cami shoves her phone in front of my face, I watch it anyway. And damn it, I'm wrecked all over again.

The video starts with me and Walker on stage at *The Black Dog*, sitting knee to knee, his guitar balanced on his thigh, my fingers strumming mine, and our mouths at the mic. The lighting is low, warm, golden, the kind that makes everything look softer, dreamier. Like something out of a movie.

Then, I hear his voice. That deep, rich, slightly rough tone that melts my insides like butter on a hot biscuit. My throat tightens as I watch. Because it's not just the way he sings. It's the way he watches me.

The slow, focused way his whiskey-colored eyes track my every move, the almost imperceptible hitch of his breath when I hit a high note, the way his fingers tighten just a little on the guitar when I lean in.

He's looking at me like I'm the only thing that exists. Like I'm something precious. Like he's completely, utterly gone for me. And it hurts.

Because right now? Things are broken between us. And I don't know if we can ever be like that again.

He's holed up in his damn cabin, working through his issues, while I'm out here trying to pretend like my heart isn't currently being drop-kicked.

I swallow, forcing down the lump in my throat. "Mack, this is a great video."

"Wow," Poppy mutters, still staring at the screen. "This is obscene."

Cami whistles, fanning herself. "I mean... damn, Violet. Watching it in person was just as hot for the record. But that's a great video. I can see why it went viral."

Maggie shakes her head, looking far too pleased. "That man is in love with you."

I let out a little laugh, pressing my hands to my face. "Well, he has a funny way of showing it."

Mack throws her hands up. "Y'all are out here acting like two emotionally constipated Hallmark characters when you could be making out and healing each other's wounds. I am suffering here."

I groan.

Poppy scrolls through more of the comments, snickering. "Violet, people are losing their *minds* over this."

I peek through my fingers. "How bad?"

Cami grins wickedly. "Oh, honey. This is *the* content the internet lives for." She clears her throat and starts reading:

"Asher Wyatt found hiding out in Bridger Falls, Wyoming."

"Violet Wilson is gorgeous, and Asher Wyatt is a walking lumberjack snack."

"Asher Wyatt and Violet Wilson need to stop playing and start making beautiful, music-loving babies immediately."

Maggie chokes on her tea.

Mack snorts. "I support this."

"Oh my God," I whisper, mortified.

Poppy scrolls again. "Oooooh, this one's good, 'Find a man who looks at you the way Asher Wyatt looks at Violet Wilson while strumming his guitar. And if you don't, stay single.'"

Cami throws up her hands. "SEE? We're not *crazy!*"

Maggie hums knowingly. "That man loves you, Violet."

I swallow hard, staring down at the video again, at how his fingers brush over the strings, at how his gaze drinks me in like I'm the only thing worth seeing.

It's bittersweet, watching this. Because for a moment, it felt real. It felt easy. Like maybe, just maybe, this thing between us was undeniable. Unshakable. Something we were both willing to hold onto. But now?

Now he's gone. And I'm here, watching this video like a

damn lovesick teenager, swooning over a man who currently thinks I betrayed him.

And now that the world knows where he lives and his privacy has been invaded, he'll probably blame that on me, too.

I sigh dramatically, handing the phone back to Cami. "I hate everything."

Mack shakes her head. "No, you don't. You love him."

Poppy nudges me. "So, what are you gonna do?"

I blink. "What am *I* gonna do?"

Maggie smirks. "Honey, that video just made the whole damn world fall in love with you two. You're going to have to face him eventually."

I bite my lip, thinking. Because yeah. Yeah, I *will*.

And maybe when he does watch this damn video, he'll miss what he threw away.

I set my glass on the table and clear my throat. "You know what? You are all right. We need to share the fundraiser. We need to do this and do it big for the ranch."

Every single head at the table slowly turns toward Mack.

She freezes, mid-bite of a biscuit, eyes darting from one of us to the next. "Why are you all looking at me like that?"

Poppy leans forward, resting her chin in her hands. "Because you are the little Queen of Virality."

Cami nods sagely. "The Social Media Overlord."

Maggie adds, "The Digital Puppet Master."

Mack blinks. "I don't like where this is going. I'm already going to be grounded for life when he realizes what I've done."

Maggie rocks back in her chair, "Your dad would never be mad if it was for a good cause, like saving Wilder Ranch here for Cami."

Part of me doesn't care right now. Walker can take his time out. I'm going to focus on Cami right now and what I can do to help. That feels a hell of a lot better than focusing on the hurt right now.

I give her a look. "Mack, can you make the fundraiser go viral?"

Mack squints at me. "You mean like cute hometown fundraiser viral? Or national thirst trap and women are booking flights to Wyoming viral?"

Maggie groans. "Lord help us all when Walker finds out."

Poppy grins. "Definitely the second one."

Mack leans back in her chair, steepling her fingers like an evil genius. "I mean, I could. But what's in it for me?"

Cami deadpans. "The survival of my family's ranch, Mack."

Mack sighs. "Ugh. Fine. Emotional blackmail always works on me."

Maggie pats her hand. "That's because you're a good person, sweetheart."

I laugh, shaking my head. "Let's start with something simple. A video explaining the fundraiser, why we're doing it, why the ranch is important—"

Mack raises a hand. "Say less. I'm on it."

We all watch as she whips out her phone, cracks her knuckles, and immediately starts typing like a woman possessed.

Poppy leans over. "What's the plan, Social Media Overlord?"

Mack grins. "Give me twenty-four hours, and this fundraiser is gonna be everywhere."

Cami sighs, shaking her head. "God help us all."

Maggie just sips her tea. "Oh, Lord. Here we go again."

Chapter 35
Walker

I wake up to my phone buzzing like a damn earthquake.

At first, I ignore it. I've been ignoring everything lately. But when it won't stop, when it keeps going like an emergency siren, I groan, grab it, and see about fifty missed calls from Will Maren.

That's... not good.

I sigh, rubbing my hand down my face as I answer. "Jesus, Will, did someone die?"

Will, already sounding exhausted, sighs. "No, but your anonymity sure as hell did."

I sit up. "What?"

Will clears his throat. "Uh, listen, so... you've gone viral."

I blink. "Viral."

"Like crazy viral."

A pit forms in my stomach. I know what's coming next. I can feel it. The same way you can feel a storm rolling in before the first thunderclap. I stand up fast, pacing. "Okay, how viral are we talking?"

Will pauses, and the hesitation immediately sends alarm

bells through my head. Finally, he coughs awkwardly. "Ten million views."

I stop pacing. The room goes deathly silent, except for the sound of my own blood roaring in my ears. I open my mouth, close it. Try again. "Where did it come from?"

Silence. A long, guilty silence. Then Will says, "Your kid's account."

I freeze. I actually lose the ability to move for a full five seconds. Then, finally, I explode. "I'm sorry—WHAT?!"

Will sighs. "Mack. She posted a video of you and Violet singing. And, uh... let's just say the internet has feelings about it."

I pinch the bridge of my nose, squeezing my eyes shut. "Of course she did."

Because of course it was Mack. Of course, my teenage daughter, who has zero concept of the words privacy, discretion, or restraint, decided to single-handedly catapult my entire life into a public spectacle.

Will chuckles, and I can hear the smug amusement dripping through the phone. "Yeah, buddy, people are thirsting over you. I got a call from People Magazine. Women are referring to you as 'Cowboy Daddy' in the comments."

I groan. "Stop."

I sit down and immediately regret my entire existence. "I hate this."

I'm standing at my cabin's kitchen counter, trying to drown my sorrows in coffee, when I hear a truck pull up fast outside. "I gotta go, Will."

Then there's banging on my door. I sigh, already knowing who it is before I even open it. And sure enough, Ollie and Jack stand on my porch, looking way too smug for my liking.

Jack smirks. "You okay, buddy? You've been real quiet lately."

Ollie nods. "We heard you were having a moment."

I scowl. "I don't need a wellness check."

Ollie sniffs the air, then nods at the empty whiskey bottle on my table. "Uh-huh. That definitely looks like a man in peak mental health."

Jack tilts his head. "So, what's the plan? You just gonna sit here and brood until the internet finds another cowboy to obsess over?"

Ollie grins. "Or are you actually gonna fix things with Violet?"

I sigh, staring at my coffee. "I don't know."

Jack crosses his arms. "Well, you'd better figure it out, because people are gonna be showing up to this town looking for their grumpy, guitar-playing Cowboy Daddy."

The realization hits me like a freight train straight to the chest. I swallow hard, my throat tight. My mind replays every single moment between them—Mack and Violet laughing in my kitchen, Mack stealing her fries at dinner like it's second nature, the way Mack looks at her when she's not even aware she's looking at her.

Violet isn't just some temporary person in Mack's life. She's family. And Mack sees her that way.

Goddamn it.

I run a hand down my face, blinking hard, trying to shove down the emotion clawing its way up my throat. I knew Violet was important to me. I knew she meant more than just some fling, more than just a woman who came into my life and made it better.

But I wasn't the only one who felt that way. Mack does too.

Ollie leans back in his chair, crossing his arms with a smug grin. "Judging by the way you just short-circuited, I'd say that hit home."

Jack, ever the instigator, smirks. "That's gotta sting a little, huh? Knowing you completely screwed this up with the woman your daughter already sees as family?"

I scowl. "I don't need a damn lecture."

Jack shrugs. "No, but you do need to pull your head out of your ass."

Ollie nods. "Because let's be real, Mack's not gonna forgive you if you let Violet walk away."

"Walker won't forgive himself either if he lets Violet walk away. He's going to regret it," Jack says.

Mack is already pissed at me. Already looking at me like I'm the biggest idiot on the planet for pushing Violet away. And she's right. Hell, they're all right.

I let my past blind me. I let Stella's betrayal twist something good—something real—into something I was too damn scared to hold onto.

And in the process? I didn't just break my own heart. I broke Mack's too. I exhale sharply, shaking my head. "I have to fix this."

Ollie grins. "Again, no shit."

Jack claps me on the back. "So, what's the move, Cowboy Daddy?"

I groan, already regretting every single life decision that led me to this moment. But I know one thing. I'm not letting Violet go without a fight.

I groan. "I hate all of you."

After way too much prodding, I finally pull up the damn video. And I immediately regret it. Because it's her. Violet.

The way she sings, her voice smooth and raw and perfect. The way she closes her eyes, completely lost in the music. The way she tilts her face toward me, just barely, as I strum beside her.

And the way I look at her. I swallow hard. Because holy

shit. I look at her like she's my whole damn world. And now? Now I've ruined it.

I thought watching this would piss me off. I thought I'd see it and feel betrayed like she knew what she was doing all along. But that's not what I feel at all. I feel like I just got kicked in the chest. Because it's so painfully obvious, I love her. And I let my own fear and insecurities drive her away.

I don't realize I've stopped breathing until Will's voice cuts through my phone. "You watch it?"

I clear my throat. "Yeah."

He sighs. "And?"

I rub my jaw. "And I need to fix this."

Silence. Then, "No shit."

* * *

The bar is quiet before opening—just me, a half-drunk cup of coffee, and the low hum of the jukebox playing something old and familiar. Mack is settled in the back with snacks and working on her homework. I've been trying to find some sort of normalcy now that everything has gone to shit.

I need silence and the space to think to figure out how the hell I'm going to fix what I broke with Violet.

But, of course, the universe isn't that kind. Because the door swings open, I don't have to look up to know who it is. I feel her presence before I see her. My skin crawls, and my stomach tightens.

Stella.

Waltzing in like she owns the place. Like she's got some goddamn right to be here. "I'm here to discuss something with you."

I sigh, dragging my hand down my face. "What do you want?"

She smirks, sliding onto a barstool like she's settling in for a friendly chat. "You always were a talented singer, Asher. You and Violet... well, I gotta admit, you're an odd pairing."

I clench my jaw. "Cut the shit. What do you want?"

She leans forward, resting her elbows on the bar. "I want to talk to her."

I freeze. "To who?"

Stella tilts her head, eyes narrowing. "Mack. To remind her who her real mother is."

My stomach turns cold. "Come again?"

She exhales, like she's bored of this conversation. "She's my daughter, Walker. Not Violet's. Violet has no right to try to take over my family."

I let out a sharp laugh. A humorless, deadly sound. "That's what you're gonna say?" I shake my head. "Yeah, you're not talking to my kid to say that."

Stella's jaw tightens. "You can't keep her from me. She's my kid, too."

I lean forward, planting both hands on the bar, my voice dropping. "Yeah, actually? I can. She's not legally your kid." She blinks, but I don't stop. "You don't have rights to her, remember? You signed them away and walked away from her."

She flinches, just barely, but it's there. Good. I hope the words sting. I hope they sink in deep and stay there.

She opens her mouth, probably to feed me some more bull-shit, but I don't let her. I step around the bar, closing the space between us, my voice turning cold.

"You left her alone in that hospital, Stella. Alone."

Her brows furrow. "The nurses were with her." She says it so matter-of-factly like it makes all the difference. Like that's the same thing. Like it wasn't abandonment.

My fists clench at my sides, my breath sharp. "That is my child," I growl. "You don't leave your child, Stella."

She finally looks uneasy, like she's realizing she stepped into something bigger than she was ready for. Like she finally understands that whatever power she used to have over me?

It's gone.

And I'll be damned if I let her get anywhere near Mack again.

I hear my daughter behind me and close my eyes for a moment. The moment Mack steps into the room, everything shifts. I know my kid. I know the way she moves, the way she reads a situation before stepping in. She's been standing back there in the kitchen, watching, taking everything in like she always does. My kid misses nothing.

I was just hoping she wouldn't come out before I could get Stella out of here.

But now? Now, she's ready.

Mack steps forward, her boots solid against the bar floor, arms crossed, chin lifted, looking so much like me it almost knocks the breath from my chest.

She doesn't look at me. She doesn't hesitate. She just zeroes in on Stella like a goddamn sniper and fires off the first shot. "What do you have to say to me?"

Stella straightens, smoothing her hands down the front of her coat as she can somehow control this moment. Like she's the one in charge here. She isn't. She opens her mouth, her voice slipping into that honeyed, condescending tone I remember all too well.

"My beautiful daughter," she starts, like she knows her. Like she has the right to talk to her like that. "I know this must be very confusing for you..."

Mack snorts. I swear to God, she snorts.

Then she holds up a hand and cuts her off. "Let me stop you right there."

Stella blinks, clearly thrown.

Mack steps in closer, her voice calm, her posture strong. "You are a DNA donor. Nothing more."

My chest tightens. She says it so clearly, so effortlessly. Like she's had this speech ready for years.

Stella flinches, but Mack doesn't give her a chance to recover.

She cocks her head, her eyes fierce, and she lays it all out. "That man right there?" She points at me without even looking at me. "That's my dad."

I stop breathing.

Mack keeps going, her voice steady. "In elementary school, he braided my hair every day before school. Drove me to soccer and all of my camps. He never missed anything. Bought me pads when I got my period and explained everything to me so I wouldn't freak out. He held me when I had bad dreams." She pauses. "And some of them? Some of them were even about you."

Stella's mouth parts before her lips press into a thin line.

Mack doesn't blink. "He has done everything for me." She takes another step forward, her voice turning sharp, deliberate, unwavering. "You? You have done nothing."

The silence that follows is so thick it's alarming. My stomach clenches because this is getting serious fast.

Stella shifts and swallows, but she has nothing to say for the first time in her life. This is a narrative she can't control or put a spin on.

I take a slow, measured step forward, my eyes locked on Stella's. "She has said her piece." My voice is low, firm, and final. "Now, here's mine."

She looks up at me, something tight in her expression like she knows what's coming next.

"You need to leave." I take another step, voice turning to gravel and steel. "Not just my bar." Another. "But this town."

I tilt my head, my eyes dark, and I say it slowly. "Never come back."

Silence.

Stella swallows, her jaw tightening. For a second, I think she might try to argue.

But then? She does the only thing she's ever been good at.

She turns. And she walks out the door.

The second it swings shut behind her, Mack takes a deep breath, shaking her arms like she just fought a war.

I turn to her, my throat tight, my heart swelling with something I can't even put into words. I step forward. "Honey."

She meets my eyes, and then she's in my arms before I can even say another word.

And for the first time in days, I feel like I can breathe again. I'm her safe space. Nothing will ever change that.

Chapter 36
Violet

I stare at my reflection in the mirror, watching as Poppy curls a perfect strand of my hair and then lets it bounce free.

"You're gonna look so hot," she announces, squinting at my hair like she's sculpting a masterpiece.

In the nail chair beside me, Cami tosses a handful of peanut M&Ms into her mouth. "Yeah, and then you're gonna get up on that stage, blow everyone's minds, and make Walker realize what an absolute dumbass he is."

Maggie sighs, lifting her sweet tea dramatically. "Beautiful."

I huff out a breath, trying to feel excited. I should be nervous. I should have butterflies, the same kind that nearly ate me alive before the performance at The Black Dog. But I'm not nervous.

I'm depressed.

God, this is worse than nerves. At least when I was anxious, I could work through it. But this? This weight sitting heavy in my chest? This ache? This is missing Walker so bad I can't even stand it.

"You know," I say, my voice too dry, "I don't think 'hot' is really the goal tonight."

Poppy raises a brow, twirling another section of my hair. "No?"

I sigh. "The goal is to raise money for Cami's ranch, not seduce the entire town of Bridger Falls."

Poppy smirks. "But why not both?"

Cami nods solemnly. "Exactly. Multi-tasking, babe."

Maggie pats my shoulder, smiling. "They're right, sweetheart. You deserve to shine tonight."

I wish I felt like I deserved it. But the only thing I feel is exhausted. I'm about to perform in front of the entire damn county, and the only thing I can think about is how Walker isn't going to be there.

I'm singing a few of my own songs, then one final one... The one we wrote together.

If I can even get through it.

Just thinking about it pricks tears in my eyes, so I blink hard, willing them away. No crying. Not today.

Mack perches in the salon chair beside me, swipes a grape lollipop across her tongue, and kicks her feet onto a footstool like she's watching a live drama unfold. "You know, you might wanna get it together before you hit the stage, Violet. You're like a sad panda."

I groan, dragging my hands down my face. "I'm perfectly together."

Mack deadpans. "You just sighed so hard it altered the air pressure in the room."

Poppy laughs.

Cami hums. "Yeah, and you keep looking at yourself like you just got dumped before prom."

I glare. "I did not get dumped."

Maggie sips her sweet tea. "So, you're saying there's still hope?"

I open my mouth and then shut it again. Because I don't know. Because Walker and I haven't spoken since everything happened. Because maybe I was dumped. I just didn't get the official text message.

Mack senses my spiral and pops her lollipop out of her mouth with a dramatic smack. "Alright, sad girl, let me distract you with some piping hot tea."

Poppy lifts a brow. "Oh?"

Mack grins. "Stella came to the bar."

Silence. Then, collectively, all of us turn to stare at her.

"She what?" Cami says, nearly choking on her M&Ms.

Maggie presses a hand to her chest like she needs a second to prepare for this emotional burden. "Oh, Lord. What did she want?"

Mack grins, licking her lollipop again like this is the greatest story she's ever told. "She told my dad that she saw the video and then said she wanted to talk to me."

I stiffen, feeling protective. "Mack..."

Mack waves me off. "Don't worry. I handled it."

Cami leans forward. "Define handled it."

Mack shrugs. "I told her she's a DNA donor, and that she needs to crawl back to wherever she came from."

Silence. Poppy cackles so loud that I jump.

Maggie gasps, then clutches Mack's face in her hands like she's just witnessed a miracle. "Sugar, you did not."

Cami throws a fist in the air. "MVP. MVP."

I choke out a laugh, shaking my head. "I'm glad you told her how you feel."

Mack beams. "Oh, I wasn't done."

Poppy leans forward in her chair. "Oh my God, there's more?"

Mack grins like the little devil she is. "I told her my dad braided my hair, drove me to soccer, bought me pads when I got my period, and held me when I had bad dreams. And that he was my parent. And she was nothing."

Silence.

Awe.

Maggie sniffs loudly, dabbing at her eyes. "That's my girl."

Cami lets out a low whistle. "Damn, Mack. You annihilated her."

I sit there, my heart somewhere in my throat.

Mack stretches her arms, completely unbothered by the emotional destruction she just delivered. "Anyway, she left town."

I blink. "Wait. Just like that?"

Mack nods. "Yup. But, uh... unfortunately when she left town, the paparazzi showed up."

Cami groans. "What? Where?"

Mack points out the window. "One of them just walked into Harvest & Honey. They're mostly camped outside my dad's driveway. And by the cabin. Watching everything."

Maggie groans. "Lord, I need more than sweet tea for this. Walker must hate this."

Mack shrugs. "They keep asking for Violet."

I frown. "But they don't know where I am?"

Mack smirks. "Nope. You've been paparazzi-free at Cami's."

Poppy peeks outside. "Uh, hate to break it to you, but I think we've been found."

We all whip our heads toward the window. Across the street, two guys with cameras sit at Harvest & Honey, pretending to eat sandwiches while zooming in on Boots and Bangs.

Mack sighs dramatically. "They're like ants. Crawling all over town."

Cami squints. "Should we go over there and accidentally spill a drink on them?"

Poppy grins. "I like how you think."

Maggie stands up, smoothing out her blouse. "I'll handle this."

We all stare at her.

Mack grins. "We're about to witness some real Bridger Falls hospitality, huh?"

Poppy nods. "Do you think she's gonna bless their hearts or threaten their lives?"

Cami sips her drink. "Honestly, both."

I watch Maggie march out the door, chin lifted, shoulders back, on a mission. And for the first time in a long time, I laugh. Because I might be sad. I might be missing Walker like hell.

But this town? These people?

They're gonna make sure I get through this.

One way or another.

* * *

I step onto the stage, the lights blinding for a second, the roar of the crowd louder than I expected. From up here, I see the Ferris wheel and rides moving and people laughing. Stalls and booths are set up, and banners and bunting flutter in the breeze. The world continues on around me, and I feel like the nerves are about to take over. I'm struggling not to let them. I know what I need to do for Cami.

I look out into a sea of people—some faces I know, some faces I don't, but all of them here for something bigger than me. Bridger Falls has transformed for the county fair, located just outside of town. People have come from all over for the fair, and normally this would be my favorite thing. But not now, not when my heart is hurting.

I'm here for Cami and for Wilder Ranch. For the place she's poured her heart into, the land she's spent sleepless nights trying to save.

I grip the microphone, clearing my throat, trying to push through the weight in my chest.

"Wow," I say, scanning the crowd, my voice shaky but strong. "This... this is incredible. First, I want to say thank you for coming. For showing up for this community. For proving, yet again, how special Bridger Falls is."

A murmur of cheers and applause ripples through the audience.

I glance over at Cami, standing off to the side, arms crossed, blinking way too fast like she's trying not to cry.

"Wilder Ranch isn't just a ranch," I continue. "It's a place of history. Of memories. Of dreams. And Cami has big ones—big, beautiful dreams for turning it into a place that serves this community. A place where kids can ride, families can gather, and life slows down just enough to remind you of what matters."

More cheers.

Cami sniffs loudly, flipping me off from the side of the stage, and I laugh. "She's gonna kill me for getting all sentimental up here, so I'll shut up now and sing."

I take a deep breath before launching into my first song. And for a while—just a little while—it feels good. I tell stories about the songs, making the crowd laugh and watching their faces as they connect with the lyrics. I forget, just for a second, that my heart feels like it's been ripped in two.

But then—

Then, it's time for the last one.

I take a breath. My throat tightens. I already know how this is gonna go. I should've cut it from the set list. I should've chosen something else. But this is the song we wrote together, and even if it breaks me, I need to sing it.

"Alright, this next one is a special one. You might have seen a video where this one was performed. Anyway, I hope you like it. It means a lot to me," I say, pretending to be able to breathe. Because right now, I'm struggling not to cry.

The first few chords hit, and I physically feel it in my chest. The crowd hushes, the weight of the moment settling over all of us. I start to sing. And it's like ripping open a wound in front of everyone.

Every word, every note, it's all him. Even though he's not here, I feel him. His voice in my ear that night, his fingers brushing mine on the guitar, his whiskey-colored eyes watching me like I was something precious.

By the last line, my voice cracks. Tears burn my eyes, spilling over before I can stop them. I let the last note ring out, my chest heaving, hands trembling.

I wipe my face, laughing weakly into the mic. "Well. That was embarrassing."

The crowd erupts, but it's all a blur. I sniff, swallowing down the ache in my throat. "Thank you for supporting Wilder Ranch."

I step off the stage, my legs wobbly and my heart shattered into a thousand pieces.

And then—then I see them.

Standing backstage, waiting for me. My parents.

Maggie steps forward first, smiling through watery eyes. "Surprise, baby girl."

I freeze. Then I'm in their arms, sobbing into my mom's shoulder, my dad rubbing my back, whispering, "We're so proud of you, Vi."

* * *

Later that night, we gather around the kitchen at Cami's farmhouse, eating leftovers and laughing, the weight of the night finally settling.

I feel lighter, even with the ache in my chest.

Mack bursts through the door, grabbing a handful of fries from Cami's plate before even saying hello. "How much money did you raise? Did you save the ranch?"

"We haven't officially got the numbers yet, but it was awesome!" Cami smiles at her and pulls her in for a hug. "How did you get here?"

Mack grins and says, "Dad dropped me off."

Silence.

I set down my drink, trying to peek out the window with no one noticing. "He didn't stay?" I ask, my voice smaller than I want it to be.

Mack shrugs. "He didn't think you'd want him to."

My stomach twists.

Maggie exhales softly.

"But," Mack continues, swallowing the last of her stolen fries, "he did ask if you'd come over tomorrow."

I blink. "What?"

Mack shrugs again, but I see a little smirk forming. "He said to meet him in the barn. Noon."

The room goes quiet. Everyone watches me. Waiting.

My heartbeat stutters. I exhale, trying to steady myself. Because I don't know what tomorrow is gonna bring. But I know one thing.

I'll be there.

Chapter 37
Walker

I've been pacing this damn barn for the past thirty minutes, kicking up dust and wrestling with my own damn thoughts.

I told Mack to ask Violet to meet me here. At noon.

It's noon. She's not here. Maybe she's not coming.

I honestly couldn't blame her. I was a jerk, and I should have handled this all better.

My chest feels tight, my heart racing in that restless way it does when I know the words that I say could change everything. God, her performance was amazing. I watched her perform from a distance, not wanting to interfere. I didn't feel like I had that right. I've really messed things up with how I handled things. But then when she was so upset at the end, I could barely handle it. I felt like I was going to lose it.

I don't know why I'm so nervous. Maybe because I know how bad I screwed up. Maybe because I've spent the past few days trying to figure out how to fix it, and nothing I come up with feels big enough. Because how the hell do you make up for breaking the trust of the woman you love? For making her feel like she wasn't worth believing in?

I lean against the stall, exhaling hard, hands shoved into my pockets. The horses shift around me, sensing my tension. Or maybe they're just judging me.

And then I hear a vehicle pull up and a car door shut.

I look up, and there she is.

My Red.

She stops just inside the barn doors, the sunlight casting a golden glow around her like something straight out of a dream.

But she doesn't look like a dream. She looks wrecked. Like she's been carrying something heavy for too damn long. Guilt pulses through me because I know I put that weight there.

I swallow hard, forcing myself to stay still, even though every damn cell in my body screams at me to go to her. But I don't feel like I've earned that right, yet.

I've missed her so bad it feels like my heart is heavy. I've spent days pretending like I needed space like I needed time to process, but the truth is, I just needed her. And now she's standing right in front of me, and I don't even know if I get to have her anymore.

She crosses her arms. "Hey, Walker."

Her voice is too careful, too steady, and I hate that. I also hate that she didn't call me Asher. She's the only person that I don't mind calling me by my name. To everyone else, I'm just Walker. And now with her, I'm back to Walker, and that feels like we're not close anymore.

I hate that I did that to us. I swallow, nervously. "Hey, Red."

Silence stretches between us. Heavy and loaded.

I should start. I know I should. I asked her here, after all. But my mouth doesn't seem to want to work. The words are caught in my throat. I'm afraid to mess this up even more.

How do I even begin to explain what she means to me? That I wake up thinking about her, go to sleep thinking about her, and every single moment in between feels lost without her in it? That she's in every song I write, every melody that's ever meant something to me? That I love her so much it scares the hell out of me?

Finally, she sighs. "Well? You gonna say something, or did you just bring me here for a staring contest?"

My lips twitch, just barely, but then I see the way she grips her arms like she's bracing for more hurt, and it damn near shreds me.

I exhale, stepping forward. "I screwed up."

Her jaw tightens.

"I should've believed you and trusted you." I run a hand down my face. "I was a damn idiot, Violet."

She crosses her arms tighter. "You were."

I nod, taking the hit. I deserve it. "I watched the video."

She stiffens.

"The one of us at The Black Dog." My throat closes up just thinking about it. "I saw how you looked at me. How I looked at you."

Her breath catches, but she stays quiet. So, I keep going.

"And then I saw you at the fundraiser. And it—" I break off, shaking my head because I can't even put it into words. It gutted me seeing her so wrecked singing our song.

Because seeing her up there, singing alone, knowing I should've been beside her? It devastated me. It was like watching the best part of my life slip away, and I was too damn stupid to grab it before it was gone.

"I should've been there with you. Instead, I was losing my damn mind over you."

Her lips part, her breath hitches, and I know I'm getting through to her.

I step closer, carefully, watching her expression. "I don't just love you, Violet."

She blinks, holding her breath.

I take another step, so close I can see the freckles dusting her nose, the way her lashes flutter just slightly when I move in.

I speak softly, letting the emotion carry the weight of my words. "I love you like my heart always knew you were the one. Like my soul didn't settle until it found yours." I shake my head, my voice thick with meaning. "I love you like you're the song I've been humming my whole life without knowing the words."

She inhales sharply, her hand lifting like she wants to touch me but isn't sure if she should.

I give her that moment, that choice, because if she's not ready, I won't push.

Because I shift closer, we both move at the same time.

And our foreheads slam together so hard I actually see stars.

"SHIT—"

Violet yelps, staggering back, clutching her face and huffs. "Are you kidding me? That was supposed to be our sexy moment."

I stumble too, rubbing my forehead. "What the hell was that? Did we just...give each other concussions?"

She glares through watery eyes. "Unreal. The first time we kiss again and we headbutt like two wild goats."

I bite back a laugh, even though my damn skull is throbbing. "You did jump me."

She smacks my chest. "Because you were taking too long with your swoony monologue!"

But then she reaches out and grabs my shirt, yanking me down, and kissing me like she's trying to make up for lost time.

And hell, I kiss her back like I'm trying to do the same.

Kissing her again feels like finally coming up for air. Like I've been drowning without her and didn't even realize how bad it was until now. I tilt my head, deepening the kiss, my hands gripping her waist, pulling her flush against me because I need to be closer. Need to feel her against me and to make up for every single second I spent pushing her away. I've missed her so much.

I chuckle, grinning down at her, and something shifts in her expression.

She tries to stay mad. But she fails spectacularly. Instead, she exhales, shaking her head, and laughs.

Softly at first. Then full-on belly laughs roll out of her until she leans into me, shaking her head against my chest.

I press my lips against her hair, still grinning.

"Guess I've got a lot to make up for, huh?" I murmur.

She tilts her head up, smiling, eyes still glassy. "Yeah, but you're getting there, Asher."

And just like that. Everything is going to be okay. I know it's not going to be easy, but nothing easy is worth it. I'm going to fight for us. Nothing will ever come between us ever again. It's Violet and me against the world.

* * *

I've played in front of thousands of people. I've faced music executives and the sheer terror of raising a teenage daughter. That last one has been the hardest by far.

But none of that prepares me for what Violet tells me right before her parents pull up to my house to meet me for the first time. And I'm already nervous.

She stands in my kitchen, arms crossed, looking nervous as well. And that's not helping any. She looks at me nervously, "So, uh... I should probably warn you about something."

I frown. "About what?"

She exhales. "My parents are... like really huge fans of yours. Huge."

I blink. "What?"

She winces. "Like... massive. Like 'Mom had a poster of you in her laundry room, and Dad considers you part of his hernia surgery recovery story' kind of huge fans."

I stare at her. "Stop messing with me, Red."

"Oh, how I wish I was."

Before I can respond, the sound of a car pulling into my driveway makes my stomach drop. What have I gotten myself into?

She grabs my wrist, eyes deadly serious. "Just...please be ready for what's coming."

"What do you mean? I don't understand."

"You will," she mutters, right as there's a sharp knock at my front door, three fast, no-nonsense raps like I owe someone money.

"Jesus," I mutter. "Am I meeting your parents or the FBI?"

Violet mutters something under her breath, but I can't hear it over the sound of my pulse as I open the door. The second I do, all hell breaks loose.

"HOLY SHIT!"

Violet's dad staggers backward, his hand flying to his chest like he's having a full-body crisis.

Her mom lets out a high-pitched gasp and smacks his arm. "Language, Eli!"

But Eli isn't listening. His wide, disbelieving eyes are locked on me. "It's—you're—Asher Wyatt?!"

Violet groans. "Dad, please don't—"

"Do you have any idea what this man means to me?!" Eli practically yells, spinning on her like she's committed an unforgivable betrayal. "Your mother and I slow-danced to 'Whiskey Sunrise' on our anniversary! This man's voice carried me through my hernia surgery!"

I blink. "Uh. Wow. That's—"

"My hernia surgery, Asher!" he repeats, as if that somehow solidifies our bond for eternity.

Violet's mom still hasn't blinked, staring at me like I might dissolve into thin air at any second. "I used to keep a poster of you in my laundry room."

Violet whimpers. "Oh my God. Mom…"

Her dad steps inside without an invitation, turning in a slow circle like he's on a VIP tour of Graceland. "I cannot believe my daughter is dating *the* Asher Wyatt."

I clear my throat. "Technically, I just go by Walker now."

"Oh, hell no," he scoffs, waving me off. "You'll always be Asher Wyatt to me."

Violet grabs her mom's face in both hands. "Can we please stop acting like I just brought home a damn rock star? He's a man, guys. A regular man. He runs a bar. He fixes things. He's got a daughter. He—"

"He wrote the best damn love songs of our generation!" her dad interrupts.

Violet's mom, Caroline, clutches her chest like she's about to faint, eyes locked on me in sheer disbelief. "I just—I can't process this. Asher Wyatt. Dating my daughter."

Her dad, Eli, lets out a slow, stunned breath. "It's like finding out Bigfoot is real and he's been living in your guest room this whole time."

Caroline nods rapidly. "It's like discovering the Mona Lisa has been sitting in the lost-and-found at a gas station."

I rub a hand down my face. "I, uh… really just live a quiet life now."

Eli scoffs. "A guy who wrote 'Whiskey Sunrise'?" He shakes his head, muttering. "I proposed to Caroline to that song."

Caroline gasps dramatically. "Eli! That is not true!"

Eli crosses his arms. "You said yes before I even got down on one knee because it was playing on the radio."

Violet groans. "Oh my God, I regret everything."

Caroline fans herself. "I need to sit down. I need a moment."

Violet pinches the bridge of her nose. "Mom. You're acting crazy."

Eli narrows his eyes at me. "Yeah? Well, this man made my wife cry in the frozen foods aisle at the Kroger in 2013."

Violet whimpers. "Dad."

I clear my throat. "Uh. Sorry?"

Caroline sighs wistfully. "It's just surreal. You were the voice of our road trips. The reason Eli started wearing cowboy boots."

"Hey!" Eli protests. "I'm a real cowboy."

But Caroline isn't done. "The reason I bought a guitar at forty-three."

"Mom!" Violet yells, looking like she's ready to throw herself out the nearest window.

Eli shakes his head, still staring at me in disbelief. "I just... never thought I'd have to look a man in the eye and say, 'Hey, don't break my daughter's heart' when that man is Asher Freakin' Wyatt."

I nod solemnly. "I get that a lot."

Violet throws up her hands. "Oh my God, please let the ground open up and swallow me whole."

Eli sighs, finally stepping forward and shaking my hand. "Welcome to the family, son. Hope you like unsolicited song requests at Thanksgiving."

Violet glances at me. "Still time to run?"

I grin at her. "Not a chance, Red."

Violet throws her hands up. "Can we please talk about us now? Maybe about how Walker and I are happy and just want to live a normal life?"

Silence.

Her mom tilts her head. "Right. Yes. That's why we're here."

But Eli is still staring at me, arms crossed, still processing all of this.

I sigh, rubbing the back of my neck. "Would you like a drink, sir?"

He lets out a long, heavy sigh. "Yeah. But only if you sing me a song first."

Violet lets out a horrified groan. "DAD."

But the man just grins at me. "Worth a shot. Come on, kid."

* * *

The grill sizzles as I flip the steaks, the smell of charred seasoning and firewood filling the air. Eli stands next to me, beer in hand, looking out over my backyard like he's been here a hundred times before.

"This is a hell of a setup," he says, nodding in approval. "Big yard, a nice grill, a fire pit. You ever think about getting some chickens?"

I glance at him. "Chickens?"

Eli shrugs. "You got the space."

"I run a bar and raise a teenager. You really think I need chickens on top of that?"

He takes a sip of his beer. "Could be fun. I mean, you already have like a million goats."

I shake my head. "You and Mack would get along with your love of farm animals."

Eli smirks. "Oh, I know we will."

Maggie's laughter rings out from the porch, where she and Caroline are parked in their chairs, drinking iced tea and swapping old stories.

"Walker, you should've seen her back in the day," Maggie

calls out, jerking a thumb toward her sister. "Caroline was the golden child, always had her life together, always followed the rules."

Caroline scoffs, crossing her arms. "That's not true."

Eli smirks. "Caroline, honey, you packed emergency snacks for our wedding day."

Caroline waves a hand. "And were you hungry that day? No. You're welcome."

Maggie sips her tea, eyes twinkling as she gazes at me. "Underneath all that brooding and guitar playing, you've always been a family man."

Caroline hums in agreement. "She's right, you know."

I shake my head, but there's warmth in my chest because, damn it, they're not wrong.

A while later I look around for Mack and finally find her. Inside the house, she and Caroline stand around, laughing in the kitchen, their voices getting louder.

"What the hell are they up to?" Eli mutters, craning his neck.

I poke my head inside just in time to see Mack holding up a wooden spoon like it's a microphone, grinning wildly at Caroline.

Caroline claps her hands. "Alright, you have to answer without thinking. Would You Rather: Fight one horse-sized duck or ten duck-sized horses?"

Mack gasps. "Oh, ten duck-sized horses for sure. I could take 'em out one by one."

Caroline doubles over laughing. "You're so right. Great plan."

Mack's face lights up at that, and I feel something in my chest pull tight—because she doesn't have many people who say things like that. People who see her and instantly just... claim her as family.

Violet nudges me, slipping her hand into mine. "You okay?" she murmurs.

I squeeze her fingers, letting out a slow breath. "Yeah." I glance back inside, where Mack and Caroline are now attempting to juggle lemons and failing miserably. "Yeah, I really am."

She leans into me, her head resting briefly against my shoulder.

I've spent years avoiding this kind of thing. The big family gatherings, the loud dinners, the easy laughter that stretches long after the plates have been cleared.

But now, standing here with Eli flipping steaks, Maggie giving me hell, Mack bonding with Violet's mom, and Violet right next to me where she belongs...

Damn.

This house has never felt more like home.

Eli slaps a steak onto a plate and nods approvingly. "Alright, Walker. You officially passed the 'meet the parents' test." He claps me on the back. "Welcome to the family, son."

I glance at Violet, who's watching the whole thing with soft, happy eyes.

Maggie laughs. "He's already been a part of this family for a long time."

This all feels like something I never thought I'd have. It's not the big things. Not the grand, life-changing moments. It's the small ones.

It's Eli standing next to me at the grill, arguing about the best way to cook a steak like we've been doing this for years. It's Mack laughing in the kitchen with Caroline, completely at ease in a way she doesn't let herself be with just anyone. It's Maggie giving me hell while secretly watching over me like she always has.

And it's Violet, her hand in mine, like she's always belonged here.

For so long, it was just me, Maggie, and Mack. And that was enough. We had our routines, our way of moving through life—just the three of us, making it work. But this?

I always thought I was meant to keep people at arm's length. That opening my home—my heart—to more than just Mack would end in loss, the way it always had before.

But tonight, I don't feel like an outsider. I don't feel like a man trying to find his place.

I feel like I already belong.

I glance over at Violet, watching as she playfully bumps Maggie's shoulder while setting the table. She catches me looking and just smiles.

And right then, I know—I've already got everything I'll ever need.

Chapter 38
Violet

The Black Dog is a madhouse.

It's supposed to be a calm, professional setting for our interview with People Magazine, but I should've known better. When Will arranged this, we mostly wanted to counteract the negative publicity we've had since Stella dropped her bombs. And we were offered a nice chunk of money from doing the interview that will go towards the startup of our new label.

This is Bridger Falls. And they know what a big deal this is, and they're taking full advantage of this and giving us hell.

The interviewer, Laura, who appears to be questioning her life choices, sits across from me and Walker at a booth, her notebook poised, her phone recording between us.

Walker, as expected, looks like he's five seconds from chewing through the wooden table to escape.

Maggie is perched at the bar, sipping her sweet tea like she's watching the best soap opera of her life. She's not holding back, adding her commentary whenever she sees fit. My mom sits next to her, and I forgot what it's like when those two conspire together. It's like double trouble.

Cami and Poppy have stationed themselves in the booth directly behind us, pretending they're not listening but failing spectacularly.

And Mack?

She's sitting in the corner with her phone propped up on a napkin holder, recording the whole thing like she's our self-appointed PR manager.

"This is historic," she mutters, typing furiously on her iPad. "I should do a live."

Walker groans. "Mack."

She grins. "Not a chance, Cowboy Daddy."

The interviewer pauses mid-question. "I'm sorry... Cowboy Daddy?"

Cami bursts out laughing.

Poppy wheezes.

I try to keep it together and be serious, but I'm practically vibrating from holding my laughter in.

Maggie clucks her tongue like this is the burden she carries in life.

Walker closes his eyes, praying for patience. "It's an internet thing."

Mack grins. "And by internet thing, he means he's a full-blown thirst trap now."

The interviewer jots something down. "So, the internet loves you."

Walker's left eye twitches. "I am not answering that."

Cami leans over. "You should see the fan pages. There's artwork, Laura."

Poppy nods seriously. "They've given him a fictional tragic backstory and everything. That's why this article is so important. I mean...no pressure, Laura."

Walker slams his forehead onto the table. "I hate this town."

The interviewer, clearly trying to regain control, clears her throat. "Right. So, let's talk about the music. Walker, you left the industry for a long time. What changed?"

Walker exhales, lifting his head, and for the first time all afternoon, he actually relaxes. His hand finds mine under the table, his thumb running along my knuckles, and my stomach flutters violently.

"She did," he says simply, nodding toward me.

My throat closes up.

The interviewer leans in. "You mean Violet?"

Walker nods, completely sure, completely steady. "She's the real deal. The best damn woman I know."

The world tilts.

Maggie sniffs dramatically, dabbing at her eyes with a cocktail napkin. "Lord above, I knew I loved you, Walker. Somebody get me my wedding hat."

Poppy clutches her chest. "Romance is alive."

Cami, grinning like a lunatic, whispers, "I *love* love."

I stare at Walker, my heart pounding so loud I swear everyone can hear it.

And then Laura, sensing the perfect moment, asks, "So what's next for you two? More performances?"

And before I can even process the question, Walker leans forward and says, "We're starting our own label."

Silence.

I blink.

The interviewer blinks.

Poppy drops her entire drink on the table.

Maggie gasps so dramatically it could win an Oscar.

Mack's phone clatters to the floor. "WHAT?"

I turn to Walker and grin. "We are."

He smirks. "Yeah, we are."

The interviewer, clearly realizing she just got the scoop of the century, scrambles for her notebook. "A record label?"

Walker nods, totally unbothered by the fact that I am currently suffering from emotional whiplash. "Red Records. We're doing this together."

My heart stutters. Because that's what gets me. Not just the label. The "we."

And we never discussed the name. But I love it. I keep it together in front of Laura, but the minute I have Walker alone, I'm kissing the hell out of him.

He says it like it was always the plan. Like he couldn't imagine it any other way. And just like that, Red Records is born.

Somehow, afterward, we get roped into a photo shoot back at the house.

Literally.

Maggie, clearly running the operation now, hands us a lasso and tells us to 'make it look natural.'

Walker, who has zero interest in being a model, is currently leaning against his horse, looking so ruggedly perfect that it's actually rude.

I, meanwhile, am trying not to pass out because Walker in his element is a lot to handle.

The photographer says, "Okay, let's get a shot of you two on your horses."

Walker smirks. "You think you can handle riding with me, Red?"

I smirk back. "I'll ride with you anytime, Asher."

Cami, from the sidelines, claps her hands. "Yes. This photo is an album cover."

Poppy nods. "Perfect photo for the magazine cover."

Mack, snapping a photo on her phone, mutters, "The internet is gonna lose their minds."

Walker chuckles, adjusting his hat. "We done here?"

Maggie waves him off. "Oh, hush, you look so handsome."

The photographer takes a few more shots before stepping back. "Alright, that's a wrap. This is going to look amazing."

Walker leans over from the saddle, eyes locked on me. "You know, Red, I think I like this whole 'working together' thing."

I grin. "Oh yeah?"

He smirks. "Yeah. Especially when you're looking at me like that."

My heart flips.

Mack groans. "Oh my God, just kiss her already."

Walker grins. "Well. Can't argue with that."

And before I can process anything, he leans towards me and kisses me, right there on horseback, with the sunset behind us while we're on our horses.

Maggie claps.

Cami swoons.

Poppy yells, "Hallmark worthy."

Mack, already typing, mutters, "This is so going viral."

And me? I just melt into Walker, surrounded by the chaos, the love, and the absolute insanity that is Bridger Falls.

Because this? This is home.

And I wouldn't trade it for anything in the world.

Chapter 39
Walker

There are two things I never thought I'd do in my own bar: Sing karaoke. And sing karaoke with Violet.

Yet, here I am, standing in front of a microphone, hand-in-hand with my girl, while her entire family cheers us on like we're about to win a damn GRAMMY.

"This is a mistake," Violet mutters under her breath, shooting me a glare as the opening chords of "It's Your Love" by Faith Hill and Tim McGraw play through the speakers.

"You say that now," I murmur, squeezing her hand. "But wait till I blow you away with my vocals."

Eli snorts from the bar. "Boy, we already know you can sing. Get on with it."

Maggie, who has appointed herself the official karaoke hype woman, waves her beer. "Less talking, more singing, lovebirds."

I glance at Violet, whose cheeks are already pink from the whiskey and the fact that every single person in this bar is watching us.

"You gonna leave me hangin', Red?" I tease.

She squares her shoulders, eyes flashing like she's ready for a fight. "Hell no."

And then I look into her eyes and start singing.

And damn if I don't forget my own name for a second.

Violet leans into the mic, voice sultry and teasing when it's her turn.

I swear to God, she winks at me, and just like that, I'm completely gone.

The crowd leans in and watches, swaying to the music. I think we did the song justice.

Caroline and Eli clap like proud parents at a school recital. Mack stands on a barstool, waving her arms like she's at a stadium concert. Cami and Maggie? They're already betting on whether we'll end up making out on stage.

And my Red?

She's fighting a smile, but I see it, the way her eyes soften, the way she leans just a little closer when I sing the next verse.

By the time we hit the last chorus, she's laughing into the mic, shaking her head like she can't believe this is happening.

Neither can I.

Because this—singing with her, the whole bar watching, the people we love cheering us on—feels like one of those moments I'll remember for the rest of my life.

The song ends, the crowd erupts, and Eli stands up, raising his glass. "I'll be damned. You kids got some major chemistry."

Mack points at us. "Y'all are gross."

Caroline sighs, all dreamy-eyed. "They're perfect."

Violet groans, grabbing my wrist. "We're leaving."

I let her drag me outside, still laughing as the bar doors swing shut behind us. The air is cool and quiet, the only sound the distant hum of the Jukebox inside.

"You didn't have to drag me out here," I tease, tilting my head at her.

She turns, cheeks still flushed, eyes bright. And then, without a word, she grabs my shirt and pulls me down into a kiss. It's fast and hot and full of the kind of energy we had up on that stage, electric, breathless, like neither of us can quite believe we're here.

When she finally pulls back, her lips are kiss-swollen, her breath uneven.

I smirk. "So, you like that? No concussions this time."

She glares, but she's smiling. "Shut up."

I tuck a piece of hair behind her ear, my voice turning softer. "I meant it, Red. I'm in this. With you."

For a second, she doesn't say anything. Just looks at me like she's realizing something big.

Then, finally, she whispers, "Me too."

And just like that, I know:

I'm never letting her go.

* * *

I've done a lot of things in my life.

Had a successful music career, became a dad, ran a bar. And now I've started a record label.

But standing in front of a damn horse, trying to figure out how to surprise my woman without making it weird, is somehow the most stressful thing I've ever done.

Stormy, the gray mare standing beside me, snorts loudly, like she's already judging me.

I glare at her. "Don't start."

She flicks an ear, completely unimpressed.

Maggie, who stands behind me with Eli, Caroline, and Mack, lets out a dramatic sigh. "Walker, honey, you're acting like you just bought an engagement ring, not a horse."

Mack perks up immediately. "Wait. Is there a ring?"

Eli grins, crossing his arms. "Well, if you're getting her a horse, a ring wouldn't be far behind."

Caroline nods. "It's a logical next step."

I groan, scrubbing a hand down my face. "I swear, y'all are the worst."

Maggie waves a hand. "Oh, hush. Now, where is Violet? I wanna see her reaction."

I glance toward the house, nerves rattling in my chest. Violet is inside with Poppy and Cami, completely unaware that I'm about to walk her outside and give her a damn horse.

Which, now that I think about it, might be an unhinged thing to do. Should I have started smaller? Maybe a nice saddle first? Too late now. I nod at Mack. "Go get her."

She grins like she's about to cause trouble, then takes off toward the house.

I adjust my hat, take a deep breath, and pat Stormy's neck. "Alright, girl. Try to win her over."

Stormy blinks at me, completely indifferent. Good talk.

The second Violet steps outside, she takes one look at Stormy and freezes. Her mouth falls open. Then, she slowly turns to me. "Walker," she says, voice suspiciously calm, "whose horse is this?"

Maggie snorts loudly. "Oh, I love this already."

I clear my throat, shifting awkwardly. "She's yours."

Violet blinks. "Mine?"

I nod. "Her name's Stormy. Figured you should have your own horse."

Violet stares at me, unmoving, for so long that I start to think I broke her.

Mack leans in toward Poppy. "She's either about to cry or kill him."

Poppy nods. "Fifty-fifty odds."

Cami sips her drink. "I love a gamble."

Violet finally shakes herself out of her daze and steps

forward, reaching for Stormy's nose. The mare nudges her gently, like she already knows she belongs to her.

Violet inhales sharply, eyes glossy with emotion. "You really got me a horse?" she whispers.

I rub the back of my neck, suddenly feeling really self-conscious. "Yeah, Red. Thought you should have one, so we can all ride together."

Maggie claps her hands together. "Lord, help me, I love a good romance."

Eli grins. "So, when's the wedding?"

Violet whirls around. "Oh my God, Dad! Can we have just one day where nobody plans my future like I'm in a Hallmark movie?"

Caroline chuckles. "Well, darling, if the boots fit."

Mack gasps as she pulls out her phone. "OH MY GOD. That should be a song! As your official PR spokeswoman, I'm writing that down for you."

I groan.

Violet, laughing now, shakes her head and turns back to me. "You really got me a horse," she says again like she still can't believe it.

I shrug, watching her as she strokes Stormy's neck, completely in love with her reaction.

"Do you love her?" I ask, keeping my voice light, but my heart is pounding.

She turns to me, smiling so soft, so bright, it knocks the wind right out of me. "I love you," she says simply. "And her."

And right there in front of Maggie, Mack, Poppy, Cami, Eli, and Caroline, she throws her arms around my neck and kisses me like she means it.

Caroline gasps dramatically. "Oh, Lord, my heart."

Mack snaps a photo. "The internet is going to die."

Maggie yells, "Put a ring on it!"

Caroline sighs. "I do love a happy ending."

Poppy nods. "Except we're not at the end, and I'm personally holding out for an elaborate proposal."

Cami grins. "Oh, definitely elaborate."

Violet pulls back, breathless, laughing against my lips, an amused grin on her face.

"We need new friends," I mutter.

She chuckles, brushing my knuckles down my jaw. "Nah, we'd be bored without 'em."

I put my arm around her and pull her close.

She sighs, dramatic as hell. "Fine. But if you ever surprise me with twenty-four goats again, we're gonna have words."

I smirk. "Damn. Guess I gotta cancel my next surprise."

Violet groans, laughing, and I kiss her again. Because Stormy might be the best damn gift I've ever given her. But having her in my life?

That's the best damn gift I've ever gotten.

Chapter 40
Violet

I have made a horrible mistake.

I thought writing songs with Walker and starting our own label would be a productive, creative, and inspiring experience.

Turns out, it's mostly him distracting me with his stupid good-looking face and even stupider hot body. Tonight, he even busted out a pair of black-rimmed glasses. How am I supposed to focus when he looks like that? So good.

We've been at it for an hour, sitting in his cabin, notebooks open, guitars out—but absolutely nothing has been written down except for a bunch of nonsense lyrics that make no sense and will never see the light of day.

And it is entirely his fault.

Walker is sitting across from me on the couch, guitar balanced on his knee, one ankle propped up on the coffee table like he has nowhere better to be.

I glare at him. "This is the worst songwriting session I've ever had."

He lifts a brow. "I dunno, Red. That last line you came up with was solid."

I scoff. "Walker, I said, 'I like the way you look in jeans, and your truck is kinda nice.'"

He nods seriously. "Country radio loves trucks and jeans. I think you're onto something."

I drop my notebook onto the table with a dramatic thud. "I can't work under these conditions."

Walker grins, setting his guitar aside and leaning forward, elbows on his knees. "What conditions?"

I wave wildly at him. "You! Being distracting. And insufferable. And entirely too attractive for me to focus on actual words."

He chuckles, running a hand over his scruff. "You think I'm attractive?"

I groan, flopping onto the couch dramatically. "You know you are. It's your whole thing. And apparently, the whole Cowboy Daddy thing has caught fire on social media, so you have that going for you, too."

He shifts, moving over to sit next to me, eyes glinting with amusement. "So, what I'm hearing is, you're too busy checking me out to write a song?"

I glare at him. "Oh my God."

He grins, arms spreading across the back of the couch. "Happens more often than you'd think."

I throw a pillow at his face. He catches it, laughing, his whole body shaking, and damn it—he's so stupidly charming I could actually scream.

After several minutes of arguing, throwing pillows, and me threatening to walk out if he didn't take this seriously, we actually start writing. And, to my shock, we come up with something good.

Like really, really good.

It starts as a joke, a playful back-and-forth about how we're both stubborn as hell and should've figured this thing out between us years ago.

But somewhere along the way, it shifts. The lyrics come easier. The melody finds itself naturally. And when we finally play through it from start to finish, neither of us says anything for a long time.

I glance over at Walker, who stares at me with an unreadable expression. I swallow. "Well?"

He shakes his head, awe flickering in his eyes. "Damn, Red."

I exhale, feeling my heartbeat faster than it should. "It's good, huh?"

He nods slowly. "Yeah."

I lick my lips, suddenly feeling way too exposed. "Wanna play it again?"

Walker's gaze drops to my mouth, and I immediately regret my choice of words. His lips curve into a slow, knowing smirk. "Oh, I got something else in mind."

And before I can even process what's happening, his guitar is set aside, and his hands are on my waist, pulling me straight into his lap.

It happens fast.

One second, I'm fully in control, completely professional, just trying to write a damn song. The next, Walker's mouth is on mine, deep and slow and borderline unfair, his hands tight on my waist, his thumb brushing bare skin under my shirt.

And that is the moment I realize we are not getting any more work done tonight.

I make a soft, breathless sound, and that's all it takes—he groans against my lips, flipping us so I'm beneath him on the couch, his weight pressing into me, his hands framing my face like he's holding something breakable.

"You drive me crazy, you know that?" he mutters, voice rough.

I grin against his mouth. "Likewise."

His lips trail down my neck, and yeah, this song is never getting finished.

I shift in his arms, trailing my fingers over his chest, feeling the slow, steady beat of his heart beneath my palm.

I tilt my head back, meeting his gaze, soft and unguarded in the early morning light.

"What do think about your future, Asher?" I whisper, barely breathing the words.

His hand lifts, tucking a piece of hair behind my ear, his thumb lingering at my jaw, tracing slow circles like he's memorizing me.

His voice is low, rough, full of something deep and certain when he finally answers—

"You look like forever to me."

I exhale sharply, because damn it, that's it. That's everything.

And when he leans in, pressing his lips to mine, slow and sure and heartbreakingly sweet— I know he's right.

Because this? This is forever.

Epilogue
Walker

Six months later.

The barn smells like fresh hay and saddle leather, the late afternoon sun streaming through the wide doors, painting everything in golden light.

It's perfect. And I need everything to be perfect today.

Stormy and Maximus are already saddled and waiting, their tails flicking lazily, ears twitching as they watch me pace like a man seconds away from losing his damn mind. Winnie gives me a look. "Hey, your kid will be home later, and she'll take you on a ride. I'm sorry, girl."

Violet should be here any minute. I run a hand down Maximus's neck, muttering mostly to myself. "You think she's gonna say yes?"

Maximus blinks at me.

Stormy snorts.

I check my watch. Four o'clock sharp.

And right on cue, I hear the familiar sound of boots on dirt, followed by the unmistakable voice of the love of my life.

"Alright, Asher," Violet calls as she steps into the barn, hair red hair glowing in the sunlight, eyes filled with love. "Are we going for a ride?"

She looks good. Boots, jeans, that green flannel I love on her, and the curious smirk that drives me crazy in the best way. Yeah, this woman is it for me. The love of my love.

I hook my thumbs in my belt loops, trying to look casual even though my heart is pounding like a drum.

"Just figured we could go on a ride," I say. "You and me."

She eyes the already-saddled horses. "A spontaneous horse-back ride?"

I shrug. "Something wrong with that?"

She narrows her eyes. "You're up to something."

I smirk. "Just get on the horse, Red."

She steps closer, Stormy nudging at her shoulder affectionately. As she runs a hand down the mare's neck, my chest tightens.

Because this right here? Seeing her with her horse, part of this life, part of my life? It feels like everything I've ever wanted.

I clear my throat. "You coming?"

She rolls her eyes but grins, throwing one last suspicious glance at me before swinging herself onto Stormy's back.

I do the same with Maximus, and then we take off.

Just the two of us.

We leave the barn together, side by side, the rhythmic sound of Stormy and Maximus's hooves against the dirt road filling the air.

It's quiet, the kind of peaceful that only exists out here—with the open Wyoming sky stretched above us, the warm wind on our skin, and the entire damn world at our backs.

She leans forward in her saddle, adjusting the reins. "Okay, I'll admit, this is nice."

I chuckle. "What, did you think I was luring you out here to leave you for the coyotes?"

She shrugs and gives me a smirk. "Maybe."

I laugh, nudging Maximus closer until our knees bump in the saddles. "I told you, you're stuck with me, Red."

She smirks, tilting her head. "Is that right?"

I grin, shaking my head, but damn if it's not true.

We ride for a while, just the two of us, the golden light filtering through the trees, the scent of wildflowers, and warm earth filling the air. When we reach a stretch of open field, I tug the reins, slowing Maximus, and reach out, catching Stormy's bridle and pulling her close.

Violet frowns, confused. "What are you—"

But before she can finish, I lean in, capturing her lips in a slow, deep kiss, the kind that steals my breath from my chest.

She sighs against me, her hands fisting in my shirt, and for a second there's nothing else.

Just her and me and this place that feels like home.

When I pull back, she blinks, a little breathless. "Wow."

I smile. "I love you."

Her cheeks are pink, her smile soft, "I love you, too."

I grin, clicking Maximus forward. "C'mon. We're almost there."

The hills roll out ahead of us, stretched wide under the open sky. The warm breeze tugs at her hair, loose strands escaping from her high ponytail, and I can't stop looking at her.

She catches me staring. "What?"

I smirk. "You just look real pretty."

She laughs. "Thanks, Asher. You're kinda pretty yourself."

We ride side by side, slow at first, just taking it in—the way the sky shifts from bright blue to that soft, glowing orange, the way the wind moves through the grass, the way she smiles at me when she thinks I'm not looking.

And for a while, we don't talk.

Riding together, spending time together, just like we've done before, I'm about to ask her to spend the rest of her life with me.

And damn if that doesn't make this ride the most important one yet.

The wildflowers stretch out ahead of us, a sea of color against the green of the hills.

Violet gasps, pulling Stormy to a stop. "Asher."

I stop beside her, watching her take it in.

Her breath catches. "This is beautiful."

I study her face, the way her eyes light up, the way the wind catches her hair, the golden light making her look like something out of a damn dream.

She's the beautiful part.

I slide off Maximus, looping the reins over a fence post, then turn to help her down.

Her hands land on my shoulders, her body sliding against mine, and for a second, I forget what I'm supposed to be doing.

She tilts her head up, watching me. "Why do you look nervous?"

I take a deep breath, reaching for her hand. "C'mon, Red."

She follows me, confused but trusting. Then, she sees it.

A picnic blanket, a bottle of wine, a small wooden box sitting next to a bouquet of wildflowers wrapped in ribbon.

She stops dead in her tracks. "Oh my gosh..." she whispers, turning to me, her eyes already glassy.

I step in close, my voice steady, certain, full of everything I feel for her. "I've loved you since the second you crashed into my life," I tell her. "And I will love you every second for the rest of it."

She inhales sharply, her grip on my hand tightening.

"I want to spend my life making music with you," I continue. "Laughing with you. Singing with you. Loving you the way you deserve to be loved."

I take a breath, then reach into the box and pull out the ring.

Violet gasps, hands flying to her mouth.

And before I can even get the damn question out, she throws herself at me.

"Yes," she breathes, laughing, crying, kissing me all at once. "Yes, yes, yes."

I catch her easily, laughing as she nearly knocks us both over.

"I didn't even get to ask," I murmur against her lips.

She grins, cupping my face. "You didn't have to."

I slide the ring onto her finger, watching as the sunlight catches the diamond. And for a moment, everything is quiet. Just the wind. The horses grazing nearby. And the woman I love, wearing my ring.

"Forever, Red?" I ask, brushing a stray curl from her face.

She smiles, eyes shining. "Forever, Asher."

And when I kiss her again, I swear, I've never been happier in my entire damn life.

We don't leave right away. We stay there for a while, talking, laughing, drinking the wine, and letting it all sink in. As the sun sets, I swing back up onto Maximus, reaching out my hand to help Violet onto Stormy.

And now, she's wearing my ring.

And damn, that does something to me.

As we ride back toward the ranch, I steal glances at her, at the way she keeps looking at her hand, smiling like she just won the lottery.

I smirk. "Still checking, huh?"

She grins. "Just making sure this is real and I'm not dreaming."

I lean over and kiss her in the fading sunlight. "It's real, Red."

She sighs, content. "I guess I get to keep you forever now, huh?"

I chuckle. "Yeah, baby. You really do."

And as we ride back, side by side, the weight of forever settled between us, light as air, I know I wouldn't trade this moment, this woman, this life for anything in the world.

Want more Violet and Walker? Check out this bonus scene for Forever To Me when you sign up for Erin's newsletter!

Scan the QR code to get your bonus scene:

About the Author

Erin Branscom is a creator of happily-ever-after's, crafting spicy, Hallmark-like romances that make readers fall head over heels for charming small towns. When she's not writing heartwarming stories, Erin can be found anywhere there are dogs, with a cup of coffee in hand, or lost in a good book. As a passionate Scorpio, she brings intensity and heart to everything she does. Dive into her world and discover love, warmth, and a touch of spice in every story.

Acknowledgments

To my family. I love you all and you are my reason for working hard every day. I'm so thankful for all of you and your support. To all my readers, thank you for always showing up for me and being excited!

Want more Violet and Walker?

Check out this bonus scene for Forever To Me when you sign up for Erin's newsletter!

Scan the QR code to get your bonus scene:

Chapter 1: Wild As Her

Cami

"Cami, is that you?" A voice calls out before I can step through the doors of the Bridger Falls National Bank. I glance over nervously and spot Maggie, our town's fairy godmother, beaming over at me.

"Oh. Hey, Maggie. How are you?"

"Well, well, Sugar. Where are you going all dressed up?" she asks, not answering my question.

"I have a meeting with Sterling," I tell her with my best smile. While I know she's supportive, I also know that word will travel that I was all dressed up at the bank for a meeting with the bank manager. She means well. But small towns are small towns. Everybody talks.

"Knock 'em dead!" She waves encouragingly and heads into Boots & Bangs, the beauty shop next door.

I take a deep breath and adjust my black blazer, smoothing down the tailored red dress beneath it that makes me feel professional. My black power heels click against the polished floor, each step confident and fueled with determination. The air smells like stale coffee and fake promises, but I'm here to save my family's ranch. Am I overdressed for a meeting at our small-town bank? Probably. Do I care? No. My ranch is at stake here.

My sleek, shiny black hair is swept into a professional chignon, and the bold red lipstick I've chosen matches my dress perfectly. The look I'm going for is professional-business-boss-lady-rancher. But really, on the inside? Yeah, I'm just a mess. I want this more than anything in the world. And I'm scared to death that they won't help me. This bank holds the keys to my future. They can choose to open the door for me or slam it shut in my face. And lately, there's been a lot of doors being slammed. I'm here to fight for the future of my family's ranch and work as hard as I can to make that happen.

I picked this ensemble so that I would look every bit the part of a businesswoman, a strong woman rancher, and a force to be reckoned with. That's my hope anyway.

In my trusty, soft, black leather satchel gifted to me from one of my favorite professors after I got my master's degree, I carry a folder with a meticulously crafted business plan, my desperate attempt to woo the bank.

The ranch will become more than just a small family-run ranch. It's going to be a gathering place. A cozy bed and breakfast with charm, trail rides with views that leave you breathless, a summer camp for kids, and a micro bakery-farmstand combo that people will drive hours to visit. It's going to be the heartbeat of Bridger Falls.

I've poured so much time and energy into this plan. It's been a nonstop dream – sometimes a fever dream – for me to put this together. This is something I eat, sleep, dream, and put into action every day with all that I do. I want nothing more than to make this come true for Wilder Ranch. And while I know that they're big dreams, I'm chasing them with everything I've got.

I think about my grandfather Wilder and wonder if he'd be proud of how hard I'm fighting for the family ranch. I remember the promise that I made to my grandpa when he was sitting in his rocking chair on the back porch of our family's home. He was near the end when he made me promise to keep the ranch in the family and do everything I can to fight for it. He and I were always very close, and my love for the ranch runs as deep as his. We were kindred spirits. I think he realized at the time that it wasn't safe with my parents, and while he hoped my mom would do right by the ranch, she didn't.

So yeah, on the outside, I probably look put together, but on the inside, my stomach churns with nerves. I won't let it show. I learned a long time ago that showing weakness does me no good. It only gives ammunition to the people who want to take me down. And no one is taking me down.

Sterling Atwood, a man in his late fifties, greets me as if he's in a hurry and ushers me into his office. His eyes don't meet mine. Instead, they rake over me like he's sizing me up, all while pretending to be a gentleman as he gestures for me to go first. I bite down the cringe clawing up my spine, fully aware he's watching every step I take as we head down the hallway toward the conference room off his office.

Any other day, I'd whirl around, call him out, and make damn sure he knew exactly how obvious he was being. But not today. I need him on my side, and biting my tongue feels like swallowing glass. Still, I keep walking, fists clenched, resisting the urge to spin on my heel and shoot him a glare that would melt the smug look right off his face.

His walls are lined with degrees, awards, and certificates that don't impress me one bit, but I pretend that they do. He gives me time to look over his accolades, and I don't miss the dick measuring contest he presents me with, making sure that I see how important he wants me to believe he is. To Atwood, I'm just a nobody here in this town. At best, someone who runs a mobile coffee trailer. He doesn't see me as the businesswoman that I am. I give him his moment, but I'm here to present my plan to him. I'm too educated for his bullshit. And my respect for him has diminished at his nonchalance towards my situation. In fact, it just pisses me off. But again, I'm not letting it show.

I smile at him and calmly lay the two folders in front of us, my bright red polished nails tapping lightly on the desk as I enthusiastically explain my plan. I tell him every step it'll to take to turn the ranch around and into the epic vision I've laid forth. My voice is strong and confident, and as I speak, I watch the boredom sweep across his face. That's when I realize that he has no intention of giving me a chance here. None. This was all for nothing. So much for the small-town bank slogan of helping out the locals. It's all a lie. He never intended to help me. I finish speaking and sit back in my chair, folding my hands in my lap.

Sterling leans back and sighs. "Miss Kendrick," he says dryly as if he's searching for the words to say.

"Just give it to me straight," I say, crossing my legs, nerves threatening to take over, but I shove them deep down and stay focused.

"That's... one impressive plan. And I'm curious as to who came up with this plan for you—."

"I did," I interrupt. "I wrote the plan."

The insinuation burns. Like I'm just some clueless woman who needed a man to swoop in and draw a roadmap for me. But I don't take the bait. I shove the fury down deep, keep my chin high, and stay locked in, cool, steady, unreadable.

His eyes widen as he nods, surprised. A sliver of hope fills me that he could still actually help me. I worked so hard on that plan. Hours and hours went into it, and I left no stone unturned for my family's ranch, taking it from red all the way to black. I *know* my plan will work.

He continues and explains it to me in the same tone he'd use if I were a child. "We've given your mother every grace period possible for the ranch. I'm sorry, but there can be no more extensions. We're all out of time here." He slides a thick folder across his desk, and the pages that slip out are highlighted in bright red with PAST DUE stamped across the pages.

"If we could just..." I stammer, desperately grasping at straws.

Sterling interrupts me with a deep sigh like I'm exhausting him. "Miss Kendrick, your ranch sold off the livestock and equipment and even attempted to lease out your land. I see that you even held a little fundraiser. You've made attempts, but... it's simply not enough to make up the past due amount, catch up on the taxes, and sustain the ranch moving forward. I am truly sorry, but we must move forward with our buyer."

My heart drops and shatters on the floor into a million pieces, but I give no outward sign of emotion. "Mr. Atwood, this ranch has been in my family for generations. I just need a little more time, please. I really need your help with this. I can fix this. Really, I can."

He shakes his head and stands, guiding me to the door. "I'm sorry, but we have run out of time."

"Who is the buyer?" I ask frantically, searching his face as it hits me that this might really be it. It's over. He knows the fate of my ranch and what will become of it.

"I'm sorry, but I'm not at liberty to share the details at this time," he replies firmly.

I clear my throat, hold my head high, and try not to cry as I turn and walk out, not bothering to say anything more. He was never going to hear me out or give my plan a chance.

I have to figure something out. Because no one is coming to

save me. I won't just give up my family's ranch. I'm going to figure this out. Just like I always do.

How? No clue. Maybe there's a Hail Mary pass out there somewhere. I rack my brain, trying to think quickly of another idea to present to him. There has to be something.

Teresa, my mom, already moved to town, leaving me to deal with the fallout. Her grand plan was to just give the ranch to the bank after she sold off whatever she could. Ollie, my brother, I love him, but he's out, too. For them, the ranch holds weighted memories that haunt them. For me, it holds a possibility for future memories. Good memories. And ones with my grandparents I refuse to give up.

I can't blame Ollie. He helped out as much as he could. He's a full-time firefighter here in Bridger Falls, and even he couldn't fix what he didn't break. I get it. It's not their dream. It's mine.

My mom is a full-time nurse at Bridger Falls Memorial Hospital and has been all my life. I'm still so angry at her about all of this. She could have told me that the ranch was circling the drain before it was too late, but she didn't. She continued to take the money that I gave her to help the ranch, never paying any bills like she said she would. When she ran out of time, she just packed up her stuff, leaving me to deal with the fallout.

This was her parent's ranch. She was raised here. After my grandparents passed away, my dad turned our world upside down in that house. He did his best to strip away every good memory he could of the ranch and our childhood. Broke everything he could, including us. Then, he did the best thing he could have ever done: he left. But really, it's only a matter of time before he's back again. And my mom will give him chance after chance, despite the chaos he's caused.

I glance back to Satan in a suit aka Atwood who smiles at me as if he won, raising his hand and waving at me. I walk out of the bank with my head held high. Screw that guy. Good luck getting your coffee somewhere else, pal. *Asshole.*

I'm not ready to go home, so I head to my coffee trailer, an old Airstream I gutted and turned into Steamy Sips. A local artist painted the name in big, swooping letters with my logo on the side, and every time I see it, I feel a flicker of pride. It might not be much, but it's mine. I source my beans from a roaster a few towns over, and if you ask anyone in Bridger Falls, they'll tell you, I serve the best damn coffee around.

I park my beat-up red truck behind it, unlock the door, and slip inside. The second it closes behind me, I lose it. Full-blown, ugly cry. I wish it helped. It doesn't.

Once I've cried myself out, I rage-clean the already spotless trailer, wiping down counters that don't need wiping, restocking cups that don't need restocking. Anything to feel like I'm doing *something.*

Because if I stop moving, if I let myself sit still, I'll unravel. And I don't have time to fall apart. Not when the ranch is slipping through my fingers.

Not when everything I've ever loved is on the line.

Wild As Her

Want more of Bridger Falls?
Scan the QR code to read Cami and Jack's story:

Freedom Valley Series
Falling Inn Love
Baked Inn Love
All Inn Thyme
Love Inn Books
Forever Inn Love
Snowed Inn

Bridger Falls
Forever To Me
Wild As Her
Always You
High Road

Non-Fiction
Writers Inspiring Writers with Jennifer Probst

Wisteria Cove
The Pumpkin Spice Spell
Mistletoe & Magic
Hexes & Honeysuckle

Cozy Creek Collection
Fall Too Well

You can find all of Erin's books on her website:
Erinbranscom.com